Trespasser

**Center Point
Large Print**

Also by Paul Doiron and available from Center Point Large Print:

The Poacher's Son

This Large Print Book carries the Seal of Approval of N.A.V.H.

TRESPASSER

Paul Doiron

CENTER POINT LARGE PRINT
THORNDIKE, MAINE

This Center Point Large Print edition is
published in the year 2011 by arrangement with
St. Martin's Press.

The text of this Large Print edition is unabridged.
In other aspects, this book may vary
from the original edition.
Printed in the United States of America.
Set in 16-point Times New Roman type.

ISBN: 978-1-61173-100-2

Library of Congress Cataloging-in-Publication Data

Doiron, Paul.
Trespasser / Paul Doiron.
    p. cm.
ISBN 978-1-61173-100-2 (library binding : alk. paper)
1. Game wardens—Fiction. 2. Traffic accidents—Fiction.
    3. Missing persons—Fiction.
    4. Young women—Crimes against—Fiction.
    5. Lobster fishers—Fiction. 6. False imprisonment—Fiction.
    7. Maine—Fiction. 8. Large type books. I. Title.
PS3604.O37T74 2011b
813'.6—dc22
                                                     2011007829

For my parents,
Richard and Judith Doiron

So full of artless jealousy is guilt, It spills itself in fearing to be spilt.

—WILLIAM SHAKESPEARE, *Hamlet*

1

I found the wreck easily enough. It was the only red sedan with a crushed hood on the Parker Point Road. In my headlights, the damage didn't look too extensive. The driver had even managed to steer the car onto the muddy shoulder, where it had become mired to its hubcaps.

I switched on my blue lights and got out of the patrol truck. My shadow lurched ahead of me like a movie monster. Right off, I saw the dark red pool of blood in the road—there must have been quarts of it, every ounce in the animal's body spilled onto the asphalt. I also noticed bloody drag marks where someone had moved the roadkill. But the deer itself was nowhere to be seen. The red smears just stopped, as if the carcass had been snatched up by space aliens into the night.

Flashlight raised high in my left hand, I approached the wrecked car. The air bags had inflated, but the windshield was intact. So where was the driver? Someone phoned in the deer/car collision. The keys were still in the ignition. Had the driver wandered off with a concussion—or just gotten tired of waiting for a delinquent game warden to arrive? It was damned mysterious.

No driver, no deer.

I was all alone on the foggy road.

The call had come in an hour earlier, near the end of a twelve-hour shift.

My last stop of the day was supposed to be the house of a very tall and angry man named Hank Varnum. He was waiting for me in the foggy nimbus of his porch light: a rangy, rawboned guy with a face that always reminded me of Abraham Lincoln when I saw him behind the counter of the Sennebec Market.

Tonight he didn't give me a chance to climb out of my truck. He just let out a snarl: "Look what those bastards did, Mike!"

And he started off into the wet woods behind his house.

I grabbed my Maglite and followed as best I could. When you are a young Maine game warden —twenty-five years old and fit—there aren't many occasions when you can truly imagine being old, but this late March evening was one of them. My knees ached from a fall I'd taken earlier that day checking ice-fishing licenses on a frozen pond, and the mud sucked at my boots with every step. Varnum had to keep waiting for me to catch up. The grocer walked like a turkey —long-legged, neck slightly extended, head bobbing as he went. But I was too exhausted to find it humorous.

Hank Varnum owned something like seventy acres of woods along the Segocket River in mid-coast Maine, and he seemed determined to lead me over every hill and dale of it. Worse yet, I discovered that my flashlight needed new batteries. The temperature had been hovering around thirty-two degrees all afternoon, and now the thaw was conjuring up a mist from the forest floor. Fog rose from the softening patches of snow and drifted like gossamer through the trees.

After many minutes, we came out of a thicket and intersected a recently used all-terrain-vehicle trail. The big wheels of the ATVs had chewed savagely into the earth, splashing mud into the treetops and scattering fist-sized rocks every-where. The ruts were filled with coffee-colored puddles deep enough to drown a small child.

Varnum thrust his forefinger at the damage. "Do you believe this shit?"

But before I could answer, he'd forged off again, turkeylike, following the four-wheel trail deeper into the woods.

I checked my watch. Whatever chance I'd had of catching a movie with my girlfriend, Sarah, was no more. Since she'd moved back into my rented house last fall, we'd been making progress reconciling our lifestyles—Maine game warden and grade-school teacher—or so it seemed to me anyway. Tonight might be a setback.

My cell phone vibrated. The display showed the number of the Knox County Regional Communications Center.

"Hold up, Hank!" I answered. "Twenty-one fifty-four. This is Bowditch."

"Twenty-one fifty-four, we've got a deer/car collision on the Parker Point Road." Most of my calls were dispatched out of the state police headquarters in Augusta, but I recognized the voice on the radio as being that of Lori Williams, one of the county 911 operators.

"Anyone injured?"

"Negative."

"What about the deer?"

"The caller said it was dead."

So why was Lori bothering me with this? Every police officer in Maine was trained to handle a deer/car collision. Nothing about the situation required the district game warden.

"Dispatch, I'm ten-twenty on the Quarry Road in Sennebec. Is there a deputy or trooper who can respond?"

"Ten-twenty-three." Meaning: Stand by.

I waited half a minute while the dispatcher made her inquiries among the available units. Hank Varnum had his flashlight beam pointed into my eyes the whole time. "Are we just about there, Hank?" I asked, squinting.

"It's right around this bend."

"Show me."

We went on another four hundred yards or so, crossing a little trout stream that the ATVs had transformed into a flowing latrine. Then we turned a corner, and I understood the well-spring of Hank Varnum's rage. At one time, the trail had run between two majestic oaks—but no longer.

"They cut down my goddamned trees!" The beam of Varnum's flashlight was shaking, he was so mad.

The stumps stood like fresh-sawn pillars on either side of the trail, with the fallen trees lying, akimbo, to the sides. Yellow posted signs were still nailed to their toppled trunks.

"First, I put up the signs," Varnum explained. "But they came through anyway. Then I dropped a couple of spruces across the trail. They just dragged those aside. So I said, 'All right, this is war.' And I strung a steel cable between the two oaks. You see how much good that did." In fact, the cable was still attached to one of the fallen trees.

I shined my light on the crosshatched tire tracks, feeling a surge of anger at the meaning-less waste in front of me. They were beautiful red oaks, more than a century old, and some assholes had snuffed out their lives for no good reason. "Do you have any idea who the vandals are?"

"That pervert Calvin Barter, probably. Or maybe Dave Drisko and that prick son of his.

There's a whole pack of them that ride around down on those fucking machines. I swear to God, Mike, I'm going to string up barbed wire here next."

Mad as I was, it was my job to be the voice of reason in these situations. "You can't booby-trap your land, Hank. No matter how much you might be tempted. You'll get sued. And you honestly don't want someone to get injured."

"I don't?" He rubbed the back of his long neck, like he was trying to take the skin off. "I never had any problem when it was just snowmobiles. It was always fine by me if the sledders used my land. They never did any real damage. But these ATVs are a different story. They *want* to tear things up. That's part of their fun." His eyes bored into mine. "So what can you do for me here, Mike?"

"Well, I could take some pictures of the tracks and the trees, but there's nothing to connect the ATVs with whoever cut down your oaks. If you could ID the riders coming through next time, we could file trespassing charges. Snapshots would help make the case."

"So that's it?"

I was about to say something about how I couldn't be everywhere at once, how I relied on citizens to help me do my job, blah, blah, blah, when I heard the roar of distant engines.

"That's them!" Varnum said.

I motioned him to get off the trail. We extinguished our flashlights and crouched down behind some young balsams and waited. My cell phone vibrated again. Lori told me that a state trooper said he was going to respond to the deer/car collision, so I was off the hook. I turned the mobile off to be as silent as possible. The snow around me had crystallized as it had melted and become granular. It made a crunching noise when I shifted my weight.

The engines got louder and louder, I saw a flash of headlights through the fog, and then, just as I was getting ready to spring, the shouts and revving motors began to recede.

Varnum jumped to his feet. "They turned off down that fire road!"

My knees cracked as I straightened up beside him. "Will they come back this way?"

"How the hell do I know?"

In a few weeks, the spring peepers would begin to call, but right now the forest was quiet except for the dripping trees. "Look, Hank, I know you're angry. But I promise you, we'll do what we can to catch the punks who did this."

He didn't even answer, just snapped on his flashlight and stormed off toward home.

I took two steps after him, and then the ground slid out from under me, and the next thing I knew I was lying face-first in the mud.

When I finally dug the mud out of my eye

sockets, I saw Varnum looming over me, his jaw stuck out, his anger unabated. He pulled a handkerchief from his pants pocket and threw it at me. "Wipe the dirt off your face."

It wasn't until I'd left Varnum at his door and gotten back to my truck that I remembered I'd turned my cell phone off. Dispatch was trying to reach me on the police radio: "Twenty-one fifty-four, please respond."

"Twenty-one fifty-four," I said.

"Do you need assistance?" Lori sounded uncharacteristically animated. She was a good dispatcher in that she usually kept her emotions in check. That's an important skill when you deal with freaked-out callers all night.

"No, I'm fine."

"We couldn't reach you."

"Sorry, I had my phone off. What's going on?"

"Four-twelve had engine trouble. He couldn't take that deer/car."

"You mean no one's responded yet?" I already knew where this conversation was heading. "Can't a deputy take it?"

"Skip's dealing with an eighteen-wheeler that went off the road in Union, and Jason's bringing in a drunk driver."

It had been at least thirty minutes since the call came through. I was mud-soaked and exhausted, with an impatient girlfriend waiting at home.

16

And now I had to go scrape a deer carcass off the road and take down insurance information. "All right, I'm on my way."

Parker Point was a narrow peninsula that jutted like a broken finger southward into the Atlantic. It was one of dozens of similar capes and necks carved out of the Maine bedrock by the glaciers during the last ice age. Ten thousand years might seem like an eternity, but in geological terms it was scarcely time enough to cover these ridges with a dusting of topsoil and a blanket of evergreen needles. Nothing with deep roots could thrive on Parker Point, just alders, beach roses, and bristling black spruces that blew over easily when the March winds came storming out of the northeast.

The houses on the point had once belonged to fishing families, but as waterfront real estate prices soared and the codfish stocks collapsed in the Gulf of Maine, these homes had been increasingly sold as summer "cottages" to wealthy out-of-staters. Or they had been torn down and replaced with new shingle-sided mansions with radiant-heat floors and gated fences. I could easily envision a time, very soon, when every Maine fishermen who still clawed a living from the sea could no longer afford to dwell within sight of it.

Because of all those NO TRESPASSING signs, the local deer population had exploded. Without hunters to control their numbers, the animals multiplied like leggy rabbits, but their lives were no easier, and they died just as brutally. The difference was that death tended to come now in the form of starvation, disease, or, as in this case, a speeding car.

The fog had gotten so thick, it bounced my headlights back at me. As I drove, I keyed in my home number on my cell phone and readied myself. But when I told Sarah I'd be late, her reaction was not what I'd expected.

"That's all right, Mike," she said in a muted voice.

"It's just that a car hit a deer in this fog," I said.

"Was anyone hurt?"

"Just the deer. Maybe we can see that movie tomorrow night."

"Amy said it wasn't a good film anyway."

Neither of us spoke for a while. Something was definitely bothering her.

"I'm sorry I missed dinner," I offered.

"It was just pea soup. You can heat it up."

I tried lightening the mood. "Why do they compare fog with pea soup anyway? It's not like it's green."

But she wouldn't play along. "I'll see you when you get home, all right?"

"I love you."

"Please be careful," she replied. It was the way she ended many of our calls.

2

The night was getting colder, or maybe it was because my uniform was damp. The sensation was that of being wrapped in wet gauze. Shivering, I got on the radio. "Lori, I'm ten-twenty on the Parker Point Road. I've located the Ford Focus, but there's no one here. Who called in the accident—was it the driver?"

"Negative. It was someone passing by. He said he'd stopped and spoken to the young woman who hit the deer. She called a tow company and was waiting for the wrecker. The caller said she was a little shaken up but uninjured. He said he wanted to make sure an officer dealt with the deer in the road."

"But the caller didn't identify himself?"

"He said he didn't want to get involved."

In my experience, this meant that the guy who'd phoned in the accident was probably driving drunk—or operating under the influence, in Maine lingo. What we had here was the Good Samaritan impulse versus the fear of being arrested on an OUI charge.

"Was the caller on a cell or a landline?"

"He was on that pay phone outside Smitty's Garage."

It was an abandoned repair shop located two

miles down the road. "Can you contact Mid-coast Towing and see if they got a phone call about this from the driver?"

"Ten-four."

The car, I noticed, was a rental with Massachusetts plates. So where was the driver? I walked up and down the road a hundred yards in either direction, shining my flashlight along the mud shoulder to see if the young woman had staggered off into the trees. But there was no sign of any footprints.

I applied myself to the problem of the missing deer.

There were hunks of hair caught under the fender and more of it floating in the viscous pool of blood in the road. This evidence established that the Focus had indeed struck a deer and not some weirdo who happened to be walking in the fog dressed like Daniel Boone.

I wondered if my anonymous Good Samaritan had been the one to help himself to the deer. Under Maine state law, any driver who hits a deer or moose has first dibs on the meat. After that, it's up to the responding officer to dispose of the carcass as he or she sees fit. Dealing with a hundred pounds of dead but still-warm animal is usually the last thing someone who's just totaled a car wants to worry about. I routinely brought the remains to a butcher who worked with the Rockland food bank or traded it to my informants in exchange for tips on local poachers. Other officers passed the meat along to families that were going through tough times.

Sometimes the underprivileged took a more active role in their own nourishment. I knew of some penniless backwoods characters who sat around the cracker barrel listening to police scanners. If they heard about a deer/car accident, they would rush to the scene to beg for free venison. Half the time, the officer was just glad to be rid of the hassle. Other times, if no cop happened to be present yet, the game thieves would abscond with the roadkill. It was possible the man who'd reported the accident fell into this category of self-help opportunists.

I decided to collect blood and hair samples for DNA evidence. Pinching someone for stealing roadkill wasn't at the top of my priority list, but the samples might come in handy if I needed to prove serial wildlife violations someday. Poaching convictions had been won on slimmer bits of thread.

I was squatting on the cold asphalt, tweezing hair into a paper bag, when I heard a diesel engine approaching. On cue, my radio squawked: "Twenty-one fifty-four, Midcoast Towing said they did receive a call."

"Thanks, Lori. The wrecker's here now."

As the truck rumbled to a halt, the driver turned on his flashing amber lights and rolled down his window. I recognized the ruddy, blond-bearded face inside. We often sat at the same lunch counter at the Square Deal Diner in Sennebec, but I couldn't remember his name. I'd been assigned to the area for only a year, and there were still plenty of days when everyone I met was a stranger.

"Warden Bowditch, whatcha got?" The inside of the truck cab smelled fragrantly of pipe tobacco.

"I was going to ask you that."

"I heard a lady from Boston hit a deer. I'm supposed to haul off her car. Hey, you look like you've been mud wrestling."

"Yeah, I took a spill. Did the woman say she needed a ride? Because she doesn't seem to be around here anywhere."

"Well, I didn't talk to her myself, you know. That's not the way it works. But I can find out for you." He picked up a clipboard from the passenger seat and held it close to his eyes to read the chicken scratch. "Her name is Ashley Kim. What's that—Korean?"

I shrugged.

"My old man fought in Korea," he said. "He hated that show M*A*S*H, though."

While the trucker got on the CB to his dispatcher, I ransacked my memory for the blond man's name. I'd learned all sorts of mnemonic tricks at the Maine Criminal Justice Academy to help recall information for my police reports, but for some reason, I never applied these strategies to my personal life. As a result, I was constantly forgetting dentist's appointments, high school classmates, et cetera. I had a vague recollection that the driver went by some odd nickname.

He swung open the truck door and hopped down: a misshapen man whose legs seemed too short for his torso, as if he'd been cobbled together out of two different bodies, a small and a tall. Just like that, his name came to me: Stump Murphy.

He wore canvas duck pants with the bottoms rolled up, a blaze orange hunting shirt, and a camouflage vest. Curly blond locks escaped from beneath his watch cap, only to be recaptured in a ponytail. On his belt, I noticed a small holster contraption holding a corncob pipe.

"Here's the scoop," said Murphy. "I guess Miss Kim said she didn't need a ride. I don't know if she was calling her husband or friend or what, but she said she already had a lift. She just wanted the car hauled off. She said she'd contact the rental company later."

I followed him around to the passenger door. He reached under the flaccid air bag for the glove compartment and groped around until he found the rental agreement. "Here you go, Warden."

Ashley Kim had reported her address as Cambridge, Massachusetts. Probably she'd been visiting someone on Parker Point.

"Did she leave a cell-phone number with your dispatcher or any way to contact her locally?"

"Nope."

"Does your phone system have caller ID?"

"I have no clue."

I worked my flashlight beam around the inside of the car, but there were no personal belongings to be seen. Same with the trunk. The situation seemed to be exactly what it appeared. "I need to fill out an accident report."

"Guess Miss Kim didn't know she was supposed to stick around," he said.

"She's not the first."

"Maybe she was afraid of the Breathalyzer."

I left Stump Murphy to refill his pipe and went to start the paperwork. My sergeant, Kathy Frost, jokingly referred to her own GMC pickup as her "office," but mine was more of a dusty shed. Inside I kept a laptop computer, toolbox, rain gear, change of clothes, personal flotation device, ballistic vest, spotting scope, binoculars, Mossberg pump shotgun, shells and slugs, tire jack, come-along, assorted ropes, flashlights, body bag, fold-out desk, batteries, law books, maps, spare .357 ammunition for my service weapon, a GPS mapping receiver, wool blankets, an official diary, and lots of bags to stuff animal parts in. If I was lucky, I might even find what I was looking for.

I had the interior dome light on and was readjusting the movable arm that held my computer in place above the passenger seat when a state trooper arrived. He pulled up behind my truck and paused awhile inside, as if making a phone call, before he finally got out. He cast a damned big shadow as he came toward me.

"What's the story, gentlemen?" He was the size of an NFL offensive lineman: shoulders a yard wide. I'm a big guy—six-two, 180 plus—but he made me feel like one of the Seven Dwarfs. He had on a heavy raincoat and that wide-brimmed Smokey the Bear hat Maine state troopers wear. At first glance, I didn't recognize him.

Murphy broke the news: "A woman hit a deer."

"So I heard." He stuck out his hand for me to shake. He could have palmed a basketball with that hand. "I'm Curt Hutchins," he said by way of introduction.

"Mike Bowditch. You're the new guy at Troop D."

"New? I grew up in Thomaston. But, yeah, I transferred over from the turnpike." His hair had been shaved so close to the scalp that he looked bald, but his face was handsome and boyish, with a big dimple in the middle of his chin. "Sorry, I couldn't get here sooner. The engine wouldn't start after I went home for supper."

"Dead battery?"

"Bad spark plugs." He pointed at the crash site. "So where's our unlucky driver?"

I told him the entire sequence of events, from the initial call I'd received from Dispatch, to my belated appearance on the scene, to Murphy's arrival shortly thereafter and our quick search of the vehicle. "I have this bad feeling I'm having trouble shaking," I admitted.

"Because somebody stole the deer?"

"Not just that. I'm just wondering where she could have gone. This is an isolated stretch of road. I'd feel better if I knew where to find this Ashley Kim."

"She caught a ride," he said confidently. "She was probably shit-faced and called a friend before the cops showed. I ran the plates just now with the rental company, and her Mass. license says she's twenty-three. Probably a party girl."

His characterization of a woman he didn't even know grated on me. "I'm thinking I'll poke around in the woods."

Hutchins didn't respond.

His silence made me uncomfortable, so I rambled on: "I just want to make sure she didn't wander off, injured.

He crossed his arms and narrowed his eyes. I could tell he'd just made a mental connection. "You're Jack Bowditch's son."

Seven months had passed, but I still couldn't escape the notoriety. No matter what else happened in my life, I would always be the son of Maine's most notorious criminal. "What does that have to do with anything?"

"Nothing. I'd just heard a rumor that you'd left the Warden Service."

"You heard wrong."

Without meeting my eyes again, he said, "I'll handle things here if you want to take off."

"What about the missing woman?"

"I'll make a few more calls, take a look around." Somehow, I doubted his intentions. After mere minutes of knowing him, Hutchins already impressed me as an arrogant asshole who operated with utter disregard for protocol. He wouldn't be the first cop to fall into that category. My own conduct during my father's manhunt had made me the poster child for the fuck-the-rules school of law enforcement. "I guarantee you she ran away before we could bust her for OUI," he said.

Stump Murphy ambled over, trailing a pungent cloud of pipe smoke. "What's the holdup, fellas? I've got other calls, you know."

"I'll file the report," Hutchins said. "It's a state police matter now."

I glanced at the wrecked car one last time. I was exhausted, cold, and slathered in mud. An hour earlier, I'd embarrassed myself in front of

Hank Varnum. Now this jerk trooper was rubbing my nose in my father's guilt.

To hell with Hutchins, I thought. To hell with this lousy night.

"It's all yours," I said.

I climbed into my truck, started the engine, and turned carefully in the road to avoid the pool of blood.

And then, God forgive me, I went home.

3

I first met Sarah Harris during our freshman year at Colby College, in central Maine. I'd fallen asleep in the back row of Chemistry 141, and she gently touched my shoulder after the lecture had ended and the classroom was emptying. "Wake up, Sleeping Beauty" were the first words she ever spoke to me. From the start, I knew I was bewitched.

Sarah had grown up in suburban Connecticut, and she'd come from money. Her father had started a profitable Web site in the nineties, during the first round of the dot-com boom, only to lose millions when the bubble burst. The specter of poverty continued to haunt her. In college, she had a recurring nightmare of the bursar kicking her out of school because her tuition check had bounced.

We didn't share many interests, beyond an insatiable sexual appetite for each other and a passion for the outdoors. Her hobbies were less bloody than mine—she was an avid hiker, swimmer, and bird-watcher—but she found it fascinating that I would get up before dawn to go deer hunting in the woods outside Waterville. Her city friends used to call me "Bambi killer" and mock my camouflage jacket and L.L.Bean boots. But Sarah ignored them. She recognized something feral underneath my clean-cut exterior, and like many good girls from proper families, she was aroused by the scent of danger.

After graduation, when I told Sarah I wanted to become a game warden, she initially took the news as a prank. When she realized I was serious, she came to the conclusion that the experience would merely be a rite of passage for me—like riding a motorcycle across Mongolia or working on an Alaskan crab boat for a season—but that eventually I would settle down and make money. Maybe move to Boston and get a law degree.

Sarah's own obsession was with kids, early-childhood education specifically. Her life's plan was to teach for a few years—"get my hands dirty," she said—then enter a Ph.D. program. She saw the radical transformation of the nation's school systems as being one of the historic imperatives of our times and talked about dedicating her life to educational reform.

Our first attempt at cohabiting fell apart when she'd realized that my interest in being a game warden seemed to be growing, rather than abating, with each night I spent crouched in the puckerbrush with a mechanical deer decoy. After many lonely evenings and at her older sister's urging, she'd moved out of our run-down shack. She was gone for three months. But then in the autumn, after my father's crime spree made the national news and I achieved notoriety for my part in the desperate search for him, we met for dinner. The next thing I knew, I was unloading from a rental truck the same furniture that I had so recently watched vacate our shared dwelling.

For my part, I tried not to psychoanalyze her motivations. It was enough that she was back in my life. Like most men, I subscribed to the hackneyed theory that women are essentially unknowable.

The house we were renting was a little ram-shackle place overlooking a tidal creek that flowed into the Segocket River. Big pines shaded the roof, and sometimes at night, a great horned owl would roost in the tallest trees to eat his dinner. In the mornings, I would find fur-and-feather pellets on the hood of my patrol truck. Once, I found the flea collar from a neighbor's missing cat.

When I got home, Sarah was already in her

flannel pajamas, sitting in front of the computer. She'd replaced her contact lenses with glasses and fastened up her shoulder-length blond hair in a scrunchie. She took one look at me in my mud-crusted uniform and frowned.

"Don't ask," I said.

"You're worse than a dog, the way you track mud in."

"Well, I'm certainly dog-tired."

"You and me both, baby."

I had to dig out the mud impacted around the laces to get my boots off, shedding dirty flakes all over the doormat. Carefully, I stripped down to my boxers and undershirt. By the time I'd finished, I was already sweating from the heat.

The house was always too warm for me now that Sarah was back in residence—we might as well have belonged to different species, polar versus tropical—but the house was also cleaner by an order of magnitude. During the months we'd lived apart, my existence had been reduced to microwave burritos, wrinkled shirts, and unwashed dishes. Now instead of bare walls, there were colorful Audubon bird prints and window-sills lined with Christmas cactuses; the refriger-ator contained fresh broccoli instead of leftover pizza. Sometimes I missed my unshaven days without a woman in residence, but mostly I was grateful. I once read that, on average, married men live five years longer than single ones, and

I could easily believe it. The human male fights the domestication process tooth and claw, but it's the best thing that can ever happen to him.

I walked over and rested my hand on her shoulder. "What are you looking at?"

She closed the browser window before I could see the screen. "Work stuff."

"Just as long as it isn't porn."

"You're the only man I've met who doesn't download it."

"I'm not going to participate in other people's degradation."

"That's very self-righteous of you." She hit the power switch, and the machine stopped humming. "Speaking of which, the Warden chaplain called for you again. She said she wants to go for a ride-along one of these days."

The Reverend Deborah Davies had been on my case for months. She wanted to talk with me again about my father's strange criminal behavior. As required by the Warden Service, I had already put in my hours with both a psychologist and the reverend herself, but I'd found counseling a waste of time.

"I don't need that woman tagging along on patrol."

"You should talk with her. It wouldn't hurt for you to open up to people about what happened." She peered at me over her glasses. "Avoidance isn't a successful life strategy."

"What am I avoiding?"

After the events at Rum Pond, all I wanted to do was move forward with my life. Meeting the retired warden pilot Charley Stevens and his wife, Ora, and seeing their love for each other, it seemed like I'd finally found an example of what a happy relationship could look like. And then when Sarah agreed to come home, I felt like I had reason to believe my luck had changed.

"If you don't know what you're avoiding, then I can't tell you," she said. "I'm going to read in bed. I made some biscuits you can have with your soup."

I watched her shuffle in her slippers into the bedroom, thinking how beautiful she looked even dressed in flannel pajamas, with her hair tied up in a frumpy knot.

In the kitchen, I poured myself a whiskey and reheated my dinner. Sarah usually corrected her kids' homework at the kitchen table. Tonight, I found some government forms scattered among the spelling quizzes. One of them was something called a Mandated Reporter Worksheet from the Child and Family Services department; the other listed signs of possible abuse or neglect: "Unexplained bruises and welts on the face, torso, and back; cigarette and other burns; mysterious fractures and dislocations; bald patches on the scalp."

I wondered now if these forms explained her somber mood.

The lights were off when I finally went to bed, but even in the pitch-blackness, I could sense that she was still awake beneath the covers. I brushed my teeth, then crawled in beside her.

"Honey?" I said.

"Not tonight, Mike, OK?"

Sex, for once, was actually far from my thoughts. "I wanted to apologize again for missing that movie."

"I'm not feeling well anyway. My stomach's been giving me trouble."

"Do you think it's the flu?"

"Every kid in my class is sick with some virus or other, so who knows?"

I turned on my side and rested my hand on her shoulder. "I saw those forms from Child and Family Services on the table. Do you think one of your students is being abused?"

In the dark, she made a sound that was almost like a laugh, but I knew it wasn't a laugh. "One of them? All my kids have cuts and bruises. I could report my entire class if I was paranoid. But no, the principal just wanted to remind us what we should be looking for, so she handed out those forms again."

When I'd first met Sarah, she was one of the least sarcastic people I'd ever met. "It doesn't sound like you had the best day," I said.

She yawned. "You never told me what happened with that car accident."

"The driver wasn't there when I arrived. I guess she caught a ride. In the meantime, somebody came by and swiped the deer."

"Weird," she said sleepily.

"The trooper who showed up was this asshole, Hutchins, who transferred over from the turnpike. He said a rumor was going around that I'd quit the Warden Service."

"You shouldn't care what jerks say."

"It just pisses me off."

"Everything pisses you off. Sometimes I think that moral indignation is your natural condition." She yawned again. "You might sleep better, you know, if you didn't have a drink before bed."

For a while, I'd dealt with my anger by throwing myself into my work, but everywhere I went my reputation preceded me. Seven months after my father's manhunt, I was still receiving crank calls (some of them, no doubt, from my fellow cops), with suggestions about where I should insert the barrel of my SIG SAUER P226 before squeezing the trigger.

Of course, you can't erase the past. You can only avoid making the same mistakes over again.

In my dissolving thoughts I saw the image of a young woman lying unconscious in the dirty snow. I realized that Hutchins never had any intention of searching the woods. But Ashley

35

Kim had told the tow company she was uninjured and catching a ride. Besides, the thought of driving back to Parker Point—to do what exactly?—was insane. While I was fretting about this woman's safety, she was probably at her friend's house, recounting her brush with death over another glass of wine.

Don't think about it, I told myself. Go to sleep.

Eventually, I did. But my sleep was a fitful one, and when I awoke in the morning, it was with the same gnawing uncertainty that had troubled my dreams.

4

Late March. Mud season in Maine. Not yet springtime but no longer winter, either—a slippery seasonal limbo. Weather even more freakish than usual. Rain, snow, ice, and sun, all within the span of an hour. A meteorologist's worst nightmare.

The only constant is mud. Mud creeping up your boots, splattering your pant legs, finding its way onto clothes you never even wear outdoors. Your fingernails jammed black with it. The impossibility of ever feeling clean. The inside of your truck transformed each day into a pigpen. Mud splashed onto the windshield, then smeared back and forth by the wipers. The wheels gummed up with mire and packed with gravel into the axles. Every car on the road painted the same shit brown.

Wherever you look, a mottled, melting landscape. Snowbanks rotting along the roadsides and meltwater streams the color of urine. Everything that was hidden is now exposed. Beer cans, trash bags, emptied ashtrays. Fur and feathers from creatures unidentifiable, things long dead.

Winter's aftermath. The dirtiest season.

March used to be a slow month for Maine game wardens. That was before all-terrain vehicles became popular. In the past, all you had to deal with were the last gasps of the winter yahoos: the foolhardy smelt fishermen venturing onto paper-thin river ice, the alcohol-fueled Evel Knievels trying, unsuccessfully, to turn their snowmobiles into Jet Skis crossing half-frozen ponds. Maybe a rabbit hunter would get lost in the woods, or you'd have to shoot a moose sick with brain worm. But traditionally, late March was a time for wardens to testify in court, catch up on paperwork, and take long overdue vacations.

Even now my sergeant, Kathy Frost, was trying her hand at tarpon fishing in the Florida Keys. A few days earlier, she'd sent me a postcard from the Hemingway house. I pictured her at Sloppy Joe's, daiquiri in hand, drinking all the barflies under the table: a Maine warden, on her March vacation, showing all those warm-weather conchs how it's done.

Those of us stuck in Maine had no such respite, not with ATVs tearing up the woods. As sales of four-wheelers skyrocketed, wardens were getting angry calls from people like Hank Varnum: landowners outraged by the damage done to their property by all-terrain vandals. This was only my second year on the job, but even I was noticing an uptick in complaints as the snow melted. What was worse, most of the local riders hadn't started gassing up their machines yet.

So I awoke at dawn, resolved to track down Hank Varnum's harassers. I showered, put on a uniform that would be filthy within five minutes of stepping outside, and left Sarah curled up beneath the covers. She'd had a restless night, tossing and turning, as if trying to wriggle free of a straitjacket.

Outside, the fog had lifted. The temperature had dipped before sunrise, and all the puddles were frozen solid. Winter wasn't done with us yet. Some of the worst snowstorms in the state's history were early-spring sucker punches. In Maine, you were a fool if you put away your snow shovel before Mother's Day.

My plan was to stop at the Square Deal Diner for a coffee and doughnut and then return to Varnum's property to have a look at the carnage by the light of day. After that, I figured I'd visit some of Hank's neighbors and see what information I could shake loose. At the very least, the word would get out that I was searching for the vandals. Fear of being caught might temper their bad behavior—or it might have the opposite effect of inspiring them to greater acts of mayhem. You could never tell with these situations.

But as I drove into Sennebec Village, I discovered that I couldn't get the name Ashley Kim out of my head. It was like a pestering fly that wouldn't leave me alone.

Outside the diner, I saw the usual lineup of commercial vehicles. Reading the names painted on the sides of these trucks was like taking a survey of midcoast Maine's winter economy. HATCHET MOUNTAIN BUILDERS. CASH & SON PLUMBERS. SNOW BUSINESS: PLOWING AND COTTAGE CARETAKING. It often struck me that most of the people in my district depended for their livelihoods on a small number of very wealthy individuals, many of whom spent only a few weeks a year in Maine.

At the counter, Ruth Libby poured me a cup of coffee. " 'Morning, Mike."

"Hi, Ruth. Where's your mom today?"

"Portland. She's got a doctor's appointment."

"Nothing bad, I hope."

"She wouldn't tell me if it was." Like her mother, Ruth was apple-cheeked and round of body. As the only waitress, she didn't have time

39

for small talk. She grabbed a molasses doughnut from the glass case and set it down on a little plate in front of me. But when she wandered back to refill my cup, I made a point of quietly asking her a question: "Does Curt Hutchins ever come in here? He's the new trooper at Troop D."

"No, Curt doesn't come in here. But I know who he is. He was in my brother Bill's class. All the girls had a crush on him."

I sipped my coffee. "What else do you remember about him?"

She set down the coffeepot and gave me a sly look. "You keep asking questions like that, and people are going to start talking."

I smiled and tried to study the room nonchalantly. It's the cop's lot in life that whenever you enter a restaurant in uniform, you give some people the creeps. I noticed one prematurely bald dude wincing at me over his newspaper, as if I'd carried the smell of dog shit into the diner with me.

I felt someone looming over me. "I want to apologize for last night," Hank Varnum said, but his craggy expression was anything but apologetic. "I shouldn't have gotten angry at you for what those punks did. I know you don't have time to stake out every ATV trail in Knox County."

He held out his hand for me to shake. It was all very theatrical.

"It's understandable you were upset, Hank," I said. "For whatever it's worth, I'm planning to talk with your neighbors this morning and see what I can find out."

"Talk to that bastard Barter first. You tell him I'm ready to prosecute whoever cut those trees to the fullest extent of the law."

"I will."

The bell above the door *clang-clanged* as he went out. Ruth Libby had been eavesdropping the whole time. "ATVers are tearing up his land?"

"Yep."

She shook her head with genuine sadness. "Damned kids," she said.

She was, at best, nineteen years old.

I sat in my truck in the parking lot and switched on my laptop computer. Up came the half-finished accident report I'd started filling out on Ashley Kim's deer/car collision. I considered calling her home number in Cambridge, but it was ungodly early, and I didn't want to step on Hutchins's toes. Instead, I looked up the addresses and phone numbers for the various law-enforcement entities in Knox and Lincoln counties. As it happened, Hutchins lived nearby, not exactly on the way to Varnum's farmhouse, but close enough to be a plausible detour. I decided to pay the trooper a visit.

It was one of the modular homes that had gone up over the winter on the Catawunkeg Road. The builders must have finished their work after the first frost, when it was too late to plant grass. Instead, they'd dropped some maple saplings into holes and left the yard a muddy mess.

Hutchins's cruiser was parked in the drive beside a shiny blue Ford F150 pickup. Like game wardens, Maine state troopers work out of their homes, reporting in to their district outposts—called barracks—only on an as-needed basis. Another vehicle, a bronze Dodge Durango, was idling in the open garage.

As I approached the door, a young woman in a business suit came hurrying out of the house toward the waiting SUV. She caught sight of me and froze. She was a short, shapely brunette with long hair pinned back behind her ears.

"Good morning," I said.

"Hello?" she said in the same wary tone one might use to greet a door-to-door salesman.

"Is Curt home?"

Instead of answering me directly, she turned and vanished inside the house. Half a minute or so later, she returned wearing a pair of sunglasses. "He'll be right out," she said, opening the door of the SUV. I watched her climb behind the wheel and back out—too quickly, in my opinion —down the drive.

Hutchins, wearing gray sweatpants and a New

England Patriots T-shirt, opened the door. His long eyelashes were crusty. "Let me guess— you just happened to be in the neighborhood."

"Something like that."

He yawned. "You want coffee?"

"If you're having some."

I followed him inside. A black Labrador retriever sprawled on a pillow in the mudroom gave me a warning growl but didn't bother to rise. Hutchins paid the dog no attention. The house didn't feel lived in yet—there was an emptiness to the rooms that spoke of boxes somewhere yet to be unpacked—and our voices seemed to echo unnaturally. He motioned for me to take a seat at the kitchen table.

"I think I startled your wife," I said.

"Katie? She's afraid of her own shadow." He poured a cup of black coffee and handed it to me without asking if I wanted milk or sugar. "So I know why you're here."

"You do?" This guy doesn't lack for confidence, I thought.

"You want to tell me I was out of line last night. I hate to break it to you, Bowditch, but you're kind of an infamous personality. There are a lot of officers who are going to have problems working with you after what your old man did. I'm not one of them. But you're never going to win any popularity contests up in Somerset County."

"Actually," I said. "I just wanted to follow up on the deer/car collision."

"You're not still worked up about that?" When he smiled, the stubble of his beard made the cleft in his chin more pronounced. "I wrote her up for leaving the scene of a collision. She'll be surprised when she learns she committed a Class E misdemeanor."

"So you never tracked her down?"

"I tried her home number in Massachusetts. Got a machine."

"You mind if I give her a call?"

He didn't bother disguising his suspicion. One of the afflictions that besets many law-enforcement officers is an inability to take any statement at face value. You're always watching for the "tell" that hints at a perp's hidden inten-tion. Then one morning you wake up and realize you're looking at your girlfriend like she's try-ing to put something over on you, too.

"What's your fascination with this? When I was working the turnpike, we got half a dozen abandoned vehicles a night."

"I'd like to talk with her about what hap-pened."

He studied me closely. "If I didn't know better," he said, "I might take that as an insult. Like you're implying I didn't do my job."

"I'm not implying anything," I said. "Maybe she knows what happened to the deer."

"The deer?" He laughed so loudly, the dog barked in the other room. "I thought you were worried about the girl. I should have guessed it was the other way around. You frigging game wardens."

There were some troopers who looked down their noses at wardens. We might have trained together at the academy, but they still didn't consider us real law officers in some essential way. Hutchins was obviously one of the elitists. I'd sensed it last night. I wanted to rip his head off, but somehow I managed to keep a bland smile on my face.

"Go ahead, give her a call," he said. "If you talk with her, though, let her know that she had some people worried about her." He grinned boyishly. "Then you can tell her about that summons."

"How's your cruiser this morning?"

I'd never heard of a trooper having engine trouble in the middle of his shift before—usually the state police kept those vehicles in tip-top condition—and that strange occurrence was yet another thing bugging me from the night before.

Hutchins seemed to sense my wariness; I saw a muscle flex along his jaw. But his voice gave nothing away. "The new spark plugs are all firing, if that's what you mean. I must have gotten some duds when I replaced them last week."

I stood up to leave. "Well, I better get on the road myself."

"Yeah, I'm supposed to meet my brother this morning in Brunswick." A bronze light came into his eyes. "That reminds me what I'd wanted to ask you. You see a lot of four-wheelers in the woods, right? You got any recommendations for a kick-ass ATV? I'm looking to do some serious off-roading this spring."

5

The rental company had provided Hutchins with Ashley Kim's home phone number in Cambridge. I drove half a mile down the road to a shuttered farm stand and dug my cell phone out of my Gore-Tex parka. After eight rings, one of those automated voices came on, instructing me to leave a message after the beep.

"This is Michael Bowditch with the Maine Warden Service, and I'm trying to reach Ashley Kim. I'm calling in regard to a car crash last night—that's March fifteenth—on the Parker Point Road in Seal Cove, Maine. It's imperative that I speak with Ms. Kim immediately. This is a law-enforcement investigation, and she is required by Maine law to provide a statement." I left my cell number, feeling doubtful she'd return my call.

By all rights, Hank Varnum's ATV vandals should have topped my to-do list. But instead, I found myself driving in the direction of Parker Point. It was a blustery, overcast day, and the wind was blowing a chop in the coves. Overhead, the tops of the spruces swayed in unison like churchgoers at an old-time tent revival.

The deer blood in the road had darkened overnight, turning a rusty red. The tire tracks from Ashley Kim's wrecked Focus were sculpted into the frozen mud. I buttoned up my parka as I roamed through the huddled evergreens and wondered again why this incident was biting so persistently at the back of my brain. What exactly had happened here after all? There was no evidence to be found amid the trees. I closed my eyes and tried to envision the sequence of events.

Sometime around dusk, a woman had been driving too fast in a thick fog on the road to Parker Point. Suddenly, a deer sprang out of the trees and smashed into her hood. The deer died on impact, the air bags inflated, but the woman emerged from the collision uninjured. She had the presence of mind to call a tow company, which sent Stump Murphy to retrieve the wrecked car.

What happened next? She told Stump's dispatcher that she already had a lift. Did she hitch a ride or call her friend on Parker Point to pick her up? How about a taxi? The nearest cab company was in Rockland, half an hour away, so probably not. Maybe she just decided to walk to whichever house she was headed.

Meanwhile, an anonymous driver arrived on the scene to offer assistance, but she refused his help. Our Good Samaritan did, however, stop at Smitty's Garage, two miles down the road, to call the Knox County dispatcher. He reported the accident and told the sheriff's department to send an officer. Unfortunately, the state trooper on duty (Hutchins) had inopportune car trouble. As a result, there was an hour delay before the responding officer (me) arrived on the scene. Sometime during the interim, an unknown person stole the dead deer. Or maybe the Good Samaritan was the game thief. Was Ashley Kim still present when the deer got snatched? Or had she already left by that time?

The logical conclusion was the one Hutchins had suggested: Ashley Kim had been drinking, she was worried about her blood-alcohol content, and so she skedaddled before the cops showed. She was probably sleeping it off in one of the swank cottages along the point. There were more than fifty properties out there. I could poke down every private drive, looking for a lighted window. That was assuming she was actually staying somewhere on the point.

My phone vibrated in my pocket.

"Hello?"

I'd been hoping it was Ashley Kim, but it was Sarah. "I wanted to remind you that we're having dinner with Charley and Ora tonight," she said. "Make sure you're home by six, OK? I don't want you showing up late, smelling like roadkill."

"Will do."

She paused awhile on her end of the phone. "I'm sorry about being cranky last night."

"I thought I was the cranky one."

"I've just got cabin fever. This weather is driving me nuts."

"Spring is on the way."

"I'll believe it when I see it," she said. "You know I love you, Mike."

"I love you, too," I said. "I'll see you tonight."

"Don't be late!"

I was genuinely looking forward to our dinner with the Stevenses. The retired warden pilot and his wife were visiting the midcoast area for a gathering of Vietnam War veterans. The last time we'd spoken, he said his knee was still in a brace but his physical therapy was proceeding well for "an old geezer." Over the phone, his spirits sounded sky-high, as usual: "Ora thinks I'm one hundred percent cured but just faking it to get rubdowns from the pretty young therapist."

"Are you?" I asked.

"At my age, son, your circulatory system needs all the aid and assistance it can get."

Sarah had taken it upon herself to arrange a dinner with the Stevenses at our house. After my talking about Charley and Ora so much over the winter, she wanted to meet them in person. I felt certain they'd enjoy one another's company. So why was I anxious?

I crouched down on the salt-frosted asphalt and plucked a tuft of deer hair from the frozen blood. I rubbed the coarse, hollow fibers between my fingers and let them blow free in the wind. Knowing my district the way I did, I probably had a better chance of locating my missing deer than I did Ashley Kim.

The first place I'd start looking was at the home of Calvin Barter, a man I knew only by his nasty reputation. My predecessor in the district had told me that Barter was a petty drug dealer and notorious game thief who never passed up fresh roadkill. I'd heard that he had an uncanny way of appearing mere minutes after a police officer radioed in a deer/car collision—ready, willing, and able to carry away the meat. Coincidentally, he was also one of the men Hank Varnum had identified as a suspected ATV vandal. So I'd be killing two birds with one stone, so to speak.

Despite all the fancy summer houses along its coast, Maine is a desperately poor state. My sergeant, Kathy Frost—who's not known for being politically correct—calls it "the fist of Appalachia shoved up the ass of Maritime Canada." I could travel just a few miles inland and see poverty everywhere: run-down mobile homes swarming with toddlers or Typar-sided shacks with junked autos rusting in their dooryards. Down every dirt road loomed a falling-down farmhouse plastered with KEEP OUT signs, as if there was anything inside worth stealing. Some of those same buildings, however, contained well-guarded meth labs and vast indoor nurseries of marijuana plants, in which case those warnings were well heeded.

The Barters' farmhouse was a rambling red brick affair with flaking white trim and rusted metal gutters. The dirt driveway up to the house led through an orchard of skeletal apple trees, and off to one side was a rolling hayfield in which various targets had been set up for rifle and archery practice. A ragged line of spruces ran along the back of the field, then crept in close behind the outbuildings.

A child was waiting for me in the drive. Her hair was a wild red tangle.

She couldn't have been older than five. The temperature was twenty-eight degrees, but she was wearing dirty pink shorts and a yellow T-shirt emblazoned with a cartoon mouse. Her lips were stained purple, as if she had just finished eating a Popsicle.

The girl watched me with enormous pale eyes as I got out of my truck.

"Sweetheart," I said in my softest voice. "Is your daddy home?"

The words that came out of her mouth sounded old beyond her years: "Yeah, but he's passed out. Ma's around back, though."

I followed the girl around the house and through a maze of scratchy bushes. Along the way, we encountered a mute toddler dressed in a denim jumpsuit and seated in a circle of petrified mud. Two more kids, a boy and a girl, both a little older, met us around the corner of the barn. Every one of them had kinky red hair. They all fell in behind us, forming a procession of sorts.

At a henhouse, three more people stood waiting. One I took to be Mrs. Barter. She was about the size and shape of a rain barrel, and she was dressed in a flowered cotton sundress with a frayed hem. Her hair was mostly gathered up in a faded kerchief, but a single gray-and-red strand had escaped confinement and now hung across her forehead. She had a cigarette clenched between her thin lips and an expression that looked as if she was barely holding in a belly laugh. A freckle-faced girl stood beside her, clutching a baby swaddled up so tightly, I couldn't be sure if it was a child or a doll. She had the beginnings of her mother's build—just give her another five years—but was dressed in shorts and a halter top. She, too, was smoking a cigarette. The last of the three was a scrawny, rusty-headed boy, maybe twelve years old, wearing a sleeveless T-shirt and jeans and holding a Daisy pellet gun. None of them seemed to realize it was a mid-March day with a wind-chill in the teens.

"Watch out, kids, it's the game warden come to take you good-for-nothings to jail," said Mrs. Barter unhelpfully.

The henhouse was a rectangle of dry dirt as large as a boxcar, with a chicken-wire fence about four feet high around it. In the back, an outhouse had been repurposed to provide the hens some shelter. Inside the pen, there were two dozen or so Rhode Island Reds. They all seemed to be engaged in the act of pecking one another's rear ends. The sour, grainy smell of chicken shit hung in the frozen air.

"I'm looking for your husband, Mrs. Barter."

"You're new around here, ain't you? What happened to that bumfuck Devoe?"

"Warden Devoe was transferred to Washington County."

"Good riddance." She took the cigarette from her lips, squashed it against the fence post, and tossed the butt into the pen, where it was quickly snapped up by one of the chickens. "Will you look at those goddamned birdbrains? It's like they got nothing better to do than peck each other in the ass."

"Can you tell me where your husband is, Mrs. Barter?"

"Oh, he's inside, sleeping it off. Give me a minute to finish with these chickens, and I'll get him."

"I shot a fox," said the red-haired boy. He pointed to the nearest tree line. "It came out of them woods. I bet it had rabies."

"Hold on, kids. Let me tell the story," said his mother.

I glanced at my watch. "If you could just get your husband, Mrs. Barter."

"This fox thing is pretty fucking funny, though."

Her son, Travis, she said, was out with his pellet gun, breaking beer bottles, when the fox walked right past him. That's how they guessed it was rabid.

"A person can get rabies," remarked the teenage girl with the baby. "You start foaming at the mouth. They give you this big-ass shot in the stomach for it."

"Now, the fox wandered right up to the hen-house as if no one else was around," continued the mother.

"That's when I shot it," said Travis, puffing up his chest.

"Well, that fox took off like its tail was on fire," said Wanda Barter with a broken smile.

"Then we look inside the pen, and damn it if my rooster t'weren't lying there dead! Davy Crockett, Jr., there killed Foghorn Leghorn!"

"It must have ricocheted off the fox," said the boy.

"Mrs. Barter," I said impatiently. "If you've got a rabid fox around here, you'd better keep your kids inside, at least for the time being."

"You ever try to keep a child indoors in the middle of springtime?"

Springtime? My nose was getting frostbitten. "Can you go inside and get your husband for me?"

She turned to her teenage daughter, the one with the baby. "Let me have one of your smokes first."

That was when I heard an ATV engine growl on the far side of the house. Before I could take two steps, it was already racing away, the sound receding into the distance as it rocketed up one of the fire roads that stretched all the way from the farm to Hank Varnum's property.

One of the children must have sneaked away to alert him.

"I guess Calvin woke up," said Wanda Barter, blowing cigarette smoke through the gap in her teeth. "Too bad you missed him. If you want to leave a card, he'll call you back."

There was no other word for it: I'd just been outfoxed.

6

In the Gospels, Jesus says, "The poor will always be with you."

I didn't realize He was speaking about me personally.

Until my mother divorced my father and spirited me away to suburbia like a stolen child out of Irish folklore, I lived in a series of leaky backwoods shacks and rusted mobile homes that were anything but mobile. All my clothes were hand-me-downs from strangers, and they were always too long or too short. At the time, I thought everyone ate day-old bread from bakery thrift outlets and shopped at stores that illegally traded food stamps for cigarettes, beer, and lottery tickets.

So what I'd found at Calvin Barter's house was like a bad trip down memory lane.

The Drisko residence was a rat of a different color. A father and son duo who were so close in age and appearance that they seemed more like twins, Dave and Donnie Drisko were ardent four-wheeling enthusiasts, frequent guests of the Knox County Jail, and self-taught martial artists. Nor were they above scavenging a dead deer from the side of a road. My gut told me that if Barter wasn't the ATV villain harassing Hank

Varnum, then it was probably the Drisko boys.

Their trailer was located at the dead end of a dirt road no sane person would dare travel. The property was walled with a makeshift fence, topped with barbed wire. The boards bore all the usual warnings about vicious dogs and the probability of trespassers being shot—although the Driskos were actually too cheap to buy real signs. Instead, they'd just spray-painted their fuck-off sentiments on the fence itself. The warning about the dog was legitimate. They owned a brindle pit bull that lived its entire existence on a rope spiked to the ground. As I drove up, it surged so fiercely against its collar that I thought its head would pop off.

I chose discretion over valor and laid on my horn. I rested my elbow against the wheel until one of the Driskos—father, son, who knew?— finally opened the door. He was, of course, shirtless.

"Jesus Christ! What the hell do you want?"

I rolled down the window. "Can you restrain your dog, Mr. Drisko? I'd like to have a word with you."

"You got a warrant?"

"I'm not here to arrest you." Technically, this was true. Of course, if I found evidence of a crime, that might change. "I just want to ask you a question."

"All right! All right! Lemme bring Vicky around back."

Drisko—I'd begun thinking it must be Dave, the father—seemed in a surprisingly obliging mood. He dragged the dog forcibly around the trailer to some spot beyond my ability to see. I waited a moment, just to be safe, before getting out of the truck.

A flatbed pickup was parked inside the fence, right beside a beat-up Chevy Monte Carlo and two mud-splattered ATVs. I took the occasion of Drisko's absence to inspect the bed of the truck. The wood bore recent bloodstains—the cold weather had preserved the redness of the hemoglobin—and frozen hunks of deer hair. Bingo, I thought. This gave me cause to search the curtilage.

Dave Drisko reappeared a moment later. He was scrawny as hell, with a black mustache and heavy bangs that fell so far down his forehead that he was constantly pushing his hair away to see out from under them. He looked like a runt, but at the Harpoon Bar in Seal Cove, the Driskos were known as the meanest drunks and dirtiest fighters in town.

"Your dog's name is Vicky?" I asked.

"Yeah, you know. She's named after that football guy, Michael Vick."

"Do you ever let her inside?"

"Hell no. She'd eat us!" He wrapped his wiry

arms around himself. "Yeesh, it's a cold one, ain't it?"

"Pretty cold."

"You want a cup of Sanka or something?"

I'd never been invited into the Drisko lair before, so the invitation raised my guard. Maybe I should have called in my location to Dispatch beforehand, but Drisko was being uncharacteristically amenable, and I didn't want to spook him. And so, I proceeded into the heart of darkness.

Imagine a bonfire fueled entirely by tobacco, smoldering cigarettes stacked twelve feet high. That was the equivalent amount of smoke I encountered within the Driskos' mobile home. Five minutes cooped up inside and I would have come down with life-threatening emphysema. The home itself was not the worst I'd visited— the carpet was no more beer-stained, the furniture no more ripped, the dirty dishes no more scattered. But a cockroach could have lived like a king there.

Donnie Drisko (also shirtless) was sprawled on the couch in front of an improbably large-screened plasma TV set. In my experience, the poorest people always seemed to find money for cigarettes, booze, and home electronics. The movie he was watching seemed to be a poorly filmed documentary on mammary glands of the largest kind.

The younger Drisko raised his shaggy head. He, too, had a wimpy mustache and pants that hung below the band of his tighty whities. If forced to guess, I would have said the father was somewhere in his late thirties and the son somewhere in his early twenties, but I might have been off the mark by years.

"Hey, it's Warden Bowden. How's it hanging, man?"

"Bowditch," I said, correcting him. "How are you doing, Donnie?"

"I'm cool. Just mellowing out."

"You want some Sanka?" Dave asked from the kitchenette. "Maybe a splash of coffee brandy?"

"I'm fine, Dave." I positioned myself against a plastic-paneled wall, keeping both father and son in view. But honestly, there wasn't a hint of hostility or suspicion about them. The vibe in the room was one of elation, fueled no doubt by coffee brandy. "Donnie, you mind pausing the movie there for a second?"

"No problemo."

"So what brings you to our neck of the woods on this fine morning?" asked Drisko the Elder.

"I thought you might be able to help me with something. You guys ever go wheeling over near Hank Varnum's property?"

"Hell no. That land's posted," said Dave, lighting another American Eagle.

"We don't ride on posted land," agreed his son.

"Then you wouldn't know who cut down two of Hank's big oak trees, one on either side of the trail."

The Driskos looked at each other as if they were about to burst out giggling. "Hell, man, it could be anyone," said Donnie from the couch. "You've got all kinds of lowlifes around here. You talk to Calvin Barter? Now that dude's a shitbag."

My throat and lungs were beginning to convulse from the smoke. I hadn't expected to get anything useful from the Driskos on the Varnum front, so I changed gears. "I'll check up on Barter. So tell me: What did you guys do with the deer?"

I could see Dave Drisko's pectoral muscles tighten. "What deer?"

"The one you picked up last night on Parker Point Road."

The two Driskos stared at each other, and I could easily believe they were communicating telepathically, like two space aliens from a rogue planet. "You lost us there, Warden," Dave offered at last.

"You guys were listening to the scanner and you heard that a woman hit a deer on Parker Point. So you jumped in your truck and shot over there to grab it before the cops arrived."

"Must have been someone else," said Dave.

"We were watching movies all night," Donnie volunteered from the couch.

"So it's just a coincidence I found fresh deer blood and hair on your truck?"

Again, the Driskos engaged in the Vulcan mind meld. I waited for them to get their stories straight via ESP. "I thought you said you wasn't here to pinch us," muttered Dave.

"And I won't arrest you if you come clean about what really happened last night." I peeled back a brittle window shade to look behind their mobile home. It was unlikely they had the deer suspended from a tree in the backyard, but criminals tend to have walnut-sized brains. I glimpsed a couple of plywood sheds in the curtilage (the yard, essentially) that could have hidden any number of things. "Was the woman still at the accident scene when you guys arrived?"

"Why don't you ask her?" Dave said.

"Maybe I will."

"Maybe you won't."

I met his eyes. They were as flat as two dirty old pennies. "What's that supposed to mean?"

"It means nobody's going to say they saw us on Parker Point last night, because we weren't there."

"Then you don't mind if I poke around. Just so I can cross you off my list."

Dave inhaled about half his cigarette before he spoke. "Yeah, we do mind."

I'd figured that might be the answer. "Maine

law says I don't need a warrant to search private property for illegally obtained game if I have probable cause of a wildlife violation."

Dave called my bluff. "You're going to have fun proving probable cause to a judge."

"When did you get a law degree, Dave? I was unaware you were an attorney." .

"Let's just say we know our rights."

Donnie propped himself up on the sofa. "And you might want to watch out for Vicky while you're in the yard. She doesn't like strangers."

There were a few ways for me to handle this scenario. As best I could tell, Drisko the Younger had just threatened to sic his dog on me. My instinct was to respond with a profanity, get out my Cap-Stun pepper spray, and prepare for a fight. But I suspected that my division commander wouldn't appreciate me escalating a minor beef into a major melee. Theft of roadkill was what, a Class E misdemeanor? Besides, two against one weren't favorable odds. For Sarah's sake, if not my own, I decided to play the diplomat.

"I still have to take an evidence sample from your truck," I said. Maybe the smoke was finally getting to me, but I felt a sudden urge to cough up a lung. "You'd better hope the DNA doesn't match the blood and hair I found at the accident scene."

Dave Drisko twirled his mustache. He couldn't decide if I was bullshitting about the lab tests;

he didn't know whether to be worried or not. "Go right ahead."

"We ain't going to stop you," said Donnie. He restarted his porn movie as I stepped outside.

His father followed me through the door, out into the frosty March morning. "You don't mind me watching you?"

I coughed, trying to force the noxious smoke out of my system. "Just as long as you leave your dog chained."

I returned to my patrol truck and searched around until I found two paper bags. I plucked a few hairs from the Driskos' flatbed and collected a shaving of frozen blood. Then I sealed, tagged, and labeled the evidence containers to put in a cooler. Eventually, I would have to fill out a chain-of-custody report when I submitted the samples for DNA testing.

Dave watched me like a starving jackal the entire time. "You're not going to come back with a bunch of wardens and bust down our door tonight?" he asked as I was packing up to leave.

"If I do, I'll be sure to knock."

"Because I've got enough going on in the legal department right now. Human Services is saying I ain't really disabled. They say I should be able to go back to the trap mill."

"What's wrong with you?" It was a question with a thousand plausible answers.

He put a hand against the small of his back.

"Back pain, man. My spine's all fucked to hell. And I got migraines like you wouldn't believe. If they take away my disability, me and my family are screwed royally."

Looking at him, I had no doubt that Dave Drisko could heave a truck tire ten feet in the air. I wondered where he stashed the neck brace he brought out when the social worker visited.

I could hear the feminine moans from the younger Drisko's porn movie through the thin walls of the trailer. "What about your son? What's Donnie doing for work these days?"

"Oh, him. He's on disability, too."

7

I decided to eat my lunch in the parking lot of the Montpelier museum in Thomaston. It was a fake mansion constructed to replicate the home of Gen. Henry Knox, a portly hero of the American Revolution and George Washington's secretary of war. The museum perched atop a hillside overlooking a cement plant on one side and the St. George River on the other.

After the Revolutionary War, the Boston-born Knox had set himself up as a British-style aristocrat—one of the so-called Great Proprietors —and eventually built an empire in the Maine woods the size of Connecticut and Rhode Island combined. His original Montpelier was one of the inspirations for Nathaniel Hawthorne's *The House of the Seven Gables*, and supposedly the character of Colonel Pyncheon was based on Knox himself. The general held his impoverished Maine "subjects" in contempt—he accused them of "idleness and dissipation"—and they responded by vandalizing his mills, burning down the homes of his agents, and even killing a few of his hired goons.

He eventually died after choking on a chicken bone.

I could never pass the Montpelier mansion without reflecting that the conflict between Maine's well-to-do newcomers and people like the Barters had deeper roots than most people understood. Life really is like a tree that way: No one considers how much history is hidden underground.

Driving home through a flurry of snow showers, I thought again of my morning confrontation with the Driskos, men whose ancestors had probably been among Knox's original rebels. I was positive that when the DNA results came back from the University of Maine laboratory, the blood I'd found at the crash scene would match the blood I'd found on their flatbed. Stealing game was a small-stakes offense, but it would justify a broader search of their property, and who knew what else we might find.

My encounter with Dave and Donnie reminded me of an event I'd witnessed as a teenager at Rum Pond; late one evening, Charley Stevens had confronted my father about a suspected poaching violation and had received an equally menacing response. The warden pilot had had the good sense to back down from the conflict. Was it a sign of personal growth that I'd managed to do the same with the Driskos?

I looked forward to sharing the mysteries of the past few days—my ATV vandals and missing deer—with Charley at dinner. I was certain the wise old owl would also have insight into the disappearance of Ashley Kim.

Without really intending to, I found myself detouring yet again to Parker Point. Why was this place pulling me like a magnet? This time, I bypassed the accident scene and drove to land's end. There was a little turnaround at the tip with a spruce-obstructed view of the Mussel Shoals islands. I got a glimpse of gray waves and gulls wheeling close to the surf, but that was it by way of a scenic vista. All of the better views lay down the end of private drives.

I'd once read that the State of Maine's coast-line, measured in a line from Kittery to Eastport, is just a few hundred miles long. But if you were able to straighten out all the inlets and peninsulas—like pulling a tangled string straight—you'd have five thousand miles of shorefront.

Parker Point was like dozens of exclusive necks north of Portland. From one main road, numerous private drives fanned out to the edge of the water. There you'd find mostly shuttered homes.

So where had Ashley Kim been going? I'd assumed she was visiting someone or had just taken a wrong turn. Was it possible that her family owned a house on the point? I doubted that Hutchins had followed this particular line of inquiry very far.

Who else might know the answer?

The town clerk, MaryBeth Fickett, had access to all the local property maps. And I knew her a little. She and her chubby hubby had shared a thermos of coffee with me while I was checking licenses out on Indian Pond. I dialed the number for the town office. After the seventh ring, I was transferred to voice mail. Maybe MaryBeth was out sick. Seal Cove was such a dinky little town that entire municipal departments could be immobilized by a bad case of the sniffles.

I left a message, saying a woman named Ashley Kim had hit a deer the night before. Her official residence was listed as Cambridge, Massachusetts, but I wondered if she owned a house in Seal Cove. I asked MaryBeth to call me back in the morning.

When I signed off, I saw that I'd gotten a text message from Sarah: "UR late 4 dinner." This adolescent infatuation of hers with texting was not one I could imagine sharing. It was true that certain gadgets—my GPS and vehicle laptop—made aspects of my job easier, but in general the WiFi age could go to hell, as far as I was concerned. Why did we need to be in constant contact with each other all the time? Whatever happened to enjoying the privacy of one's own thoughts?

I reversed course for home. The cigarette stench from the Driskos' trailer had penetrated through my pores. Maybe if I bathed in tomato juice, the way you wash skunk spray off a dog, I might emerge cleansed.

I found Sarah rushing around the kitchen, trying to do five things at once in preparation for Charley and Ora's visit. The house smelled pleasantly of the salt pork and onions she'd used to start her fish chowder.

"What kept you?"

"I got caught up in that deer/car thing from last night. I'm still trying to track down the driver. But I think I know who stole the deer."

"Can we talk about it later?" She gave me a repulsed look. "You stink of cigarettes."

"What do you want me to do?"

"Get out of your uniform, for one thing. Maybe you should hang it outside. Then help me figure out how we're going to get a woman in a wheelchair up the front stairs."

Ora Stevens was paralyzed from the waist down, the result of a plane crash that had left her husband—a seasoned pilot, who'd been teaching her to fly at the time—largely uninjured. Though Ora had been at the controls, Charley blamed himself for her injury. On several occasions, I'd seen him watch his wife wheeling herself around, and there was no doubt in my mind that he was reliving that terrible day for the thousandth time. Even those glacier green eyes of his couldn't hide his abiding guilt.

By the time I'd showered and changed, Sarah had moved from the kitchen to the bedroom. She was standing in her underwear in front of the open closet—filled from end to end with dresses, blouses, pants, sweaters, and shoes—and chewing on a cuticle. She'd been a competitive diver in high school and still had taut muscles in her shoulders and thighs. "What should I wear?" she asked.

"I'm happy with what you've got on."

"Be serious, Mike."

"It doesn't matter. Charley and Ora aren't exactly what you would call formal."

She turned, giving me a peek at her flat stomach. "Sometimes I'm stunned about how little you know about women. Of course it matters."

"How about jeans and a nice sweater?"

She waved her hand at me and went back to

studying the closet. "Get out of here. Go scrape the ice off the porch steps or something."

Charley and Ora drove up in their van two minutes before six o'clock. Mainers of their generation are, I believe, the most punctual people on earth.

Although we'd spoken on the phone, the last time I'd seen them was on the day of Charley's return from the hospital. He'd been wounded in the arm and leg, and his skin had been marbled with bruises from his ankles to his shoulders. Coming home for the first time since his accident, he'd shaken off all my offers of assistance and made his way on crutches up the ramp of their cabin with a look of iron determination on his face. "I've always been a bear for punishment," he'd said.

Now, in the phantom light of my porch, I watched him hop out of the driver's side of their Dodge Caravan. "Hello, there!" he called, a big smile cracking his weathered face. He looked hale enough, but he came at me with a new limp that couldn't be disguised.

His grip, as we shook hands, was as strong as ever. "Good to see you, young man."

"How've you been, Charley?"

"Fair to middling. I'm still doing the physical therapy, you know."

"Well, you look great."

One thing I'd noticed about Charley was that he seemed to own essentially a single outfit. Every piece of his wardrobe was some shade of green, as if he'd spent so many years in a warden's uniform, he couldn't imagine dressing in any other color. As always, his thick hair was barbered in such a way as to make me think of the brush they use on horses. And the knife-sharp intelligence in his eyes was a warning to anyone who might underestimate him. Charley Stevens would drop dead before he ever got senile.

The automatic door of the van slid open and the vehicle seemed to kneel as a ramp tilted out from the side.

"Pardon me while I help the Boss," he said.

"Hello, Mike." Ora waved from inside the van. Her wheelchair was held in place beside the driver's seat by a system of ratcheting straps. It took Charley mere seconds to loosen them.

Who was it who said that you get the face you deserve as you grow older? By that standard, Ora Stevens, had one of the most beautiful souls on the planet. It wasn't just the snow-white hair and Nordic cheekbones. She had a way of listening to you with full attention and constant eye contact, making you feel simultaneously fascinating and foolish.

"It's so good to see you," she said.

"Thank you for coming all the way down here."

"Don't be silly."

Charley clapped me on the back. "Take ahold of that side of the chair, and we'll tote this contraption up those stairs."

Ora herself didn't weigh much, but her automated wheelchair was cumbersome, and once again I was struck by Charley's surprising strength.

Sarah had put on black jeans and a washed-denim top that brought out the blue in her eyes. She seemed nervous, fidgety. Something about the thought of meeting Charley and Ora intimidated her; I could see the anxiety behind her welcoming expression.

"This is Sarah Harris," I said.

"Well, I certainly hope so," said Charley. "Or else you got us down here on false pretenses."

"We brought you this, dear." Ora held out a pan wrapped in a napkin. "It's an Indian pudding I baked this morning."

"Thank you. Mike has raved about your cooking," said Sarah. "I hope you won't be disappointed in my fish chowder."

"I was just saying it's a night for chowder." Charley winked at me. "Hasn't it been a cold winter, though?"

"Can I get you something to drink? I'm having a whiskey."

Charley waited for his wife to answer.

"I would have a whiskey and soda, please,"

she said. The choice pleasantly surprised me.

"Black coffee," added the old pilot. It was all he ever drank.

After I fetched the drinks, we all sat down in the living room. I'd cranked up the woodstove, knowing that Ora tended to feel chills deeply. It wasn't long before I felt my face growing ruddy from the heat and alcohol. We made some small talk about the long drive from their winter home in Maine's western foothills to Sennebec and about the tidy little motel they were staying at behind the Square Deal Diner.

"You have a lovely house," Ora told Sarah.

"It wasn't so lovely when I was living here by myself," I said.

"Men are such foolish creatures," said Ora. "When I first met Charley, he used to do his laundry by tying his clothes to a rope and towing them around the lake behind his canoe."

"Good old-fashioned ingenuity," said her husband.

After a few minutes of chitchat, I spotted my chance to turn the conversation in a different direction. "So what's going on in Flagstaff?" I asked. "The last I'd heard, Wendigo was going to exercise its option on all the leases around the lake. Are they really forcing you out of there?"

The Stevenses had owned their waterfront cabin for three decades, but under a vagary of Maine law, timber companies had always held title to the land beneath the house. The latest owner, Wendigo Timberlands, LLC, was a Canadian corporation with a history of clear-cutting forestlands and then selling off the denuded lakefronts as real estate holdings. Last year, they'd announced their plan to "sell" the leased lots in Flagstaff to their current occupants at outrageous prices.

"We can't afford to stay," admitted Ora.

"I'd say the Wendigo directors took the murder of their spokesman last year somewhat in stride," said Charley with a sour smirk I'd never seen from him before.

"So they're just taking over the whole town and forcing everyone out?" said Sarah with genuine horror. "How can they do that?"

"It's their land," I explained.

"They've got the deed, that's for sure, but I'll bet that CEO couldn't find Flagstaff, Maine, on a map." Charley took a deep breath to calm himself. "I suppose we shouldn't abandon all hope just yet."

"That's been my advice all along," said Ora. "Desperate times call for hopeful measures."

"I've fought for many a lost cause before and seen it come through," her husband agreed, but there was the timbre of defeat in his voice.

"Will you buy another cabin somewhere?" I asked.

"We still have Ora's mother's house in

Farmington, but I can't live in town without going stir-crazy," said Charley. "Civilization has lost its appeal for this old bird."

"It *never* appealed to you," said his wife. "You just endured it for the sake of the girls."

They exchanged uncharacteristically disapproving glances, as if Ora's remark concealed some veiled meaning. It made me wonder about their two daughters. They were estranged from their younger girl, Stacey, who still blamed her father for the plane accident that had crippled her mom.

Sarah leaned her elbows on her knees. "Where will you go if you leave Flagstaff?"

"A fellow I know has offered us some good land over toward Machias," said Charley. "I was posted in eastern Maine when I was a young warden and have always liked the people. Once you get past Bar Harbor, the Down East coast is more like the whole state used to be back at the dawn of time."

"You told me not to live in the past," I said. "You said I'd miss out on the present if I did."

Charley flexed the arm my father had shot as if it were giving him trouble. "I guess you could say that recent events have spoiled me on the present tense."

"Let's talk about happier subjects," suggested Ora.

But her husband's expression remained grim.

8

We'd just about finished dinner—Ora's Indian pudding was as delicious as advertised—and Sarah was talking about the kids in her fourth-grade class. Two glasses of Pinot Grigio had made her a little tipsy, and now her complexion was glowing. "You never know what they're going to say," she was telling us. "And you don't know if anything you say will have repercussions in their life. Everything is formative with them. And yet they can be so resilient, too."

"Those children are lucky to have you for a teacher," said Charley.

"There are days when I feel more like a social worker. I had to go buy a winter coat for one little girl who came in during a blizzard wearing just a sweater—and then her mother sent it back! She said she didn't want charity."

"That sounds like my mom," I said. "When I was a kid, she never wanted to admit how poor we were."

A phone rang in the next room. I'd left my cell in its holder, still attached to my gun belt. The sound carried from the bedroom closet: a worrying, faraway cry of alarm.

I set down my beer bottle.

Sarah put both hands on the table. "You're not on duty tonight, Mike."

The phone rang again. Everyone was staring at me, waiting for me to react.

"Please, let it go," Sarah said.

I was positive the call concerned Ashley Kim. Was she phoning me back finally? Or had Hutchins managed to track her down? Maybe it was MaryBeth Fickett, calling from the town office. I found myself turning to Charley for backup. "I'm expecting a call about a deer/car collision I'm investigating," I explained.

The phone rang for the third time.

"I don't see any harm in him taking it," the old pilot said to his wife.

I nearly kicked over my chair, I rose so quickly. "Excuse me for just a minute."

"Please, Mike," Sarah said, her voice rising.

But I was already gone.

The caller was MaryBeth Fickett. In the darkened bedroom, I glanced at the luminous green numbers on the alarm clock.

"I hope you're not still working at this hour," I said.

"If I am, it's your own fault." The Seal Cove town clerk was a very large woman who had the helium-pitched voice of a little girl. "Did you honestly expect to leave that message and not pique my curiosity? The answer to your question is, I don't have a record for anyone named Kim owning property on the point. But you said this woman lived in Cambridge, Massachusetts, didn't you?"

"That's right."

"Well, there's a Hans Westergaard from Cambridge who has a summer place out on the point. It's that big new house at the end of Schooner Lane. I know because Bill was the stone-mason on the project. He says Mr. Westergaard is a professor at the Harvard Business School."

"It can't be a coincidence."

"No, I wouldn't think so," said MaryBeth. "I have his home phone number in Massachusetts. His wife gave it to Bill because she kept changing her mind about the design of the fieldstone chimney. Mrs. Westergaard is a . . . perfectionist."

"I thought you were going to use another word."

She tittered in that girlish voice of hers. "I was."

The overhead light snapped on. Sarah stepped through the doorway of the bedroom and closed the door behind her.

"What did you say his telephone number was again?" I reached for the notepad beside the bed and scribbled the number down on a piece of paper.

"You'd better let me know what you find out!" said MaryBeth.

"I will," I promised.

Sarah waited until I'd hung up before she spoke. Then it all came out in a torrent. "I can't believe you just got up from the table like that. I don't mind you working. I've come to terms with your job. But when you're off duty, I expect you to make an effort at being emotionally present."

"The call was about that missing woman from last night. I think I know where she is."

"But you already said it was a state police matter. You swore you'd stop this cowboy shit if I moved back here, remember?"

"I remember."

What else could I do except follow her? But first I tore off the note with the Westergaards' phone number on it.

Charley and Ora were waiting silently at the table. From the set of her chin and his own cowed expression, I wondered whether my friend had just gotten a scolding, too.

"Sorry about the interruption," I said.

"I hope it wasn't an emergency," Ora said.

Sarah neatened her napkin, spreading it flat across her knees again. "No, it wasn't anything important."

The room was roasting. On my way to the table, I made a detour at the woodstove. "Does anyone mind if I turn down the heat?"

"Not at all!" said Charley.

I was dying to call Professor Westergaard and ask him about Ashley Kim; I just needed to concoct an excuse to leave the room again.

Ora put her hands on the place mat and began twiddling her thumbs. "So, Sarah was telling us she was approached about a fellowship down in Washington, D.C."

Before she moved back in with me, Sarah had applied for a yearlong position with the national office of the Head Start program. To her surprise, she was offered the job, which she rejected. I hadn't asked her to turn down the fellowship, but I hadn't encouraged her to accept it, either. When she informed me of her decision to stay in Maine, I was secretly overjoyed.

"Is it something you're going to pursue?" Charley asked Sarah.

"No, not right now."

Ora touched Sarah's sleeve. "Why not, dear?"

"I couldn't possibly move to Washington," replied Sarah. "It would be a fantastic opportunity, but after what happened, I just can't—" She wouldn't look at me, but I could see that her eyes were watery. "Well, you know. After what happened, I just can't leave Mike here alone."

I went to take a sip from my beer bottle but found it empty. "I'm going to get another beer. Would anyone like anything?"

Charley rose stiffly to his feet. "Let me help you with some of these dishes."

He followed me into the kitchen with a stack of bowls and plates.

"So what's the scoop with that phone call?" he whispered.

"It's a long story."

He wagged his thumb at the door leading out to the back porch. "Well then, let's step outside. It's hotter than the devil's armpit in here."

The temperature had plunged after darkness fell, and there was a crispness in the air that harkened back to the depths of winter. Overhead, the constellations were as clear as illustrations in a textbook. It took no imagination at all to connect the dots and see Orion, the hunter, with his lethal club and broad belt.

As concisely as I could, I told him about Ashley Kim's disappearance and my tense encounter with the Driskos. He listened carefully, rubbing his lantern chin the whole time, the very model of thoughtful attention. "So you suspect the young woman was headed out to this fellow Westergaard's house?"

"It makes sense, doesn't it?"

"And these Drisko fellers showed up to snatch the deer?"

"I don't know if they arrived before or after she left—but yes."

"Do you have Westergaard's phone number?"

"I have his number in Massachusetts." I reached into my pocket for the note I'd scribbled in the bedroom. I heard the door creak open behind me and felt warmth from the kitchen rushing out into the night like a hot breath upon my neck.

"What mischief are you men up to out here?" asked Ora. She had to lean forward in her wheelchair to hold the door ajar.

"Just getting some fresh air," her husband said.

"Could you come inside for a moment, Mike?"

"Sure, Ora."

"Don't stay out too long," she told her husband.

Charley snatched the note from my hand and gave me a wink. "You'd think I spent my life as an accountant and not a game warden."

In the bright light of the kitchen, I towered over Ora. I'm not sure how she stayed active, paralyzed as she was, but she radiated the vitality of a woman who swam a mile each morning. The house was strangely quiet.

"Where's Sarah?" I asked.

"Oh, she's in the powder room. I think she needed a moment to herself." She paused deliberately. "Is she feeling . . . all right?"

"She's had some stomach issues."

Whatever Ora was fishing for, she hadn't hooked it. "I wanted to ask you about your mother."

"My mom?" The request took me by surprise. During the hunt for my father, it seemed the whole world believed he was guilty—everyone except his son and ex-wife. I'd realized that my mom still loved my dad in a twisted way that defied understanding. "I haven't seen much of her," I explained. "We didn't have a service for my father. The state took care of the body—cremated it. They asked me if I wanted the ashes, but I said no."

"What about your mother?"

"I don't know if she took the ashes."

Ora frowned with consternation, as if I was failing to understand an obvious question. "I mean, do you know how she's doing? Your father's death must have been very difficult for her."

The concern in Ora Stevens's wide-set eyes made me feel embarrassed that I'd been so slow to catch her meaning. "She was still emotional when I saw her in Scarborough over the holidays," I explained. "In her heart, she sees my dad as a tragic figure and blames Brenda Dean for turning him into a monster. We haven't really spoken about what happened, to tell you the truth."

"You should," Ora said with sudden vehemence. "Grieving comes to people in a variety of ways. I've seen it in my own family. And, of course, Charley and I have watched friends pass as we've gotten older." She reached out for my hand. "Have you spoken to anyone yourself? You must know Deborah Davies, the Warden Service chaplain. She was very helpful to Charley."

"Charley?"

"After our accident, she came to see him."

I found this revelation startling. "He never told me."

"I think you'd find the reverend easy to talk to."

I squatted down on the linoleum so that I was at eye level. She smelled of whiskey and rose water. "I appreciate your concern, Ora, but I'm OK."

"Forgiveness can be hard," she said in a tone that made me wonder if she was speaking of the plane accident that had paralyzed her or of something else. "It takes real effort."

I shook my head with disdain. "I can't ever forgive my father."

"I'm not talking about your father, Mike. I'm talking about you."

At that moment, the door blew open and the gust carried Charley into the room. I spotted a cell phone in his hand. "Mike and I need to go out for a bit."

"What's happening?"

"I'll explain when we get back."

"Of course, Charley. Whatever you need to do."

Sarah appeared in the kitchen door, looking flushed, anxious, and confused.

"Mike and I need to take a ride, Sarah."

"A ride? Where?"

"Parker Point," said Charley. "I think something might have happened out there."

9

We grabbed our coats and stepped out again into the frigid night. I'd fastened my badge and my holster to my belt—the Warden Service required that all wardens be armed whenever we drove our state trucks. The rules also prohibited us from reporting to duty while impaired by alcoholic beverage, but I felt perfectly sober. As I reached into my pocket for the keys, however, Charley clamped a hand around my wrist. "Are you all right to drive?"

The question irked me. "What do you mean?"

"You've had a few pops."

"I'm fine, Charley." But my telltale breath drifted in the cold air.

He looked hard at me but didn't speak again until we were backing out of the driveway. "I couldn't find a local number for Hans Westergaard, so I tried him at home in Massachusetts."

His insatiable curiosity always amused me. "You just can't help yourself from butting into these situations, can you?"

"My mother always said I had an inquisitive nature."

"Was Westergaard home?"

"No, but his wife was."

"Uh-oh."

"She told me Ashley Kim was her husband's research assistant."

"That's a new term for it." The truck hit a frost heave, which brought the seat belt tight against my chest. "I'm guessing there's more."

"Mrs. Westergaard said he left yesterday for an international monetary policy conference at Bretton Woods in New Hampshire. She hasn't heard from him since."

"What makes you think this is anything more than a case of him screwing around?"

"There was a tone in her voice."

"I bet there was!"

Charley raised his collar up around his throat and rubbed his gloved hands together. "It was something else. She seemed panicked. 'Is Ashley missing, too?' she asked. I thought that was an odd word for her to use, *missing*."

"Should I call the dispatcher?"

"Let's see what we find first," he said. "Hopefully, we'll discover those two lovebirds snuggled up in their nest, and that'll be the end of the mystery."

"If we do, I'm going to give her hell for leaving the scene of an accident. You can bet on that."

"I have no doubt." Charley laughed.

The drive from my house in Sennebec down the peninsula to Seal Cove usually took twenty minutes, but I kept my foot on the gas and we made it in fifteen. The headlights cut a narrow path through the dark, making me feel as if I were wearing blinders. We passed the accident site after we turned onto the Parker Point Road. I indicated the ill-omened stain in the road. Charley gave a solemn nod.

The sign for Schooner Lane was brand-new and marked PVT for private. The road had been plowed and sanded over the winter. I figured that Professor Westergaard employed one of the local caretaking companies that watched over the seasonal homes in Seal Cove. The snow had thawed and refrozen a few times since the plow last went through; the lane was as slick as a bob-sled run.

There were no other homes on Schooner Lane, just a dense, bristling mass of spruces. At the bottom of a slight hill, the road curved and came to rest in the driveway of a large cottage. The remaining snowbanks along the edges of the drive showed that the caretaker had made a visit after the last big storm. No vehicles were visible, but a car might very well have been tucked away inside the three-bay garage.

As we rolled to a stop, a motion-sensor light sprang on, illuminating the impressive building from the fieldstone foundation to the fieldstone chimneys. The mansion was obviously new. The building frame and casements had recently been painted a deep kelly green, and the cedar shingles still retained a pinkish hue. The architect's design might have been an attempt at a post-modern Maine cottage, but something about the place brought to mind the House of Usher.

"There's a light on upstairs." Charley pointed to the second story where the faintest hint of illumination brightened one window.

The rest of the house seemed utterly dark.

I reached into the backseat and found the Maglite. It was as long as my forearm and as heavy as a steel club.

When we slammed the truck doors, the sound echoed like gunshots in the night. I followed Charley up the frozen drive—someone had recently sanded it—to the front door. We paused a moment on the granite step and exchanged quizzical expressions. Then Charley pushed the bell, saying, "Let's see who's home."

We could hear the muffled, electronic chime of the bell through the glass transom above the door.

In the quiet, I became aware of the crashing of waves in the dark beyond the house. The ocean was an unseen but uneasy presence that made me think of a dragon sleeping in a dark cave.

After a minute of silence, Charley tried again.

I dug my bare hands into my pockets. The air was sharp and cold and stung my cheeks.

After another long minute, Charley hit the bell

three times in quick succession. Impatient, I pounded my fist against the door as hard as I could.

Still, there was no response.

"It doesn't look like anyone's around," said Charley.

I glared up at the lighted window on the second floor. If nothing else, it told me that the house hadn't been abandoned for the winter.

The old pilot stamped his feet to warm them. "The women won't be too happy we flew out here on a wild-goose chase."

"This house has got to be where Ashley Kim was headed," I insisted.

"Maybe she and the professor drove up to Camden for a romantic dinner," Charley said. "I suppose we could wait, but who's to say when they'll be back?"

"I'm going to look in the windows." I stepped into the brittle snow and began making a circuit of the building, pressing my forehead against every pane of icy glass and squinting to see what I could. Most of the windows had curtains to prevent a burglar from doing exactly what I was doing, but there were slits between some of the drapes that afforded a glimpse inside. The interior of the house hid itself in shadows. I could make out the bulked silhouettes of furniture and floating gray rectangles demarcating windows on the far side of the home.

"We should probably get back to the ladies," called Charley.

The night before, I'd left the scene of an accident without quieting my doubts. I wouldn't make the same mistake again.

A long porch stretched along the ocean side of the house, suspended on steel pilings driven into the ledge. Below me, waves splashed against the rocks, turning from ink black to foaming white as they exploded against the shore. I mounted the steep ice-coated steps and climbed carefully up to the porch.

The doors were all of glass. Like dark mirrors, they reflected the harbor behind me: a phantom seascape lit by watery stars. Again, I peered inside. Heavy drapes barred my view. I moved to the last window and found the curtains parted. Inside, all was blackness. Nothing to be seen.

I switched on my flashlight and, shielding my eyes with my hand, began moving the beam around the inside of the room. On the other side of the window, at the level of my feet, there was a pale carpet that might have been light gray or bluish white. My light encountered the legs of a coffee table. I moved the beam to the right and found a couch. The carpet stretched on into the darkness.

Something sparkled. I directed the cone of light back a few feet and focused it on a distant patch of rug. Tiny prisms lit up, like quartz crystals scattered on the floor. A lamp had fallen from a table. It lay broken in pieces. I saw that the cord had been pulled out of the wall socket. There was something else there, too, at the edge of the flashlight beam. Beside the toppled lamp —a large reddish stain.

"Charley!" I swung the Maglite around in my hand and drove the heavy butt down against the door. The glass shattered. I reached inside to turn the lock. A jagged shard sliced through my parka and into the meat of my forearm. I saw the blood but didn't feel any pain; it was as if my arm had been unplugged from my nervous system.

The lock turned with a sharp click and I shoved the sliding door open. I unholstered my service weapon.

The inside of the house was very warm and as dry as a desert. I felt the hot air on my face as I entered the room. Someone had cranked up the thermostat. I could hear the furnace murmuring in the basement. I crouched over the stained carpet. It was unmistakably a splatter of congealing blood.

I glanced up, unsure what to do or where to go. "Police!" I shouted. "Professor Westergaard?"

The only answer was the ominous hum of the furnace.

A hallway receded ahead of me, a long Persian carpet disappearing into the shadows. I followed it past a guest room with a stripped mattress and white sheets draped like shrouds over the bureaus. The door of the first-floor bathroom stood ajar, but the room was empty.

In the kitchen, I saw granite countertops and sinks, pots and pans hanging from hooks. Reflected light bounced back at me from the brushed aluminum face of the refrigerator. My eyes searched for clues.

Atop a stone island in the center of the room was the knife block. A knife was missing.

Charley called after me, down the hall, "Mike?"

Steps led up to the second floor. The hall light was burning. "Upstairs!"

I sprang up the stairs, taking two at a time. Behind me came a pulse of light as Charley found a switch on the kitchen wall.

The house was huge. There were so many doors. I pushed open one after another before I reached the master bedroom. I turned the knob and swung the door into the room. Before me was another bare mattress. But this one was splattered with blood. I circled the bed, aiming my weapon at the center of the flashlight beam.

On the floor reposed a naked woman. She lay on her side, with her arms bound together behind her, not with rope but with sailor's rigging tape. She was very small. Black hair almost completely masked her face, but I could see her chin was painted with blood and her neck was covered with purple spots. Her body was white except where a knife had cut bloody letters into the skin.

The overhead light snapped on as Charley entered the room. I heard the old pilot gasp out loud.

I slid my SIG back into its paddle holster and knelt beside the dead woman. Rigging tape was wrapped over her nose and mouth. I brushed the hair out of her eyes. They were open, lifeless. On the woman's cheek was a small *S*. Between her breasts was a larger *L*. The word continued down her torso, a bloody signature that ended above the dark triangle of pubic hair.

"Don't touch her!" said Charley.

He yanked me away, but not before I had pushed the dead girl onto her back. By then, I knew the inscription the killer had carved into the body of Ashley Kim.

SLUT, it said.

10

As a child, I had a fierce and powerful faith. My mother instilled in me a deep connection to the Catholic Church, taking me to Mass each Sunday morning while my father lay hungover on the couch.

I was baptized and received my First Communion at the Church of Saint Sebastian in the gritty papermaking town of Madison. I said my first penance there, too, whispering through a screen to a priest whose role in this arcane ritual I didn't comprehend. I had known Father Landry all my young life, but I was now supposed to believe that he wasn't actually present in the confessional. The heavyset man who seemed to glide down the aisle during Mass had been transformed into God's earpiece. At age eight, I couldn't figure out why the Lord needed a surrogate, especially since my previous conversations with Him in prayer had been so direct. But I surrendered myself to the sacrament, promising not to trespass again and saying the ten Hail Marys that Father Landry gave me as punishment for my childish sins.

I emerged from the confessional, unsure of what had taken place. The unsatisfying ceremony made me feel *more* distant from Him, rather than less. Still, I continued in my Catholic faith, taking my father's name, John, in confirmation.

It was only many years later, when I had real sins to confess, that I began to wonder where God was hiding. One of us had gone missing, but I couldn't have told you which.

By the time of my father's rampage, I had parted ways with the supernatural. In the weeks following my return from Rum Pond, when the Warden Service chaplain, Deborah Davies, first came to see me, I remembered feeling vaguely sorry for her. She seemed like a kindhearted person, and I was glad that she derived comfort from her beliefs. But when she asked me if I'd spoken to my parish priest recently, it was all I could do to keep from rolling on the floor.

I did not believe in ESP. I did not believe in ghosts or crystal balls or future events foretold in tea leaves. If she had asked me, I would have told her that the prophets of the Old Testament were schizophrenics and that the voices that spoke to them out of the desert were electro-chemical misfires in the brain. Human beings are not transmitters of their intentions, I would have said. Angels do not whisper in our ears. Predestination is a fairy tale, a bedtime story for adults scared of meaningless death. Those were the articles of my adult faith.

So how could I explain the deep foreboding that preceded my discovery of Ashley Kim?

When I arrived at Hans Westergaard's house, I didn't suspect the woman was dead or fear she was dead. I *knew* she was dead. The certainty had been with me for hours—like an animal lurking beyond the campfire light—but I hadn't recognized the premonition for what it was. Maybe I didn't want to admit to myself the meaning of the portent. I didn't want to open the confessional door after so many years and find God present once again, but in a shape I no longer recognized.

With a grip like eagle talons, Charley pulled me from the Westergaards' bedroom. He guided me back down the stairs, his voice soft in my ears, encouraging me to retrace my original footprints, until we were once again standing beside my truck in the driveway.

"It's a crime scene now," my friend said. "We don't want to muck it up any more than we have."

In the sharp, cold air, my senses returned. I found my cell phone in my jacket pocket. I started to key in the direct number for the Knox County dispatcher, when I heard a car coming down the drive behind us. Flashing blue lights made hallucinatory patterns in the trees. Then a blinding spotlight snapped on, pinning us both in place. An electronically amplified voice boomed out, "Don't move."

Charley and I exchanged befuddled looks. How had a cop gotten here so fast, before we'd even called in the homicide?

A car door slammed and I heard a familiar voice. "Bowditch?"

Trooper Curt Hutchins came striding toward us out of the light. "What the hell are you doing here?"

"There's a dead woman inside," I said, as if that were any explanation.

"What?"

"We came over here looking for a missing

woman whose car struck a deer last night," said Charley in an even tone. "We had reason to think she might be inside this home. We found her body upstairs. She seems to have been sexually assaulted before she was killed."

"It's Ashley Kim," I said.

"You need to get an evidence team over here, sonny," said Charley.

"Who are you?" Hutchins asked.

"Charley Stevens, Maine Warden Service, retired."

The big state trooper had positioned himself so that we couldn't see his expression; he was just a silhouette against a wall of light. "I know you—you're that daredevil pilot."

I squinted to see his expression. "How the hell did you get here so fast, Hutchins?"

"You triggered the silent alarm. What were you doing, breaking down the goddamned door?"

"I looked in the windows and saw signs of a struggle," I replied. "I was justified. Blood was in plain view."

"But what were you doing here in the first place?"

"Will you just stop asking us questions and call for some fucking backup here? There's a dead woman inside who's been raped and mutilated."

There was a heavy pause. "I'm going to go take a look."

"We already disturbed the crime scene," said Charley. "Please take our word for it, Troop. The evidence-recovery techs need to cordon off this entire building."

"I'm going to go take a look." He breezed right past us, moving purposefully up the walkway.

"Fuck it," I said. "I'm calling Dispatch."

Lori was working again. As briefly as I could, I told her where we were and what we'd found. "You need to get some detectives down here ASAP," I said. "And the state police CID, too."

"You said it's the same woman who hit the deer last night?" asked Lori.

"I think so."

"And there was a word carved in the body?"

"Yes."

"Oh God," the dispatcher said mysteriously. "Not again."

After I'd hung up, Charley brought out his own phone. "We need to tell the women we're going to be late."

I listened as Charley fibbed to my girlfriend. "Oh, he's fine, Sarah. But we've stumbled onto a pretty bad scene here, and the police are going to need our statements. I don't know how long this process is going to take."

He then moved out of earshot to converse privately with his wife.

"You should have been a diplomat," I said when he returned.

"I was—every time I met a man with a loaded gun." He gestured toward my arm. "It looks like you cut yourself back there."

"It's nothing."

"You should have an EMT look at it all the same."

My head was spinning in circles. I closed my eyes and tried to make it stop. I visualized a roulette wheel slowing. The wheel landed on a red number.

"Westergaard," I said.

Charley understood. "There was no sign of him, unless he was hiding in a closet."

I dialed information and asked for the hotel at Bretton Woods, New Hampshire. A minute later, I had my answer.

"There's a conference going on all right," I told Charley, "but Westergaard isn't at it. He canceled his reservation two days ago."

"That makes the professor the prime suspect, I'd say."

"But why carve that word into her?"

The old pilot glanced up at the lighted windows. "I've been on this earth nearly seven decades, and I don't think I'll ever understand the abominations men commit against women."

Hutchins came down the walk slowly, with his wide-brimmed hat in his hands and his face empty of meaning. Looking at him, I felt an upwelling of anger at this arrogant, incompetent man. He tried to slide past us, but I blocked his way.

"Good work, Trooper. Nice job finding that missing driver."

"Shut up, Bowditch."

" 'She was probably shit-faced and called a friend before the cops showed'? That's what you told me. Maybe if you had actually looked for her, she'd still be alive."

He looked down at me, eyes flat, jaw tight. "You smell like booze."

"Boys," warned Charley. He knew where this was headed.

For an instant, I thought Hutchins might punch me. Instead, he turned one of those wide shoulders into my chest and flicked me aside like a bull tossing a picador. I practically fell over into the snowbank as he stormed back to his cruiser. We could overhear him on his police radio, although his exact words were lost to us.

"I'm not sure that was called for," said Charley.

"He just pisses me off."

The wind shifted direction and swept in suddenly off the sea. Charley's teeth began chattering like castanets. "I'm guessing we're going to be out here awhile."

"I'm sorry for dragging you into this."

"I'm not sure who dragged who into what," said my friend with a humorless smile. "But I'm thinking I'd better buy myself a rabbit's foot, quick. My luck's definitely taken a left-hand turn since I made your acquaintance, Warden Bowditch."

It was Charley's idea to meet the detectives at the top of the driveway. "They're going to want to spray wax on the tire tracks," he told me. "And we don't need any more cars coming down this hill."

We left Hutchins standing like a statue beside his cruiser and pushed our way uphill through the broken-branched trees, taking a circuitous route and checking the thinning snowpack with our flashlights every few feet to be certain that no one else had recently come this way. It had begun to dawn on me how thoroughly I had contaminated the crime scene by breaking into the house.

The first responder to arrive was a Knox County deputy. Another soon followed. The police lights made revolving blue shapes in the spruces, turning all our faces blue.

The county sheriff himself was the next to show up. He was a short man with two chins and smoothly shaven cheeks. He had recently won election to the job after working at a desk in the Maine State Prison. Somehow, back in November, he had managed to convince a majority of voters that his background in corrections qualified as sufficient law-enforcement experience. Most of the jail guards I'd met didn't have a clue about the niceties of community policing. I wasn't optimistic Dudley Baker would be the exception to the rule.

"Tell me what happened," he said, peering out at us from behind photochromatic eyeglasses.

"The house belongs to a Professor Hans Westergaard of Cambridge, Massachusetts," I stated. "There's a dead woman named Ashley Kim inside, but no sign of the professor. We think they were lovers. If I were you, I'd put an APB out on Westergaard immediately."

He was wearing a fur-lined parka with the hood up. The effect of which made him look like an Eskimo. "You're Bowditch, right?"

"Yes."

"And you're Charley Stevens."

"Pleased to meet you."

He glanced back and forth between us, frowning. "You need to explain this to me. What the heck are you guys doing here? Why did you break into this house?"

"Maybe we should wait for the state police before we get into all the gory details," Charley said in an amiable voice. "There's no point in us telling our story twice." In Maine, with the exception of the largest cities, all homicides are investigated by the state police's Criminal Investigation Division. The sheriff's department would merely assist in the case.

Baker sniffed and thrust his hands into his

pockets. "Fine," he said. Then he went off to speak with his underlings.

"You need to put an APB out on Westergaard!" I called after him.

It took another half hour for a state police detective to arrive. As he climbed out of his sedan, my stomach did a flip-flop. Even in the swirling light of the police cars, I recognized the spark-plug physique and do-it-yourself crew cut. Detective Antonio Menario recognized me, too. "Bowditch," he muttered, not bothering to hide his contempt.

"Detective."

He glared at Charley with coal black eyes. "You're a long way from home, Stevens."

"I'd say the same for you," said the old pilot.

Maine state police detectives are assigned to designated regions, and it was my understanding that Menario worked out of the western foothills and mountains, given the role he had played in investigating my father's case. The detective had never wavered from his theory that my dad had killed those men, and he had treated me with disdain when I'd argued for the possibility of other suspects.

"What are you doing on the coast, Menario?" I asked.

"I'm on temporary assignment so Pomerleau can have another kid. Explain to me what you two are doing here."

"We found the body."

Menario tilted back his head and breathed out steam. "Of course you did."

Sheriff Baker returned and launched into a situation report for the detective. "We've put up a perimeter. Your man Hutchins is down at the house, but no one besides these two wardens has gone down the driveway or otherwise disturbed the crime scene. The medical examiner is on his way. My DA is down in Portland, so I'm not sure when we'll see him tonight. I put in a call to Assistant Attorney General Marshall."

"What do you mean, they disturbed the crime scene?"

"I guess we should explain what happened," Charley offered.

"Now would be the time," said the detective.

I left it to Charley to tell the tale, figuring Menario hated my guts already, so what was the use? The detective listened with arms crossed, occasionally asking a curt question to clarify a point, sometimes sighing audibly in disgust. He appeared to me like a man with a terminal case of constipation.

After Charley had concluded, the detective fell silent. Then, out of the blue, he said to me, "What did you do to your arm?"

Blood was dripping to the ground, but I felt no pain whatsoever. "Oh, I cut it on the glass door."

Menario scowled. "We're going to need samples from both of you," he said. "Blood, hair, fiber, DNA, boot prints. The evidence-recovery techs will take those at the jail. Tomorrow, we're going to need you to go through the video we shoot of the house, so we know exactly which rooms you fucked up." He turned his basilisk gaze on me. "We're impounding your truck, in case you carried any contaminants from it indoors."

"Anything else?" I asked.

"Signed statements. And keep your mouth shut about what you saw here until I say otherwise."

A deputy stepped out of the shadows. "The caretaker's here."

"Let him through," the sheriff replied.

The deputy brought over a very tall, very thin man with small eyes and a bony face. He was wearing a black watch cap pulled over his ears, a dark peacoat, oil-stained work pants, and heavy rubber boots. I thought I recognized him from somewhere but couldn't recall the circumstances of our meeting.

"This is Stanley Snow," said the deputy.

Menario measured the man from head to toe, as if trying to guess his exact height. (I would have estimated six-five.) "You're the caretaker?"

"Yes, I am." Snow had a higher-pitched voice than I would have expected, given the acne-scarred roughness of his features. "Can you tell me what's happened here? I was asleep when your dispatcher called."

"When was the last time you spoke with Hans Westergaard?"

"He called three days ago and asked me to get the house ready."

"What did he mean by that?"

"Make sure the driveway was plowed and sanded. Check the pipes and furnace." He smiled in a way that suggested the answer should have been self-evident to anyone. "Hans or Jill always call me before they drive up from Massachusetts."

"By Jill, you mean Mrs. Westergaard."

"Yes."

"Did he say he'd be bringing anyone with him?"

"No."

"How did he sound to you?"

Snow cocked his head, as if he was having a hard time hearing Menario clearly. "I don't understand the question."

"You didn't notice anything unusual in the tone of his voice? He didn't say something that struck you as out of the ordinary?"

"No," the lanky man said. "We only spoke for a few minutes. He asked how my winter was going—it was just small talk—and then told me he was coming up for a couple of days and needed the house to be ready."

107

"When was the last time you visited the house?"

"Three days ago, like I said."

I'd been listening to the interrogation with a growing sense of impatience. When was Menario going to cut to the chase? "Do you know a woman named Ashley Kim?" I asked point-blank.

Because he had no neck to speak of, Menario had to turn his entire body to fix me with a reprimanding glare. I think he'd been so focused on grilling the caretaker that he'd forgotten all about us. My unwelcome question had broken that spell.

"I don't think so," Stanley Snow said in answer to my question.

Menario raised his hand like a traffic cop signaling a car to halt. "Hang on a second, Mr. Snow. Sheriff, can you arrange for the wardens to get a ride to the sheriff's office to give their statements? Their presence here is no longer required."

11

The office of the Knox County sheriff is located in the same building as the jail, down the end of an obscure road near the sulfurous Rockland city dump. The deputy who drove us there, Skip Morrison, was a friendly acquaintance of mine, a freckle-faced beanpole prone to chattering. Charley rode in the passenger seat, while I was stuck in back, where the doors had childproof locks.

"So it looks like Westergaard is the perp," said Skip, speaking loudly over his shoulder.

"I think it's too soon to say that with certainty," Charley said.

I realized that my old friend was technically correct. The circumstances appeared damning for Hans Westergaard, but at this point, who could say where the evidence might lead?

Skip was not persuaded. "I'll give you odds right now that Westergaard's our guy. In these things, it's always the boyfriend."

In spite of my better judgment, I found myself siding with Skip.

At the jail, a state police evidence tech made us change into orange jumpsuits and slippers while he bagged our clothing and shoes. My forearm was still bleeding, so I found a first-aid kit, rinsed the wound under the bathroom faucet, and wrapped it tightly with a gauze bandage.

The state had our fingerprints on file, but the technician drew my blood, swabbed my tongue, and carefully plucked several hairs from my head. Then we were given access to computers so that we could type in our statements. Menario and his detectives would certainly question us about these documents, and AAG Marshall would need to sign off on them, as well. I felt a ponderous responsibility to choose my words carefully.

At the Maine Criminal Justice Academy, we'd been taught to fill out incident reports with short declarative sentences. Don't elaborate. Don't hypothesize. Just stick to the facts.

But what, exactly, were the facts of my involvement in this murder investigation? How was I to explain my daylong infatuation with the missing woman? Or my itchy mistrust of Hutchins?

When I reached the section in the report where I was supposed to describe my discovery of the body, my fingers hovered over the keyboard. The image of Ashley's naked body, bound with rigging tape, cruelly sliced, and defiled by that disgusting profanity made me nauseous. Why the hell would Westergaard torture her that way? And why leave her corpse in his own bedroom? Was he trying to make it look like the act of a random psychopath? Under the fluorescent lights of the patrol office, my head began to ache. The hour was too late for so many questions.

I became aware of someone standing at my shoulder.

It was Sheriff Baker. His L.L.Bean parka was folded over his arm, and I saw that he was wearing a pressed oxford-cloth shirt tucked into pleated chinos. His hair was wet and freshly parted. He looked neater than any man should look at three in the morning.

"Can I have a word with you, Mike?" he asked. "If you're done with your statement."

From across the room, Charley raised his red-rimmed eyes at me without expression.

I followed the sheriff into his office. The dull walls were adorned with plaques and awards bearing the names of various fraternal and community service organizations. The air smelled of furniture polish: a lemon/beeswax aroma.

"Have a seat."

He moved a pen from the stand beside his blotter and began turning it in his nubby fingers. "We're going to want you to come back here tomorrow morning to look at some videos of the house."

"That's what Detective Menario said."

The sheriff continued: "I put a call in to your division commander earlier to inform him of your involvement in the investigation. He said he'll be in touch with you." His chair gave a squeak as he repositioned his oversized rear end. "I didn't realize you've only been a warden for such a short time. Lieutenant Malcomb thinks you have real potential."

That was a backhanded compliment if ever I'd heard one. I could only imagine how irked the lieutenant would be over my involvement in another murder investigation. Once again, through my impetuous actions, I had managed to put my career under a cloud.

"Sheriff, how can I help you here?"

Baker smiled ever so briefly again before his features reset—in the law-enforcement trade, it's called "a microexpression"—and cleared his throat. "I fully understand that the state police have jurisdiction in this investigation, just so you don't misinterpret my interest. You mentioned that the victim was naked and bound with some sort of tape?"

"My guess is that she asphyxiated from having her mouth and nose taped shut, but that's a question for the coroner."

"And you said that she had a word cut into her skin?"

"Slut." Even saying it made me sick to my stomach. "That was the word."

"Interesting." He blinked at me from behind his tinted glasses.

"Is that it?" I asked. "Is that all you wanted to ask?"

He inserted the pen back in its stand. "Detective Menario said I should send you home after you were done with your statements. But you need to go to the hospital first."

"What for?"

"You're bleeding on my chair."

It was true; blood had seeped through the gauze bandage, staining the jumpsuit and dripping onto the floor. "Fuck," I said.

"I'll arrange a ride for you to Pen Bay."

"Charley's going to need someone to take him back to my house," I said. "That's where his van is, and his wife is waiting for him there."

He picked up his desk phone. "Morrison can drive him."

"So we're done?"

He held the phone in midair, as if waiting for me to leave. "Thank you. Yes."

I wandered back out into the patrol office, wondering what had just happened. Why did Baker seem so antsy? Maybe it was just the brutality of the crime and the prospect of having a sexual predator loose in his county for the first time since his election. But why did he ask me about those specific details? When he had mentioned the rigging tape, a fleeting memory had flashed in my head. There was something vaguely familiar about the circumstances of this murder.

I decided to get some coffee in the break room before checking back in with Charley.

The Knox County Jail was usually where I brought anyone I happened to arrest. Most of my cases seemed to be Class D or E misdemeanors. Rarely did I have an occasion to drag some idiot to jail in handcuffs. So I wasn't used to hanging out in this part of the building, let alone dressed in inmate garb.

In the hallway, a middle-aged woman with

saffron-tinted curls and wearing a sheriff's uniform that squeezed her breasts and hips was washing a carafe in the sink. She did a double take at the sight of me.

"Mike! I didn't recognize you."

"Hi, Lori."

Lori Williams was a dispatcher at the 911 call center. She'd been the one to radio me about the deer/car collision the previous night, and she'd taken my call from the Westergaard house when I phoned in the murder.

"They took my clothes for fiber samples," I explained.

"What happened to your arm?"

"Just a cut." I forced a smile. "Is there any coffee?"

"I was just making some." She filled the carafe with water from the tap. "That poor woman! I've been thinking about her all day."

"That makes two of us."

She set the pot on the burner. "There was something about that anonymous caller that gave me the creeps."

In the rush of the night's events, I had almost forgotten how everything had begun—that a caller had phoned 911 to report a deer/car collision but refused to leave his name.

"Do you think the man I talked to was the killer?" Lori asked.

"It's possible."

At the moment, the focus of the investigation was on finding Hans Westergaard, so I doubted anyone would pursue this particular lead immediately. In any case, it would have been nonsensical for Ashley Kim's abductor to report the accident. "I don't suppose you recognized the voice?"

"I think he might have had a glove or something over the receiver," she said. "His voice sounded muffled."

"Then it won't help the detectives to listen to the nine one one tapes."

"You never know." She looked up from the coffee machine, and suddenly her expression softened. "Oh, Mike, you look so tired."

"I'm not a night owl like you." Something Lori had said pushed its way into my thoughts. "Do you remember when we were on the phone earlier? I told you that there was a word cut in the victim, and you said, 'Not again.' What did you mean by that?"

She licked her rose-painted lips and glanced at the door as if afraid of being overheard. "I was thinking of the Jefferts case."

"Erland Jefferts?"

Suddenly, I understood what it was about the Ashley Kim killing that had seemed familiar. I'd just finished high school when Jefferts's arrest and trial became front-page news across Maine.

"He used rigging tape to smother the Donnatelli girl," Lori said. "And he carved a word in her body, too. I'm sure all those nuts who think Jefferts is innocent are going to pounce on this girl's death."

At that moment, Charley appeared in the hall. His brow was deeply furrowed and his eyes were baggy. "I've been looking over hill and dale for you," he said.

"They're sending me to the hospital to get stitched."

He looked at my red and dripping arm and shook his head in amusement. "I would hope so!"

"Morrison is supposed to give you a lift back to my house."

"Can I speak with you in private before we go our separate ways?"

"I need to get back to my APU," Lori said. "Take care, Mike. Get some sleep."

After she'd left, I said, "What's up?"

"I thought you might like to see this." He handed me a piece of paper printed from a computer; it was a screen shot from the Web site of the Harvard Business School:

Dr. Hans Westergaard is a Harvard Business School Professor of Management practice. He holds degrees from the the University of Copenhagen, the

Harvard Business School (M.B.A.), as well as (Econ) from the London School of Economics (Ph.D.). He has been a Senior Research Fellow at the Stockholm School of Economics and is the author of the book *Magt Fordærver: Svig og Fejl i de Multinationale Corporation (Power Corrupts: Fraud and Failure in the Multinational Corporation)*. Dr. Westergaard has been identified in a variety of rankings and surveys as one of the world's most influential thinkers on leadership and accountability in the financial services industry in the context of the financial crisis.

The accompanying photo showed a dignified older man in a black suit. He had thick silver hair that looked expensively styled, a prominent nose, and puckish gray eyes. I wouldn't have identified him as a European except for his open collar—no power tie for Hans Westergaard—and rimless eyeglasses.

"He doesn't look like a sexual psychopath," I offered.

"Most of them don't." Charley gestured for me to take a seat at the table in the training room. "You're going to hear this anyway, and I figure it should come from me."

"What is it?"

"Do you remember the Erland Jefferts trial?"

"Lori and I were just talking about it."

"I didn't want to spout off back at the house, because I don't believe in leaping to conclusions. But there are certain resemblances between the two homicides."

"But Jefferts is still in the Maine State Prison," I said. "No wonder Baker is nervous. People have been claiming for years that he's innocent. Either there's a copycat killer out there or those fanatics were right and Jefferts was imprisoned for a murder he didn't commit."

Charley fell silent. He leaned his knobby elbows on the table and pressed the fingertips of both hands together. It seemed as if he was searching for the right words to tell me some bad news.

"Is there something else?"

He nodded. "I heard a deputy talking. He was down to the Westergaards' house when Walt Kitteridge was examining the body. You know Walt? He's the state medical examiner. According to the deputy, Walt said that rigor mortis was still progressing in the deceased. It hadn't reached its peak."

In the back of my mind, a half-recollected textbook triggered an alarm. "What does that mean in terms of time of death?"

"It could mean a lot of things, but I guess there was still some residual body heat in the inner organs." His voice was hoarse and he paused to get some saliva going. "The indication is that Ashley Kim didn't die last night after the accident. She was probably killed sometime this afternoon."

The realization was like a hand closing around my throat.

I could have saved her.

12

Seven years ago, a pretty waitress named Nikki Donnatelli disappeared on her way home from a late-night shift at the Harpoon Bar in Seal Cove. The next morning, while searching for the missing girl, the cops instead found Erland Jefferts passed out behind his steering wheel on an isolated woods road.

A local lobsterman known for his dashing good looks and substance-abuse problems, Jefferts had been bounced out of the Harpoon for making lewd advances to Donnatelli. Fearing the worst, the Maine state police and game wardens began an extensive search of the surrounding forest. The hunt took the better part of two rain-soaked days, but eventually Warden Kathy Frost and her cadaver dog, Pluto, located the body of the lost girl. Nikki had been bound with rigging tape to a tree, tortured, and raped. Because of the presence of a petechial hemorrhage, the medical examiner determined that she had died from asphyxiation after Erland Jefferts taped shut her nose and mouth.

Or so the prosecution claimed. The defense argued otherwise, and there were certain inconsistencies in the evidence to back up Jefferts's story. Problems with the autopsy, a plausible alibi placing the accused in police custody at the medically determined time of death, some shucking and jiving by one of the investigating detectives on the witness stand—there were holes in the prosecutor's case, but not enough to persuade the jury of Jefferts's innocence. When the judge sentenced the handsome and articulate lobsterman to life imprisonment in the Maine State Prison without the possibility of parole, a group of his supporters began organizing to prove his innocence and secure his release. They called themselves "the J-Team."

For seven years, they'd worked with a pro bono legal team to hire private investigators, write letters to newspapers, and file friend-of-the-court briefs to secure a new trial. But it was all for nothing. Erland Jefferts was still rotting away in his cell. And no more beautiful girls had gone missing in Knox County in all the years since.

That was before Ashley Kim took a wrong turn on a fog-darkened road on Parker Point.

• • •

I still remember the morning I first read the story. It was the summer following my graduation from high school, a rainy July day. My stepfather, Neil, was at his law office and my mother was having lunch with one of her tennis friends when I shuffled into the kitchen. The *Portland Press Herald* was spread out on the breakfast table. The headline read

WAITRESS MISSING IN SEAL COVE

The story was sensational, but what caught my attention was the accompanying photograph. It showed an achingly beautiful brunette, a few years older than I was, smiling at the camera. I knew from the moment I saw her that Nikki Donnatelli was dead. My heart didn't care. I was smitten by a ghost.

That summer, I was working as sternman on a lobsterboat out of Pine Point. The previous year, I had gone to work in a remote sporting camp in the North Woods, where my estranged father lived, to wash dishes and scrub floors. Mostly, I had gone to be with my dad. The experiment had proved a disaster. So the next year, I decided to try my luck at sea. The sternman acts as the lobsterman's assistant, which means you do all the shitwork—emptying the rancid bait bags and throwing the decaying remains to the gulls,

121

rebaiting the mesh sacks with "fresh" herring, coiling the algae-slick lines, stacking the brick-weighted traps. You don't actually get to haul traps or pilot the boat, or at least I didn't. And while my employer earned a small fortune, he paid me only a flat wage. Still, I preferred lobstering to selling sneakers at the mall.

Most lobstermen listen to country-and-western music while they work, but my boss preferred talk radio. All the news that summer was about the beautiful Nikki Donnatelli and her despicable killer, Erland Jefferts. As a result, I found myself following each development in the case as the story shifted daily.

Nikki Donnatelli was twenty years old. Her family resided most of the year in White Plains, New York, but they had a summer cottage in Seal Cove. I have a vague memory that her father was an investment banker at one of those too-big-to-fail firms. Whatever he did, the Donnatellis had plenty of money.

The Harpoon Bar was a dive bar of a certain type you find in coastal towns. The decor tended toward lobster buoys and fishnets slung along plank walls. As the only saloon for miles, it attracted a diverse clientele. I always figured that the suntanned summer people got a thrill from drinking gin and tonics next to windburned guys who reeked of fish, sweat, and desperation. Fights broke out at the bar on weekend nights, but no one ever got shot or stabbed, so there was only a mild aura of danger to go with your fried clams. The appeal of dining and drinking at the 'Poon was that it made you feel like a local, even if you spent only a month in town each summer.

Nikki Donnatelli had just finished her junior year at Brown, where she was majoring in art history and planning a course of postgraduate study in Italy. She was described by various sources as intelligent, playful, and feisty: a young woman who had traveled alone across Europe and could take care of herself. The Harpoon's owner, Mark Folsom, said Nikki enjoyed the attention she received from the younger lobstermen, but he claimed she confidently resisted their crude advances. She had a boyfriend in Florence, to whom she remained faithful, Folsom later testified.

Erland Jefferts was twenty-three that summer and a local kid. His mother's family—the Bateses —had lived in Seal Cove since the town's founding, and there were a number of landmarks in the neighborhood bearing their name. Little was known about Jefferts's deadbeat dad. He had been a merchant mariner who had departed for seas unknown when young Erland was in diapers. The boy had largely been raised by his mother's sizable clan. And when he later went on trial for murder, it was the Bates family who packed the courtroom.

From a young age, Erländ had been called sensitive and intelligent. He'd started college at the Maine College of Art but dropped out after a year to follow the rock group Phish on its transcontinental wanderings. Eventually, he drifted back on the tide to Seal Cove. Before Nikki Donnatelli was murdered, he was working as sternman on a local vessel, the *Glory B*, owned by one Arthur Banks, and renting a room over the general store.

Jefferts had a reputation as a ladies' man. Even the worst photos of him showed an impossibly handsome young guy with a sculpted jaw, piercing eyes, and wavy blond hair. Prior to the murder, his claim to fame was that a photographer from *GQ* had used him in a photo shoot. The magazine dudded up a few rugged lobstermen in expensive sweaters and designer peacoats for a fashion feature. Erland's reputation as a small-town Casanova would later become a central point in the case against him, as well as an argument in his own defense.

The night of Nikki's disappearance was a balmy Friday evening in mid-July. An approaching high-pressure front from the southwest had pushed a mass of subtropical air into Maine, making Seal Cove feel as hot and steamy as the Caribbean. As a result, the deck outside the Harpoon Bar was packed with merrymakers. The owner, Mark Folsom, later testified that everyone in town seemed to drop by that night for a cold drink.

In Erland Jefferts's case, it was more than one drink. His liquor of choice was Jagermeister, and his capacity was legend. Even so, there was a line where his charm began to curdle, and he crossed the sloppy meridian around nine o'clock, according to witnesses. He'd been flirting with Nikki Donnatelli for weeks, and the pattern continued right up until the moment he grabbed her ass. Nikki complained to her employer, a former Marine who served as his own bouncer. Folsom applied a headlock to Jefferts and dragged him through the door. Outside, the bartender flung him bodily to the pavement. A small crowd watched Erland burn rubber as he fled the parking lot.

Why didn't Folsom phone the police? That question took prominence at the trial. The barman's confession was that he was worried about losing his liquor license, since Maine law prohibits serving drinks to anyone who is visibly intoxicated, and it was no secret that Jefferts had consumed the better part of a bottle since sundown.

After Jefferts left, the fiesta started up again. There were no more fights. Last call was at twelve-thirty, and then at one o'clock, Folsom locked the doors, and he and his staff went home.

With one exception.

Nikki Donnatelli lived less than a quarter of a mile from the Harpoon Bar. A notoriously poor driver who had just wrecked her car, she typically walked home or caught a ride from Folsom or one of the waitresses. But with the night being warm and the moon shining in the harbor, she made a fateful decision to take the shore path that stopped by Compass Rock. She was never seen alive again.

Several hours later, her mother, Angela, awoke from a nightmare. Because the walls of the summer house were cardboard-thin, she always heard Nikki washing her face and brushing her teeth, she told authorities. Angela roused her husband, Nick, and they agreed to telephone the police. The dispatcher informed them that Nikki couldn't properly be termed *missing*. People her age frequently spent entire nights out without informing their parents, despite the Donnatellis' assurances that their daughter would never do such a thing. The dispatcher eventually agreed to write down a physical description of Nikki, promising to alert sheriff's deputies and state troopers on patrol in the area. "If anyone sees her," the dispatcher said, "we'll let you know."

Shortly before dawn, a first-year sheriff's deputy with the odd name of Dane Guffey was patrolling a stretch of isolated road about five miles from the Harpoon Bar when he decided to check out a forested ATV trail popular with teenagers looking for privacy. He had received word about Nikki Donnatelli, and he had a hunch that she might have sneaked into the woods with some Romeo. At the very least, he hoped he might surprise some amorous teens. Interrupting a couple having sex is one of the beat cop's prurient pleasures.

The dirt road was heavily rutted but passable to four-wheel-drive vehicles, and Guffey had been assigned one of the county's new SUVs. About half a mile into the forest, he was surprised to find a rusted blue Ford Ranger parked with its tailgate down and driver-side door ajar. He recognized the truck as belonging to Jefferts.

Guffey hit his spotlight, bathing the scene in brilliant whiteness, and announced his presence as a police officer over the radio loudspeaker. There was no movement, no response. He took his flashlight and, resting his right hand on the grip of his pistol, carefully approached the vehicle.

In his report, he wrote that the first thing he noticed was a pile of greenish vomit near the passenger door. His testimony evolved over time. At the trial, he testified that his eyes went first to a roll of marine rigging tape resting oddly on the tailgate, as if someone had just set it there.

Inside the vehicle, Guffey found Erland Jefferts

passed out across the passenger seat. He was curled into something resembling a fetal position and would not awaken when the deputy called his name. Guffey said he had to shake Jefferts's leg hard repeatedly before the intoxicated man awoke with a groan.

The deputy asked Jefferts if he had been drinking and received a firm no. Guffey then pointed to the pile of vomit outside and indicated the strong odor of alcohol filling the cab. At this point, Jefferts relented. Yes, he said, he had been drinking—but just a shot and two beers.

Why was he parked here in the woods? the deputy asked.

Jefferts's confused explanation was that he had been returning to his apartment from a house party, where he had eaten some clam dip that disagreed with him. He felt that he needed to throw up, and so he drove down the ATV trail, looking for privacy. After he had puked, it occurred to him that having an empty stomach might boost his blood-alcohol level, and since he was fearful about being arrested for operating under the influence, he decided to take a nap until he was safe to drive again. That, he said, was when the deputy had found him.

Jefferts seemed excessively agitated, Guffey later testified. His eyes were wide and jumpy, and his upper lip was slick with perspiration. He kept glancing at his truck as if it might reveal some falsehood in his story and incriminate him.

The deputy decided to radio the dispatcher to find out if Nikki Donnatelli had returned home. It was then that he discovered that Angela had telephoned Nikki's employer, Mark Folsom, and that the bar owner had reported the earlier run-in with Erland Jefferts as cause for concern.

Guffey asked the dispatcher to send backup.

The first officer to respond was a veteran Knox County detective, Joe Winchenback, whose testimony would be the linchpin of the case against Jefferts. It was Winchenback who took the young lobsterman aside and asked him if he knew Nikki Donnatelli.

No was the answer.

"She's a waitress at the Harpoon Bar," the detective informed him gently. Wasn't it true that he'd been drinking there earlier that very evening?

No.

There were many witnesses who said that he had, in fact, been present at the bar, explained Winchenback.

Maybe he was there, Jefferts admitted.

Wasn't it true that he had touched Nikki in an inappropriate way?

Absolutely not.

Would he at least admit that Mark Folsom had thrown him out of the bar because of something Nikki claimed he did.

Folsom was an asshole and a liar, responded Jefferts.

The detective changed his approach and asked the lobsterman if he had seen Nikki after he left the Harpoon Bar.

He couldn't remember.

Did he know what time Nikki usually left the bar?

One a.m. That was when the bar closed.

Did he happen to know where she lived?

Yes, because she had told him once.

With Jefferts having changed his story several times, Winchenback made a decision to inform Jefferts of his Miranda rights. The process was just a technicality, he said, but he didn't want to get into trouble with the sheriff for not going by the book. Jefferts asked what crime he was being accused of, and the detective said suspicion of operating a motor vehicle under the influence of intoxicating liquor.

Was a breath test really necessary?

Maybe not, said the detective. If Jefferts could be helpful in finding Nikki Donnatelli, it would improve his situation. Nikki hadn't come home, and her parents were very worried. They just wanted her back safe and sound, so if Jefferts had any information about where she might be found, the police would be in a better position to help him on the drunk-driving matter.

Jefferts lowered his voice to a whisper. "What if I know where she is?"

These were the words the detective was waiting for. "Do you?" he asked.

Maybe he had seen her at the party, Jefferts admitted.

What would happen if they were to search his pickup truck? Winchenback asked. Would they find evidence of Nikki's having been in it?

He had given her a ride home one night, so yes.

The detective pointed out that earlier in the interview, Jefferts had claimed never to have met Nikki Donnatelli.

The young man became angry. He said he was confused because he was tired and he wasn't feeling well. He was having trouble remembering things. He felt the police were harassing him for no good reason and that he probably shouldn't say anything more without a lawyer.

Winchenback responded that a girl was missing, and time was of the essence. "If you know something and don't tell us," he said, "it will haunt you forever. You wouldn't want that on your conscience, would you?"

"No," said the lobsterman.

Winchenback saw another opening and walked through it. "Do you remember what you did with Nikki?" he asked.

"What if I said yes?" replied Erland Jefferts.

Winchenback would later swear—and the prosecutor, Assistant Attorney General Danica Marshall, would argue in court—that Jefferts's words were tantamount to a confession of guilt.

Seven years ago, I never would have imagined my future connection to any of these people. Like the rest of Maine, I'd found myself caught up in the mystery of a photogenic girl gone missing and a model-handsome lobsterman under suspicion. But my fascination was rooted more in hatred than in prurience. I fantasized driving to Rockland and shooting Jefferts with a deer rifle as he was being taken in chains from the courthouse. If I were Nikki's boyfriend, I wondered, would I have had the guts to seek revenge?

But of course I wasn't her boyfriend. I was just a testosterone-crazed kid. And frustrated lust, of the kind Jefferts must have felt for Nikki Donnatelli, was an intimate sensation for me, even more than my teenaged self dared to admit.

13

Being a game warden is an old-fashioned job. As professions go, it seems to belong to some lost and legendary age, right along with black-smithing, lamplighting, and the harpooning of sperm whales. The Sheriff of Nottingham is history's most famous game warden. What does that tell you?

Even among my friends and family, the widely

held belief was that my job was all about animals. And in certain moments I did see myself as the heroic protector of voiceless creatures. Without wardens in the woods, how many more deer would be slaughtered? How many more ducks would be killed? There was nobility in what we did, even if our salaries were paid for by the sale of hunting and fishing licenses. So in our case, you could say that death subsidized life. Game wardens represented society's recognition that humans need to be protected from their own predaciousness. That bloody desire to kill and keep killing. The inability to ever stop.

Ultimately, my job wasn't about animals at all. It was about people—and the cruelties they will commit when no one is watching.

Ashley Kim had needed protecting. Tomorrow the newspapers would say the responsibility to safeguard her had belonged to Maine state trooper Curtis Hutchins. A young woman goes missing on a darkened road after an automobile accident and the investigating officer does *nothing?* In law enforcement, you pay as much for your sins of omission as you do for your sins of commission. Sometimes you pay more. Hutchins had either just reached the ceiling of his career or the floor had dropped out from beneath his scaffold. An internal investigation would determine which of these descriptions proved most apt.

At the moment, I was torn between pitying him and hating his guts.

But what about my own responsibility?

As I waited in the emergency room to have my forearm stitched, legs dangling from a steel table, I kept returning to the scene of the accident on Parker Point. When I shut my tired eyes, I saw Hutchins staring out from beneath the brim of his wet trooper's hat, saying, "It's a state police matter now."

What was my response? "It's all yours."

And then I had driven home.

The ER doctor was a little guy in a big white coat and sneakers, with blond hair and a pearly-white smile. He didn't look a whole lot older than me when he finally appeared to suture up my arm.

"And how are we doing tonight?" he asked brightly.

Sarah was in the waiting room when I came through the automatic doors. She had a *Parenting* magazine open on her lap and the television was broadcasting an infomercial, but she wasn't paying attention to either. Her eyes were soft and unfocused, and I knew that she had gone some-place deep inside herself.

I had to call her name to get her attention.

Without a word, she threw her arms around my shoulders and pressed her face against my chest.

When she looked up at me, my shirt was wet where her cheek had been. "I should have listened to you," she said.

"Let's go home."

Driving back to Sennebec in her little Subaru, neither of us spoke. The blower pushed hot air into our faces. Behind us in the east, the sky had turned a plum color, a harbinger of the false dawn.

"I don't want to know the details," Sarah said at last. "I'll find out eventually. Everyone will be talking about it. But right now, tonight, I don't want to know what that maniac did to her. OK?"

"OK."

I thought that would be the end of the conversation, but she went on. "I feel responsible somehow. You kept saying you were worried about her, and I just thought it was you working too much again. It made me mad." She sniffed back a sob. "If I had listened to you, maybe you would have found her sooner."

I reached for her hand. "The state police will catch whoever did this."

"Will they?" she said, wiping back a tear. "Because they don't always."

How far could Westergaard run before someone spotted him, before he had to use his credit cards? "They will."

"You shouldn't promise things like that."

She was right. Menario's investigation was beyond my power to influence, and Maine had its share of unsolved mysteries. There were too many cases, most involving women, where the police knew beyond a shadow of a doubt which dirtbag had committed the crime but lacked the evidence to make a charge stick. In horrific cases like Ashley Kim's, was it any wonder that cops might push the limits to get a conviction? When your responsibility is bringing a monster to justice, who's to say that the ends don't justify the means? Not me.

"Charley came by to get Ora," Sarah said absently. "A deputy dropped him off as I was leaving."

"How did he seem?"

"Like he'd just come from a murder scene."

Sarah had left every light burning in our house. I could see it from a long ways away, glowing like a beacon through the pine trees. Inside, though, the untended woodstove had grown cold, the rooms were drafty, and the brightness seemed like just another false promise of comfort.

There was a message on the answering machine from Lieutenant Malcomb, asking me to give him a call in the morning. He said he had volunteered my assistance to the state police to help in any way possible. But with my direct supervisor, Kathy Frost, still on vacation, we would need to coordinate certain bureaucratic details, since I had my own duties to perform in the district, and the cash-strapped Warden Service needed to be prudent with its overtime allowances. Even a murder investigation ultimately came down to money.

I peeled off my jail jumpsuit and tossed it in the trash. "How was Ora?"

"Worried. I can't imagine what their marriage has been like for her."

I let that one drift by on the breeze.

"I think she's having problems with one of her daughters," continued Sarah.

"It's probably Stacey." Charley had led me to believe that his younger girl was something of a wild child. The last I'd heard, she'd become a part-time whitewater-rafting guide out west, after graduating with a degree in biology from the University of Maine.

Sarah removed her wristwatch and set it in a box where she kept her jewelry in the closet. "When I asked Ora about her children, she changed the subject."

In the bathroom, I inspected the bandage on my arm—the disinfectant had already stained the gauze—and I brushed my teeth. When I returned to the bedroom, I found Sarah standing, fully dressed, at the window. With the lights going, you couldn't see outside; the glass was a mirror reflecting her stricken expression.

"Why don't you pull the shades and get undressed," I said.

"I was just thinking that the person who killed her is out there right now. He might be a few miles away."

"Well, he's not coming here."

"Maine seems like such a safe place compared to New York, and then something like this happens, and it makes you rethink all your assumptions," she said. "People live so far away from one another in this town. If somebody broke in while I was alone, nobody would hear me cry for help."

"Come to bed."

"You know, I've never fired a gun in my life."

I turned off the lamp beside the bed. In the dark, I saw her silhouetted as she turned away from the window. "I've offered to teach you," I said.

"I'm not that kind of person."

She didn't budge from where she was standing.

"Is there something else bothering you?" I asked.

"You mean beside a young woman being brutally raped and murdered?"

"Why don't you come to bed. It's too late to have a conversation."

For some reason, what I'd said made her chuckle.

"What's so funny?" I asked.

"Too late is right." She turned around, but in the darkness I couldn't see her expression.

"What do you mean?"

"Never mind."

When she was naked under the covers with me finally, I put my arms around her, but her whole body remained rigid. Then she started to shake. At first, I thought she was crying again, and then I realized it was laughter.

"What are you laughing at?"

"Nothing."

"Tell me."

"Do you know what I saw on my way home this afternoon? A turkey vulture. Talk about an ill omen."

Bird-watching was one of Sarah's great joys in life. She kept a list of every species she had ever seen and recorded the date in the springtime when each of the migrant warblers returned from its southern vacation. The happiest I had ever seen her was one bright morning as we stood on a sunlit hillside listening to the first redstart of the season, a vivid black-and-orange bird singing from atop a distant tree.

"Vultures are some of the first birds to come back after the winter," I said, repeating something she'd once told me. "So it was just a sign of spring."

"Tell that to Ashley Kim," she said, rolling away from me.

14

I almost never remember any of my dreams. Sarah says that my eyelids twitch like any normal person engaged in REM sleep, but as a matter of course, I awaken each morning with no nocturnal memories. A psychologist would probably say that this amnesia is a symptom of some deep repression, but it just happens to be the way I sleep—like a machine being turned off for six or seven hours a night.

When I do recall a dream, it always startles me. The temptation is to search for profound meanings, as if my subconscious is so accustomed to being gagged that it must be screaming at me from the depths of my brain.

Take this one: I am walking through a forest of birches, trees as white as bone. I'm not lost, but I have no idea where I am headed. After a while, I become aware of footsteps in the leaves behind me. I turn, and there is a young Penobscot Indian woman with braided hair following me, and I feel a shudder because I know that she is dead. But the expression on her face is passive. We walk on together for a while. I look over my shoulder again. Now a man with a black mustache and a red spot over his heart is part of our silent procession. The trail begins ascending a steep hill and a breeze whispers through the leaves. Glancing farther back now, I see a sight that should terrify me, but it doesn't. It's a shambling corpse whose face has been blown to smithereens. Where are we all headed? I look up the hill and there is my father's cabin at Rum Pond. Smoke is rising from the chimney. The door opens before me, and I step inside. But it is my own house I am entering, and no one is there.

There was a knock at the door. A shaft of sunlight streamed through the window. I flopped over and found Sarah's side of the bed empty. I had been so exhausted that I'd slept through her leaving for school.

She'd sounded so strange the night before. The shock of the murder had affected her almost personally. And she hadn't even seen the corpse.

The knocking at the door continued with greater emphasis. From the bed, my view of the driveway was blocked. If I wanted to discover who was bothering me, I'd have to get up.

I slipped on some jeans and shambled out to greet my visitor.

On my steps, in the freezing cold, stood a stocky gray-haired woman. She wore the standard uniform of a game warden, with one noteworthy exception—around her throat was a white clerical collar. Along with the Reverend Kate Braestrup, Deborah Davies was one of the

Maine Warden Service's two female chaplains. An ordained Methodist minister, her job was to counsel the parents of children lost in the woods, the families of victims of careless hunters, and wardens like myself who had suffered some trauma in the line of duty. She wore her hair cut fashionably short and spiky, and the red frames of her eyeglasses made her look like a refugee from a New York ad agency. In her hands, uplifted, she bore a doughnut box and a cup of coffee.

" 'Then the Lord said to Moses,' " she intoned, " 'Behold, I will rain down bread from heaven for you.' "

"No thanks," I replied. "I've already eaten."

Her smile didn't falter. "You're not going to make me eat *another* doughnut, are you? I've already had two honey-dipped and one chocolate-glazed. Show some compassion for an over-weight woman with weak willpower, will you?"

Without really thinking about it, I accepted the greasy box and the cup. We regarded each other across the threshold.

"I thought I'd invite myself on a ride-along," she said with a flash of teeth.

"Today's really not the best day, Reverend."

"Lieutenant Malcomb said I needed to drag my keister over here and park it in your passenger seat."

So this was an order from on high, then:

142

Comply or else. "I'm not even sure if I'm going out on patrol. I'm supposed to go over to the jail to watch some video taken of the Ashley Kim crime scene. I'm assuming that's why you're here. To talk with me about last night."

She shrugged, never losing that megawatt smile of hers for an instant. "I can keep you company either way."

"I haven't even showered yet."

She removed a Rite in the Rain notebook from her pocket. "I'll work on my Sunday sermon while I wait."

Resisting Deb Davies was obviously futile. "Come on in," I said, stepping aside.

In the shower, I stood under the stream of hot water and thought about the blood-spattered diorama I'd discovered at the Westergaard house the night before.

I wondered if they'd nabbed the professor yet. It was only a matter of time until they did. "It's always the boyfriend," Skip Morrison had said.

So why had Charley seemed unconvinced? He always cautioned me against jumping to conclusions. But who else could have killed Ashley Kim? I supposed the Driskos needed to be considered suspects, especially if the DNA evidence came back linking the deer blood on their truck to the sample I'd taken from the road. Those bastards seemed capable of murder—

although the timing didn't make sense. I'd visited their trailer before Ashley Kim was murdered. It scarcely seemed possible that they could have been hiding her somewhere without giving themselves away.

Then there was the anonymous caller who had initially reported the collision. He, too, had been at the scene. But I doubted Menario was investing time or manpower in tracking down the Good Samaritan.

Who else? The caretaker, Stanley Snow, had keys to the house. Add his name to the list.

The philosophical principle called Occam's razor argues that the simplest explanation is almost always the right explanation. By that reasoning, the murderer had to be Westergaard. Why else would he go missing if he hadn't killed her?

· The eerie similarity of this homicide to the Jefferts case defied my ability to understand. What was the point in Westergaard making the murder look like a replay of the Donnatelli slaying, especially if he was going on the lam? Occam was no help with that question.

When I got out of the shower, I heard the growl of a vacuum cleaner. The Reverend Deborah Davies was, incredibly, vacuuming my living room carpet.

"What are you doing?" I asked, buttoning up my uniform shirt.

"I tracked some mud in."

This was a fib. Her boots were spotless. "Do you always come into someone's house and start cleaning?"

"I'm a neat freak." She wrapped the cord in perfect loops. "But I've come to terms with my addiction and admitted I have a problem. That's the first of the twelve steps. Just eleven more to go."

"I thought you were writing a sermon."

"Finished! Do you want to hear it?"

"Not particularly."

"I'm going to talk about Dante's *Inferno*."

"Sounds uplifting."

She laughed a little too raucously. "Did you ever read *The Divine Comedy*?"

"I was supposed to read it in college."

"It's actually pretty funny in places. Dante used his poem to settle a bunch of personal scores. He devised all sorts of elaborate tortures for his enemies in Hell." She eyed the cardboard box on the coffee table. "Are you going to eat that last doughnut? I get the feeling you don't really want it."

"Go ahead."

More and more, I was coming to the conclusion that Deborah Davies was one of the oddest ducks in the pond. But Ora had told me how helpful she'd been with Charley after their plane crash. I just couldn't square the idea of a cleric with this chirpy little woman. In my life, I'd known plenty of Roman Catholic priests. Some of them were cold fish, some were a little creepy even, but none was a Bible-quoting, hyperactive goofball.

Outside, the air smelled of snow. The sky had a pewter cast, which erased the shadows from under the trees, and the mud had grown tacky with the falling temperature. I noticed that the reverend's personal vehicle was a lemon yellow Volkswagen Bug. It glowed from the end of my driveway like a miniature sun.

Davies raised a quizzical eyebrow. "What's the matter?"

"My patrol truck is still at the jail. The technicians were going to vacuum it for fibers." One happy consequence of the situation dawned on me. "It looks like we'll have to do that ride-along some other day."

The reverend removed an iPhone from her pocket. "Why don't you call the jail? Maybe the tech people are done with your truck. I can give you a lift over there."

The next thing I knew, Davies had connected me with the sheriff's secretary, who informed me that, yes, the state police were done collecting fibers and I could now retrieve my truck from the jail garage. I looked at the chaplain's Volkswagen, imagining the sad picture of me riding in the passenger seat of that ludicrous vehicle. Her vanity license plate read REVDD.

"Don't be such a sissy," Davies said, once again exhibiting her uncanny ability to read my mind. "Hop in."

I obeyed.

Fastening my seat belt, I had a premonition of the reverend using the circumstance as a trap to investigate the inner corners of my emotional state. My intuition proved correct.

"Michael," she began. "I deal with lots of people in pain. That's my area of expertise. You know the one thing that never works? Bottling up your emotions."

I squared around. "Look, Reverend. I appreciate what you're trying to do, but you're not going to get anywhere with me. I'm kind of an atheist."

" 'Kind of an atheist'?" She gave me a dazzling flash of teeth. "That's like being kind of pregnant. Are you an agnostic?"

"I don't believe in God," I said flatly.

She seemed to ignore this comment. "Remember what I was telling you about my sermon on Dante. In the *Inferno*, he condemns suicides to the seventh circle of Hell. In the poem, he transforms people who have killed themselves into thorny trees that bleed when a branch is broken off. It's a horrible image of souls condemned to suffer forever, unable to move or defend themselves from torment because of the offenses they've committed against their own bodies."

"Why exactly are you telling me this?"

"Even an atheist has to admit it's a powerful metaphor. I think you feel responsible for more than you let on, Michael. Your father especially. No one should carry that amount of guilt."

I cracked the window so the wind would drown her out. "Who says I feel guilty?"

Davies reassessed her approach. We drove along for five minutes through a brown-and-gray wasteland. Some flakes of light snow began to fall, salting the windshield. She flicked on the wipers, but the crystals blew off on their own.

Finally, she spoke again: "Monhegan Island is part of your district, isn't it?"

"Yes."

Located ten miles off the Maine coast, Monhegan is the glacier-scraped top of a submerged mountain; nothing but sheer cliffs and twisted spruces soaked in perpetual fog, alone in a howling ocean. In 1614, Captain John Smith claimed the island for the English Crown. Today, Monhegan is home to fifty or so year-round residents who make their livings lobstering through the bitter winter months and then catering to tourists all summer.

The reverend continued: "I don't suppose you go out there much?"

"There's no real reason to. There's nothing to hunt except sea ducks and a few pheasants. I leave it to the Marine Patrol."

"Something you said made me think of a story," Davies explained. "You weren't around for this, but in 1997, the islanders hired a sharp-shooter to kill every deer on that island."

"I know this story."

Back in the 1950s, the locals had arranged to ship some white-tailed deer to Monhegan, the idea being to provide meat and sport to the local populace. At the time, the island's only resident wild mammal was the Norway rat.

For many years, the deer were considered local attractions. They foraged in the village and nibbled apples from the hands of small children. But over time, the pets became pests. Islanders were forced to fence their vegetable gardens with barriers at least six feet tall. Entire species of wildflowers were eaten to extinction. And in-breeding among the deer began to produce deformed antlers and stunted growth: real freak-show specimens. The last straw was when the deer and the rats began passing ticks back and forth. The ticks carried Lyme disease, and by the 1990s an epidemic of the illness plagued the island.

"What you don't know," said Deb Davies, "is that I was the island chaplain—every year there's a different volunteer who gets to spend the summer out there—when the town debated the issue of what to do about the deer."

"That must have been pleasant."

"The island was totally divided over the issue. On the one hand, you had people concerned about the public health risk and the general nuisance factor. On the other hand, you had people who couldn't imagine Monhegan without its deer. The town meetings were so contentious. But in the end, the discussion kept coming back to all the people who'd gotten Lyme disease. Still, it was a close vote, and I'm not sure folks out there have entirely forgiven one another for what was said. There was some talk at first of just capturing the deer and transporting them to the mainland, but they were dealing with more than a hundred animals, and the cost was just astronomical. So the islanders asked the state to find a sharpshooter."

"I know the man they hired," I said. "He's a biologist from Connecticut who specializes in controlling nuisance animals—'the world's best deer killer.' "

"That's what he calls himself." Davies smiled at me. "The sharpshooter set up feeding stations around the island to get the deer used to gathering in the same places. A month later, he returned with a couple of assistants and an ATV to haul out the carcasses. The men worked after dark, using silencers. I was told that if you stayed away from the shed on Lighthouse Hill where they butchered the animals, you would never have known what was happening."

I had the sense that the reverend was drawing near to the moral of her sermon, so I let her finish.

"It took three years to kill them all," she said. "They shot seventy-two that first winter, thirty-five the second, and six the third. I wasn't on the island when the last deer was killed, but I heard about it from a lobsterman friend. After a fresh snow in March, the sharpshooter and his team returned to Monhegan. They scouted Cathedral Woods and located the tracks of a doe and two fawns. And then they killed them. Today, there are no more deer on Monhegan."

We crossed the border between Thomaston and Rockland. The reverend put on her blinker.

"My friend the lobsterman, he'd grown up living with deer. Every year, between the Harvest Moon Ball and Trap Day, he would go hunting for them. He was a hunter, but no one loved those deer more. On his mantel, he had a photograph of a little doe that had wandered into his living room and settled down on his couch. He loved those deer, but in the end he voted to exterminate them, because he didn't want his family getting Lyme disease."

The Volkswagen turned into the jail parking lot.

"I remember my friend calling me the week those last deer were shot," she said. "It was unusual for him to call, because he's never been much of a talker. Lobstermen are like game wardens that way." She piloted the car into a parking space outside the main entrance and brought us to an abrupt halt. "After he told me what had happened, I asked him if he felt guilty, and do you know what he said?"

I knew the response she was calling for. "He said, 'Why should I feel guilty?' "

The reverend gave me a sly smile and turned the ignition off.

15

There was a television and digital video player set up in the training room, waiting for me. At the reception window, I'd managed to shake loose the Reverend Davies with a promise to continue our conversation later, only to be shepherded quickly by the receptionist into the cluttered, brightly lighted room. I sat alone at the table for a while, examining the ringed Olympics pattern made by a series of coffee cups. Finally, Detective Menario and Assistant Attorney General Danica Marshall came in. The detective, baggy-eyed, unshaven, had on the same wrinkled shirt and trousers from the night before.

I'd glimpsed Danica Marshall in the Knox County Courthouse on a few occasions when I was giving testimony at trials, but we'd never been formally introduced. Her office was located in Augusta, the state capital, but as one of several prosecutors assigned to murder investigations in Maine, she got around a lot, leaving a trail of lewd comments and dirty jokes in her wake. This was my first look at her up close.

My impression had always been that Danica Marshall was a stunner, but there was something severe about her deep-set eyes and cheekbones under the fluorescent lights of the training room. She was petite: five four tops, with a lean body that suggested lots of hours on the elliptical machine. She wore heavy blue eyeliner, an open-throated blouse, heels, and a raven black suit, which matched her hair. I guessed her to be in her late thirties, ten years older than me at least. Her hair was mussed in a way that made you think she'd just climbed out of bed. Maybe it was the hairstyle that explained her reputation as a court-house sex symbol.

"Let's start with your statement," said Danica. (All the deputies and wardens called her by her first name behind her back, and I couldn't stop myself from doing the same in my head.) "We'd like you to explain in your own words how you discovered Ashley Kim's car and the steps you took that resulted in you and Warden Stevens breaking into the Westergaard house."

They'd positioned themselves on either side of me, so I was forced to keep swiveling my head back and forth to converse with both of them. It was going to be like watching a tennis match. "Have you actually read my statement?"

"We read it," said Menario. His voice was gruff from lack of sleep.

"I tried to offer a detailed explanation for all of my actions."

"Just walk us through it, will you, Warden?" Danica gave me a polite smile, but her beryl blue eyes were as distant as a woman's eyes could possibly be.

I started from the beginning: the 911 call, the missing deer, Stump Murphy and Curt Hutchins, the DNA samples I'd taken, my discovery of the Driskos' presence at the scene of the accident, the information MaryBeth Fickett had provided me about the Westergaards also being from Cambridge, and finally the rush out to Parker Point. I held nothing back.

They let me ramble with minimal interruptions until this point.

"Let's return to Trooper Hutchins," said Danica. "You said he arrived at the accident scene approximately fifteen minutes after you."

"I wasn't looking at my watch, but that sounds about right."

"Did he tell you why he was delayed?"

"Something about bad spark plugs."

"Did you believe him?"

The question took me by surprise. So did my answer. "No."

"Why not?" asked Menario.

I craned my neck around to meet his gaze. "It just seemed like an odd excuse."

Why were they asking me about Hutchins? Was there an inconsistency in his statement? Maybe they were already laying the groundwork for an internal affairs investigation.

The muscular detective radiated heat like a pizza oven. "Hutchins says you were in a real hurry to get out of there."

"I wouldn't put it that way. He told me it was a state police matter and that I should go home."

"But you didn't stick around to help him look for the girl."

"I'd already done so before he arrived. It's in my statement."

"You walked up and down the road." His tone suggested he considered my actions inadequate.

"How would you describe your relationship with Trooper Hutchins?" Danica's eyes had grown opaque.

"We don't have a relationship. I've only met him a few times."

Menario gave me a blast of stale coffee breath. "You don't like him, do you?"

"I have no opinion of him," I replied, lying.

"Did you or did you not have an altercation with Trooper Hutchins last night?" asked Danica.

"I wouldn't call it that. We were outside the

Westergaard house, waiting for backup. I was angry, and he sort of pushed me."

"Why were you angry?"

"He'd told me at the accident scene that he would assume responsibility for finding Ashley. He didn't do squat. As a result, she ended up raped and murdered."

"So you blame him?"

"Yes, I blame him—and myself." I made an impatient gesture with my hands and looked squarely at the prosecutor. "I should never have gone home that night. I knew something was wrong."

The detective and the prosecutor regarded each other over my head. My T-shirt was damp under the arms and down the back, from where I'd been leaning against the chair.

"Will you excuse us for a moment?" asked Danica.

With that, the two of them left the room. I rubbed my mouth and chin. Why had I confessed to feeling guilty over my conduct on the night of Ashley Kim's disappearance? Was I intent on making myself a scapegoat, too? It must have been that stupid sermon Deb Davies gave me.

After several long moments, the door swung open and the detective and prosecutor returned. They brought with them a gray-eyed, gray-haired, gray-faced man who introduced himself as Detective Atwood of the Knox County sheriff's department. He then parked himself in a corner and never spoke another word during the remainder of my time in that room.

"We're going to play a video," Danica said pleasantly.

"We want you to show us where you trashed the crime scene," explained Menario.

This time, I didn't rise to the bait.

Menario tried to run the video machine but quickly became exasperated by its unwillingness to bend to his command. A deputy was brought in to steer us through the house.

We started outside the building and moved carefully up the walkway, just as Charley and I had done the night before. At the front door, I indicated the place where my footprints left the steps and forged off through mud and snow around the corner of the house. Detective Menario scribbled furiously into a notebook as I narrated. The video tech had spent a lot of time photographing the broken window where I'd busted in—the broken glass shining from the carpet, and a few specks of what must have been blood from my arm. Each spot had been numbered and marked by an arrow, with a ruler beside it for scale. We lingered awhile in the kitchen, zooming in on the knife block with its missing blade, before proceeding upstairs. I couldn't help but think of a cheap horror movie, the shaky camera stalking the hall as if from the killer's point of view.

The images of Ashley Kim were even more gruesome than my memories. I found myself focusing on details I had missed—the frayed and bloody edge of the rigging tape over her mouth, the uneven depths of the letters inscribed into her pale flesh, the rawness of her genitals. I told the detective and the prosecutor how the body had been positioned when I discovered it and how I had turned the corpse over to read the word scrawled into her skin.

"We found your fingerprints on her shoulder," said Menario.

"Did you find any others?"

"Your role here is as a material witness," explained Danica. "We can't share information about what we've discovered without undermining your usefulness to us when this case goes to trial."

So I was being frozen out of the hunt for the murderer. I should have expected as much. Still, my curiosity was such that I couldn't keep myself from making one last attempt. "I heard the medical examiner estimated the time of death to be yesterday afternoon."

"Those results are preliminary," said Menario without thinking.

Danica Marshall turned her blue death ray on him. "The medical examiner has issued no findings, so whatever you heard is gossip." She gave me a tight smile. "I wouldn't put any stock in it."

"People are going to talk," I said. "It's inevitable in this town."

The deputy—a young guy with acne scars and pale, watery eyes—smirked. I was glad I was amusing someone. As I glanced about the room, I became aware of Detective Atwood again, hanging silently in the background like Hamlet's dead father.

"Well, *you'd* better not talk," said Menario. "I'm not shitting around, Bowditch. You keep your mouth shut about what you saw in that house. That means no talking to the press. It means no talking with your girlfriend. Understand?"

Again, Danica interjected: "As a law officer, you appreciate that principle, I'm sure."

I tilted back in my chair. I felt that I had a certain leverage. "Has Ashley's family been notified?"

"That's not your concern," said the detective.

"What about Westergaard. Have you found the professor yet?"

"No comment."

"What if Mrs. Westergaard calls me?"

Menario glanced at a sheet of paper in his hand. "According to your statement, you didn't speak with Mrs. Westergaard. Charley Stevens did."

Danica intervened. "If you are contacted by Mrs. Westergaard—or anyone else—you should just refer them to Detective Menario or the state police public-information officer. Does that clarify things?"

"Yes."

"The early hours of an investigation like this are absolutely critical," Danica said, lecturing me. "We need everyone to be on the same team if we're going to find the monster who killed Ashley."

"In other words, I don't want you and Charley Stevens going off the reservation again," Menario snapped.

"Would you use that expression if Detective Soctomah was in the room?"

Menario's supervisor was a Passamaquoddy Indian who'd grown up on sovereign tribal lands in easternmost Maine.

"Fuck you."

The prosecutor rose to her feet. "Enough with the testosterone. We're finished here."

There was just one more lingering question on my mind. "I understand that there are similarities between this killing and the Erland Jefferts case."

When I spoke that name, a look came over Danica Marshall that startled me. Her eyes hardened and her mouth drew taut. It was as if all the glamour had been sucked out of her, leaving her own death mask where her face had been. "There are *no* similarities between these killings," she said. "And if you go around saying there are, you will be very sorry. Do I make myself clear?"

Both Menario and the evidence tech visibly shared my surprise at her transformation. Even ghostly, expressionless Atwood shifted his weight from one foot to the other.

"Yeah," I said.

"Say it."

"I never heard of Erland Jefferts."

"Now take your truck and go."

But as it turned out, I was going to have trouble keeping my promises. After I left the training room, I paused outside the reception window and checked my cell phone for messages. There were two. I had expected to hear from Sarah, but neither of the voice mails was from her. Instead, I had a call from Lieutenant Malcomb, asking me to report in once I'd finished at the jail.

The second message was a curveball. The caller was a woman who identified herself as Lou Bates. "I represent a group called the J-Team," she said in one of the thickest Down East accents I'd ever heard. "We've learned that an Oriental girl got killed last night in Seal Cove and you discovered the body. It is our belief that you might have information that would exonerate my nephew, Erland Jefferts, of the wrongful accusation and conviction against him. I would very much appreciate a callback at your immediate and absolute convenience."

Now, how in the hell did this woman find me? I wondered. The local constabulary wasn't known for having the tightest lips around, and I was fairly certain MaryBeth Fickett had been working the phones all morning. In a small town, gossip travels literally at the speed of sound. But who would have connected me with this so-called J-Team?

I was puzzling over this phenomenon when I felt a hard tap on the shoulder. Behind me stood a blond woman I'd never seen before.

"Warden Bowditch? I'm Jill Westergaard."

16

She was tall, with high breasts that seemed too big for her narrow hips. Her blond hair was held back from her forehead by sunglasses that she had pushed up there for that purpose. There was no hint of a wrinkle on that forehead. She had large brown eyes that were red around the edges, as if she'd been up all night drinking or crying, or both. She wore a khaki raincoat over a high-throated brown sweater that hid her neck from view. Her chocolate-colored slacks were tucked into L.L.Bean boots. If I had to guess, I would have put her age somewhere in the late fifties, although she was doing everything in her power to tell the world she was actually a decade younger than that.

"Mrs. Westergaard, I can't talk with you."

She ignored my statement. "Warden Stevens told me I could find you here. He said you were the one who found Ashley."

Of course Charley had told her where I'd be. That troublemaking old coot liked nothing better than to stir the pot.

"Do the detectives know you're here?" I asked.

"I just drove up from Cambridge."

Greater Boston was a four- or five-hour car ride from Seal Cove, depending on the season and the time of day. With her husband missing, and seemingly guilty of a violent crime, I could understand her wanting to be at the center of the action, although I doubted the investigators would open her house anytime soon.

I glanced through the locked door that led back to the sheriff's office. "Mrs. Westergaard—"

"Jill," she said.

"I really can't talk with you. This is a murder investigation, and I'm a material witness."

Her large eyes got even larger, but her forehead remained placid. "Please."

"I'm sorry."

I tried to step around her, but she reached out and grabbed my sleeve, not with any force, but just pinching the fabric of my uniform. The timidity of the gesture made me pause.

"We can talk outside," she whispered.

"It's not that," I said. "I'm bound by my oath not to interfere in an open investigation."

"Hans didn't do this terrible thing."

"Mrs. Westergaard—"

"He couldn't have done it," she said in a tremulous voice.

The desperation in her eyes provoked a strange emotion in me. I'm not sure how to describe the feeling except to say that it wasn't sadness or pity; it was more like empathy. From my own experience, I knew how love can blind a person to certain vicious truths.

"Please," she said again. "I need your help."

In Jill Westergaard's mind, she was the only person who could convince the police of her fugitive husband's innocence. What would this poor woman do when they finally caught him and he confessed to every last bloody detail?

"I'll meet you outside," I said.

After she had left, I tied and retied the laces of my boots, thinking that what I was about to do was stupid and reckless. And yet I felt impressed by the nobility of my intentions. I might not be able to persuade Jill Westergaard of anything, but she would remember our conversation with gratitude.

She was waiting for me in the parking lot, wearing her sunglasses now and leaning against the hood of a sand-colored Range Rover, as if she might topple over without its support. The tone of the vehicle perfectly complemented her hair. This woman considers all her decisions very carefully, I realized.

She beeped open the SUV's doors. With a quick backward glance at the jail, I climbed into the passenger seat. The interior of the vehicle still smelled of the automobile showroom. But there was a musky hint of perfume, too.

Jill Westergaard swiveled around to face me. "I need to know what you saw."

The demand took me by surprise. I had expected her to continue her defense of her husband's innocence, with me in the role of truth-hardened counselor. With her sunglasses down, I felt that she had me at a disadvantage. Given the immobility of her brow, I could read her expression only in the movement of her mouth.

"Mrs. Westergaard, I can't tell you that."

"No one will."

So at least Charley had been mum on that point. "It's a crime scene," I said, trying to explain.

"But it's my *house.*"

I leaned back against the cold window. "I know this must be extremely difficult."

She shook her head, so that her long hair swayed. "You don't understand. I designed that house. I'm an architect. I put my entire soul into its creation."

MaryBeth Fickett hadn't told me that detail. I'd been left with the impression that Jill Westergaard was just another rich bitch from Boston who kept changing her mind about the specifications of her dream home.

"You really need to speak with the detectives," I said. "It would be inappropriate for me to tell you what we discovered."

"But you broke inside my home."

"We had to."

"Why? I don't understand what you expected to find."

This was a question for which I actually had no good answer. "I'm afraid I can't say."

She let out a wounded-sounding sigh.

We sat quietly for the better part of a minute. I realized that I could hear her labored breathing.

"Hans didn't do this terrible thing," she said, using the same words she'd uttered inside the jail.

"If you know where your husband is, you owe it to him to tell the detectives."

"But he didn't do it. I know Hans."

"Then you knew he was coming up here."

"He often came to Maine to work if he needed to focus."

"So why did you tell Charley he was missing?"

She wrapped her left arm around the leather steering wheel. "I'd expected Hans to call me earlier from the conference. I wasn't suggesting anything sinister. He's brilliant, and he can be a bit spacey at times. He was a chess prodigy in Copenhagen. He beat a Russian grand master when he was twelve! I'm sure he just forgot to call me. I was a little worried, but if I'd known that using that word would lead to people suspecting *him* of murder . . ."

She left the sentence unfinished. I could see her mind already building a house of cards.

"Did you know he was arranging a liaison with Ashley Kim?"

I didn't mean the question to come out so pointedly, but she winced and shrank back against the steering wheel.

When she spoke again, it was with iron certainty. "Hans wasn't having an affair with Ashley."

"Then what was she doing here?"

"I don't know."

Her naïveté made me feel compassionate toward her again. She seemed once again like a wife under an impossible delusion and less like a woman used to getting her way regardless of the circumstances.

"Your husband's research assistant was murdered in his home, and now he's disappeared," I said in as gentle a tone as I could manage. "You have to see how that's going to make him a suspect."

"Never in a million years would Hans have an affair with Ashley."

I exhaled. "Mrs. Westergaard—"

"Let me tell you about Ashley," she said, showing her teeth. "She was a funny girl. Hans said she drew political cartoons for the *Yale Daily News* when she was an undergraduate. We had her up here last summer, and I enjoyed her company. When she had anything to drink, her speech got surprisingly profane. You would never have guessed it, given what a little mouse she was normally."

"She was attractive," I ventured.

She flicked her fingers at me, and I noticed that her manicured nails were painted maroon. "She was a nerd. You know how some of those Asian kids are." She caught herself. "She had no social life, no social *skills*. She was extremely intelligent, and she could be witty, yes, but there is no way that Hans would ever have *desired* her. There was nothing remotely sexual about the girl! He would never have chosen Ashley Kim over me, for God's sake."

It was no surprise that she was vain or that she was in denial about her age. The Botox, the breast implants (those things couldn't possibly have been real), the care she took managing every aspect of her appearance—somewhere beneath that elaborate facade lived a secret fear. Was it any wonder that she was deluding herself about her husband's extracurricular activities and maybe about his capacity for violence?

"Mrs. Westergaard," I said. "I don't mean to be blunt, but I think you should consider the possibility that you're letting your love for your husband cloud your judgment."

"You think that's what I'm doing?" She was incredulous.

I'd never intended this discussion to become an argument. "I'm just cautioning you against leaping to conclusions."

"That's quite ironic."

"I'm sorry?"

"You don't know the first thing about my husband. Yet you're already convinced he's a cold-blooded sex killer."

I'm sure my face had grown red. "Well, I hope I'm wrong about him, but it would be better if he turned himself in to the authorities and made his own case."

"You really don't get it, do you? Something has *happened* to Hans. Has it even occurred to the police that my husband might have been abducted? I'm terrified out of my mind right now."

She believed he was another victim.

"Do you have any idea who might have killed Ashley?" I asked.

"No."

"What about your caretaker, Stanley Snow?"

She gave me another of those imperious smirks. "Stanley is the gentlest person I've ever known."

"He has the keys to your house."

"And that somehow makes him a killer? Why don't you accuse me of murdering them while you're at it? You people really are a bunch of bumpkins."

You people? I knew I shouldn't let this unpleasant woman push my buttons, but if she held me in such contempt, I no longer felt protective of her feelings. "Well, someone raped and murdered Ashley Kim, and the evidence points to your husband."

She squared her shoulders. "Get out."

I opened the door. "Go talk to the detectives, Mrs. Westergaard. Tell them what you told me."

"I intend to."

I rested my hands against the cold roof of the SUV and peered back at her brittle mask of a face. "I hope you're right, and that they find your husband safe and sound."

"Do you? Do you really?"

17

I went back into the building and retrieved my truck keys without any rigmarole from the attending deputy, which was lucky for him. My blood was already boiling.

How had I ever pegged Jill Westergaard for a damsel in distress?

It was entirely possible she would rat me out to Detective Menario and AAG Danica Marshall, informing them that I had violated my duty as a material witness not to talk about the case. Christ, I was an idiot.

It would be better if I made myself unavailable for a while. As I drove back toward Sennebec, I punched in Charley's number and waited for him to answer.

"Howdy do," he said.

"I can't believe you told that woman where to find me!"

He chuckled. "I'm assuming you're referring to Mrs. Westergaard."

"Of course I am."

"I thought an encounter with her might be a good test of your tree fiber." In the background, there was some soft murmuring that must have been Ora. "You and I need to talk, young feller."

"I'd say so."

"How about we get some lunch?"

The clock on my dashboard said it wasn't even ten o'clock. But I knew that Charley rose religiously before dawn, so for him, this was already the middle of the day.

"Why don't I meet you at the Square Deal," I said. "That way, I can say good-bye to Ora before you drive home."

"I was going to suggest the very thing."

The sky had a gray and arbitrary cast. In March, the daily question was always whether the next batch of precipitation would fall as snow, ice, or rain. Every morning, Mother Nature rolled the dice.

I barely recognized my formerly messy truck. It was as if the cleaning fairy had waved a magic wand and transformed it from a pumpkin back into a proper law-enforcement coach. That's one benefit of having your vehicle impounded for inspection, I thought.

As I drove, I summoned the courage to telephone my division commander. Lieutenant Malcomb was on his way to a meeting with the Warden Service colonel in Augusta. As such, he was already in a pissy mood. The two men disliked each other intensely from having worked together for twenty-plus years in the field. Or so my sergeant, Kathy Frost, had told me. Malcomb himself would never have confided his personal sentiments to a rookie warden, especially one as trouble-prone as me.

"How the hell did you get wrapped up in this investigation?" he demanded before I could squeeze in two words.

"I don't know, Lieutenant. It just seemed to happen."

"That's always the way with you." He was a chain-smoker, and you could hear the damage to his lungs in his every utterance.

When I mentioned how Charley Stevens had gone with me to the Westergaard house, the lieutenant let loose with a gravelly groan. He and the warden pilot were dear friends, but he believed that Charley and I goaded each other on to deeds of greater recklessness. We were mutually bad influences, in his opinion.

"If it's any consolation," I said, "the AAG says she's pretty much done with me—until she goes to trial."

"Good, because Frost is back tomorrow. She can be your liaison with the state police going forward. You've got enough on your plate."

"Yes, sir."

"Just do your job for once."

That last comment stung. For all my occasional misadventures, I'd begun to consider myself a competent law-enforcement professional. I had a high conviction rate on my arrests. My activity reports were all up-to-date. And the only formal complaint against me—by an obnoxious boater from Massachusetts named Anthony DeSalle, who had accused me of harassing him and his son last summer—had collapsed under its own weight.

Of course, this glowing assessment of my character conveniently failed to take into account my maverick actions during the period of my father's manhunt. Among the power players at the Maine Department of Inland Fisheries and Wildlife, hearing that Warden Mike Bowditch had bumbled his way into another murder investigation would be nobody's idea of a surprise.

At the Square Deal Diner, heads turned as I walked through the door, and every conversation in the room stopped. The gruesome murder on Parker Point was undoubtedly the topic of the day. And now who should arrive but the man of the hour himself.

Charley had settled down in a corner booth, as far from the lunch counter as possible. I'd expected that Ora would be with him, since the motel was just behind the diner, but he was alone. No one said anything to me as I crossed the room, but you could feel the curiosity quotient rise by ten degrees.

"Goddamn you, Charley," I said in a hushed voice.

He rose to shake my hand—he always shook

my hand when we met—and nearly crushed my metacarpals. "I am here to beg your forgiveness."

"Granted."

His expression turned solemn. "How did your interview go?"

"You mean my interrogation?" I unrolled the paper napkin from around the knife, spoon, and fork and spread it across my knee. "I'm assuming Menario brought you in earlier to go over your statement."

"They showed me some video."

"Me, too."

"It's a bad business, no doubt." He studied me from beneath his bushy eyebrows. "You seem to have survived your encounter with Mrs. Westergaard with gonads intact."

"The less said about that, the better."

Ruth Libby came over with a coffeepot and a down-turned mouth.

"Everyone's talking about what happened on Parker Point," she said.

"What are they saying?" asked Charley.

"That a girl got killed in one of them new mansions. And that there was some gross sexual stuff." She lowered her voice. "So you guys found the body, huh?"

"No comment," I said.

She glanced at the men seated along the counter. "That's what I've been telling the peanut gallery. I told them that cops are sworn to silence. But you know how those guys are."

"What else are they saying?" It was predictable that Charley would throw discretion to the wind.

She turned our cups over and poured them full of black coffee. "Everybody's talking about Erland Jefferts. They said this girl died the same as Nikki Donnatelli. Some people say it's a copycat. Others say it just proves Erland was wrongfully accused the first time." Her eyes flitted back and forth between us, looking for confirmation, but neither of us responded, so Ruth decided to take a new tack. "Those Westergaard folks come in pretty regular in the summer."

Charley raised the cup to his mouth. "Do they now?"

"They always come in Sunday nights for pie and coffee. I guess they think we're kind of quaint."

"What makes you say that?" asked Charley.

"They told my mom we're kind of quaint. That's OK, though. In Maine, Mom says, being *quaint* is good for business."

"How is your mother?" I asked.

Once again, Dot was nowhere to be seen. She was such a constant fixture at the diner that her absence seemed all the more unnerving.

"She's waiting for the test results. She thinks it's probably cancer."

Like her mother, Ruth was one of the most genuine people I'd ever met. But even I was taken aback by her bluntness. I couldn't imagine Sennebec without Dot Libby's garrulous, sprightly presence.

"Tell her that I'm thinking about her," I said.

She nodded but said nothing.

Charley leaped boldly into the void. "I'm curious about those Westergaard folks. How would you describe them, in your uncensored opinion?"

"Well, he's foreign," Ruth said. "And they're very rich, but that's nothing unusual around here. They both drive Range Rovers the same sandy color, his and hers. And they dress kind of *Town & Country*, if you know what I mean. My mom thinks he's handsome for an older dude, and his wife is very glamorous. She's taller than him. I know she bleaches her hair, because she came in once with the roots showing a little. I told her about Wendy at Shear Perfection, but she didn't thank me or nothing."

"You've got a good eye for details, young lady," said Charley. "You should consider becoming a detective."

"I don't need the hassle. What can I get you?"

I ordered an egg sandwich and a molasses doughnut, since it was still breakfast time by my reckoning. Charley requested the tripe.

"You don't see it on menus much anymore," he observed.

"For good reason!" I said.

"When I was a youngster, we had tripe twice a month."

"Well, you're the first one who's ordered it in a while," Ruth replied with characteristic candor.

Charley shook his head in mock sorrow. "What's wrong with tripe?" he asked once Ruth had left.

"It's fallen out of culinary fashion." I swirled the cream around in my coffee and decided to stop procrastinating. "Jill Westergaard is in total denial about her husband. She told me he'd never cheat on her with a 'mouse' like Ashley Kim."

He dabbed the corner of his mouth with the napkin. "Under the circumstances, I'd cut the woman some slack. She's had a terrific shock, you know."

I frowned in disagreement but moved on anyway. "What do you make of the similarities to the Erland Jefferts case?"

"That's a can of worms no one wants to open."

We both sipped our coffees. The warm cinnamon smell of baking pies drifted out of the kitchen as Ruth Libby opened and closed a door.

"I thought Ora was going to join us," I said.

"She's got a wicked headache."

"I hope she's not coming down with something."

"It's not that kind of headache."

The wooden booth creaked as I leaned back against it. Something Sarah had said the night before flashed in my mind. "So how are your daughters doing?"

He winked at me, impressed by my powers of deduction. "Ann's husband just got a promotion over to Bath Iron Works, making destroyers. As long as people keep blowing each other up, he should be comfortably employed."

I remembered meeting Ann's husband at Charley's hospital bedside: a tubby, neatly barbered guy with an American flag lapel pin and a tone of certainty in his every utterance. My guess was that Charley and I shared the same view of him.

"What about Stacey?" I asked.

Stacey was the younger of Charley and Ora's two daughters, the one I'd never met. My understanding was that she blamed her father for the terrible plane accident that had left her mother paralyzed. As a result, they hadn't spoken for a number of years. I was curious whether her father's recent brush with death had changed the equation.

"She's been getting her graduate degree in biology at the University of Colorado. She was studying mountain lions. Leave it to Stacey to have a soft spot for fierce creatures."

"Sounds like her old man."

"Fortunately, she takes after her mother in the looks department."

"So what's happened?" I asked.

He threw back his head and guffawed. "You're like a hound dog on a scent when you get going."

"It's not all that mysterious, Charley."

"The long and the short of it is that Stacey got kicked out of the university."

That explained Ora's headache. "What happened?"

"She punched out her faculty adviser. Knocked him cold, in fact."

"What happened?"

"She says he groped her, but there's no proof, since she never filed a grievance. She just clocked him. That makes her the aggressor, according to the university."

"Can't she appeal?"

"My estimation is that she was looking for a reason to come back to Maine." He looked over my shoulder at nothing in particular. "It's causing Ora fits, in any case. We owe the school some money, and the Boulder DA is still considering an assault charge. Before you came in here, I was just thinking that Kim woman was the same age as Stacey."

I'd wondered how long it would take for us to return to the matter at hand. "What did the detectives ask you this morning?"

"The usual questions. That Menario is some hotheaded character. He makes a bull look timid by comparison. But at least he doesn't play games. That pretty prosecutor is another story."

"Danica."

His eyes widened in such a way that I could tell my use of her first name had caught his attention. "She's a sweet peach," he agreed. "But don't assume that she's on your side just because she's a prosecutor."

I recounted my ordeal in the training room that morning. He listened, stroking his chin the way he did when he was mulling over a problem.

"So what should I do?" I asked.

The old pilot cleared his throat carefully. "I'd advise you against talking with Mrs. Westergaard to start."

"Too late."

"Menario's going to be looking at Hans Westergaard as the perpetrator until such time as the professor is located. But your DNA evidence also places those Drisko fellers at the crime scene."

"I think it will, yes."

"In that case, you'd do well to give them a wide berth."

"That will be difficult if they really are the ones tearing up Hank Varnum's land with their ATVs." Ruth arrived with our plates. I watched Charley slather ketchup on his tripe and instantly lost my appetite. We waited for the waitress to leave before I continued. "I don't see how the Driskos could have done it anyway. If the medical examiner is correct, then I was at their trailer just before the murder."

"You're assuming they didn't have her stashed somewhere. For all we know, they had her tied up back at the Westergaard house and were just waiting for dark."

"I guess that's possible. But they didn't seem like two guys who were about to go rape and murder someone."

"How did they seem?"

"I don't know. Happy?"

"Those things aren't mutually exclusive, I hate to tell you. Who else do you reckon was at the scene?"

I nibbled my sandwich. "There's the anonymous guy who phoned in the accident to nine one one."

"There's something queer about that call. I hope Menario pokes around a bit. Who else?"

"Me and Stump Murphy. I could add Hutchins to the list."

The old pilot sucked on his teeth. "I think that's one theory you're better off keeping to yourself."

"Hutchins has a stick up his ass. Wouldn't you agree?"

"You can't tell by the looks of a frog how far he'll jump," Charley said.

Sometimes my friend's lumber-camp sayings were too much even for me. "What the hell does that mean?"

"It means that reading people is more art than science, in my experience."

We chewed our food for two minutes. He was correct that I had, thus far in my life and career, proven to be a monumentally bad judge of character. Every time I expected someone to do one thing, they did the opposite.

Charley wiped both corners of his mouth neatly with his napkin. "I have a delicate question I've been meaning to ask you."

"Shoot."

"Is Sarah pregnant?"

I almost spit out my coffee. "What?"

"Ora suspects she is."

"No," I said. "Absolutely not. She would have told me if she was."

He nodded his head very slowly, as if he didn't really believe me but was trying to pretend he did. "Maybe Ora is mistaken."

I studied his poker face. "Did Sarah say something to her?"

"No, but Ora's usually a good judge of these things."

Suddenly, Sarah's strange behavior the previous few days came into focus: the nausea, the preoccupation, her anguished response to what had happened to Ashley Kim. I felt like the dumbest man in the world for missing the clues. But if she was pregnant, why hadn't she told me? Could she be waiting for the right moment? The past few days hadn't provided many opportunities for intimate conversations.

"There's no way she's pregnant." I draped my napkin over my half-finished sandwich. "Do you think I should buy her some flowers?"

He leaned back in the booth, a smile spreading across his leather face. "Son, you should always buy a woman flowers. It never matters the reason." He waggled his thumb at the diner's door. "Why don't we go over to the motel room and see how the Boss is weathering the family storm." Then he waved for the waitress and ordered a cup of herbal tea to go.

The Square Deal Motel was tucked behind the diner. The little motor court consisted of six small cabins, each painted white, with orange doors and green shutters—the same color scheme as the restaurant. All of the other cabins seemed unoccupied, which was no great shock, given that this was mud season.

Charley had pulled the van around to the spot in front of the first cabin. As we approached the door, I noticed that the shade was drawn.

"Probably I should do some reconnoitering first," said Charley.

I waited on the cabin's small porch while he

slipped soundlessly inside. Could Sarah really be pregnant? My friends who had children told me that kids changed your life in unbelievable ways. At the moment, having a baby—really having one, with Sarah, in my run-down house, with my poor-paying job—was beyond my powers of imagination.

After several minutes, Charley emerged with a worried expression. "She's on the telephone."

With Stacey, no doubt.

For all his backwoods guile and wiry toughness, Charley impressed me as one of those men who derived genuine, as opposed to metaphorical, strength from the woman in his life. She sustained him in ways that were beyond my own understanding or experience. It didn't surprise me that her anxiety would unsettle him so greatly.

"Give her my love, please," I said. "And apologize again for my whisking you away last night."

"She's used to my shenanigans. She's forgiven me for worse episodes."

"Maybe she should talk with Sarah."

"That girl loves you, son. Don't you doubt that." Charley clapped one of his big hands on my shoulder. "If she has news to tell, I'm sure she's just waiting for the right time. My advice is that you make her a big supper tonight and even fix her a bubble bath if that's what she wants. Treat her like a queen. Let the detectives worry about unsolved homicides."

We shook hands once more on the porch before Charley opened the door to return to his lovely bride. Then he remembered one more thing. He turned and in a loudish whisper said, "And buy her some goddamned flowers, pronto!"

The door closed. The wind blew cold against my cheeks. And in spite of everything he'd just said, I stood there for a long time, unable to move forward.

18

After leaving the Square Deal, I drove into Waldoboro to visit a florist. The cramped and steamy store smelled like someone had spilled a vat of cheap perfume on the floor. I wandered in confusion among the lavish displays and gazed dumbly at the frosted refrigerator with its bins of long-stemmed roses before the elderly clerk took pity on me.

"I need to send some flowers to my girlfriend," I explained.

"Do you know what kinds of flowers she likes?"

"No," I said honestly.

The woman frowned at me over her reading glasses, as if I'd failed a test. "How much would you be interested in spending?"

"A lot," I said, then clarified: "Fifty dollars."

"I see." The way she crinkled her nose told me that she was finished sizing me up. To this old shopkeeper, sending flowers was more likely to be a neglectful man's way of asking forgiveness than a genuine expression of love.

I paid the bill for the bouquet and gave her the name of the school where Sarah was teaching.

My mother and father's marriage hadn't exactly prepared me for a lifetime of conjugal bliss.

For the first years of my life, I thought that most couples communicated with each other through drunken screams, thrown dishes, and slammed doors. I believed that one of the police's primary responsibilities was to mediate late-night arguments over misspent paychecks and accusations of adultery.

When my mother married my stepfather, Neil, I learned a different example. For a while, during the early years of her second marriage, my mother would continue to throw tantrums, but to less effect. Neil was a tax attorney and well-off, we had moved into his spacious suburban home, and there was always enough money now for new cars and clothing. Neil didn't provoke her the way my dad had, either. He would patiently wait out her moods, speaking to her in the reassuring tones a cowboy uses on a spirited colt. After a time, my mother's temper would cool, and that would be the end of it.

As I got older, I began to feel as if Neil was treating my mother like a child. He was a handsome man with broad shoulders and a dignified touch of gray at the temples—he projected the rugged vitality of a man in an advertisement for erectile-dysfunction pills—and people commented frequently what an attractive couple he and my mom made. But something seemed to be missing between them. They rarely touched each other in my presence, and because Neil went to bed two hours before she did each night, and he left for work before she was even awake, I wondered when they actually had time for sex. Not that I cared to imagine it.

If my mother minded this arrangement, she didn't show it. After those hot-blooded years with my dad, maybe she'd decided that trading passion for BMW sedans and diamond earrings was a bargain she was finally ready to make.

I wasn't entirely certain what to do with myself for the rest of the somber afternoon.

Technically, I was still on duty. But every time I paused at a stop sign, I found my mind wandering back to the house on Parker Point. Not knowing what was happening made me feel pissed off and powerless. I listened closely to the police radio but heard no intel about Hans Westergaard. I felt like I had been amputated from the investigation.

I rode by Calvin Barter's farm. There were NO TRESPASSING notices posted along the fence posts. Since they hadn't been there before, I interpreted the signs' sudden appearance as a personal warning that I'd better not roam around the property measuring ATV prints, not unless I wanted a faceful of buckshot. If I was going to nab Barter, it would be red-handed or not at all.

Lieutenant Malcomb had said that Sgt. Kathy Frost was returning from vacation the next day. I could easily imagine how she would react to my latest escapade: *"I go away for a week and you find a body!"* But aside from Charley, my district supervisor was the closest thing I had to a confidante. Over the past few days, I'd found myself missing her potty-mouthed lectures.

After a couple of hours of driving down dead-end roads, I decided to go home and finish some paperwork. Under the Warden Service's core shift system, I was required to put in eight hours of work over a twelve-hour period: four days on, two days off. How I accounted for my time was up to me.

Besides, as long as Ashley Kim's killer was at large, I knew that I was going to be unfocused, irritable, and otherwise next to useless.

I was surprised to find Sarah at home so early. She had started a fire in the woodstove and was reheating the leftover chowder from the night before. I looked around for the flowers as I came in, expecting to see them in a vase on the coffee table or kitchen counter.

"Didn't you get a delivery at school?" I asked with all the casualness I could muster.

"No," she said. "Why?"

"I sent you flowers."

She narrowed her eyes in a playful way. "What trouble are you in now?"

"Nothing! I just thought it would be romantic."

"Oh, honey." She laughed. "That's really sweet. I took off early. I'm sure they were delivered after I left. They'll be in my classroom tomorrow."

"Tomorrow is Saturday."

"Maybe a janitor can let me in."

"I paid extra for the delivery."

"I appreciate the effort. You get a gold star." At least she seemed in a good mood. She'd changed into blue jeans and one of my oversized Colby sweatshirts and was padding around in ridiculously fluffy slippers, which made her look like she had a pink rabbit glued to each foot. Given my own miserable childhood, I was never entirely certain what a happy home life was supposed to look like, but this scene seemed like a good approximation.

I wanted to tell her about Ora's suspicion, but how do you ask your girlfriend if she's pregnant without accusing her of misleading you? I had no idea how to broach the subject.

My cell phone rang. I removed it from my belt and held it to my ear. "Hello?"

"Michael Bowditch?" The woman's accent was as thick as a Down East fog bank.

"Yes, this is Warden Bowditch. Who's this?"

"My name is Lou Bates. I left you a message previously. It was about the unfortunate girl who got killed last night and a miscarriage of justice I need to bring to your attention."

Christ, it was Erland Jefferts's crazy aunt. Sarah was gazing at me expectantly, curious who it might be. I rolled my eyes to indicate it was just another crank.

"Yes, ma'am," I said in my best cop voice. "I'm afraid I'm not permitted to speak about the matter."

"I want to talk with you about a wrongfully persecuted individual named Erland Jefferts."

"I can't talk about him, either."

She ignored my response but launched into what sounded like a well-practiced speech. "Warden Bowditch, Erland Jefferts's supporters ask only for a new trial. Prosecutors at the attorney general's office are fully aware that they could never win a trial where jurors hear *all* the evidence, not just what they are willing to disclose. They have done everything in their power to prevent an innocent man from ever having a chance at justice. He has been in prison for seven years, and unless the desperate desire of those prosecutors is overcome, he will remain there until he dies."

"Mrs. Bates—"

"We, the J-Team, are currently petitioning the governor, the chief justice of the Maine Supreme Judicial Court, and the attorney general of Maine, requesting a complete, fair, and independent investigation of the Erland Jefferts case. This travesty of justice must not be allowed to stand."

It took me a few moments to realize that she had reached the end of her speech.

"Mrs. Bates," I said. "I appreciate your commitment to your nephew's cause, but I just can't say anything at this time about any open investigations or pending legal matters. Please respect my position and don't call me again."

I switched off the phone and stuck it in my belt holster. I removed my gun belt and hung it in the bedroom closet, unbuttoned my uniform shirt and sniffed the underarms to see whether I could get away with wearing it again, decided not, and tossed it into the hamper. Then I went into the kitchen to pour myself a whiskey.

Sarah was stirring the chowder. "So who was on the phone?"

"A crazy lady who thinks I can somehow help get her nephew out of prison."

"How would you do that?" she asked.

My supposition was that Sarah was unfamiliar with the Erland Jefferts case. The murder and trial occurred while she was still in high school in Connecticut, although the antics of the J-Team still got enough ink these days in the local newspaper.

"She says her nephew was wrongfully convicted seven years ago and believes the real killer murdered Ashley Kim last night. For some reason, she thinks I can help her."

She put the spoon down next to the burner and started to sob.

"Sarah." I stepped forward and put my arms around her.

A shiver rippled down her spine. "I'm sorry. I've been doing this all day. All the teachers were talking about the murder. That's why I left school early. I kept breaking into tears and didn't want the kids to see." She reached for a dishrag to wipe her nose and eyes. "Go on. What were you saying?"

"It was nothing important."

She shook her head, so that her blond hair swayed just like Jill Westergaard's had that morning. "I want to hear what you found out from the detectives."

I took my glass and sat down at the kitchen table and sipped my whiskey. "The state police are still looking for this Hans Westergaard, who owns the house. They think the killing was a rendezvous that somehow went really, really bad."

"So this professor was the one who murdered her?"

"In these cases, it's almost always the boyfriend," I said, parroting Skip Morrison's words.

"But the detectives don't know for certain?"

"The probability is high."

"But there's a chance it was someone else? It could be some random psychopath who happened on the accident scene and offered to give her a ride."

I gulped down the rest of my whiskey. "I don't think there's a random psychopath in Seal Cove."

Sarah dished me a bowl of chowder and set it on the place mat. "The teachers were saying—" Her voice caught in her throat again, but this time she managed to recover herself and continue. "We were saying how scary it is for women to drive alone at night on some of these back roads. What happened to that woman, it could have happened to me."

This conversation seemed poised to become another indictment of our living situation. Sarah had made it abundantly clear that she would have preferred renting an apartment up the road in swanky Camden. I dug into my dinner. "Well, it didn't."

"You think Ashley Kim was just unlucky."

"Basically."

"That's how you and I are different." Sarah had

been raised as an Episcopalian and still considered her parents' family priest a trusted friend. She was a person of faith, just as I was a person of doubt. On the question of happenstance, she saw destiny's hand instead of random luck. "I don't believe in accidents."

At dinner, I kept waiting for Sarah to break the news to me, if there was news, but she ate quietly, lost in her own head.

Finally, as we were washing the dishes side by side at the sink and my inhibitions had been lowered by two more whiskeys, I just blurted out the question. "So how's your stomach?"

She focused on what her hands were doing in the soapy water. "It's still giving me trouble."

I waited for her to say more, but that was the beginning and the end of the subject.

As I refolded the napkins, I sneaked a look at Sarah's midsection. I wasn't sure what I expected to see, but her abdomen was as flat as the tabletop. If we had a baby and it was a little boy, I realized I could teach him everything my father had failed to teach me. That possibility of having a second chance at childhood, if only vicariously, appealed to some deep emotion I couldn't even name.

She must have picked up on one of my brain waves. "Was your father always like that?"

"Like what?"

"Self-destructive."

"I don't know," I said. "My grandmother used to tell me he was different before he went to Vietnam."

"Different how?"

"I'd rather not talk about my dad."

"I understand." She nodded knowingly and put a hand on my shoulder. "There's something I've been meaning to ask you." She hesitated, looking at me intensely out of the corners of her sky blue eyes. "It's kind of strange."

Now I was genuinely nervous. "What is it?"

"Did you vacuum the rug?"

"Yes," I replied, lying.

"You actually cleaned something in this house?"

"Yes."

She laughed and tossed the wet dish towel at me. "Who are you? And what did you do with my boyfriend?"

19

The phone rang very early the next morning. Sarah reached across my naked back to answer it.

"It's Kathy Frost," she mumbled.

I raised myself off the mattress with a groan. "Jesus, Kathy," I said, blinking at the darkened window. "Do you know what time it is?"

"I don't know. Early?"

"It's five o'clock on a Saturday morning."

"I must still be on Key West time."

"Florida is in the same time zone as Maine."

"Oh, yeah." A dog was whining plaintively somewhere in the background. "Well, now that you're bright-eyed and bushy-tailed, how would you like to get some breakfast? I brought you a souvenir."

I sat up and swung my stiff legs off the bed. The floorboards were cold as ice beneath my heels. "OK. Where?"

"How about my place? I've got a sick dog here. I don't know what shit Devoe fed him, but it's been coming out both ends all night long."

I rubbed the flakes from my eyelashes. "I'll see you in an hour."

"Bring doughnuts! And coffee!"

So my sergeant had somehow conned me into driving forty miles to her house in the predawn light, on my day off no less, and paying for breakfast in the bargain. What was it about women that made me agree to their most out-landish requests?

I left Sarah dozing in bed and shuffled, naked, into the bathroom. The harsh light above the mirror showed a drawn, stubbled face, making me wonder whether I'd done the Rip van Winkle thing and overslept by a decade or two. My head ached from the three whiskeys I'd consumed before bed. I needed to cut back on those, I decided. And my pubic bone was sore in a spot I rarely had reason to consider. I'd been surprised by Sarah's sudden playfulness the night before. One moment she'd been all sad and teary, and the next she was reaching for my zipper. She hadn't seemed like a woman worried about an unplanned pregnancy.

When I'd toweled off after the shower and was pulling on my pants, I found Sarah leaning sleepily against the doorjamb, holding the phone. She, too, was naked. "It's for you again," she said, yawning. "It's Hank Varnum."

She handed me the phone and collapsed once more onto the bed.

I took the call in the kitchen. A gauzy gray light had begun seeping through the windows. The room was so cold, I could see my breath when I spoke. "What's going on, Hank?"

"You need to get over here, Mike!"

"I'm not on duty today. Do you want me to call John Farwell? He's covering my district."

"No, I want you to arrest that pervert Calvin Barter."

I settled my aching bones down at the table. "Tell me what happened."

"That pervert just dragged away my mailbox! I was still asleep when I heard the ATVs ride across my front yard. There were two of them, a big one and a little one, and they were whooping and hollering. I grabbed my revolver and ran outside, but they were already racing down the road, dragging my mailbox by a chain."

"And you're sure one of the two riders was Barter?"

"Yes! I'd recognize that big pervert anywhere."

"Why do you keep calling him a 'pervert'?"

"The man's a child molester! Everybody in town knows that."

When I'd moved to the midcoast last year, I'd reviewed the list of sexual predators—the registry of local child molesters, Peeping Toms, public masturbators, and statutory rapists—but Calvin's name hadn't jumped out at me. There were lots of Barters in these backwaters. It wasn't until this conversation with Hank that I finally made the connection.

"All right," I said. "I'll drive over to the Barter place. I'll arrest him on the spot if I have cause, but I can't just haul him into jail on your say-so. Please promise me that if he comes back over here later, you won't do anything rash."

"I'll defend myself and my property."

"I don't want this turning into a feud between you two."

"It already is!"

With that, he hung up.

I changed out of my Carhartts and put on my wrinkled uniform. Peering into the darkened bedroom again, I saw that Sarah was snoring softly. I looked longingly at her spread-eagled backside, but instead of waking her again, I left a note on the kitchen counter, promising to be back by noon. We were scheduled to drive to Portland to visit her older sister, Amy—the one who hated my guts. Wait till she heard I'd knocked up Sarah.

The sun hadn't even risen yet, and already this was shaping up to be one hellacious day.

Outside, there was a sting in the air that made my cheeks feel as if they'd both been freshly slapped. Clouds sagged down on the treetops, and the smell of imminent snow made me dread the long drive to southern Maine later that afternoon.

The cab of the truck always took an eternity to heat up. There were many mornings when my vehicle seemed like a four-wheeled icebox. It actually felt warmer standing outside in the open air.

On the drive over to Barter's farm, I weighed the idea of calling Kathy or Farwell for backup. But I wanted the satisfaction of confronting Calvin on my own. Like Varnum, I was having trouble not taking this as a personal offense. If Barter wanted a fight, I'd gladly give him one. It didn't matter if he was the size of Andre the Giant.

I drove past the NO TRESPASSING signs and through the orchard of bony apple trees to the dooryard of the farmhouse. Most of the windows were dim, but I saw a light in a lower room, probably coming from the kitchen. I got out of the truck and carefully closed the door, not wanting to spook Barter into fleeing again.

The cold snap had hardened the mud underfoot. The frozen earth was contoured and crusted into waves that crackled with every step I took. I pounded my fist against the flaking front door. I heard muttering inside and saw a light flick on in the entryway.

The door opened, and Barter's teenaged, red-headed, chicken-shooting son glared out at me from the hall. He wore muddy jeans and nothing else. His jutting ribs reminding me of an inmate recently released from a concentration camp.

"What do you want?" he sassed.

"Go get your father."

"He ain't here."

"I don't believe you, kid." The mud-splattered pants told me who Barter's ATV companion had been.

The boy pushed a heavy red bang out of his eyes and sharpened his sneer. "Didn't you read them signs?" he asked.

"I read them. Now go get your father."

"You don't tell me what to do."

"Travis!"

Wanda Barter, dressed in a shapeless smock that might once have been a circus tent, came storming down the hall. She already had a cigarette fired up and tucked between her cracked lips. Her reddish gray hair was fastened forcibly back from her forehead by a cruel array of pins. She shoved her son by the head, so that he stumbled away from the door. Then she stepped forward as if to block my entrance should I consider barging into the home. I felt vaguely like Theseus up against the Minotaur.

"What do you want?"

"I know your husband's inside, Mrs. Barter." Glancing behind the barrel-shaped woman, I saw the boy down the hall. I raised my voice so that it could be heard throughout the house, in case someone was eavesdropping from the top of the staircase. "We've got another warden in the woods behind the house, so Calvin can forget trying to give us the slip again." It was a blatant lie, but I was sick of Wanda's bullshit.

She studied me through the wafting cigarette smoke. "I guess you didn't see the 'No Trespassing' signs we put up out front. Or maybe you don't read so well. You didn't strike me as the intelligent type the other day. Those signs mean the same as 'Keep Out.' "

When you grow up in poverty, as I did, you develop a complicated attitude toward the destitute, the shiftless, and the genuinely needy. You remember your own frequent visits to the food bank and the squalor of your playmates' mobile homes, and you feel an upwelling of sympathy that lasts until the moment some redneck spits in your face. And then you start thinking that ultimately we all deserve the hand we're dealt.

I counted to ten. "Someone just committed criminal mischief on Hank Varnum's property for the second time in a week. I know it was your husband who did it."

A random redheaded toddler wandered out of the shadows and stood behind its mother, or grandmother, or whoever the hell she was. There were too many homes in these parts where the family trees defied easy diagramming.

"Calvin's away on business," she said.

Business? The man didn't work. "We both know I'm going to catch up with Calvin sooner or later. Do I really have to get a warrant to talk with him?"

"Yep." She blew two massive lungfuls of smoke in my face. "You really fucking do. Now why don't you get the fuck off my property before I really lose my fucking temper."

She didn't close the door on me, just crossed her brawny forearms and made it clear that the conversation was officially over. We both knew that I had no recourse. She hadn't threatened me, and without a warrant specifying probable cause for a search, I had no business lingering on private property. Once again, Wanda Barter had me by the short hairs, and she damn well knew it.

"I'll be back," I said, but the threat sounded hollow even to my own ears.

She merely leered at me while the blank-faced toddler peeked out from between her formidable legs.

I didn't fully turn my back on the house until I had climbed into my truck. I swung around the circular driveway fast and accelerated through the leafless orchard, furious and tempted to take out a few fence posts along my way. My spinning tires churned up loose gravel, which rattled around the underside of the chassis, and for an instant, I thought I heard a pinging sound.

It was only fifteen minutes later, as I was getting out of the vehicle at the Square Deal to buy Kathy her doughnuts, that I realized where the noise had come from. My side window was cracked in an unmistakable spiderwebbed pattern, one that could only have been produced by a pellet gun.

20

I was never cut out to be a comedian. I know only one Maine joke, and it happens to be tasteless. "What does a Maine girl say during sex? 'Ease up, Dad. You're crushing my smokes.'"

There were too many houses I visited where the truth behind that punch line lurked in creepy silhouettes behind drawn window shades. Wanda Barter's farm was one. Two days ago, I had found the woman and her redheaded band of offspring vaguely amusing. Now the thought of Barter and his brood gave me a major case of the willies.

I needed to nab this asshole. Most game wardens were assigned all-terrain vehicles, but budget cuts and the geographical peculiarities of my district—all those rocky peninsulas and marshy rivers—had precluded me from getting one. Maybe I could borrow Kathy's, I thought. I relished the possibility of meeting Calvin Barter alone on a darkened trail.

Whatever the expression on my face was as I entered the Square Deal Diner, it caused Ruth Libby to blanch. "What's wrong?" she asked.

"Could I get a dozen doughnuts to go? And two large coffees?"

"We're calling them 'grande' coffees now."

"You are?"

"Heck no." She winked, trying to lighten my mood.

I appreciated her intent, but I wasn't especially eager to let go of my rage. Like the men on my father's side of the family, I seemed to enjoy getting angry—the heat of the blood pulsing through my temples affected me like a dangerous intoxicant.

Out of the corner of my eye, I became aware of a couple watching me from a corner booth, the very same booth Charley and I had occupied the previous day. They were an older, mismatched couple. The man had a shock of white hair and glasses with thick black rims. He wore a black blazer over a black polo shirt that hugged his heavy paunch. The woman was whip-thin, with close-cropped gray curls, a long nose, and deeply set eyes that put me in mind of a stalking heron. As I waited for Ruth to fill my order, the man and women consulted each other in whispers and then rose ceremoniously to their feet. I saw that the man was lugging a file box that looked stuffed to overflowing with documents.

"Oh shit," whispered Ruth. "Those are the ones who were asking about you."

"Warden Bowditch," said the woman in a thick Down East accent I instantly recognized. "My name is Lou Bates. I spoke with you on the telephone. This is my associate, Mr. Oswald Bell."

"Call me Ozzie." His voice was parched and raspy, probably from a lifetime's worth of cigarettes. His own accent said Rockaway, New York, rather than Rockport, Maine.

"We're here on behalf of my nephew, Erland Jefferts," explained Lou Bates.

I noticed they were both sporting white buttons on their lapels with the words FREE ERLAND JEFFERTS. I tried to muster a modicum of politeness. "As I told you yesterday, I can't talk with you, Mrs. Bates."

"Five minutes of your time," said Bell. "You can give us five minutes, right?"

"No, Mr. Bell, I'm afraid I can't."

"Make it three minutes, then. You've got that. While they ring up your order."

"This isn't a negotiation," I said. "How did you know to find me here?"

"Our sources told us that you frequent this establishment on a daily basis," said Lou Bates.

"Your sources?"

"My nephew is being wrongfully incarcerated in the Maine State Prison for a crime he didn't commit."

"Basically, we consider Mr. Jefferts a political prisoner," declared Bell.

Lou Bates continued: "It is our belief that you have evidence that can help exonerate him and secure his full pardon and release."

Bell raised the heavy cardboard box in my

direction, as if he expected me to accept it as a gift. "If you'll just look at these files, you'll see Erland has gotten royally shafted. There are state secrets in this box—information the prosecution refuses to make public."

"I told you that I can't talk with you." The entire diner had fallen silent. A voice in the back of my head told me to cool down fast, before the consequences spiraled out of control. "I need to use the rest room."

All eyes followed me into the bathroom. Inside, I leaned both arms against the sink and stared into my own burning reflection. Did these J-Team nuts really think that I was some sort of crusader for the unfairly accused? I started the tap water running and splashed my face. Get a grip, Bowditch. Pay for your doughnuts and hit the road.

When I opened the bathroom door, I found everyone in the restaurant gawking at me. But Ozzie Bell and Lou Bates had disappeared.

"I told them to leave, or else I'd call the police," Ruth explained.

"Thanks," I said, and paid my bill.

Outside, I scanned the parked cars to see whether my two stalkers were lying in wait, but they seemed to have vanished. I approached my patrol truck, coffee and doughnuts in hand, but did a double take as I drew near. There in the bed was Ozzie Bell's box of top secret files.

• • •

Kathy Frost lived in a two-hundred-year-old farmhouse in the rolling hills of Appleton, at the northern edge of my district. Blueberry barrens, which turned crimson in the fall, cascaded down from her doorstep. The undulating fields were crisscrossed with stone walls and strewn with scorched boulders. In the summer, after the last berries had been raked, immigrant workers would set fire to the fields, blackening the barrens so that the bushes would blossom with greater fruitfulness in seasons to come.

I rarely had cause to visit Kathy at home. My sergeant didn't go out of her way to encourage visitors. At Division B, she had the reputation of being an odd breed of hermit: a funny, sociable, and utterly uninhibited person who nevertheless kept her private life private. She'd been married a long time ago to some dude named Frost, but the marriage hadn't stuck, for one reason or another. It occurred to me that I knew very little about Kathy's social life despite having spent countless hours in cold, cramped circumstances with her on search parties, night patrols, and stakeouts. Our relationship was a strange mixture of intimacy (I knew how she smelled without deodorant) and aloof professionalism.

As I drove up to the house, a dog began baying inside. That was Pluto, Kathy's grizzled coonhound. I took a moment before I turned off the engine, trying to get the lay of the land. She had a nice spread. There were stately old elms here that had survived a century of blight, along with some big maples fit for sugaring. Kathy's GMC patrol truck was parked in the dooryard. I also spotted a muddy all-terrain vehicle behind the house—exactly what I'd been looking for.

The doorbell was broken, so I rapped against the glass. Pluto came loping down the foyer, barking all the way. I tried to talk soothingly to him through the glass, but he just kept yowling, as if we were strangers.

After a moment, Kathy appeared, tanned and grinning, and jerked the door open.

Kathy Frost was in her forties, although whether she was in her mid- or late forties, I could never have told you. She was six feet tall, with long, strong limbs. Her bobbed haircut didn't flatter her, but she had fetching hazel eyes. She wore blue jeans, muddy work boots, and a flannel shirt that had survived a thousand trips through the washing machine. Her trip to Florida had left her with a remarkable tan, as if she'd been dipped head to toe in bronze.

"Took you long enough," she said.

I presented her with the coffee and dough-nuts. "Don't start, Kathy. I've had a shitty morning."

"Yeah, yeah, yeah."

I followed her into the depths of the old house

—the chilly air had a vaguely doggish scent—and into the kitchen. Pluto trailed us slowly down the hall and then collapsed with a wheeze on a hand-hooked rug beside the oven. As one of her duties, Kathy oversaw the Warden Service's K-9 units, training officers and their dogs to assist in search and rescue operations. Pluto looked like an unassuming old pooch—thick of body and grizzled of snout—but he was a retired celebrity in law-enforcement circles. Over his working lifetime, he had located dozens of lost people, alive and dead.

We sat down at an antique table, which tilted when you set your elbows on it, and opened the box of doughnuts.

"First, I want to hear about Key West," I said.

"It was hot and crowded. I caught a tarpon."

"That's it?"

"The daiquiris were overpriced. Also, I bought you a souvenir."

She handed me a paperback book from the counter. It was *Men Without Women*, by Ernest Hemingway. "I saw the title and thought of you."

"I don't think that's a compliment, Kath."

She shrugged her broad shoulders. "So tell me about this dead girl of yours. I've got to hand it you, Grasshopper. You don't waste any time. I go away for a week and suddenly you're up to your crotch again in a murder investigation. And

211

somehow you found a way to involve Charley Stevens in this, I hear. That old geezer must consider you his personal ace of spades." She sipped from her cold coffee. "Malcomb gave me the rundown last night, but he left out the juicy stuff. Clue me in."

"I don't see the point. Menario already informed me that my role in the investigation is finished—until this thing goes to trial, if it ever does."

"Menario?"

"He got transferred to the coast to run the investigation."

She waved a cruller at me. "Come on, tell me the inside dope on what's going on here. I'm your sergeant, and I command you to share all your gossip on this case with me."

I titled back in my creaky chair with a grin. "You can't order me to do that."

"Are you sure of that? What does the policy manual say?"

"I have no idea."

"It's on page seventy-seven: 'Wardens are required to tell their supervisors about all the interesting shit that happened while they were on vacation.' "

In truth, I was relieved to go over it again. Telling the story to Kathy Frost from the beginning gave me a chance to reexamine the details, and I was glad to have another interested person to help me make sense of the mystery, especially now that Charley had decamped. I started my story with my arrival at Hank Varnum's house three nights earlier and went on from there, trying to include every halfway relevant detail in my account. Kathy could be a wiseass, but she had a well-trained mind. If there was a hole in my reasoning, she'd find it, and if I was deluding myself in any way, she'd let me know that, too. Kathy listened seriously, rocking back in her chair with arms folded as I told my tale.

"Can you believe those freaks left that box of files in my truck?" I said by way of conclusion. "I'm the last person anyone should want defending an accused man's innocence."

"You've become the Saint Jude of hopeless criminal prosecutions."

Pluto, meanwhile, had fallen asleep and was in the midst of a vivid dream that caused him to growl and twitch. We both looked at him with eyebrows raised in amusement.

"You know Pluto and I were the ones who found Nikki Donnatelli," Kathy said, licking doughnut grease off her fingers.

"I wanted to ask you about that."

"All of our K-9s are extensively trained for SAR. But Pluto is primarily a cadaver dog, meaning that he's good at sniffing out dead people. We only take him into the woods these days when we're pretty sure we're dealing with human remains instead of a living, breathing person. Some animals are just better suited to one or the other—recovery versus rescue. Pluto has a nose for death."

"Maybe that's why he doesn't like me. I think I must carry the smell of it or something."

"Don't flatter yourself. He also eats his own shit. Still, he's got one hell of a morbid gift."

We both glanced at him again, but the dog's dream had passed and he was snoring peaceably again.

"What was it like coming across her body?" I asked.

She switched to her stern sergeant's voice. "Promise me you're not going to get involved with this Erland Jefferts conspiracy. The guy's guilty. There might be some copycat thing going on here, but another girl getting tied up with tape doesn't mean pretty-boy Jefferts is innocent."

"I just want to hear what happened."

"Let me make more coffee." She turned on the tap, filled the teakettle, and set it on a burner. When the flame ignited, an acrid smell wafted through the room. Kathy was an infamously bad cook. From the odor, I deduced that she had burned some cheese-related dish and never cleaned it up.

We reused the Styrofoam cups for our instant coffee and sat down again at the antique table, and then Kathy told me her version of Maine's most infamous murder case.

"I'm assuming you know the general outline of the story. How the Donnatelli girl disappeared on her way home from work and then the next morning they found Jefferts passed out in his truck in the woods? Well, the state police brought us in pretty quick. They have their own K-9 people, but they know we're better at searches. One problem we had right away was that it began to rain like Mother Nature was taking a wicked piss. No dog can track well under those conditions. And it's no picnic for the searchers, either."

A sudden gust of wind shook the kitchen windows. The day seemed to be getting dimmer, although the clock hadn't yet struck noon. Through the glass I watched snow showers blow past. The brown fields in the background looked like a watercolor painting left out in the rain.

"You've been on those searches," Kathy continued. "You know the drill. We had about a hundred volunteers—personnel from the Brunswick Naval Air Station, the Rockland Coast Guard station. The National Guard sent a helicopter with a Forward Looking Infrared camera so they could search for Nikki's body heat from treetop level.

"Malcomb was in charge of designing the

search criteria, based on what we knew about Nikki and the rough time line the state police had established. One logical place to begin the search was where Jefferts had parked his pickup. And we needed to double-check the shore path. There are quarries all over that peninsula, too, and we didn't know if she might be at the bottom of one of those disgusting pits. As always, the problem was, Where do you start looking?"

None of this came as news to me. I'd been trained extensively in the science of finding lost persons. But I wanted to hear the story, in light of how I'd discovered Ashley Kim.

Kathy was lost in her own memories now. "The setup of the search had to be defined, maps drawn up, assignments given. Every team needed to know its waypoints and specific instructions about ground to be covered, as well as the general details—like the spacing for the grid searches. Anyway, the overall situation that day was the usual controlled chaos, with the rain not helping. You always get lots of hits with the K-9s, but most are false alarms. Each time, though, you have to figure out if it's a bust or not. There are just all sorts of bad smells and dead critters out there for the dogs to find."

Kathy had spoken with me about becoming a dog handler—district wardens often acquire an area of specialization, in addition to their usual responsibilities—but I was leaning toward the dive team. Charley, meanwhile, wanted me to follow in his footsteps and become a warden pilot, but I found his several near-death aerial experiences less than inspiring.

"We gave Pluto a good whiff of Nikki's clothes, but that didn't do the trick," she said. "In those circumstances, you try all kinds of things. Her shampoo, perfume, soap. Ultimately, it was the rigging tape that did it, the roll from Jefferts's truck. I smelled the tape myself. It had a strong fishy odor, like it had come off a lobsterboat.

"That first day was just a blur. It seemed like her body should have been somewhere right there, along that dirt road, but it wasn't. God, the weather was miserable, hot and rainy. The mosquitoes were plenty happy we were out there, though. Malcomb called us in after dark. Pluto and I could have kept searching—we wanted to—but that wasn't our call. The Donnatellis were waiting at the command post with Deb Davies. I'll never forget the look on the father's face. It was as if someone had ripped his heart out of his chest and he hadn't yet realized it."

She excused herself to use the bathroom, leaving me in the drafty kitchen listening to the windows rattle in their casements. Retelling this story had robbed Kathy of her high spirits. I felt bad about that, knowing she'd just returned from a much-needed vacation.

After a few minutes, she returned and squatted down next to Pluto on his rug and began scratching his throat. "So the next day, we went back out again," she said, "and it was still raining like Noah should have been building an ark somewhere. We were all exhausted by midafternoon. The adrenaline leaves your bloodstream, and all those hours in the field catch up with you. Well, suddenly we got a message over the radio. It turned out someone had made an error assigning the search areas. We'd missed this big swampy swatch of forest. They shifted my group south to have a look at it. Within half an hour, Pluto started running a track. He nearly pulled me off my feet. When he hit that hard, I knew it was Nikki."

She paused and collected herself before continuing.

"She'd been tied with her arms around the tree, so he could get to her from behind, if you know what I mean. I remember seeing her white body through the rain and thinking she might be alive. She was on her feet and sort of looked like she was resting her shoulders against the trunk, but that was just the way he'd tied her. I told my search party to stay back. I wanted to preserve a single path to the crime scene and keep everyone from trampling over the evidence."

Exactly what I had *not* done at the Westergaard house.

"Her jeans were pulled down around her ankles. The rest of her clothes had been cut away, none too gently. She had all sorts of bloody little wounds on her, and this red mark on her forehead where Jefferts must have clobbered her. They never did find her underwear. Her eyes were wide open, but the flies had already been at them. She'd died knowing she was suffocating, and she still had that look of terror and disbelief you see with so many corpses. Death is never real to some people until the moment they realize it's happening to them.

"I called her name, but I knew there was no point."

She took a breath, and I saw the toll it was taking on her to revisit this day, which had been one of the worst in her life. I wanted to ask her a question, but I felt inhibited by the grief I was witnessing, so I just sat there and waited for her to continue.

"My partner from the state police radioed in the Code Blue to the command post," she said. "The next time I saw her, she was in a bag strapped to a stretcher.

"The trial was a circus, as you know. But fortunately, I wasn't the focus of the defense's attention. Jefferts's lawyer—I forget his name—was a total doofus. On cross-examination, he tried to suggest that I might have fucked up the crime scene in some unspecific way. Time of death was what he was arguing—that it would have been impossible for Jefferts to commit the murder, since he was somewhere else when Nikki died, based on the ME's own testimony. But Danica Marshall squashed that argument like a bug. I was surprised that the AG had assigned her to such a high-profile case, since she was just a kid at the time. But when I saw her in the courtroom, all my doubts went out the window. Jesus, that little cutie has bigger balls than you do." She paused for comic effect. "No offense."

"Offense taken," I said.

The joke had loosened her mood again. She leaned her elbows on the old table, which caused it to creak in complaint. "It sounds like whoever killed this Kim woman took a few pages from Jefferts's playbook, but I can tell you we nailed the right perp seven years ago. Erland's exactly where he belongs—at the prison. If I were you, I'd drop that box of files they gave you in a Dumpster on your way home."

"Don't worry," I said. "I'm not joining the J-Team." I cracked my knuckles while I considered whether I had the guts to ask her the question buzzing in my head. "What word did Nikki Donnatelli have written on her body?"

Kathy looked as if I'd just punched her in the solar plexus. "What?"

"Ashley Kim also had a profanity carved into her skin."

"Jesus H. Christ."

I could see the color rising beneath her tanned cheeks and knew I'd struck pay dirt. "Just tell me the truth, Kathy. I promise you I'm not on another mission to prove anything."

"It was *slut*." When she spoke again, it was in a tough voice she reserved for arrests. "That was the word on Ashley, right? So I've indulged your curiosity. Let's talk about your job. What the hell have you been up to anyway?"

I stood up. "Well, I've got some ATV vandals harassing Hank Varnum."

"So are you planning on catching them or what?"

"That's why I came over here," I said. "Can I borrow your four-wheeler?"

21

The snow was turning to sleet as I drove my overloaded truck along the sloping, slippery roads from Appleton to Sennebec. Kathy had helped me set up two boards to drive her ATV up into the bed of my pickup. The weight of the four-wheeler gave my truck excellent traction, but it made me feel a bit top-heavy whenever I rounded a curve, which was every thirty seconds or so.

I wasn't sure if the snow made it more or less likely that Barter would be venturing out again this evening. Hopefully, the new powder would serve as an enticement. There wasn't quite enough of the white stuff anymore for snow-mobiling, but a person could have some fun skidding around on an all-terrain vehicle.

The story Kathy had told me about the search for Nikki Donnatelli kept intruding on my thoughts. I looked over at the passenger seat, where I'd moved Ozzie Bell's box of files. Kathy had advised dumping them in the trash on the way home, but somehow I had managed not to do so.

Kathy's pursuit ATV was a real beast. It had a 71-horsepower engine with an auto-locking front differential and dynamic power steering. She told me that, if properly handled, her Can-Am/Bombardier could go as fast as the fastest four-wheelers on the trails. She'd empha-sized the words *properly handled* when she'd given me the keys, as if she doubted the likeli-hood of my delivering her prize toy back to her in a single piece. She had reason to worry. Like most overgrown boys, I loved the sensation of going really, really fast.

I parked my truck in the woods half a mile from Varnum's place and inspected the armor Kathy had loaned me. Her plated riding boots wouldn't fit, so I was stuck with my own field boots and work gloves. Fortunately, I could squeeze my big head into her helmet and goggles. I knew my uniform was going to get trashed from flying mud and roost—the grit and rocks an ATV's wheels churn up—but there was no way around that.

I unfastened the tailgate and propped up the ramps Kathy had given me. Then I climbed up into the bed and started the engine. The machine gave a large, harsh growl.

Traveling backward on a four-wheeler is a funky art. I could just imagine explaining to Kathy how I'd flipped her ATV over while getting it out of my vehicle. Like most quads, hers had a winch on the front to pull it out of mud holes, but that wouldn't do me any good if I found myself pinned beneath the machine.

I did a couple of circuits on the nearest stretch of trail, trying to regain my muscle memory. Posture is everything when riding an all-terrain vehicle, and I needed to get loose, relaxing my shoulders and elbows and tilting my knees into the gas tank. The machine fought against my efforts to master it. The handlebars pulled against my forearms when I tried to turn them, and the vibration from the engine sent a shock wave up my spine that crashed against my cerebellum. The sleet, mixed now with freezing rain, began falling more heavily, screwing with my vision through the plastic goggles.

After getting comfortable in the saddle, I turned the ATV in the direction of Barter's farm and revved the throttle. The woods were a blur as I raced along the cold-hardened trail. The forecast for the coming week was for warmer weather, but two nights of subzero temperatures had hardened the mud into shit cement. The conditions made for a jarring ride. The freezing rain was sliding its cold, wet fingers down the back of my neck. And it was getting dark.

As best as I could tell from my DeLorme GPS, Calvin Barter had only one direct-access point into the trail system that connected his property with that of the Varnums. A single path exited his farm before forking off in several directions across the peninsula. When I arrived at the fork, I paused and looked around. The local trees were all hardwoods—maples and oaks mostly, with their usual tatters of dead leaves—affording me little in the way of cover. But there was a knoll to one side of the trail that I could perch atop. Dressed as I was in an olive uniform and riding a mud-crusted machine, it was unlikely Barter would spot me if he came racing past at forty-five miles per hour. I leaned forward and down-shifted to climb the little hill, then swung the ATV around in a tight circle until I was facing the fork in the trail. I turned off the engine and removed my goggles and helmet.

The freezing rain pelted my bare face like

bird shot. It took several minutes for my hearing to return to normal, and even then a ghost echo of that loud engine lurked behind my throbbing eardrums. I became aware of the sound of the icy rain on the frozen snow—an insistent *shhh,* as if the sky were telling the earth to be silent.

I removed a glove and reached inside my soaked parka for my cell phone. I tapped in Wanda Barter's number and waited.

"Hello?" The voice was female, Wanda's daughter maybe, the one with the baby.

"This is Warden Bowditch. I want to talk with Calvin Barter."

"Go fuck yourself."

"Tell him I'm coming with a warrant." I wasn't certain I got out the last words before she hung up.

Now there was nothing to do but wait. The prospect of actually catching Barter in the act of vandalizing Hank's place seemed pretty remote, so this was the only way I could see to play things. Maine law provided a nice assortment of offenses—from speeding to suspicion of operating under the influence of intoxicating liquor—that I could use to stop Barter on the trail. After that, I'd have to hope he said something stupid or otherwise provoked me in such a manner that I could make a bona fide arrest. It was possible I could connect his ATV tire treads to the prints I'd collected at the Varnum house, so the district attorney would feel confident pressing charges, but I doubted it.

I didn't have long to wait. In the distance I heard the insect whine of engines. The noise began to grow. I was definitely hearing two machines— Barter and who else? I put my helmet and goggles back on and restarted the ignition. The ATV sent a shudder through every bone in my skeleton.

In less than a minute, I saw the lights. The first figure was very large, almost too large for the vehicle beneath him. The second was ridiculously small, riding what looked like a toy version of a four-wheeler—like something out of a cereal box.

I kept my lights off until the last possible second, when they were just about to fly past me, I hit the pursuit lights.

I saw the two riders turn their heads in my direction and then, without even a pause to consider the situation, they took off.

Bending forward so that my weight was over the back of the seat, I started down the slope. The machine seemed to slide beneath me, and I squeezed the brakes hard, swerving to avoid a tree that seemed to materialize out of nowhere.

Barter and the other, smaller rider—it had to be the teenage boy, Travis—were already disappearing into the distance. Between the driving ice and the trees themselves, the visibility absolutely sucked, but clouds of snow and smoke lingered behind the two machines, and their tire tracks showed clearly in my headlights. I realized I might have trouble overtaking them, but I could certainly follow. At the moment, the riders were headed for Hank Varnum's land.

In front of me I could see their lights growing smaller. I gunned the engine. I'd forgotten how physically exhausting it was to drive one of these quads. The process seemed to involve long-forgotten muscles in my thighs and lower back.

Suddenly, with just a split second to act, I noticed a huge log in the path. Barter and the boy had turned off into the woods to avoid it, but I was flying along at a speed too fast to do the same. I stood up in the seat and throttled hard. For an instant, I felt a lifting sensation in my stomach, as if I were about to tumble ass over teakettle across the handlebars, but then the front wheels grabbed the bark and I found myself launching into space. I threw my weight back when the rear wheels hit, landing so hard, I almost veered off trail. I had to yank the handlebars back in line to avoid smacking into a birch.

The path began to climb sharply. I stood up in a crouched position on the foot rests, trying to regain an attack stance so that I could move forward, sideways, or to the rear—depending on what I saw coming at me in the headlights. It was a steep and nasty hill that Barter had chosen. I charged up the slope, staying on the gas and leaning forward to keep the front end down.

Even so, I felt the machine begin to loop out. I was about to wheelie back on myself with hundreds of pounds of metal crashing down on top of me. I threw my weight to the right, turning the front wheels downhill, and made a U-turn, swerving through an obstacle course of birch and beech trees. Their branches pawed at me, seeking to knock me loose, but I held on with all the strength my hands could muster. Somehow, I managed to circle around to the base of the hill.

I braked hard and stared up at the steep trail. Barter knew what he was doing. He had chosen this path because he suspected a rider unfamiliar with it would have problems climbing the hill. Looking for a detour would probably mean I'd lose them for good.

Try again, I decided. I swung the ATV around to give myself a longer approach this time. I shifted into a lower gear and gassed it, aiming for as much momentum as possible and hoping to hell my wheels didn't lose traction on the icy surface.

Again, I felt the engine revs bogging me down, and again I threw my weight forward, throttling the machine for all it was worth. For a second, I felt myself poised as if on a teeter-totter. The slightest shift in my weight would send me forward or back. This time, I committed to the hill. The front wheels grabbed hold, and I jerked ahead, topping the crest.

The tracks from the two ATVs led off through the descending storm.

Where will they go next? I wondered if Barter might decide to play cat and mouse with me, leading me through his own private obstacle course in the hope I'd give up or wreck my machine. His other choice was to circle around behind me.

For the moment, I decided to proceed ahead cautiously. I might not be able to catch him, but maybe I could outsmart him.

The sleet had changed over entirely to freezing rain. I could feel the subtle rise in air temperature on my bare nose and throat. Ice was starting to weigh down the boughs of the spruces. Mist was beginning to push back the beam of my headlights, and with each passing minute, the landscape was becoming more and more crystalline. I moved methodically forward down the slope—no longer at top speed—searching for clues.

What I discovered next surprised me. At the far side of the ridge, the trail entered a pool of half-frozen mud. A taut surface of ice stretched from one side of the path to the other. Both all-terrain vehicles had gone surging through this watercourse, but only one had made it across. In the middle, a small yellow ATV sat submerged. The handlebars projected above the surface, but the rest of the vehicle had broken through the ice and sunk down into the gluey mud at the bottom. Its lights were still on, shining fuzzily forward across the pond, but it was apparent to me that the boy's engine had drowned out.

I paused for a moment and unhooked the Maglite on my belt, then shined it to either side of the pond. There was a chance the boy was hiding somewhere in the trees, but I saw no trace of him. That meant Barter had taken the boy on the back of his own vehicle. The additional weight would slow them down now and having a passenger would probably make Barter less aggressive in his efforts to elude me.

I reached into my parka for my GPS. From this spot, there was no easy way back to Barter's farm via the trail system. With the ice storm picking up in intensity, it made sense for them to seek cover. The only alternative was to cut through the woods to the nearest road and then follow it back to the farmhouse.

If I caught Calvin Barter riding his ATV down the middle of a paved road, I would have a misdemeanor to charge him with, and if he was carrying a child on the back of his four-wheeler, I could add endangering the welfare of a minor to the list of offenses.

I plotted an intercept course from my current location back to the farmhouse.

First, I'll need to go back down that horrible hill, I realized with a pang.

I throttled up the ATV and spun a tight circle back up the ridge. The storm had begun leaving miniature icicles along the opening in my helmet, and my wheels seemed to be spinning more than ever, as if the treads were gunked up with frozen slush.

I arrived at the top of the·hill again and realized the angle was such that I couldn't get the headlights to shine down the descending trail. From this vantage, it seemed as steep as a cliff. How the hell did I get up here before? I wondered. And how the hell will I find my way down now?

Go slow, I told myself.

A lot of good that did. Within just a few seconds of beginning my descent, I could feel the tires start to skid on the slippery surface of ice. I became aware of the back end of the ATV beginning to pirouette out to my left side. There was a levitating sensation that started in my toes and traveled up my sciatic nerve, and I knew the quad was about to flip on top of me. For a moment, I hesitated and pulled as hard as I could on the handlebars, but it was all in vain. The machine's center of balance lurched under my feet. Instinctively, I sprang off the seat into the air. I tried to tuck and roll, but when I came down, my right hand hit first, hard and fast, and I tumbled headlong down the slope. Glancing to one side of me, I was aware of

Kathy's four-wheeler pursuing a parallel course before it slammed into a tree trunk.

I knew my hand was broken even before I had come to rest. I'd broken bones before, and the sensation—as if one's raw nerves were being attacked by hornets—was unmistakable.

I lay for a while on the frozen ground, feeling the icy rain pressing on every inch of my body. The tumble had filled my helmet with snow. I cradled my right hand against my chest.

"Shit, shit, shit, shit, shit, shit, shit."

The collision had knocked the wind out of me, and it took a long time before I had the strength to sit up. I saw Kathy's ATV lying on its side at the base of the hill. A young poplar tree rose up from the snow beside me. I grabbed hold of the flexible swaying trunk and used it to gain my footing. The nerves in my right hand were all in a riot.

Back at my truck, I had a pliable splint I could use to immobilize the wrist, but I needed to limp my way there first. I stumbled over to Kathy's wrecked quad and removed the keys from the ignition. The engine died abruptly. The sound of the pattering rain swept suddenly over me. I pried loose my goggles and hung them and the helmet from a handlebar. I unzipped the front of my parka and tucked my injured hand against my heart, then zipped it back up again. Not as good as a sling, but better than nothing.

From the GPS, I knew that the nearest road was less than a quarter of a mile to the west. I removed my DeLorme from my pocket and took a bearing and then began to stumble in that general direction. After what seemed like an eternity, I broke through a wall of ice-tipped spruce boughs and stepped into a flooded ditch. Before me was the road. It stretched north and south.

Which way was my truck?

North, I remembered.

I climbed up onto the glazed road and began to hoof it back toward the Varnum place. It was a country road, with no lights along the telephone poles. The plow hadn't come by yet, and it was hard going.

After a few minutes, I turned a corner and saw rain-blurred headlights and bright flashing orange lights up ahead. I knew at once that it was a plow truck, but the hulking shape wasn't moving. It just seemed to be stopped in the middle of the road.

As I approached, I saw the silhouette of a man standing on the edge of the road, looking down into the woods. Had the plow struck a deer?

"Hey!" I shouted.

Slowly, the man's head turned. I moved faster, and now I could see that he was a young guy, wearing a red plaid jacket and heavy Sorel boots. His head was bare, and he seemed to be wearing a cap of ice from the way his wet hair had frozen in the cold.

"Maine game warden!"

The man mumbled something, but I was still too far away to hear him over the idling engine of his plow truck.

"What?" I asked.

"I didn't see them." His eyes were wet and pleading. "They didn't have their lights on."

I unfastened the Maglite from my belt and shined the beam into the ditch. An ATV lay on its side in a mud-splattered snowbank. Beside it sat a big bearded man—dressed from head to toe in a black snowmobiling suit—cradling a red-haired boy in his arms. The boy's head was back, his neck was limp, and there was blood flowing from his nose.

Calvin Barter stared up into the beam of my flashlight, his pupils huge and black. "Call nine one one!" he shouted at us.

22

I slid on the edges of my feet down the icy slope and ordered Barter out of the way. Maybe because he didn't know what else to do, he handed the boy to me. I felt beneath the jaw for the carotid artery. There was no pulse. I bit down on the icy tips of my glove and yanked it off with my teeth. The bare skin of my palm detected no breath from either the nose or open mouth.

Carefully, I placed the boy flat on the frozen ground. I eased my broken hand out of the parka and spread my screaming fingers below Travis Barter's sternum. I pressed my good hand atop the shattered one, gulped down a big breath, and began a series of thirty compressions. The intensity of the pain made me grit my molars, but I continued CPR. After I'd completed thirty compressions, I wiped my eyes and tilted the boy's head back gingerly. I covered his mouth with mine and administered two rescue breaths.

Still no pulse.

Heedless of the pain, I started pumping the boy's chest again. Thirty compressions, followed by two rescue breaths. Then feel for a pulse. Thirty compressions and two rescue breaths. Then feel for a pulse. I wondered how long I could keep going before I passed out from the agony.

I pressed two fingers to Travis Barter's neck. Blood was moving through the artery. The pulse was faint. I pressed my ear to his mouth and felt the damp heat of his breath.

The boy was alive, but for how long?

It took half an hour for a deputy to arrive on the scene and half an hour more before the emergency medical technicians showed up. Cars were off the road all over the peninsula, the deputy told me. Frozen branches were snapping everywhere, bringing down electrical wires. Power lines were sizzling and snapping, rendering roads impassable. The ice storm was shaping up to be the worst in years.

I watched the EMTs secure Travis Barter's neck and head with a brace and carefully strap him to a stretcher. His body was as floppy as a sock puppet. The medical people exchanged worried looks.

While the ambulance crew ministered to the injured teenager, Calvin Barter stood beside his ruined vehicle, muttering obscenities. His long black beard grew high on his cheekbones, so that little of his face showed beside his coal black eyes. His chest and belly wanted to burst loose from his mud-splattered snowsuit, and his boots were sizable enough for Bigfoot to wear. Even his hands were gargantuan. I wondered how those thick fingers could ever button a shirt.

I waited for the deputy—my buddy Skip Morrison—to set up some emergency beacons. Then I took him aside. I explained about the ATV vandalism case and how I'd chased Barter and the boy through the woods. I told him about crashing my sergeant's ATV, and he gave me a pitying look. I didn't mention my broken hand, just kept it tucked inside my parka, out of sight.

My fingers were throbbing. I could feel the knuckles beginning to swell.

Skip left me for a while to go take a statement from the plow truck's driver.

Barter insisted on helping the EMTs levitate the stretcher with the boy on it out of the ditch. No one dared refuse the giant man. In truth, he probably could have lifted the heavy gurney on his own and toted it all the way to the hospital in Rockport on his back.

As the EMTs were packing to leave, Skip came slipping and sliding back to me. "The plow driver says they were riding in the middle of the road with their lights off, for some reason."

"They were fleeing from me," I explained.

"You saved that kid's life, Mike."

"Let's hope so."

"Do you want me to help you arrest Barter?"

"Not here," I said. "But I'd appreciate your filling out the accident report."

"Sure thing. That guy is seriously bad news. I think half the high school kids around here get their pills from him." He wiped melted water from his chin. "Did you hear someone sighted Westergaard?"

It took a moment for the name to register. "What? No."

"They got a report about his Range Rover being seen in Massachusetts. But it's not definite."

I knew this was potentially big news, but somehow I couldn't bring myself to care. Between the kid and my hand, I had enough on my mind. "I'm going to follow the ambulance to the hospital."

"Maybe you should get a doctor to check you out," he said. "You look a little green."

I caught a ride with the plow driver back to the tote road where I'd hidden my truck. He was a greasy-haired, pimple-faced dude, scarcely out of high school, and he didn't say a single word to me while we were on the road together.

"Don't blame yourself," I told him. "They shouldn't have been in the road like that with their lights off."

The driver looked at me as if I'd just muttered something to him in Swedish.

"Are you going to be OK?" I asked him.

"No," he said.

The ice had encased my pickup in an opaque shell. I had to chip away at the seams of the door with my multitool before I could pry it open. Once inside, I ran the heater and defrosters full blast, hoping they would melt the windshield ice and spare me the labor of scraping it clear. I cradled my right hand on my lap. Very carefully, tugging each finger one by one, I removed my glove. Every little twitch sent jolts of pain up my forearm. My fingers were visibly swollen. The image that came to mind was of hot dogs expanding in a microwave.

I used my cell phone to call home.

Sarah picked up immediately. "Mike? Where the hell are you?"

"I got sidetracked. I'm sorry about missing Amy's party."

"She canceled it on account of the storm. I've been worried about you. The roads are horrible!"

"I'm going to be a while longer," I said through clenched teeth. "That guy I was looking for—Hank Varnum's ATV vandal—crashed his machine. I'm following the ambulance to the hospital. A boy who was riding with him was injured."

"A boy? What's his name?"

"Travis Barter."

"Oh my God! I have the Barter twins in my class—Jud and Julie. What happened to Travis? Is he going to be all right?"

"I don't know."

She took a long time to respond. "Your voice sounds strange."

"The ambulance is leaving and I need to get going."

"Call me from the hospital. And please drive safely. It's such a dangerous night. I've had this feeling of foreboding all afternoon."

"I'll be home soon."

I checked my voice mail. There was a message

from Kathy Frost, asking for an update. I'd call her later. Maybe by then I'd have an excuse for demolishing her ATV.

There was also voice mail from Charley. "I picked up some info on the q.t.," he said. "The state police found a print on that telephone outside Smitty's Garage. It belongs to Mark Folsom, the owner of the Harpoon Bar. That's an interesting wrinkle, don't you think? Give me a call when you can, young feller."

The defroster was having no effect whatsoever on the rimed windshield. I got out and started scraping the glass until, at long last, my truck emerged from its frozen chrysalis.

I could barely process Charley's message. Was the anonymous caller who reported Ashley Kim's accident Nikki Donnatelli's former boss? At the moment, I was in no condition to chase that particular rabbit down the trail.

I drove myself one-handed to the hospital. Sarah and Skip were right: The road was treacherous. At intervals, I felt as if I were driving on sheer glass. Falling rain glittered like diamonds in my headlights. There was an eerie beauty to this night. Every tree branch and hanging wire seemed coated with a pastry glaze.

On my way off the peninsula, I passed several cars off the road and slowed down for each one, but the drivers had disappeared as utterly as Ashley Kim. For their sake, I hoped they had met real Samaritans on the road instead of the monster I knew to be lurking somewhere in the darkness.

At the hospital, I parked in a surprisingly crowded lot and dragged myself through the automatic doors of the emergency room.

The white-haired woman behind the admissions desk looked up from her computer screen with a tentative smile, as if she recognized my face but couldn't quite place where we'd met. "Can I help you?"

"An ambulance brought in a boy just now. The name's Barter. He was in an ATV accident. I need to know how he's doing."

She pursed her cracked lips. "I'm not supposed to disclose the status of any patients— even to law-enforcement officers."

"Can I speak to the nurse supervisor or a security guard?"

With a sweep of her hand, she motioned me to a row of chairs. "Please have a seat, and someone will be with you shortly."

The ER waiting room was peopled with the usual motley crew of injured, ill, and intoxicated persons. Some were casualties of the storm— people who had fallen on the ice or careened their vehicles into snowbanks. But others were just poor folk for whom the emergency room was the only means of getting medical care. A single television set provided the official entertainment, but the remote control was in the hands of a chunky girl with a pierced nose and attention deficit disorder. She would linger on a channel for five seconds and then move on, unsatisfied, to the next.

The security guard arrived first. He emerged through the sliding doors with an expression of alarm. He was a heavyset guy, but he looked strong in the way that some fat men are, impressively muscled beneath the blubber.

"What's the problem, Warden?"

With my functioning hand, I pointed to an unpeopled corner of the room, beyond the Coke machine. "Can we talk over there?"

When we were out of earshot of the other patients, I explained. "An ambulance just brought in a boy named Travis Barter, who was injured in an ATV crash down in Seal Cove. He's here with his father, a guy named Calvin Barter. I need to arrest the old man on a bunch of charges, but the boy is in bad shape, and I don't want to drag his father from his bedside. On the other hand, this Barter guy is potentially dangerous, so I need you to call the Rockport police and get an officer over here. I want to wait for the mother to show up before we bust the father."

"What did the guy do?"

"Endangering a minor, failure to stop for an officer, driving to endanger, felony vandalism—

it's a long list. Tell the responding officer to meet me in the waiting room. You might want to hang out in the ER in the meantime. Take my word for it. Barter's trouble."

The guard had been listening attentively to me the whole time, and I had the impression that he was good at his job. "Ten-four," he said.

I returned to my place between the ADD girl with the remote control and a drunk-looking guy pressing a bloody ice pack to the side of his head. The television stations flashed by overhead—infomercial, black-and-white movie, basketball game. The drunk guy stared at the screen, spellbound by the kaleidoscopic effect.

Frayed magazines and yellowed newspapers were fanned out across the table in front of me. I glanced absently at the covers, trying to keep my mind off the pulsing sensation in my hand. A headline from the *Boston Globe* brought me up short:

BAY STATE WOMAN FOUND MURDERED IN MAINE

The picture of Ashley Kim that accompanied the article showed a face I barely recognized, a cute young woman with intelligent eyes and a wry smile—as if the photographer had captured her enjoying a private joke.

The story said that Ashley Kim was twenty-three years old, a native of San Jose, California, now a resident of Cambridge, and a graduate student at the Harvard Business School. She had told friends that she was going cross-country skiing in Maine, which was unusual, since no one knew she skied.

The article reported, accurately, that she had called the rental company about hitting a deer shortly before she vanished. It named Trooper Curtis Hutchins as the responding officer and questioned why he hadn't gone to greater lengths to search for her. In response, there was a quote from the spokesman for the Department of Public Safety, who said that it was Trooper Hutchins's understanding that Ashley was uninjured and that she had left the scene of the accident willingly. The spokesman also noted that an internal investigation would review the actions the trooper had taken or failed to take. The choice of those particular words doesn't bode well for Hutchins, I thought.

The article said that Kim's body had been found at the summer home of one of her Harvard Business School professors, Hans Westergaard, of Cambridge. According to investigators, Westergaard was "a person of interest," and the public was asked to report any information they might have about his whereabouts. His wife, Jill, hadn't responded to phone calls.

"You wanted to see me?"

I looked up from the paper at a strong-looking woman in blue-green scrubs standing over me. She had wiry black hair, thin lips, and dark circles under her eyes.

"You're the head nurse?" I asked.

"I'm the ER supervisor, and I'm extremely busy. We've got a packed house tonight. What can I do for you, Warden?"

Both the ADD girl and Mr. Ice Pack were gawking at us. I hobbled over to my familiar corner behind the Coke machine. "You admitted a boy a while ago named Travis Barter," I said. "He was seriously injured in an ATV crash. How's he doing?"

"You know that's privileged information."

"Look, I was chasing him at the time. The ATV he and his father were riding was struck by a snowplow because they were trying to get away from me."

The taut line of her mouth relaxed and the small muscles around her eyes softened. "The kid was thrown pretty hard," she said. "That's really all I can say."

"I understand." I removed my right hand from the inside of my warden's parka. The knobby fingers had started turning black. "I think I hurt my hand."

"Jesus Christ!" she said.

"It's bad, then?"

She cocked an eyebrow at me. "When an ER

245

nurse says 'Jesus Christ,' it usually means it's bad. We need to get a doctor to look at you. Have you filled out an admissions form?"

"No."

"You need to do that first."

I hobbled back to the admissions desk and my girlfriend behind the counter.

"I told you you'd have to wait your turn," she said triumphantly.

After I had been formally processed at the admissions desk, I returned to my perch beside the guy with the ice pack. The ADD girl had vanished. By coincidence, she had left the TV tuned to a show about real-life cops. On the screen, a documentary crew was riding in a squad car through the mean streets of Denver. The shaky camera followed two officers as they arrested a series of belligerent, moronic, and inebriated lowlifes who resembled, in many ways, the people seated around me.

I was entranced with the show by the time the outside doors slid open and Wanda Barter and her red-haired clan blew in on a cold and damp gust of air. There were six of them, from the freckled teenager with the freckled baby down to the little girl who had greeted me the first day I visited their farm. I recognized the twins, the boy and girl Sarah had mentioned were students in her class. Despite the storm, not a single one of the children was wearing a winter coat.

"Where's my baby?" Wanda wailed at the admissions clerk. "Where's Travis?"

I considered approaching Mrs. Barter to convey my sadness about the tragic turn of events but then thought better of becoming the outlet for her considerable anger. After a few minutes of Wanda's shouting and wailing, a nurse appeared from the trauma center to take the Barter family into the ICU to see the injured boy.

Instead of the Rockport cop I was expecting, I was surprised to see Kathy Frost appear at the hospital door. She stepped in out of the rain and pushed back her wet hair from her streaming face. She spotted me within seconds and came striding across the room, boots squeaking, with the scowl of an irate mother. "Where's my ATV?"

"I crashed it."

"You what?"

"I crashed it while pursuing Calvin Barter. It's in the woods near Hank Varnum's house. How did you know to look for me here?"

"I called Sarah, and she told me about Barter's boy. How is he?"

"They won't say."

Water was dripping down her forehead into her eyes, causing her to blink. "Goddamn it, Mike. How could you crash my ATV?"

"I rolled it on an icy hill." I held up my

mangled paw. "I think I broke my hand."

Her lips pulled away from her teeth. "Yeah, I'd say you did. Jesus, that's disgusting. But it doesn't get you off the hook."

What happened next was so abrupt, it caught me entirely off guard. One of the Barter kids must have noticed me sitting in the waiting room, because suddenly Calvin Barter came rushing out of the trauma center, shouting obscenities. Kathy scarcely had time to dodge to one side before the bearded ogre threw himself at me.

"Fuck you! Motherfucker!"

I put up my good hand to defend my face from the punches he was hurling at my head, but I ended up falling backward onto my injured wrist. A burst of pain from my hand turned my vision bloodred. Then a punch connected with my temple, knocking me against the seat back.

I kicked hard at Barter's knee while Kathy sprung on him from behind, wrapping her forearm around his windpipe. The fat security guard was suddenly there, too, pulling at one of my assailant's forearms. All three of them went down with a crash, breaking the legs of the magazine table.

By the time my vision had cleared, I saw Kathy cuffing Barter's hands behind his back while the overweight guard sat on his head.

An hour or so later, I was sitting on a high table waiting for a doctor to examine me. My hand had swollen to the size of a catcher's mitt.

At last, the ER doctor popped around the curtain. He was the same little blond guy who'd stitched up my arm a few nights earlier.

"And how are we doing tonight?" he asked.

23

The X-rays revealed that I had broken two bones in my right hand—the first metacarpal and the radius—in addition to whatever insults I had committed against the ligaments. Because of the intense swelling, the doctor fitted me with the largest splint available, size extra-extra-large. He said that we'd have to wait for the hand to shrink back to near-normal size before they could outfit me with a standard plaster cast. I was told I would have my choice of colors.

"Even green to match your uniform," the doctor said with a pearlescent smile.

I found my sergeant waiting for me outside the trauma center, arms crossed, snapping her gum.

"What happened to Barter?" I asked.

"I handed him off to the Rockport cops. Come on, I'll give you a lift home."

"Thanks," I said. "But I can drive myself."

She gave me a doubtful sort of smirk. "I'm not sure that's such a smart idea, Grasshopper. The doc didn't give you any drugs, did he?"

My parka was draped over my left shoulder, since my right arm was now in a sling. "He wrote me a prescription for Vicodin."

"That's heavy-duty stuff."

It was after midnight now and the waiting room had grown relatively quiet except for the mindless chatter of late-night television.

"How's the boy?"

"Too soon to tell. I guess the docs want to evacuate him to Boston, but the weather has all the Life Flight choppers grounded. I don't know if they'll chance driving him in an ambulance."

My coat began to slide off my shoulder. Kathy caught it.

"So it looks like I'll be taking a few sick days," I said at last.

She studied the bruised fingertips sticking out from my splint. "I'd say that's a safe bet. You won't be able to go on patrol as long as you're wearing a splint or a cast. Maybe we can put you behind a desk in Augusta after you get back from disability leave."

Well, at least Sarah wouldn't have to worry about me out on patrol.

Kathy followed me to my truck. The temperature had climbed a degree or two while I was shut up in the hospital, and the precipitation was now drifting down lightly as plain warm rain. Still, the surface of the parking lot remained as slick as a hockey rink. Under the wet and swirling arc light, my sergeant rearranged my drooping parka back onto my shoulder and raised my collar. "I still can't believe you crashed my fucking ATV."

Despite my wishes, Kathy followed me most of the way home. The snowplows had salted and sanded the main roads, but the driving conditions were as bad as I'd seen in ages. At the turn off to Sennebec, Kathy blinked her high beams at me and kept going.

The image of that redheaded kid in a hospital bed seemed to float beyond the limits of my headlights.

I stopped my truck beneath the frozen pines at the end of the driveway and tried to puzzle out what I was going to tell Sarah. Why hadn't I called her from the hospital and told her about my broken hand? It was because this latest accident was further proof how unreliable I was going to be as a father—if I was going to be a father.

The front windows were dark. When I opened the door, I heard her call my name from the bedroom.

"It's me," I said.

I struggled to remove my wet parka and hang it on the hook by the door. Then I began fiddling, one-handed, with the ice-coated lacings of my boots. It took me forever to get my soaking feet out of them.

I found Sarah reading in bed. As I limped through the door, she began to smile sleepily until she caught sight of my sling and splint. Then her eyes widened and she sat up so suddenly, her book dropped to the floor.

"Michael, what happened?"

"I crashed Kathy's ATV chasing Calvin and Travis Barter. I broke two bones in my hand."

She jumped out of bed. "Are you in pain?"

"No," I lied.

"Let me see." She examined my wounded fingers with an expression of deep concern. "Oh Mike, your hand looks awful."

"It could be a lot worse." I sat down beside her heavily on the bed, so heavily the springs groaned in protest. "I could have broken my neck."

She sat beside me and clasped my good hand with both of her small ones. "Why do you keep hurting yourself like this? I worry that there's something self-destructive in you that makes you take these risks. I'm scared for you all the time."

"Well, I won't be going on patrol for a while, so you needn't worry."

"What will they have you do?"

"Take sick time at first, disability, and then I really don't know." I took a deep breath from my diaphragm. "There's something else I need to tell you. Travis Barter has a serious head injury. The doctors are evacuating him to Boston."

She put a hand over her open mouth in horror.

I found that I couldn't meet Sarah's eyes as I recounted the evening's events, but kept staring down at my grotesque hand in its ridiculously oversized splint. She didn't ask any questions or interrupt me, but I could feel her emotions rising in the way her grip tightened.

"You can't blame yourself for what happened to that boy," she said after I'd finally lapsed into silence.

"I don't blame myself." I used my good hand to push myself off the bed and onto my wobbly feet. "I blame his goddamned father for driving on the goddamned road."

"Don't you want to talk about what happened?" Sarah said.

"I'm too tired," I said, and went into the bathroom to take a Vicodin.

Power was out all along the midcoast. We were among the few fortunate households to have electricity. We heard on the radio that linesmen were assembling from all over New England to assist with the emergency. We spent the day after the storm with Sarah shielding me from phone calls while I slept in the darkened bedroom, knocked out on Vicodin.

Except for alcohol and some extra-strength Tylenol prescribed for previous broken bones and stitched wounds, I had never taken drugs before. Somehow I had negotiated my adolescence without ever smoking a joint. Having a crazed drunk for a father is a pretty good advertisement for sobriety in that respect.

So the spell that the Vicodin cast over me was profound. I drifted in and out of consciousness, unable to tell wakefulness from the hallucinations of my sleeping mind, feeling as if I were submerged at the bottom of a lake, watching lights and shadows dart across the ceiling like quick-moving fish. It was not an unpleasant experience. The pills made the pain in my hand vanish, and I would stare at my splint as if it belonged to some unfortunate person sitting on the bed beside me. Poor fellow, I thought.

Sometime during that first long, drugged afternoon, Sarah appeared with a bowl of minestrone and a plate of crackers. The brightness of the overhead light stabbed into my brain.

"How are you doing, honey?"

"Fine," I said.

"Maybe you should get up for a while and walk around."

"No thanks." I was impatient to return to my languorous existence at the bottom of the lake.

"You should at least eat something."

She plumped up the pillow behind my shoulders so that I could eat off the tray. I obliged her while she told me of the events that had taken place in the world outside my bedroom.

"The phone's been ringing nonstop," she said.

"Haven't heard it."

"You got calls from Lieutenant Malcomb and Kathy Frost, both wanting to know how you're doing. Charley, too. That chaplain, Deb Davies, also called. I guess word travels fast through the Warden Service. You got this weird call from some guy named Oswald Bell earlier. He had this thick Long Island accent. He wanted to know if you'd read the files he gave you. I told him I had no idea what he was talking about. There were a bunch of hang-ups, too."

"The Barters."

"God, do you think? Are they going to come over here? What should I do?"

"They won't come over. They know I'd shoot their whole fucking family."

She removed the tray from my lap and set it on the bedside table. Her eyes seemed a different color from what I remembered—I felt like I'd never truly seen them before.

"How many of those pills did you take?"

"Just what the bottle said."

"Your voice is slurred. I don't think you should take any more."

"OK."

She put a hand on my forehead and then ran her fingers through my crew cut. "I'm worried about you, honey."

Her concern struck me as misplaced but very

sweet. I felt a sudden desire to share some of the insights I'd recently experienced. "Do you remember your First Communion? There was all this big buildup to it in the Catholic Church. We had these CCD classes—I don't know what CCD stands for—it was like Sunday school, except it wasn't on Sundays. The idea of eating the body of Christ—what's a kid supposed to make of that?"

"Mike . . ."

"The wafer was just this dusty round piece of paper. I don't know what I thought would happen—maybe that I'd see a vision of God with beams of sunlight and angels. But instead, there was *nothing*. So which church should we raise our kids in? Catholic or Episcopal? I guess you'd be the one to take them, so you should decide."

She got up from the bed and lifted the tray. She seemed to be swaying dreamily herself, uncertain on her feet. "Get some rest."

After she'd left the room, I stared at the shimmering light beneath the bedroom door. It seemed to ripple like waves of heat rising off hot desert sands. Sarah hadn't understood what I was getting at. These revelations were peculiar to me. No one else could understand them.

24

On Monday morning, after Sarah had left for school, I awoke to a sensation in my right hand. It might best be compared to an elephant sitting on all five of my fingers. I stumbled into the bathroom and began rummaging through the medicine cabinet. The little orange vial of Vicodin had disappeared without a trace.

I telephoned Sarah's school and left a message. I told the receptionist it was an emergency. Then I waited in my pajama bottoms on the edge of the unmade bed, cradling my bad hand in my good one.

After an eternity, the phone rang. "Mike, what is it? Did you hear something about Travis?"

"I can't find my pills."

In my mind's eye, I saw Sarah easing the receiver away from her ear until she could decide how to respond. "Did you look in the medicine cabinet?"

"Of course I looked in the medicine cabinet."

"Maybe you got up in the night and misplaced the bottle. You might have dropped it on the floor. Did you check behind the toilet?"

"No."

A paranoid idea popped into my head: I wondered if she had hidden my pills during the night. Her voice had risen to a higher pitch over the course of our brief conversation. At the police academy, I had learned that was one of the telltale clues to dishonesty.

"I'm sure they'll show up eventually." Sarah sounded like the patient schoolteacher she was. "Why don't you take a shower and get dressed? You need something to occupy your attention. You could read that book Kathy gave you." She seemed to be making a conscious effort to humor me. "The principal told me she's transferring the Barter twins from my class as a precaution. Everyone here knows about you and their father."

"*He* attacked me."

"It's unfair, but people blame you for what happened to Travis. You're the district game warden."

"Great," I said. "That's just what I need."

"Mike, you didn't do anything wrong. You were just doing your job. If you find your Vicodin, please just take half a dose, OK?"

"OK."

After we signed off, I set to work rooting through her underwear drawers and closet shelves in search of my painkillers. I had the thought she might have stashed the vial in a coat pocket or the toe of a boot. But no matter where I looked, I found nothing.

I was still rummaging around the bedroom

when there was a knock at the door. It was the mailman with an express package from my mother in Naples, Florida. Inside was a get-well card, signed "With Love," telling me she hoped the enclosed present would help occupy me while I healed. She'd sent me a video game, Cabela's Big Game Hunter for PlayStation 2. I didn't own a PlayStation machine. I didn't even own a television.

I dropped the video game in the trash. Ora was right that my mother and I would eventually need to have a serious talk about my dad. But I had a gut feeling that discussion would be a long time coming.

Why had I been such a jerk to Sarah? A broken hand was no excuse. She'd never made a habit of lying to me. And yet she had been behaving so strangely lately. I had been so quick to believe Ora's suspicion that Sarah might be pregnant. I needed to get past my self-pity and paranoia.

I downed a handful of ibuprofen with a glass of tap water. Then I pulled a bread bag from a kitchen drawer and, after stripping naked, wrapped the plastic around my splint and awkwardly fastened it into place with a rubber band. Even with the bag secured this way, moisture from the shower found a way of seeping in and dampening the brace.

I put on a flannel shirt and some oil-flecked Carhartt pants and then made myself the simplest breakfast imaginable—dry toast and orange juice. I ate it at the kitchen table. Looking out at the tidal marsh, I saw a red-winged blackbird, another early migrant, alight briefly atop a swaying stalk of phragmites before winging down the river.

Fishing season kicked off next week, and I wondered who would cover my district. The first day of open-water fishing was one of my favorite days of the year to be a warden. For a moment again, I felt oppressed by my infirmity.

There was another knock at the door.

In my irritable convalescent state, I wasn't sure who I was expecting, but it surely wasn't the Knox County sheriff, Dudley Baker.

When I opened the door, I felt a mild brush of wind on my face. Much of the snow and ice had already dropped from the frozen branches. Our little patch of forest was loud with the staccato *drip-drip* of gravity pulling water down out of the trees.

The sheriff looked, as always, like a man whose entire appearance was sealed neatly into place; he seemed to begin each morning by coating himself from head to toe in immobilizing hair spray. His jowly cheeks bore a flush of color from the morning air. As we spoke, his tinted eyeglass lenses misted over, so that he had to wipe them with the corner of a pressed handkerchief.

"I hope I haven't disturbed you," he said, knowing full well that he had.

"I just finished breakfast."

"How's your hand?"

"Could be worse."

He nodded his two chins. "Do you mind if I come in?"

We sat across from each other beside the expiring woodstove. I didn't offer him coffee, tea, or even a glass of water. The sheriff had driven to my house for a specific reason, and I wanted to hear what it was.

"I thought I should give you an update about the Barter boy myself," he said. "The doctors decided to fly him down to Boston. He's in a drug-induced coma. There was extensive damage to the anterior frontal lobes of his brain. It's too early to predict his prognosis."

I didn't know how to respond to this news. "So what are you doing with Calvin?"

"We're holding him on some bench warrants, in addition to his ATV offenses. Unpaid traffic violations, failure to appear—that sort of thing. He's going to be my guest for a while unless he can muster bail."

"Morrison told me Barter's been dealing pills to teenagers," I said.

"Roofies are his specialty."

"I guess it makes sense that a registered sex offender would traffic in date-rape drugs."

"It's all just hearsay. A kid we busted said he bought the pills off Barter. We can't pin anything on Calvin."

I had the distinct impression the sheriff was beating around some kind of bush. "So, I heard Hans Westergaard's car might have been spotted in Massachusetts?"

"I can't comment on that."

If I kept pressing, I wondered if I could tease some information out of him. "A man just doesn't disappear into thin air. Whoever killed Ashley left that house in a hurry. If Westergaard was panicked and on the run, he would have used one of his credit cards by now."

"You know I can't go into any of the investigative details." He readjusted his glasses on the bridge of his nose. "Mrs. Westergaard told Detective Menario that she spoke with you outside the jail."

I gave a mirthless laugh. "I figured she would."

"You should expect that AAG Marshall is going to come after you for tampering with a witness."

"I'd say Jill Westergaard tampered with *me.*"

The sheriff licked his lips. "May I have a glass of water?"

"Help yourself. The glasses are to the right of the sink."

Even in my altered state, I understood that Baker was behaving oddly.

He returned from the kitchen with a jelly glass full of water and a look of resolve in his moist eyes. The conversation seemed to have taken a wrong turn in Baker's mind, and now he was determined to get it moving in the right direction. "You know I worked at the Maine State Prison for many years before I ran for county sheriff."

"I don't mean to insult you, but that's one reason I didn't vote for you," I said. "Your opponent had real community policing experience. I'm sorry, but it's the truth."

For the first time, the tidy little man seemed to bristle. "I've heard that criticism before. You'd be surprised how many people at my own church have apologized for not voting for me. But it doesn't matter. I won the election."

"Where's your church?"

"First Pentecostal." He set down the glass and put a small pink hand on each knee. "Do you worship locally?"

"No, but I was raised Catholic."

My answer seemed to deflate him, causing his shoulders to shrink. "I learned a lot about human nature working in the prison," he said out of nowhere. "In my experience, most corrections officers are literal-minded individuals. That's as it should be. It's not a prison guard's responsibility to second-guess judges or juries. Our job is to execute the law without prejudice or preference."

"Sheriff, I'm really not equipped to have a philosophical conversation at the moment." I displayed my black fingertips to bring the point home. "Could you please tell me what you want?"

His eyes darted around behind their amber lenses, but they didn't leave mine. "I know Ozzie Bell and Lou Bates left certain documents with you. Have you had a chance to read them yet?"

The question spun my head around 360 degrees. "Don't tell me you're a member of the J-Team."

He made a not very convincing show of clearing his throat. "As the sheriff of Knox County, I can't engage in public crusades on behalf of convicted criminals."

"I don't believe it—you actually think Erland Jefferts is innocent."

He sipped his water so lightly, I wasn't even certain he had consumed any. "When you work at the prison, you get to know certain prisoners. I found Jefferts to be a remarkable young man. He's a painter, a gardener, and a mentor to the other prisoners. He's helped inmates learn to read, and he's organized Bible-study groups."

"He also raped and murdered a young woman, I seem to remember."

Baker shook his head with such vigor, I feared his glasses might fly off. "You're jumping to conclusions."

"The man was convicted by a jury of his peers!"

"Anyone who researches the prosecution of Erland Jefferts will have their faith shaken in Maine's legal system."

I was losing patience now. "But what does this have to do with me?"

"You found Ashley Kim."

"I found her mutilated corpse."

The sheriff, sensing my growing irritation, attempted yet another fresh approach. "Unlike Trooper Hutchins, you recognized that Ashley Kim was in danger, and you took action to find her, even though it wasn't your responsibility as a game warden to do so."

"That's a flattering way of saying I'm not a very good law officer."

"I think you have the aptitude to become an outstanding law officer. That's why we'd like your assistance."

"By 'we,' you mean the J-Team?"

He refused to bite. "There's a chance that if you looked through Bell's files, you might spot a detail we've overlooked."

"Look, Sheriff," I said. "If you think Jefferts was wrongfully accused and Nikki Donnatelli's killer also murdered Ashley Kim, then *you* prove it. That's your job, not mine."

He smiled benevolently. "You're not as cynical as you pretend to be."

"Is that so? What am I, then?"

"You're a brave young man who believes in the cause of justice."

I stood up unsteadily. "I need to take a piss."

What had Kathy Frost called me? The patron saint of hopeless criminal prosecutions? From Jill Westergaard to Dudley Baker, I was suddenly attracting gullible saps like a picnic basket attracts wasps. I stood over the toilet and marveled how my life had taken this bizarre twist.

This murder investigation was no longer any of my business. My only involvement would be as a witness at Professor Westergaard's trial. And yet the spectral image of that murdered girl just wouldn't leave me be. I'd begun to fear it never would. I didn't trust Menario to find Ashley Kim's killer, whether it was Hans Westergaard or not. The idea of adding her name to Maine's list of unsolved homicides filled me with a red rage. I owed it to that poor woman to do *something* on her behalf.

By the time I returned to the living room, I'd decided on a course of action. "I'll look through Bell's files," I said with a theatrical sigh. "On one condition, though. You have to promise to share information with me about the Ashley Kim investigation."

Baker's fat neck flushed scarlet. "I won't share anything that might compromise the case."

"Does Westergaard have access to a private plane? I know he's rich. Is there any way he could have slipped out of the country? Back to Europe or something?"

"I'm not at liberty to reveal those particular details."

I pressed my splint against my chest. "Just tell me who Menario has interviewed, then."

He puffed out his cheeks. "Mark Folsom, the owner of the Harpoon Bar in Seal Cove. We pulled one of his fingerprints off the pay phone outside Smitty's Garage."

Charley Stevens had called me with that news. "Folsom was Nikki Donnatelli's employer."

"And a suspect in her murder. But he claims that he's used that phone on several occasions, and there's nothing to place him at the scene of the accident on the night of Ashley Kim's disappearance."

"What about the Driskos?"

"So far, they've refused to talk. The state police are expediting the DNA tests on that blood and hair you collected, but it seems certain that the Driskos stole the deer from the road. Menario can't arrest them until he has proof of it, though."

"How about the Westergaards' caretaker—Stanley Snow?"

"He has alibis for the entire day Ashley was missing—people who swore they'd seen him at the Square Deal and around Seal Cove. He's also offered to take a polygraph."

I remembered what Jill Westergaard had said about Snow—that he was the gentlest man she'd ever met. The caretaker was either supremely confident or supremely stupid if he had volunteered to take a lie-detector test to prove his innocence. But polygraphs were not infallible, and they could be beaten. There were sites all over the Internet that taught you techniques on becoming an artful liar.

"Who else are you looking at?" I asked.

"Menario's team has been going down the list of sex predators for Seal Cove, although it's possible it's someone who's never been registered. If it was just some random person passing by at the wrong time, it's going to be very hard to solve."

"Is that why you came to me—because you're grasping at straws?"

"You might say that."

The admission squeezed some sympathy from me. "I'll take a look at Ozzie Bell's files," I said, rising and motioning my good hand toward the door. "If I notice anything noteworthy, I'll give you a call."

"As sheriff, I can't have a public connection to this."

"You mean I should call Lou Bates instead?"

His rabbit nose crinkled when he smiled. "Lou is—how should I put it?—a very zealous person. I'd recommend that you speak with Bell."

268

I escorted him to the door. "I'm curious what changed your mind about Jefferts's innocence."

Very carefully, he buttoned the front of his jacket with his short fingers. "Read the evidence, and you'll see."

"You made it sound like your own conversion was personal," I said. "Like Saint Paul on the Road to Damascus."

He perked up at my New Testament allusion. "Even before I read Bell's report, I had doubts," he admitted. "The junior staff at the prison—they assume everyone is guilty because a jury convicted them. But the older guards, they develop their own views, based on personal interactions over time. These guys have a list of inmates they'd personally set free if they could. At the top of that list is Erland Jefferts."

25

It took some doing, but I managed to manhandle Bell's box of files out of my truck and lug them as far as the mudroom. I pried open the dented cardboard cover and extracted the first document: "Rush to Judgment: The State of Maine's Rigged Case Against Erland Jefferts."

This is going to be good, I thought.

Ozzie Bell's box included the complete trial transcript (1,334 pages) of the *State of Maine v.*

Erland R. Jefferts; the report of Knox County sheriff's deputy Dane Guffey on finding Jefferts and his truck on the night of July 12, 2004; the handwritten notes of Detective Joseph Winchenback, recounting the circumstances and exact wording of Jefferts's "confession," which disagreed with the investigator's sworn testimony at trial; a printout from the Maine Sex Offender Registry listing every convicted predator within a ten-mile radius of the crime scene (Calvin Barter's name was circled, for some reason); a photocopied map showing the location of Jefferts's truck in relation to both the Harpoon Bar and the swampy spot where Nikki Donnatelli's body was later located; an inventory of items recovered from his pickup; the report of Warden Katherine Frost concerning the search and discovery of the dead girl's body; the final report of the state psychologist on the sanity of Erland R. Jefferts; the autopsy report of the state medical examiner, Dr. Walter Kitteridge; snapshots of Jefferts with his J-Team supporters in prison on the occasion of his thirtieth birthday; a letter from Louise Bates to the presiding judge, pleading for mercy for her nephew; and a statement by Maine's attorney general denying an investigation into prosecutorial misconduct. And that was just half of it.

I decided to read in bed, with my inflamed hand elevated against my chest.

As I rearranged the lumped-up sheets, I found my bottle of Vicodin under a pillow, where I must have tucked it. I swallowed a pill and settled down to immerse myself in a juicy conspiracy theory.

As best I could tell, the J-Team's argument was that the state's case against Jefferts was entirely circumstantial and made in bad faith. Investigators hadn't framed Erland per se, but they'd bent the law to convict a man they believed from the start to be a sex killer. Winchenback had fabricated a confession, the prosecutors had conspired to conceal exculpatory evidence from the defense and jury, and forensic science proved beyond a shadow of a doubt that Erland Jefferts could not have committed the crime.

The J-Team stipulated that, yes, Erland had been intoxicated on the night of Nikki's disappearance. But they took issue with Mark Folsom's ex post facto statement that he had bounced Jefferts out of the Harpoon for making lewd remarks to Nikki. In fact, patrons remembered the bar owner dragging a stumble-drunk Jefferts into the parking lot, but no one could attest to the exact reason why. After Erland was arrested, however, the story that he had groped Nikki became the accepted version of the event.

Furthermore, Erland Jefferts had no record of violence. So what had made this affable man, so well liked in the community, commit such an atrocity? A credible motive was therefore a problem, according to Ozzie Bell.

Then there was the question of opportunity. The time-of-death evidence indicated that Nikki—like Ashley Kim—was kept alive for some hours before being murdered. She even had a bump on her head that seemed to have been inflicted many hours before her other wounds.

"Somebody played Mr. Jefferts for a patsy," his attorney said at trial. "They found him passed out in the woods and planted the rigging tape to frame him."

Typically, sexual predators take an object from the body of their murdered victims, panties being especially popular. So where was Nikki's underwear if Jefferts didn't have it in his possession?

When forensic technicians examined Nikki, they found traces of blood beneath her finger-nails. But the DNA didn't match Erland's. It belonged, instead, to an unidentified male. Dr. Kitteridge countered that there was no reason to surmise it came from Nikki's assailant. She could have picked it up anywhere.

Bell found this statement ridiculous, and it showed in his overheated prose. "Why is some other man's DNA in the blood under Nikki Donnatelli's fingernails, and why did investiga-tors focus on Jefferts to the exclusion of other suspects, including a well-known predator who lived nearby and had recently been arrested for sexually abusing a teenage girl?"

That person was Calvin Barter. Given his criminal record, he was high on the J-Team's list of alternate suspects. But so was Nikki's employer, Mark Folsom, along with a bunch of other people, some of whose names I recognized (such as Dave Drisko) and some I didn't. Reviewing the list of sexual predators—more than sixty within ten miles of the crime scene—made me nauseous. As a game warden, I saw Maine's crushing poverty and hidden depravity every day, but the sheer number of local perverts stunned me.

Reading through these twice-baked documents, I began to form an opinion of Ozzie Bell. As a "retired" big-city reporter, he had an undisguised contempt for small-town rubes. Dane Guffey, the deputy who found Jefferts, was a "cue ball–headed kid with a cynical streak a mile wide." Joe Winchenback, the detective who took Erland's "confession," was a "bulbous-nosed man with a penchant for telling off-color tales." I knew neither of these individuals, but I did know Danica Marshall, whom Bell described as an "ice-blooded beauty who might have walked straight out of a cheap film noir." The one adjective he used for Warden Kathy Frost was "mannish," which was accurate in the sense that my sergeant could have kicked Oswald's ass from here till Sunday.

Bell's worst vitriol was saved for the medical examiner, Dr. Walter Kitteridge, who, more than anyone else, in his view, bore the blame for Erland Jefferts's wrongful conviction.

Determining the time of death has been described as both an art and a science, and there are many techniques at a medical examiner's disposal. The temperature of the body is one method, but Kitteridge never measured Nikki's. Nor did he record the ambient temperature of the forest in which the corpse was found. He also failed to conduct a standard test of her eye fluid, which can indicate the hour of death.

Then there were the blowflies.

In his trial testimony Kitteridge was quoted as saying, "With a cadaver found in the woods in July, I would have anticipated seeing more fly activity, especially after two days. Flies land and lay eggs on the body at sites of injury, as well as the eyes." That statement suggested, in Bell's mind, that Nikki hadn't been dead quite as long as the coroner claimed—and the longer she'd been alive, the more the case against Erland Jefferts fell apart, since he'd been in police custody for a full day before Pluto sniffed out the dead body. So the fly evidence might have been exculpatory.

There was only one problem: The forensic lab had somehow, mistakenly or deliberately, discarded the fly larvae collected at the scene.

In the end, Dr. Kitteridge based his estimation

of time of death exclusively on rigor mortis, the extreme stiffening of the body that follows death. From my course work, I understood the process to be a chemical change in the muscles —something about the stoppage of the blood flow causing various proteins to begin locking up in weird ways until digestive enzymes start the process of decomposition.

Bell described the progression: "In an adult, under general conditions, rigor mortis begins in about two hours after death, spreads through the skeletal muscles within ten to twelve hours, and resolves within thirty-six hours after death before the muscles become flaccid again." Hot temperatures can speed the process up. Body size and physical condition play roles, too. There are innumerable variables, but generally speaking, a body that still shows signs of rigor hasn't been dead all that long.

When Kitteridge examined Nikki Donnatelli's body, he reported that "rigor mortis was easily broken." In the J-Team's interpretation, this meant that it was scientifically impossible for Erland to have killed Nikki, since he was under police supervision during the entire window of time when she might have been murdered.

Unfortunately for Jefferts, his country bumpkin attorney had failed to pick up this bombshell. And now the lobsterman was serving a life term without the possibility of parole.

Ozzie Bell described himself as an unwilling recruit to the cause. He hadn't known Jefferts or Donnatelli. But as a former newsman from Queens who'd retired to quiet Seal Cove, he couldn't help but take an interest in such a heinous crime. He began researching the evidence, spoke with Lou Bates and the principals on the other side, but it was only when he encountered Dr. Kitteridge's testimony that he had his eureka moment: "The state's own forensic evidence proved that Erland Jefferts couldn't possibly have murdered Nikki Donnatelli!"

I didn't know enough about rigor mortis to share Bell's certainty. And I had more than a few questions of my own. What about Jefferts's confession, for example?

"Do you remember what you did with Nikki?" Detective Joe Winchenback had asked him.

"What if I said yes?" replied Jefferts.

Bell and the J-Team waved off this statement. Jefferts had been confused, half-drunk, sleep-deprived. Winchenback never taped Jefferts's "admission," and his own contemporaneous notes contradicted the exact phrasing he used in court. Therefore, the detective must have been lying on the witness stand. The primary investigating officer had coerced a vaguely worded confession out of a suggestible young man who couldn't remember his own actions on the night of Nikki's disappearance. In effect, Erland had been bullied into making a hedged admission, which the prosecutors instantly held up as proof positive of his bloody deeds.

It makes for one whopper of a story, I thought sleepily. But I doubted any of it was true. It didn't surprise me that the cops might have conducted a messy investigation. Half my own arrests were fucked-up in one way or another. Had Danica Marshall used every weapon in her arsenal to shoot a rocket up Jefferts's ass? Of course she had. When a prosecutor got a sex killer in the courtroom, and there was a chance he might walk free, what else was she supposed to do?

I swung my legs off the bed and crossed the creaking floor to the box of files. I leafed through the contents until I came to the collection of photographs I'd noticed earlier. They were pictures of Jefferts having a birthday party in prison with the J-Team. The convict had put on weight over the years, but he was still devilishly handsome, with wavy blond hair and a Hollywood smile.

Attached to one of the photos was a poem.

Solitary

I don't know why
A man can't cry.
Holding on to his father's pain
That will become his son's in time.
The only legacy left now.

Imprisoned in himself first
And in four walls second.
Iron bars for an iron soul.

From yourself there's no escape.
No time off for good behavior.
No parole or earthly savior.

Hours go by
And become days.
Days become months.
Months become years.

Walled up in this place
Without sunlight or air.
We are all dead here.
We just don't know it.

BY ERLAND R. JEFFERTS

The thought of this handsome con man selling his bullshit story to naïve friends and family infuriated me. Nothing I could say to Lou Bates or Ozzie Bell would change their minds about him. Those fools were absolutely convinced of Erland's innocence, just as Jill Westergaard was certain her missing husband was a model of fidelity.

But I knew what kind of a monster Jefferts was. Better than anyone, I knew.

I found the phone number I was looking for on a business card stapled to a folder. I dialed the seven digits and waited until a man with a thick New York accent answered.

"Oswald Bell here."

"Mr. Bell, this is Mike Bowditch. I read the files you gave me. I'd like to meet Erland Jefferts."

26

The world was melting. The next day, the sun reappeared, as if it had suddenly remembered it was springtime now and no longer winter. The tidal creek behind the house was swollen with runoff from the dripping ice, and the chickadees in the pines were singing a libidinal tune.

I didn't tell Sarah where I was going. I let her leave for school in the belief that I planned to spend my day on the couch reading the Hemingway book Kathy had brought me from Key West. I knew that if I told her about my call to Ozzie Bell, she would assume I was meddling in the Ashley Kim investigation—which I was.

Dressing yourself with one hand is harder than you think. After trying for ten minutes to button a flannel shirt, I switched to a military-style sweater. I didn't even bother attempting shoelaces, but tugged on my neoprene boots. Inspecting myself in the mirror, I thought I looked like a sickly duck hunter about to venture onto the frozen flats. I wondered if the prison guards would discern the opaque Vicodin glassiness in my eyes.

I wasn't accustomed to driving with my left hand, having to reach across my body to shift gears, using my bad hand to hold the wheel steady. I'd arranged to meet Bell at a gas station up the road from the prison, where he would leave his vehicle. The two of us would ride in my Jeep, we'd agreed.

He stood waiting outside a blue Nissan about the size of a golf cart. He was dressed in exactly the same clothes he'd worn to the diner—black pants, black polo shirt, and black blazer lightly dusted with dandruff along the collar. His glasses were enormous, with heavy plastic frames, and his thick white hair was styled and swirled in a manner that made me think of a soft-serve ice-cream cone.

"Warden Bowditch! Or can I call you Mike?"

"Mike's fine," I said.

"Thanks for coming. Yowza, what happened to your hand?"

"I was in an all-terrain-vehicle accident."

"What—like a go-cart? One of those things the kids ride?"

"Something like that."

He coughed suddenly, a phlegmy sound that rattled wetly around his throat for a long while before he managed to gulp it down. "Cigarettes," he explained at last. "What was it Norman Mailer said? 'It's easier to give up the love of your life than quit smoking.' It took me forty years, but I finally did it. I knew Mailer back at the *Voice*. If there was a real newspaper editor in this backwater state, Erland Jefferts wouldn't still be behind bars, I'll tell you that much."

I glanced at my watch for effect. "I'd like to get going, Mr. Bell."

"Call me Ozzie. I appreciate your taking the time for this, Mike. But you won't be sorry you did! If you don't leave today convinced an innocent man is behind bars . . ." He trailed off, paused to collect his thoughts, and then began again. "You're going to like Erland. You remind me of him a little. Not physically. But you've got the same inner strength. I'm a good judge of people. Every real journalist has a fool-proof bullshit detector."

When he climbed into my passenger seat and watched me reach across my body to shift gears, the peculiarity of the situation seemed to dawn on him. "Maybe we should take my Nissan. You shouldn't be driving with a hand like that."

"Thanks," I said. "But I can manage."

The Maine State Prison in Thomaston used to be a landmark on Route 1, a brick and razor-wire edifice that some called "Shawshank." Then in the 1990s, the state built a massive complex on a wood-shrouded hilltop in the nearby town of Warren. Except for the distant spotlights, which gave the night sky an ocher glow, the new prison was largely hidden from the view of passing motorists. Out of sight, out of mind seemed to be the architectural and governmental intent.

"So you read the files, then?" Bell asked me as we turned up the hill toward the immense cream-colored structure. "You understand that the scientific evidence is indisputable. Kitteridge's own report proves Erland could not have killed Nikki Donnatelli."

I smiled at him. "You seem to have a low opinion of Dr. Kitteridge."

"The guy's a disgrace."

"In your report you wrote that he threw away the fly larvae collected from Nikki's eyes."

"Threw it away! We don't even know if they were Calliphoridae or Sarcophagidae." Bell shook his hands in the air as if they were wet and he needed to dry them. "And he never measured the hypoxanthine in the ocular fluid. The least he could have done was to take the body and ambient temperature! All he did was a bullshit test for rigor mortis."

I flicked a glance at him. "He testified rigor was passing off when he examined the body."

"Which proves that Erland couldn't have killed her, because he'd been in police custody for the previous thirty-six hours."

"My understanding of rigor mortis is that there's lots of variation depending on body size, temperature, and other factors."

"Yes, yes. But Nikki was a small girl, and it was a hot day. Based upon the state's own findings, there can be no question about the time of death."

"I guess that's what puzzles me," I said.

"How so?"

"Well, you say that Dr. Kitteridge is incompetent, and you cite all these mistakes he made at the autopsy. But if he's such a quack, why are you willing to take his word about the rigor mortis? How do you know he didn't get that part wrong, too?"

He stared at me through those Coke bottles. "I don't follow you, Mike."

"It just seems like you're trying to have it both ways. You don't want to believe anything Dr. Kitteridge says except when it validates your theory about the time of death."

Bell pointed a big finger at a building. "Park over there," he said, disregarding my argument.

The rules at the Maine State Prison require that all inmate visits be scheduled twenty-four hours ahead of time and that new visitors complete a detailed application form. But someone—I suspected Sheriff Baker, with his deep prison connections—had greased the skids for me. They let me in with just a glance at my driver's license, warden's badge, and a cursory pat-down. As for

Bell, they led him away to a special room. As a perennial pest, he was probably subjected to cavity searches on a routine basis—how else to find the bug up his ass?

Before we were permitted into the visitation room, a stern-faced guard with the long torso of a weasel ran down the visitation rules with us. "There shall be no profane or loud language. Nothing may be passed between the visitor and prisoner. The hands of the prisoner and visitor must be visible at all times. The visitor and the prisoner may embrace or kiss briefly at the beginning and end of the visit. Prisoners and visitors may hold hands during the remainder of the visit. Visitors are not allowed to use the rest room in the visit area unless it is an emergency or undue hardship. Visitors are encouraged to use the rest room prior to their visit. Prisoners are not allowed toilet privileges during their visit under any conditions."

I tried to picture the circumstances under which I might want to kiss Erland Jefferts, but my imagination failed me.

A tall guard with coffee-colored skin and hands the size of bird-eating tarantulas then escorted us into the visitation room. He greeted my companion with what appeared to be genuine affection. "How are you doing today, Mr. Bell?"

"I am well, Thomas. And you?"

"It's good to see the sun."

"You and I are fortunate to see the sun! The men in here are not so lucky."

"Them's the choices they made."

"Not all of them, Thomas. Not Erland Jefferts."

The towering guard laughed as he showed us to Visit Booth 2. "So you keep telling me, Mr. Bell."

After he'd gone, Bell leaned close to me. "I call him 'Doubting Thomas.' He's not a thug like some of the others. That skinny man outside—Tolman—he's a thug. But Thomas is not too bright, either, and he's very young. All the experienced guards, the ones with smarts, they know Erland is innocent."

So Sheriff Baker had told me.

The protocol was for Bell and me to sit on the same side of a table—every item in the room was bolted to the floor—while the guards went to fetch Jefferts. The long wait gave Bell a chance to return to his dissertation on rigor mortis.

"I think you're missing the important point about the time of death," he said in his smoke-strained voice. "Maybe you didn't have a chance to read the trial testimony in full, so I don't blame you. Danica Marshall—I call her 'the Black Widow'—is an expert prosecutor. She builds her cases very methodically, like spinning a web. I wasn't present for Erland's trial, but I've watched her in action since I joined the J-Team. I wanted to study her approach the way an entomologist studies a spider."

"A spider is an arachnid," I said.

Either he didn't hear me or he didn't find the correction worthy of acknowledgment.

"The Black Widow leaves nothing to chance. She studies every scrap of evidence and coaches each witness for the prosecution. She uses her looks, too, but that's neither here nor there. I suspect she was raped as a young woman. That would explain her hatred of men."

I kept my eyes on the door through which they would soon be bringing the prisoner. Bell and his relentless lectures had begun to annoy me.

He continued anyway: "In every murder trial, the prosecutor asks the medical examiner, 'Based on your examination, at what time did death occur?' And the ME specifies between which hours it might have taken place. The prosecutor wants to prove to the jury that the victim died at a certain hour, when the defendant had an opportunity to commit the crime. But the Black Widow didn't do that! She asked Kitteridge if he had reached a conclusion about when death occurred, and he said, 'Probably thirty hours or more.' Why be so fuzzy? Because she *knew* Erland couldn't have murdered Nikki, and she wanted to confuse the jurors."

"What would be the point in her railroading an innocent man?"

"You are a game warden, so perhaps you feel a certain loyalty to the prosecution. But you are intelligent and open-minded. I know you attended Colby College. You see, I have studied you, too." Was I supposed to feel flattered or stalked? "And you must admit that there are times when the cops fixate on a suspect too quickly. They *know* in their bones that so-and-so is guilty, but they don't have the evidence to convict. What happens then? If they are professionals, they keep investigating until they find the evidence. Or they admit they are wrong and begin looking at other suspects. But not all detectives and prosecutors are so scrupulous. Some are lazy, like Winchenback and Marshall, who just decide that Erland Jefferts is guilty, and then do everything within their powers to convict him—even by withholding evidence and misleading the jury."

It was at this stage of his diatribe that I'd begun to wonder whether coming to the prison had been such a smart move on my part. Then the doors slid open and the guard whom Bell called Doubting Thomas emerged. He was leading by the arm a handsome blond-haired man in a light blue work shirt and jeans.

"Erland!" Bell exclaimed, rising to his feet.

27

The two men did not kiss, but Bell did wrap one heck of a bear hug around the prisoner.

"It's always good to see you, Ozzie," said Jefferts, taking a seat across from us. He seemed slightly shorter in real life, but his eyes were an aqueous blue and the strong jawline was familiar to me from the *GQ* photo shoot.

Bell waved his arm like a magician gesturing at an empty cabinet from which his assistant has just vanished. "Allow me to introduce Warden Michael Bowditch. He's read your case file and would like to assist us in getting you a new trial."

I put my functional hand on Bell's arm to slow him down. "That's not entirely accurate. But I did want to meet you."

"I don't get many visitors." He had a lobster-man's accent—not as strong as his aunt's—but it branded him as a native Mainer. "What happened to your hand?"

"I broke it."

"That sucks." He settled back in his chair and made unblinking eye contact with me. "I recognize your name. When your old man was on the run, it was all over the TV. We get to watch the news sometimes. But mostly they try to keep us ignorant in here."

"Erland is the exception," Bell interjected. "He has used this opportunity to better himself. He's learned more about Maine law than half the attorneys in the state. I bet he could pass the bar on the first try."

I held my tongue. It's an old cop trick. People don't like speechless intervals. Keep your mouth shut, and eventually they begin to babble. I wanted to see if my silence unnerved the convicted killer.

Erland Jefferts stared right back at me with a canny smile.

"So you must have questions for Erland," Ozzie Bell blurted out.

"Just one," I said. "Did you kill Nikki Donnatelli?"

"No."

There was no hesitation, not a twitch around the mouth or a blinking of the eyes. Jefferts was either telling the truth or he had convinced himself of a lie he'd told repeatedly over seven years. The third alternative was that he was a stone-cold psychopath.

"So who killed her, then?" I asked.

He began to pick with his fingernail at something in his teeth. "I thought you had only one question."

"I lied."

He smiled broadly. "Here I thought cops always told the truth."

"Sadly, we know that's not the case," said Bell.

"So who killed her?" I repeated.

"Hell, man, it could have been lots of guys. Didn't Ozzie show you his list of local perverts? At the moment, I'd look at that Westergaard guy if I were you. He's still missing, right? Have you checked out his whereabouts seven years ago?"

I leaned back and rested my splint on the table. "I'm guessing you have someone else in mind, though. Someone other than Professor Westergaard, since his name isn't in Ozzie's files."

Jefferts let his eyes go blank. He had no intention of answering me.

Bell jumped into the conversation. "Erland is not required to do the police's job. The defense only needs to suggest that other individuals had the means, motive, and opportunity to commit the crime. And our affidavits do that."

I tried circling around for an unobstructed shot. "What happened at the Harpoon Bar? Why did Folsom throw you out?"

"Because I was flirting with Nikki." His hard tone told me he was still carrying a grudge. "Folsom didn't like it because he wanted to bang her himself."

"Describe Nikki to me."

"She was a spoiled little cock tease. We made out in my truck a few times—which is why they found her hairs and clothing fibers in it—but she wouldn't let me touch her between the legs. Not at first. She said she had a boyfriend in Italy." He laughed. "You think I'm incriminating myself by saying that we fooled around a little."

He was right that the admission had thrown me for a loop. Was this apparent candor a ploy to win me over? "Tell me what happened after you left the bar."

"I didn't see Nikki again."

"That's not what I asked."

A pink flush rose along his pale throat and spread across his cheeks. "I've been interrogated about this a thousand times before, you know."

I could feel waves of nervousness rippling off Bell beside me. This wasn't how he'd expected our conversation to go. "Mike, I don't follow your line of questioning here."

"I'd like to hear Erland's version of what he did that night."

"I'll answer his questions." The rosiness drained from Jefferts's face as quickly as it had appeared. "I drove around awhile, called some buddies on my CrackBerry to see what was going on. There was this house party out on Graffam Point. I hung out there for a while, had a few drinks, got a blow job in the bathroom."

This was news to me. "From who?"

"Some drunk chick, a college girl from out of town. The next thing I remember is being on the road again, and I'm starting to feel sick. So I pull down this dirt road—it's that one with the big tree with all the initials carved in it—and I start throwing up. I guess I passed out after that."

"So you have no memory of what happened next?"

"No."

Was it any wonder the jury had doubted him? Alcoholic amnesia didn't make for a convincing alibi. I couldn't figure out Jefferts's game here. Was he so sure the forensic evidence exonerated him that it didn't matter how guilty he looked?

"What's the next thing you remember?" I asked.

"I woke up and some deputy had his flashlight shining in my eyes. I didn't even recognize him as that turd Guffey. Pretty soon, other cops started showing up, and I'm talking to this prick Winchenback. He wants to know the last time I saw Nikki Donnatelli. And I'm thinking, *Nikki? What the fuck?* I'm still buzzed, for Christ's sake. I'm scared shitless that the cops are going to bust me for OUI. It doesn't even occur to me that this dick thinks I abducted her—that's how wasted I am."

"Winchenback claimed you confessed to having done something to Nikki."

For the first time, Jefferts's voice rose in anger. "That's bullshit! What he asked was if I *might* know where she was. And I said, 'Yeah,' because I thought I might have seen her at that party.

And then suddenly he's putting me in handcuffs, like I just confessed to killing her." Jefferts appealed to Bell. "You showed this guy the forensic stuff, right, Ozzie? The state's own evidence proves I was in police custody when some motherfucker raped and killed her."

Bell nodded emphatically. "Yes, I shared all the files with Mike. He knows abut the rigor mortis evidence." He turned to me again. "I'm afraid I don't understand the prosecutorial tenor of this conversation. I thought we were in agreement that Erland was wrongly convicted."

Jefferts leaned back in his chair. "Something tells me the warden doesn't care about my guilt or innocence."

"You'd be right on that score," I said. "What I care about is a girl named Ashley Kim."

He motioned at the cement walls. "I got an airtight alibi on that one, Warden."

He had me there. But I couldn't shake the feeling that Jefferts knew some telling detail he refused to disclose. "Tell me about your relationship with Dave and Donnie Drisko."

"They're assholes."

"And Calvin Barter."

"Ditto."

"Did you ever buy drugs from him?"

Like a ventriloquist, he barely moved his mouth when he spoke. "No comment."

Ozzie Bell put both of his palms down on the

table, fingers spread wide. "You shouldn't answer any more of his questions."

But Erland Jefferts was beginning to enjoy himself. Laugh lines showed around his handsome eyes, and the corners of his mouth curled. "I know what's going on here," he said. "Warden Bowditch has a problem, and he wants me to solve it for him."

"Really?" I said.

"You think I murdered Nikki Donnatelli because you're a cop, and you refuse to believe your buddies shafted me for no good reason. But if I'm guilty as charged, then how is it possible the Oriental chick was killed in the exact same way as Nikki?" He paused for a time, studying my deadpan expression as if it were a Rorschach test. "Unfortunately, I was locked up here last week, so unless I'm the great Houdini, it wasn't me that did it. That means it must have been the same guy who killed Nikki. But you don't want to buy that theory because it proves the attorney general's office screwed me over."

I felt blood warming my cheeks as he spoke, not just because he was correct in his analysis—Bell was right about Jefferts's intelligence—but because I'd come here intending to see through his bullshit. Instead, he'd seen through mine.

"I could offer a few other possibilities," I said bitterly. "Maybe you told one of your cell mates about how you killed Nikki, and now he's on the outside continuing your handiwork. Or maybe you had an accomplice seven years ago, and he's still at large. For all I know, it was a whack job from the J-Team who was willing to kill another girl on your behalf to win your release."

Bell sprang to his feet. "I resent that! I resent that!"

Jefferts, however, remained seated, with his hands folded on his swelling belly and a darkening expression. "Just because your old man was a killer doesn't mean I'm guilty. You can try to convince yourself of that, *Mike,* but you and I both know it ain't true. So thanks for coming in here and wasting my time."

I stood up. "Get used to it. The rest of your life is going to be a waste of time."

"Fuck you, too."

Bell pinched my shoulder and called out to whoever was waiting for us to finish. "We're done here! We're done!"

Bell waited until we were outside the prison walls to fully lay into me: "You brought me here under false pretenses!" he said. "I'm ashamed of you, sir. Deeply ashamed."

"Calm down, Ozzie."

Driving down the hill from the prison, I noticed patches of greening grass amid the expanses of brown on the southern slopes. We tend to think of spring as a time of rebirth. But this lawn had never truly been dead. I wasn't sure why that realization came to mind, but it did.

At the gas station, I pulled in beside Bell's microscopic Nissan and idled the engine as he got out. "Clearly you are no friend to Erland Jefferts," he huffed. "I'm extremely disappointed in you, Warden Bowditch. I thought you were a better man than this. The truth is going to come out, and when it does, your guilty conscience will haunt you for the rest of your life. Good-bye!"

I watched the old reporter climb into his Matchbox car and back hurriedly out of his parking spot, nearly sideswiping a gas pump. What I hadn't told Bell was that being haunted by my conscience would hardly be a new experience.

It was only after he'd sped away that I realized I'd forgotten to return his files. The office box was still in the cargo bed of my Jeep. Sooner or later, the J-Team would want them.

I sat behind the steering wheel, trying to decide what to do next. I was afraid to check my cell phone, in case Sarah had left a message. How would I ever explain to her my escapade at the Maine State Prison with Oswald Bell?

I felt depressed and depleted. Overhead, I watched billowy clouds, a sign of an approaching fair-weather system, crawling eastward out to sea. Along Route 1, the heaped snowbanks were crusted with a litter-strewn layer of grime: a winter's worth of sand pushed up into dirty, frozen walls.

I decided to go inside the gas station and buy a cup of coffee.

When I opened the Jeep's door, I smelled a pungent odor on the breeze. Somewhere nearby, a vehicle had recently flattened a skunk. I thought of this unfortunate animal that had hibernated peacefully through blizzards and ice storms, safe and secure from harm. It had returned to life on a glorious spring night, shaken off five months' worth of slumber, and ventured out in search of earthworms and fresh grass in which to dig for them. Heedless, it waddled out onto a belt of asphalt. Then *wham!* Death arrived at sixty miles per hour.

28

As I drank my coffee—too bitter from the pot —I played back my conversation with Erland Jefferts. I had assumed there was no direct link between the murder of Nikki Donnatelli and what had happened to Ashley Kim, that it was all just misdirection and sleight of hand. Hans Westergaard was a Harvard professor and a genius. He undoubtedly knew the tangled story of Erland Jefferts. What better plan for killing your mistress than to smother her in a way designed to mimic the notorious Seal Cove scandal? But if that had been his intention, why had he disappeared? Wouldn't it have made more sense to call the cops himself, saying he'd just arrived at his summer house and stumbled upon a bloodbath. Maybe Westergaard had started down that road but lost his nerve.

Was there a chance Erland Jefferts really had been railroaded? I didn't want to believe it.

So what was the connection between these two homicides? Jefferts had dropped a comment that surprised me, but I couldn't remember what it was. Something offhand.

The thought of waiting at home for Sarah depressed me. It was a relief to feel some sunlight refracted through the windshield after two days wasted on the sofa. I'd already put my head on the chopping block by visiting the prison. Why not poke around a bit more?

I called my friend Deputy Skip Morrison on his cell.

"Jeesh, you should have told me about your hand. I would have given you a lift to the hospital."

"I thought I'd just sprained it," I said. "What can you tell me about Dane Guffey?"

"Guffey? That guy was way before my time. Why do you ask?"

"His name came up in conversation. I realized I'd never met him."

"That's no surprise. I hear he's kind of a hermit now."

"What's he doing?"

"He's a wood-carver. He makes sculptures of birds, I think. They're supposed to be very realistic. He's won awards."

"Do you have any idea why he quit being a cop?"

"I think he quit after his first year, after that Jefferts stuff. I guess he figured he wasn't cut out for the work."

"Do you know where he lives?"

"Now you've got me curious. What are you fishing around for, Bowditch?"

"Just tell me, Skip."

"He lives down in Seal Cove with his father. I guess the old man has Parkinson's or something. Dane takes care of him and carves his wooden birds."

"Can you give me a street address?"

Skip paused to look up the information on his laptop. "Now this is interesting. Guess who Guffey's neighbors are? It's your friends the Driskos."

I wasn't sure how Dane Guffey would react to my showing up unannounced at the door of his sick father's house, but it didn't strike me as a coincidence that he had resigned after Erland Jefferts's trial. He knew something dangerous.

I cracked the window for the drive down the peninsula to Seal Cove. The wind whistled like a panpipe in my ears. A week earlier, the landscape had looked thoroughly drab, but now I noticed a blush of color in the swelling buds of the birch trees and maples. I saw turkey vultures wheeling, in the company of eagles and ravens, in high circles above the poultry farm where the farmer dumped piles of chicken guts behind the barn. As I'd told Sarah last week, vultures were harbingers of spring in Maine, whatever else they were. On a day like today, with crocus spears poking up through the dirty snowbanks, you could almost convince yourself that this godforsaken world could rise from the dead.

The drive took me off the major roads and down a few winding country lanes. In every thicket I noticed gallon milk jugs hanging from the gray trunks of sugar maples. Early spring is sugaring season in Maine. Because we'd had so many freezing nights and thawing days, the sap was running well this year. A big tree can pour out buckets a day, but it takes something like thirty gallons of sap to make one gallon of syrup. A stand of sugar maples is called a "sugar bush," a bawdy term that always brought out my inner eighth grader.

I'd just passed one of these stands and was driving through a more densely forested lowland, thick with shaggy spruces and firs, when something Jefferts had said came back to me: "the big tree with all the initials carved into it."

I hit the brakes of the Jeep hard and slid to a squealing halt in the middle of the road. I unhitched my seat belt so that I could contort my body to grope around behind the passenger seat. It took me a few moments to find what I was looking for: a weather-stained topographical map of the quadrant around Seal Cove.

When I'd first been assigned to this district, I'd spent hours roaming around with that green-and-brown map, exploring every marked road and dirt trail, trying to get my bearings. A game warden has to know every path a poacher might use, every sand pit where teenagers might smoke pot, every boat launch where closeted gay men might sneak into the woods for anonymous sex. I'd made pencil notes all over this document, but rain and time had smudged some of them past the point of readability. When the new topo maps came out, I'd consigned this wrinkled artifact to the back of my Jeep.

On these maps, a line of dashes indicates an ATV trail. The one I wanted lay half a mile behind me, near the end of an unimproved road—the place where Deputy Dane Guffey had discovered Erland Jefferts passed out behind the wheel of his truck. I was tracing it with my left index finger when I heard a horn blare behind me and felt the Jeep shake and shudder as a seafood delivery truck came barreling past at warp speed.

The driver had a right to be pissed. What kind of moron stops in the middle of the road?

Taking better care, I made a quick three-point turn—or as quick a turn as I could manage with one hand—and headed back from whence I'd come. The trail had been marked with an *X* on Ozzie Bell's photocopied map. I remembered it was the same place I'd once found a bearded flower child running naked in a mushroom-induced euphoria. His trip ended in a puddle of vomit at the Knox County Jail. So much for the magical mystery tour.

Near the paved road, there were a few ranch-style homes and a squalid house trailer, but as I crept farther down the dirt lane, the going got rougher. The frost had pushed big rocks to the surface and the rain had spooned out deep furrows filled with water the color of milk chocolate. I couldn't tell whether anyone else had driven a vehicle on this road recently; the sleet and drizzle had washed away all evidence of human activity. But I could see that a big buck had wandered through. His cloven prints meandered down the lane awhile before something scared him and he bounded suddenly into the evergreens. If I'd cared to look, I probably would have found the place where he'd landed about thirty feet away. A stag is nature's champion long jumper.

Eventually, it became clear that if I ventured any farther, my Jeep was likely to become a permanent fixture in the landscape, at least until the end of mud season.

I stopped, turned off the engine, and got out. The day had felt warm in the light of the resurgent sun, but here beneath the spreading spruce boughs, the temperature was probably ten degrees colder. I shivered and reached behind the seat for my green wool jacket. I had a hell of a time getting my splint down the sleeve.

The air carried the aroma of balsams, like those muslin sachets you sometimes find in the bottom of steamer trunks. The Maine woods smell different—duller, you might say—in winter than in spring, or at least the human nose has a harder time discerning scents. But as I breathed in, I detected a faint fecund odor, which told me the season was turning. In a few weeks, this same trail would reek of skunk cabbages.

It felt good being outside after days cooped up in bed. Despite the Vicodin numbing my nerve endings, I could remember my former self again. The tree Jefferts had mentioned, an ancient sugar maple in which generations of teenagers had carved hearts, initials, and occasional profanities, loomed over my head. Down the road, I heard the white noise of a rushing stream.

The ATV trail left the dirt lane just before a washed-out bridge and ran roughly parallel to the creek about a mile into the woods. The mushy ground would be baked to a hard crust by mid-July, hard enough for a pickup truck to drive on.

I could tell from the depth of the prints that an SUV had struggled to make it this far. The storm had washed away most of the tracks, but Kathy Frost had tutored me in the fine art of reading tire treads. I spotted the serpentine pattern of a pickup or SUV in a sheltered spot, where the arching tree boughs had functioned like an awning to keep out the rain.

I couldn't say it shocked me to find the sand-colored vehicle. What surprised me was that, given the similarities between the Ashley Kim homicide and the one seven years earlier, no one else had thought to investigate the place in the woods where Dane Guffey had apprehended Erland Jefferts. I crouched down and studied the SUV from a distance, trying to make out the license plate. Was it his or hers? Ruth Libby had said that both Westergaards drove the same model.

I remembered that the wife had a vanity plate —WGAARD, or something like that. But this plate was just a meaningless string of letters and numbers. So that report Skip Morrison had given me—that Hans Westergaard's SUV had been sighted in Massachusetts—was a case of mistaken identity after all.

My mouth had gone suddenly dry; I couldn't have spit if I'd wanted to.

The stream seemed very loud here. The noise it made, slipping around rocks, plunging softly over ledges, was like a crowd of people whispering: a chorus of hushed words I couldn't quite catch.

After a moment, I blew all the air out of my lungs and then refilled them. I took long, purposeful steps straight toward the driver's door. I had no weapon, nothing to protect myself, but I had a hunch that I wouldn't need one. That presentiment proved correct.

The window was misted over from the inside, but the splatter of red on the glass told me all there was to tell.

I pulled my left hand back into my sweater sleeve like a turtle pulling its head back into its shell. I didn't want to contaminate the handle with my own fingerprints.

As I expected, the door was open. And as I expected, Hans Westergaard was inside.

He sat upright behind the steering wheel, his face chalk white, his eyes open but frosted. Ruth Libby was correct that he was a handsome man. He had a strong jaw, a Roman nose, and a head of silver hair I recognized from his portrait on the Harvard Business School's Web page. He wore a chambray shirt and chinos, but no shoes or socks. Like the Rover's leather upholstery, all of his clothes were now stained a deep, indelible red.

On the seat beside him was the kitchen knife someone had used to cut his throat.

29

"What the hell brought you here?" asked Danica Marshall.

"It was a hunch," I said.

She was dressed in an electric blue down jacket, making her eyes that much more vivid, black denim pants that flattered her legs, and shiny black boots. She had a skier's golden tan —new since the last time I'd seen her.

We were standing around my Jeep—Danica, Menario, Baker, and me.

Somewhere in the darkening woods, the state police evidence-recovery techs were performing their painstaking work while the medical examiner inspected the corpse. Under the Maine attorney general's Death Protocol, the body couldn't be touched or moved until Dr. Kitteridge had made his preliminary assessment. I was willing to predict the ME would attribute death to a severing of the carotid artery, but I was less certain about the timing. The Range Rover had certainly been mired in place since before the ice storm.

"We know you came here straight from the prison," said Menario.

I'd taken a Vicodin after I called in my grisly discovery and now felt a mellow self-confidence. "News travels fast."

"A guard called to tell me there was an off-duty game warden speaking with Erland Jefferts," said Danica. "I didn't need to be Perry Mason to figure out who it might be."

"What were you doing with that asshole Bell?" asked Menario.

I noticed that Sheriff Baker had slid his hands into his parka pockets and kept gazing dreamily off into the trees. He needn't have worried. I had no intention of squealing on him.

I cocked my head. "Which question am I supposed to answer first? What brought me here? Or why was I at the Maine State Prison with Oswald Bell?"

"Don't be a joker," said Menario.

"We know you spoke with Jill Westergaard, too." Danica tried to stare me down, to no effect.

"Is that a third question?"

"Are you on something, Bowditch?" asked the detective, looking into my undersized pupils with suspicion.

This was the first question that actually provoked a nervous reaction in me. I had no idea how impaired I was by the Vicodin in my system. I was fortunate that Kathy Frost had been summoned that morning to Aroostook County to help look for a lost girl. The only warden on the scene was Ruth's cousin, Mark Libby. At the moment, he was off in the woods with the CID techs.

"I went to meet Erland Jefferts at Ozzie Bell's request," I said.

Danica opened her mouth and shook her head in disbelief. "Didn't I warn you about Jefferts?"

I looked over at the sheriff, who was doing his best imitation of an invisible man. "I'm not joining the J-Team, in case you wondered," I said. "I know Erland is guilty, but I wanted to meet him. You wouldn't understand."

"You're right there," she said. "What is with you anyway? Do you have some kind of career death wish?"

I rested my body against the cold hood of my Jeep. "I was curious about Jefferts. I wondered why seemingly sane people flock to his defense."

The detective and the prosecutor waited. They were expecting me to drop a pearl of wisdom on them.

"Go on," said Menario finally.

"He's a con man," I said.

Sheriff Baker coughed into his fist. When he had arrived on the scene, I knew from his glare that Bell must have told him how abusive I'd been to the J-Team's beloved convict.

"That's an amazing insight," said Danica Marshall.

I let the sarcasm roll off my back. "After I spoke with Jefferts, I started thinking about the similarities between the two homicides. He said something about an old tree the kids carve their initials in. I figured this place might be another point of connection to the Nikki Donnatelli killing. Being the district game warden, I decided to investigate. I recognized the tire tracks, found the vehicle, and called you in."

Menario gave me one of his patented eye rolls. "The district game warden? You're on sick leave!"

"But this is still my district."

"Not for long," said Menario.

I was unimpressed by his bluster. "What are you going to do, punish me for finding the most wanted fugitive north of Boston?"

"I'm having a hard time understanding your personal obsession with this case," said Danica without animosity. She was genuinely perplexed, and I couldn't blame her.

I was still formulating a response when a state police evidence tech came running down the trail. "Detective!"

"Don't go anywhere," said Menario, stalking off toward the crime scene.

After a moment of indecision, Sheriff Baker hurried along behind. As a clandestine supporter of the J-Team, he wanted to overhear every possible conversation.

I thought maybe Danica Marshall would follow the two men, but evidently she didn't want to let me out of her sight. She reached into her ski jacket for something. It turned out to be lip balm, which she applied overgenerously to her wide mouth. "I don't get you at all," she said. "How long have you been a game warden? Two years?"

"Less than that."

"I have no idea what to make of you. On the one hand, you have the highest conviction rate of any warden in the service, according to your lieutenant. On the other hand, your colonel is taking bets in Augusta on when you'll quit or be fired. You strike me as a world-class fuckup, and yet you keep doing Menario's job for him."

"Does it really matter what you make of me?" I asked.

"Not anymore."

"What do you mean?"

"I was worried before about putting you on the stand. Now it doesn't matter whether you're an unreliable witness."

I understood what she was hinting at. "There's not going to be a trial."

"Not if it's a murder-suicide."

"But Westergaard didn't kill himself," I said. "Someone else did."

She inspected the painted nails on her left hand, pretending I hadn't offered an objection. "What did Bell tell you about me anyway?" she asked casually.

"I'm assuming you've read Bell's dossier," I said. "He thinks that you suborned perjury by

Detective Winchenback and suppressed evidence at the Jefferts trial."

"The attorney general and a three-judge panel say I didn't. You know the J-Team has been shot down on every appeal."

"Maybe that's why Bell calls you 'the Black Widow.' "

When she smiled, I could see that her teeth had been professionally whitened. "The Black Widow. I like that."

For an instant, the beauty of her smile and the playfulness in her voice almost took me in, but I caught something in her eyes—a calculation behind the seductiveness—that made me bite my tongue. Even candor was just another pose for this woman.

"This peninsula is crawling with sexual predators," I said. "How come you never looked at anyone else?"

Her eyes narrowed; her lips tightened. "Excuse me?"

"I think Jefferts is guilty, but I also question whether he got a fair trial."

Instantly, she began oozing venom again. "I've devoted my career to punishing men who victimize women. I'm the president of the Coalition to Prevent Domestic Violence. I volunteer at shelters for battered women. So don't talk to me about that sick predator's rights. I got into this job to put scum like Erland Jefferts behind bars."

I sensed that this was just the beginning of what was meant to be a longer tirade, but luckily for me, Menario and Baker appeared again, walking side by side out of the deepening shadows. They were both short guys, but while the detective was all muscle, the sheriff was as soft as an eclair.

"Well?" Her voice echoed loudly through the woods.

Menario was the one who answered. "From the blood splatter, Kitteridge says it could be a suicide."

"What?" I said.

"The angle of the wound suggests he might have cut his throat with his right hand," he explained.

"It's a ridiculous theory," spat Dudley Baker. The sound of his voice seemed to startle us, as if a dog had been given the gift of speech. "What kind of person cuts his own throat to commit suicide?"

Danica settled back on her boot heels. "The kind of person who rapes a girl, smothers her with tape, and then cuts an obscenity into her skin."

"It's only a preliminary assessment," Menario said.

"An assessment that makes no sense!"

For the first time, I was impressed with my new sheriff. The puffy little man was voicing my exact objections to Kitteridge's theory.

"Calm down, Dudley. I'm not saying it's what definitely happened."

In the dim light of the trees, Baker's photochromatic glasses had grown clear, and his eyes were wide and fierce. "Are you prepared to tell the media that Hans Westergaard raped and murdered his girlfriend in a manner identical to the Donnatelli homicide, and then he drove to the exact spot Erland Jefferts was arrested, only to commit suicide?"

"Maybe Westergaard had some sort of fascination with the Donnatelli case," offered Danica. "It could have been a sex game that went wrong, and he killed himself out of remorse."

"That's absurd."

"For whatever it's worth, there's an empty bottle of brandy in the vehicle," Menario told Danica. "The guy was pickled when he died."

I had a sudden memory of Jill Westergaard's frantic voice and tear-filled eyes. From the first, she'd believed her husband was a victim. I owed her an apology.

A cell phone rang among us. All three of my colleagues reached instinctively for their pockets. It turned out to be Danica Marshall's BlackBerry. She didn't bother to excuse herself, just walked behind my Jeep, out of earshot.

"Come on, Menario," I said softly after she'd left. "You know this thing is a crock."

"Stay out of this, Bowditch."

"Let him talk," said Baker.

"You're a professional," I continued, trying some flattery for a change. "This setup with the Range Rover is obviously meant to distract you from the real killer."

The detective crossed his powerful forearms. "Are you guys deaf? I'm just reporting what Kitteridge told me offhand. Nothing has been decided here."

"Both Marshall and Kitteridge have an interest in closing this case."

"What the fuck does that mean?"

"Neither of them wants the Erland Jefferts investigation dredged up again. We all know they cut corners to convict him. The last thing they want is for the media to start asking over-due questions or for Jefferts to get a new trial."

"That's right," said the sheriff, flying his J-Team flag for the first time. "They have a conflict of interest."

"I can't believe I'm listening to this baloney," said Menario with palpable heat. "You think the state medical examiner is going to call a homicide a suicide to save himself from *embarrassment?* I've known Walt for fifteen years."

I decided to play my trump card. "Don't let a murderer outsmart you."

Menario didn't answer. His face was brutal with anger, but I thought I detected some doubt in his rapid blinking.

"I said the case was still open," he replied finally.

Danica had finished her call and strode purposely back to us with a down-turned mouth. Whatever news she'd just gotten hadn't been happy. "That was the attorney general," she said. "He wants a full status report. I have to drive back to Augusta."

"We've got to wait on the autopsy anyway," said Menario.

Danica glared at me with those magnetic eyes of hers; no matter how hard you fought, they inevitably pulled you into them. "Don't be surprised if you get a personal call from the AG," she warned me. "He's as puzzled as the rest of us why you keep popping up at crime scenes before anyone else does."

The prospect of that conversation gave me heartburn. Being hauled in front of the attorney general was not my idea of fun. Lieutenant Malcomb had already warned me about meddling in this case. There was a good chance I could be fired here.

"I'm prepared to justify my actions," I said flatly.

"That's good," Menario said. "Because you're going back to the sheriff's office now to give another statement. You're going to be there awhile."

30

Darkness was falling by the time I finally left the sheriff's office. I'd just given my statement to a young detective with the same crew cut, musculature, and bad attitude as his boss. I knew that I had embarrassed Menario's team by finding Hans Westergaard, but I wasn't going to make excuses for using my brain.

As I stepped outside, I saw a bird shoot up from the alders across the parking lot. It rocketed high into the air and then came spiraling down, making a twittering call that sounded like a rapidly dripping faucet. It was a male woodcock showing off for the females. Every species has its own bizarre mating ritual.

It took me a few minutes to muster the courage, but I finally called Sarah.

"Where are you?" she asked with audible concern and anger.

"I'm at the Knox County sheriff's office."

"Why? Did something happen to you?"

"Something happened, but not to me." The only thing to do was explain my day from the start. "Please listen to the whole story before you get mad at me."

Needless to say, I didn't get very far.

"Wait a minute," she said, interrupting me.

"You mean you've been *driving* with a broken hand? Mike, you're taking Vicodin."

"I know it sounds bad, but let me explain."

I tried to paint my crusade in a positive light, but I received no understanding or forgiveness for my efforts.

"Mike, this is just so amazingly self-destructive," she said. "It's everything I asked you not to do."

I confessed that none of it probably made sense.

"You shouldn't drive while you're taking a narcotic," she said. "I'm going to come get you."

"I haven't taken a pill in hours."

"Just come home, then. And do not take another Vicodin. Your judgment sucks enough as it is."

"I love you," I said.

"So you keep telling me."

Whoever killed Hans Westergaard and Ashley Kim was still at large.

I believed Menario when he said that Dr. Walter Kitteridge would never submit a dishonest autopsy report, but if Bell's files proved anything, it was that Maine's elderly medical examiner was prone to lapses in concentration. I had less faith that Danica Marshall would conduct an objective investigation. Her career would be ruined if it came out that she'd railroaded Erland Jefferts while the actual murderer escaped, only to kill again seven years later.

As for Detective Menario himself, I had no idea. He'd promised the sheriff that he was continuing the investigation. With Westergaard dead, that meant reviewing other suspects. But how doggedly would he follow up with them?

The almost illegible note I had scribbled with Dane Guffey's address sat on my dusty dashboard. The fact that he had resigned as a Knox County deputy shortly after the Jefferts trial seemed significant. Something had driven the man to become a virtual hermit.

My right hand had begun to throb again, and I heard again the siren song of the painkillers in my pocket. The instructions said not to take more than six pills in twenty-four hours, but I had lost count during the long day. Despite what I'd told Sarah, the chemicals were still screwing with my head.

Fuck the pain, I thought.

I started the engine and set a course for the seedy corner of Seal Cove: the unlighted cross-roads where Dane Guffey's street intersected with the Driskos'.

I promised myself that it would be a quick detour. I would stop briefly at Guffey's house and ask him a few blunt questions. Most likely, he would slam the door in my face, and then it would be straight back home to Sarah.

It's astonishing the lies we tell ourselves.

On the drive down the peninsula, a barred owl swept across the hood of my Jeep. It swooped down out of the black trees, its body thick, its wing beats heavy, and then disappeared into the darkness across the road. The occurrence happened so suddenly that, for a moment, it seemed like another of my recent hallucinations. To the ancient Greeks, owls were symbols of wisdom, but I doubted this interpretation applied to my own unwise quest.

When Morrison had given me the address I knew exactly which house belonged to the Guffeys; I'd been past the dump many times, wondering who lived there and whether it might be abandoned. So many of the old ones in town had been given over to ghosts. Theirs was an ugly two-story building that had been painted white many decades ago and then left to mold and rot in the salty sea fogs that invaded the peninsula at night. The windows were all shaded, but one room on the first floor emitted a sickly yellow glow.

As I crossed the lawn to the front door, I noticed the shadow of a big barn behind the house. Was that where Dane did his wood carving? The temperature had dipped below freezing; I knew because the grass crackled under my boots.

On the door, there was an ancient cast-iron knocker that should have had Jacob Marley's face carved into it. With my good hand, I used it to announce my presence. The sound echoed off into the darkness.

I waited a long time for someone to answer.

Eventually, I heard a faint shuffling, as if someone was descending a flight of stairs. Then a light snapped on above my head. The door opened a crack but was impeded from further progress by a chain. Looking through the illuminated slit, I found myself facing an old man wearing a drab bathrobe.

I could see only one side of him, but I recognized at once that he had Parkinson's disease. The single eye that examined me was nearly all pupil, and his entire body was shaking like a streaker at the North Pole. He had a shiny dome for a head and a set of oversized yellow teeth that might have been dentures.

"Mr. Guffey? Is Dane at home?" I saw my breath shimmering in the cold air.

"No-o-o-o."

"Do you know where he is?"

The man made a gurgling noise.

I tried another question: "Do you know when Dane will be back?"

"No-o-o-o."

"I'm Mike Bowditch, the district game warden." I fumbled in my pocket for one of my business cards. It was a white rectangle that bore the seal of the State of Maine. "When your son gets home, can you have him call me at the bottom number? That's my cell phone." Why am I speaking to this man as if he were a child? I wondered. Parkinson's doesn't affect the brain. "Please tell him it's important."

I tried to hand the card to Mr. Guffey, but it slipped through his quivering fingers and drifted like a leaf to the floor. It was still lying there when he closed the door on me. In the silence that followed, I heard a bolt shoot home.

The pain in my fingers and wrist was excruciating. The temptation to pop another Vicodin whispered to me from the back of my skull. *What's the purpose of needless suffering?* it hissed.

I turned on the ignition and reached across my body to shift gears while bracing the wheel with my splint. As I pulled onto the paved road, my headlights lit up the dirt drive that led to the home of Dave and Donnie Drisko. Since my journey to the Guffey house had been such a bust, I felt a sudden urge to check in with my two game thieves.

If I hadn't recognized it before, I should have realized then that my thinking was seriously impaired.

During my convalescence, I figured, the Driskos needed to know they were being watched. Already I was certain that word had gotten around that the local warden was out of commission. A surprise visit, I reasoned, might give them a healthful shock.

Stupidly, I headed up the rocky road, past the homes of a couple unfortunate neighbors who probably lived in fear of the local hell-raisers. If I had a house near the Driskos, every window would be barred, and I'd keep a bazooka in the umbrella stand. I crept quietly forward until my lights just touched the edge of their property line.

I unlocked my glove compartment and found the pistol I kept there. It was a Walther PPKS .380 that I'd purchased on my eighteenth birthday because—hilariously, in retrospect—I'd wanted to be like James Bond. Today, it served as my off-duty carry weapon. Every so often, Sarah and I would be traveling somewhere, and she'd want something from the glove compartment—tissues, maybe, or a mint. When she'd see the pistol, she'd give a shriek, as if it were a big spider.

I ejected the magazine and checked the chamber. With a set of five butter fingers encased in a bulky splint, even this simple task became a difficult and painful act. There was no way I could accurately discharge the weapon with my right hand, and as a lefty, I'd never been able to hit the broad side of an aircraft carrier. With the Driskos, though, you could never be too careful.

The moon was nearly full, but the pale disk was shrouded by clouds and it cast a pellucid light on the road. I'd taken only two steps or so before the Driskos' pit bull began growling from the other side of the fence. Some dogs bark viciously, as if they very much wish to bite you. Vicky sounded like she wanted to dismember me limb from limb. I half-imagined her breaking through the fence, leaving a dog-shaped opening like you see in old cartoons.

A heavy padlock hung on a chain wrapped around the handles. Because the gate was locked from the outside, it meant that my friends, the Driskos, were not at home. I had a feeling the swinging singles might be out on the town.

It didn't take Sherlock Holmes to deduce where Dave and Donnie might be at this hour. The Harpoon Bar was a quick jaunt down the road.

When I got back to the Jeep, there was a new message on my cell phone. The unfamiliar voice belonged to a man, and from his first words I could tell he was apopleptic: "This is a message for Warden Bowditch. This is Nick Donnatelli —Nikki's father. I've heard you're one of the bastards trying to set Erland Jefferts free. The man is a psychopath! He raped and murdered my baby in cold blood. It's bad enough for my family to be subjected to seven years of harassment by lunatics. But you're a law-enforcement officer, for God's sake! Who the hell do you think you are?"

I pushed the erase button. Someone must have contacted him. Maybe Danica Marshall thought a phone call from the grieving father would appeal to my conscience and dissuade me from my quixotic quest.

I should have returned Mr. Donnatelli's phone call, if only to explain my intentions: I was on a mission to discover the truth, not just for Ashley Kim's sake but for his own daughter's, too. It was the only way for justice to be served and for both women to rest in peace. He needed to know my heart was just.

I should have called Nikki's father back, but I didn't.

31

The houses in the fishing village of Seal Cove clung like barnacles around a perfect vase-shaped harbor. Mariners knew it as a hurricane hole: a safe haven where they could tie up their boats if ever a monster storm came crashing down the coast. In August the cove would be a watery parking lot where sloops and lobsterboats angled for every available mooring, but in March the only boats were a few lonely commercial vessels glowing white in the moonlight. You could fish for lobsters year-round along the Maine coast if you didn't mind scraping ice off every hawser and venturing out on subzero mornings through breath-stopping clouds of sea smoke.

But now with spring officially here—on the calendar, if not in fact—more lobsterboats would begin to emerge from beneath their shrink-wrapped skins. Soon the harbormaster would motor out to set the summer moorings. One morning the cove would be placid and empty; the next it would be dotted with floating volleyballs.

The Harpoon Bar occupied an entire wharf on the waterfront. It was a sprawling dead whale of a place that looked like it might someday slide back into the brink. When I got there that night, the parking lot was full, and the joint was jumping. During mud season, there wasn't much to do in this ghost town but drink.

Close to the water, the air felt raw, but the smell of the ocean was stronger than I remembered: another seasonal sign of change. That pleasant briny odor was caused by breeding plankton. In July you could breathe in the sea from miles away, but in the winter it was just a faint scent that drifted like a windblown memory of some long-forgotten summer.

Even before I opened the door, I could hear loud rock music and shouted conversations. I stepped into the bar and paused on the threshold to absorb the maritime spectacle.

The Harpoon took its nautical theme seriously —fishing nets were hung decoratively from the ceiling, and the walls were made of weathered panels that might have been salvaged from wrecked pirate ships. It was the kind of place where the bathroom doors were labeled BUOYS and GULLS. The signature harpoon itself hung above the fully stocked bar, which was where I seated myself.

Despite all the packed bodies inside the bar, the air was as cold as a fish locker; it smelled of fried seafood, spilled beer, and various strong perfumes and colognes.

The bartender took a while to find his way to me. He was engrossed in a spirited conversation with a middle-aged woman wearing a UConn sweatshirt. The TV above their heads showed a fast-paced basketball game. I was so caught up in my own obsessions that I'd forgotten about the other March madness.

I spun around on my stool. All the tables seemed to be full. I recognized many of the faces—men and women I'd arrested for growing pot or driving drunk—but there were just as many people unfamiliar to me. I spotted the mustachioed Driskos in the far corner. They were seated with a balding man who sat with his back to the room.

"What'll you have?"

The bartender leaned across the damp bar. Despite the cloistered chill of the room, he wore a T-shirt that exposed his massive biceps, one of which was emblazoned with a United States Marines tattoo. I guessed him to be in his late thirties, maybe early forties, a veteran of the first Gulf War. He might have been handsome if not for the flattened nose and thinning sandy hair.

"A beer and a menu," I said.

"What?" He needed to shout to be heard above the thudding bass of Lynyrd Skynyrd.

"Allagash White!" I shouted back. "And a menu!"

He poured me a pint and returned with a grease-slicked menu. "What happened to your hand?"

I wriggled my black fingers for him. "Crashed my ATV!"

He bobbed his eyebrows at me. "You're that game warden!"

I should have figured the town bartender would be a link in the local gossip chain. "Folsom, right?"

"Yeah!" he said, displaying enough suspicion to tell me that he was no dope. "What do you want to eat?"

"Hamburger!"

He stared at me for a moment as if he hadn't heard what I'd said, then wandered down to the end of the bar, past the row of beer taps and ice sinks, to punch my order into a computer.

After a while, Folsom drifted down to me again. There was a mirror behind the shelf of liquor bottles, and it showed a hairless spot on the crown of his head.

"Can we talk somewhere?" I was tired of shouting.

"Why?"

"I just need a minute!"

He motioned down to the end of the bar, where a set of swinging doors led into a brightly lit kitchen. I grabbed my beer and followed. The jukebox was still loud in the kitchen, and there was the added clatter of plates and the wet hum of the dishwasher. But you could at least converse at a near normal volume.

Folsom grabbed a pretty waitress by the shoulder. "Watch the bar for me."

She sighed and disappeared back into pandemonium.

The bartender bobbed his head at me as if he'd already reached the limit of his patience. "So what can I do for you?"

"I'm looking for Dane Guffey."

"Guffey? He only comes in for lunch sometimes." He played with a few strands of his wispy forelock. "What do you want with him?"

"Police business." The words sounded ridiculous as soon as they left my mouth. "I need to talk with him about Erland Jefferts."

"Jefferts? What the hell is this about?"

"I think you know."

Folsom crossed his Popeye forearms. "If this is about that Asian chick, I have nothing to say. Besides, I thought they found the guy who killed her. It's been all over the news tonight."

"I wouldn't believe everything you hear. The case continues to be under active investigation."

"Are you saying I'm still some kind of suspect?"

"There's evidence linking you to the death of two young women."

The bartender leaned close enough that I could smell liquor on his breath. Folsom was one of those barkeeps who helped himself to his own spirits. "So I used Smitty's pay phone a few times? So what? I wasn't anywhere near Parker Point that night."

"The J-Team doesn't care. As far as they're concerned, these new killings just prove Nikki's murderer is still on the loose. And your name is on their list."

"I never committed a crime in my life." Folsom's muscled chest had begun to heave, and he seemed on the verge of tears. "Do you know what it's like being called a sex killer? It nearly killed my mom to read that shit in the papers." One of the waitresses dropped a plate, which shattered on the floor. We both watched as the cook scolded her for her clumsiness.

When Folsom looked at me again, his eyes were dry. "What does it matter to you anyway?"

"I was the one who found Ashley Kim. I think there's some connection between her death and what happened to Nikki Donnatelli." I framed my next words with care. "Jefferts and Nikki had a sexual relationship, didn't they?"

"That's a lie," Folsom sneered. "Nikki was a good girl from a good family. She wouldn't have been interested in a scumbag like that."

I sensed that he wasn't being entirely truthful. "How can you be so sure?"

He narrowed his eyes. "Because I knew her, and you didn't. I resent your talking about Nikki like she was some kind of slut."

Interesting choice of words, I thought. But I didn't want to provoke a fistfight with a former Marine, especially with one hand tied behind my back, so to speak. "What do you think happened to Nikki after she left work that night?"

"For seven years, I've been asking myself that question. Jefferts must have surprised her or something." He pinched his nostrils as if to keep them from running and looked down at the greasy kitchen floor. "You don't know what it's like having people think you're a murderer."

"Actually, I do."

Folsom shook his head as if I was just being agreeable and not stating an essential truth of my life. "I was having a good night tonight," he said. "Why'd you have to come in here and fuck it all up?"

I suspected the bartender was withholding information about Erland and Nikki. But whatever Bell thought of him, Mark Folsom didn't strike me as a man capable of raping and murdering a young woman. If anything, he seemed like a man carrying a heavy grief. I wondered if he blamed himself for Nikki's death.

I reached for my wallet. It was then that I felt a certain lightness inside my skull. The beer seemed to be affecting me in a profound way. "What do I owe you?"

Folsom waved his hand. "Nothing. Just get the hell out of here."

On my way out the door, I glanced over at the Driskos' table. Father and son were alone now, laughing and backslapping as if they'd just won the lottery. The man they'd been sitting with had vanished.

Dave spotted me, nudged his son, and pointed in my direction.

I pointed back at them, making a pistol of my left hand and pulling my thumb down as if firing it.

I needed to make a detour to the rest room. I stood in front of the urinal for what seemed like half an hour, emptying my bladder.

While I was there, another guy came in and

stood beside me at the next urinal. He unzipped but seemed to have a hard time getting going. When I flushed, he flushed, too, and began washing his hands at one of the sinks. We looked at each other in the dirty mirror. He was lanky, prematurely bald, and the bones in his face were very prominent, from his cheekbones to his jaw.

"You're Stanley Snow," I said.

"Warden Bowditch," he said in his surprisingly high voice. "I heard you were the one who found Hans."

"Yes."

"Thank you for doing that." He wadded the wet paper towel in his hands into a ball. "The cops finally let us back into the house. But Jill said she can't stand to sleep there, so she's staying at the hotel. I think she's going to sell the place."

"Please give her my condolences."

He gave me a closed-lipped smile and tossed his paper towel at the trash can. It landed on the floor instead, but he ignored it and went back out to the restaurant.

I looked at the wadded piece of paper for a moment and then stooped and retrieved it and dropped it in the trash. People's thoughtlessness never ceased to amaze me. Then I wandered back out to the saloon.

When I passed the bar again, I noticed Folsom

making a call on his cell phone. He gave me a dark glance, which raised the hairs on my neck as I stepped outside.

I met the Driskos again in the parking lot. They were both seated casually on the hood of my Jeep. How they knew it was my vehicle was a mystery.

"Warden Bowditch!" the son slurred. "It's a surprise to see you here."

"We didn't figure you for a barfly," said Dave, looking glassy-eyed and sour.

My left hand went into my jacket pocket and found the textured grip of my pistol. "Get off my Jeep."

"Is this yours?" said Dave. They laughed simultaneously and, without even looking at each other, slid off the hood in unison.

"Dude, what happened to your hand?" asked Donnie.

"I was in an ATV accident."

"That was you? Fuck! We heard it on the scanner. Barter's little kid is like a vegetable or something."

"You must feel like shit," said his father. In the moonlight, his mustache seemed to be crawling like a black caterpillar along his upper lip.

"If you ever need an ATV lesson, you should give us a call," Donnie added. "We can teach you how to ride better."

These men had absolutely no fear of me. Their disrespect ate at my heart.

"Do you know what I just realized?" said Dave with sudden vehemence. "Now all three of us are on disability!"

Father and son looked at each and started to cackle.

"You boys seem happy," I said.

"You have no idea, man," said Dave. "You have no idea."

"You might want to talk with the detectives sooner rather than later," I said. "The DNA evidence I took is going to show that you swiped that deer."

"Misdemeanor," said Donnie with a smirk.

"That ain't an admission of guilt by the way," added his father.

"Well, I would expect to get a visit from Detective Menario if I were you."

"Cops are assholes," said Dave. Then he added with a smoke-stained smile, "Present company excluded."

I advanced on Dave, who stood probably half a foot shorter than me. "I don't appreciate hearing you talk that way about law-enforcement officers."

"You'd better get out of my face," the runt warned.

"Or what?"

"Or you'll be sorry is what." Donnie stepped forward to present a unified front.

I didn't back down. "I think you boys have been lying to me from the start, and I bet you know a lot more about what happened to Ashley Kim than you're admitting."

"Fuck you." Donnie made fists of his hands.

"Back off, Donnie," I said.

His father, being older, wiser, or just less intoxicated, shoved his son. "Listen to the warden, Don."

"The deer blood places you at the scene of the accident at the time of Ashley Kim's disappearance," I said. "That makes you prime suspects in her murder."

"What about her dead professor boyfriend?" Dave gave me a sly smile. "Yeah, we heard about that. Or maybe someone else was there that night, too. You ever think of that?"

"What's that supposed to mean?"

"Figure it out, asshole."

"If you boys know what happened to that girl—"

Disregarding my warning, Dave and Donnie sauntered toward the bar entrance.

"Have a good evening, Warden!" Dave called over his shoulder.

I bit my tongue rather than let loose with some profanity.

I thought that was the end of it. But as I was fiddling with the keys to my Jeep, one of them gave a loud shout: "Don't drink and drive, Warden!"

●　●　●

Inside my vehicle, I tried to make sense of what had just gone down. For scrawny little men, the Driskos definitely had hog-size balls. What did Dave's crack mean about someone else being at the crash scene the night Ashley Kim disappeared? Was he referring to the man who made the anonymous 911 call?

Trying to start the ignition, I dropped my set of keys on the floor. Sarah was absolutely correct: My judgment sucked. Driving to Seal Cove was the textbook definition of *reckless.* And to top it off, I hadn't even gotten my hamburger.

I started the engine, backed carefully out, then headed back up the peninsula. After just a few minutes, I was passed by a Maine state trooper's patrol car, a powder blue Ford Interceptor, moving in the opposite direction. The trooper continued around the piney bend behind me without decreasing speed.

A few moments later, I glanced into my rearview mirror and saw the patrol car behind me. It didn't have its blue lights going, nor was it gaining velocity. It just tagged along at a distance of about a quarter mile, pacing me.

You think that cops spot impaired drivers primarily because drunks speed or weave across the center line, but just as often you can spot someone who is intoxicated because they are driving too slowly, overcompensating for their diminished capacities. As such, I kept close watch on the speedometer, maintaining a constant forty-five miles per hour.

But it was to no avail. As I crossed the line into Sennebec, the trooper suddenly accelerated and switched on his pursuit lights.

There was nothing else for me to do but steer carefully onto the mud shoulder and wait. The trooper pulled in behind me at an angle, as all law officers are trained to do, and paused there, reporting my tags, assessing my movements.

I decided to remove my splint. The pain was excruciating, but I thought it would look better to be driving with a blackened hand than with a splint. I retrieved my auto registration and proof of insurance from the sun visor, but I had a hard time getting my wallet out of my pants with one hand. My fingers found the Vicodin in the pocket. Quickly, I tucked the bottle under the seat.

The trooper emerged from his vehicle. Looking in my side mirror, I watched him approach closely along the side of my Jeep. He rested his right hand on his holster.

I rolled down my window.

"Can you step out of the car, please?" said Curt Hutchins.

32

I'd known it was Hutchins all along. He regularly patrolled this peninsula. The question was, had someone called him from the bar? A conviction for operating under the influence—or even its lesser cousin, driving to endanger—would mean the end of my law-enforcement career.

His voice was a monotone. "I need you to step out of the car."

I climbed awkwardly out of the Jeep. "Jesus, Curt, is this necessary?"

"I need to see your license, registration, and proof of insurance."

Never once making eye contact with me, he examined the papers I gave him as if he expected them to be riddled with errors. I'd forgotten how large a man he was. "How much have you been drinking, Warden?"

"Just a beer."

The trooper was exuding anger from every pore. "What are you taking for the broken hand?"

"Ibuprofen." At that moment, I remembered the loaded Walther in my pocket and my heart skipped a few beats. As a game warden, I had a permit to carry a concealed weapon, but I was obliged to disclose that I was carrying. More important, I was prohibited from packing a gun while consuming alcohol or certain prescription medications.

I decided to keep mum.

In the process of handing the papers back to me, Hutchins deliberately dropped them in the mud. It's a trick we all use. Lack of coordination is another marker of intoxication. To secure a conviction, you needed probable cause to do a Breathalyzer or blood test. I bent down awkwardly and gathered them.

"So what do you want to do first, the nystagmus test?" I asked, figuring my only way out of this mess was to be bolder than he expected.

He stared out from beneath the crisp brim of his trooper's hat. He appeared drawn and tired. There was a patch of stubble on his throat that he'd missed when shaving. He didn't respond.

"Or do you want me to recite the alphabet," I continued. "Which way—forward or backward?"

A white pickup sped past, the driver slowing down to see what we were doing. I glanced at Hutchins's cruiser and figured he had the video camera on his dashboard rolling. To a prosecutor, a tape showing a drunk trying, and failing, to walk a straight line was like money in the bank.

"I'd cut the wiseass shit if I were you," he said in a flat tone.

"I know what's going down here. You're

hounding me because you're pissed about that night at the Westergaard house."

"You think so, huh?"

"Your career is in the shitter because of Ashley Kim, and you're guessing this is your chance to flush me down with you."

"You really don't know when to shut up, do you?"

"People tell me that."

He peered into the front and back of my Jeep, looking for God only knew what. I wondered if he would search the vehicle; he would be within his rights to do so. He circled the Jeep, and then without a word, he returned to his cruiser, leaving me standing there along the side of the road to wait and worry.

My mind was racing. So what would happen after he busted me? He'd take me to the Knox County Jail for a blood test. Then would come the mug shots and fingerprinting. I'd have to call Sarah to bail me out. The union might be able to protect me until a guilty verdict came in —if it came in—but how long would that take? In the meantime, Colonel Harkavy would find some excuse to fire me. It wasn't like I was the beloved mascot of the Maine Warden Service.

I was fucked, in other words. Maybe Sarah was right about self-destructiveness being hard-wired into the Bowditch genes. And now, for all I knew, she might be bringing another generation of us boneheads into the world.

Hutchins climbed back out of his Ford, fastened the chin strap on his hat again, and came striding in my direction.

"Go home," he said.

"What?"

"Get the fuck out of here." His mouth became a sneer. "I think you're probably impaired, and I could give you some field sobriety tests. Maybe you'd fail the blood test for real. But if you didn't, it would look like I'm harassing you. And you're right: My career is in the shitter anyhow. Busting you isn't going to help me with Internal Affairs. So get in your car and drive home . . . slowly."

I was speechless.

"Get in your car, Bowditch. Go home."

Before he could change his mind, I slid back behind the wheel of my Jeep. And then, driving five miles under the speed limit and wondering the whole time if he was toying with me, I steered a course for home.

Hutchins followed me the entire way, stopping finally beneath the copse of white pines at the top of my muddy driveway. Sarah's car was parked in the dooryard. Beside it was a bright yellow Volkswagen. *What is Reverend Davies doing here?* I wondered. I fastened my splint back on, gritting my teeth against the pain, then pulled the sling out of the glove compartment and arranged it around my right shoulder. I glanced in the rearview mirror. The blue Ford was still parked at the edge of the drive. Stiffly, I climbed out of my Jeep.

I opened the door, to find my girlfriend seated on the sofa beside Deb Davies. Sarah was in her pajamas. Her eyes were wet when they fastened on me.

She jumped to her feet. "Mike! Where the hell were you?"

"I got held up."

"Hello, Michael," said Davies. She wasn't sporting her uniform or clerical collar. She was wearing jeans, a fuzzy purple sweater, and her signature eyeglasses. She rose more slowly.

"Reverend," I said. "What are you doing here?"

"She came to see you," said Sarah.

Davies's forehead was creased with worry. "Sergeant Frost told me about Professor Westergaard."

I wriggled free of my coat and hung it on a peg beside the door. The coat was heavy from the Walther pistol still hidden in the pocket. "Did Kathy and Pluto find that lost girl?" I asked with affected casualness.

"Yes," Davies said. "The little girl is all right."

"Kathy's been trying to call you," said Sarah. "We all have."

"I didn't receive any messages." I stuck my hand in my pants pocket, but the cell phone wasn't there. Nor was it in my wool coat when I checked. "I must have left it out in the Jeep."

"I can't believe you've been driving with a broken hand," Sarah said.

"I managed all right." Then I sat down on the bench and began to tug ineffectually at my boots.

Sarah watched me struggling for a while and then came over to help pull them off. As she leaned close to me, her nose twitched. "Have you been drinking?"

"I had a beer with dinner."

She covered her eyes with her small hand. "Are you crazy? Mike, you're taking Vicodin. What the hell is happening to you?"

"I'm fine," I insisted.

"You're not fine!"

I went to the front window and parted the curtains. Hutchins's cruiser was still parked there. What was he waiting for?

Sarah peeked over my shoulder. "What are you looking at?"

I turned to block her view. "I should have told you I was going to see Erland Jefferts," I said. "I shouldn't have been driving with a broken hand. I shouldn't have stopped for a beer."

"That's it? That's your apology?"

"Perhaps I should go," said Davies. "Please feel free to call me—either of you."

"Thank you, Reverend." Sarah opened the door for her.

I peered outside at the top of the hill. It was hard to see from the light spilling out into the dark trees. Hutchins's cruiser was no longer there.

"Take care," said Deb Davies. I sensed that she was speaking to my girlfriend, not me.

"Good night," I said.

After she closed the door, Sarah spun around. "I am so mad at you, I can't even think straight."

"I'm sorry," I said again.

"I don't want your fake apologies." Her shoulders were rigid. "Ever since that woman disappeared, you've been like another person. And you've only gotten worse since that boy was injured. You've been avoiding your phone calls. Charley's probably called ten times since your accident. And what about Kathy? You can't just blow off your sergeant."

"I told you, I misplaced my phone." I knew she was right, but there was something afire inside me. "What do you want me to do, Sarah? Tell me, and I'll do it."

"I want you to get help."

"From who? Reverend Davies?"

For a moment, I thought she might step forward to embrace me, but the pain in her eyes made me terrified to touch her. "Michael," she said softly. "You can't let yourself be destroyed by guilt or whatever this is. We've been through too much for you to fall apart now."

"I told you, I'm fine." I walked past her toward the bedroom.

"Michael?"

"I'm going to call Charley."

I didn't mean to slam the bedroom door. But I did. Through it, soon, I heard the sound of Sarah crying.

I sat on the bed, dialed Charley's cell-phone number, and waited for him to pick up. For the life of me, I couldn't understand why I was so mad. I didn't even know who I was mad at. Sarah had been correct about everything. Over the past week, despite all my best efforts to move forward, I'd become someone I scarcely recognized. Maybe I really was my father's son.

"Charley?" I said. "It's Mike."

"Hello there!" said the old pilot. "I guess it's true that a good man is hard to find. I heard about your accident from Lieutenant Malcomb. How's the broken claw?"

The sound of his voice made me realize how much I'd missed the old fart. I could feel my heartbeat slowing down, returning to its usual rhythm. "I guess I'll be joining you in physical therapy."

"That bad, huh? It's a shame about that Barter boy. How are you holding up?"

"I don't know." It was probably the first honest thing I'd said all day. "I've been a bastard to Sarah."

He hesitated. "Has she said anything to you about her condition?"

"No."

"Maybe Ora was mistaken." He coughed away from the receiver. "So you found the missing professor, I heard. That's some smart detective work."

"Tell that to Menario."

"Don't worry about him. He's just exercised because you keep embarrassing him in front of his superiors."

"There's no way Westergaard killed himself, Charley."

"I'm inclined to concur."

"There's some connection to the Erland Jefferts case, but I haven't figured out what it is yet."

"You might want to ease up on the pedal and let someone else get behind that wheel."

"Spare me the folk sayings, Charley."

"I just worry about you. The state police will crack this case with or without your assistance. If I were in your boots, I'd stick closer to home for the time being."

I paused and moved the phone away from my ear. Through the door, I could no longer hear Sarah weeping. The house had fallen completely silent.

33

Sarah slept on the couch that night. I offered her the bed, but she wouldn't take it. By the time I'd finished my conversation with Charley, her sadness and pity had hardened once again into a firm resolve.

"Tomorrow morning," she said in a calm, flat voice, "I want you to call Kathy Frost and arrange to set up an appointment with the Warden Service psychologist. Ask her to drive you there. If she doesn't, I will. I don't want you driving anymore."

I agreed to do what she asked. "I'm sorry, Sarah. I really mean that."

"I'll believe you when you finally get some help."

She left me alone in the bedroom.

I popped two Vicodins before turning in and started the Hemingway book to get my mind off Ashley Kim. I might have read a single page before I passed out. In the night, I dreamed that Sarah was in the bathroom and couldn't stop vomiting. When I awoke from my coma the next morning, she had left for school, the paperback was spread open across my chest, and the phone on the nightstand was ringing insistently.

"Hello?" My speech was thick and dry. I desperately needed some water.

"Warden Bowditch?" It was a woman's voice, a familiar one.

"Yes?"

"This is Jill Westergaard."

I sat up against the pillow and tried to cough the phlegm out of my throat before continuing. "Mrs. Westergaard. I'm very sorry for your loss."

"I wondered if you would meet me at my house. I need to speak with you."

The request startled me. Stanley Snow had said she was having a bad time of things. I could see how she had suffered a double wound in the last few days. First, there was the hard truth of her husband's affair with his teaching assistant. Then there was my discovery of his lifeless body in the woods. Despite the unpleasant way our last encounter had ended, I felt compassion for Westergaard's widow. I also wondered whether she was clinging to some piece of information that might lead to his killer or killers.

Charley's advice about leaving the investigation to the professionals murmured in my head. But what was the point of sticking close to home if Sarah was at school?

"I've had an accident since we last spoke," I said. "I really shouldn't drive."

"Please," she said. "It's very important that I see you."

I told Jill Westergaard I would meet her in an hour.

I rinsed my face in the bathroom sink and brushed the fur from my teeth. I swallowed two ibuprofen tablets with a glass of orange juice. Then I put on the same mud-splattered pants I'd worn the previous day and a faded flannel shirt. As I grabbed my coat, I felt the weight of the pistol and remembered my missing cell phone. Where the hell was it?

I went outside to look in the Jeep.

There were new tire tracks in the driveway. I squatted down and examined them. They had been made earlier that morning, after Sarah had left for school, by a big vehicle—either a pickup or a very large and heavily loaded SUV. The tracks led toward the house and then back out again, so whoever had come to visit me hadn't chosen to stick around. Probably just some lost driver looking for another house, I thought.

My mobile was nowhere to be found. All I could think was that I might have dropped it somewhere the night before, either outside the Guffey house or at the Harpoon Bar. Maybe it had fallen out of my coat when Hutchins stopped me on the road.

As I was rummaging through my vehicle, I noticed that my hand, while still a ghoulish mottle of purple, yellow, and black, was a bit smaller than it had been previously. I trudged back inside. I used our landline to set a date with the orthopedic hand specialist at Pen Bay Medical Center to be fitted for a hard cast. The sooner I moved on to that stage of my recovery, the better.

After I'd finished with the hospital, I considered the promise I'd made to Sarah. I was supposed to have Kathy make an appointment for me with the psychologist. I started to dial my sergeant on the landline, then stopped. Instead, I found myself punching in my own cell-phone number to see if someone had found it. But all I got was voice mail.

My hand was abuzz. I was tempted to take a Vicodin but resisted the urge for the moment. I tucked the vial inside my shirt pocket and set out for Parker Point.

It had rained lightly during the night, the ditches were again running with meltwater, and I spotted fewer patches of snow in the shadows of the trees along the road. The ice storm had distorted the forest into some grotesque version of its previous self, with birches and willows bent over like whipped slaves and snapped limbs lying strewn about the landscape in a mass dismemberment.

I turned on the police scanner I kept in the Jeep and listened to the chatter, but it sounded like a slow morning in cop land. Driving around like this, I could almost fool myself that I was on patrol, headed to Indian Pond to see whether the last smelt shacks had been hauled off the ice, as required by law. In reality, my destination was a house I had been warned to avoid in the strongest-possible language.

What I discovered at Schooner Lane took me by surprise. A big moving van had backed down the Westergaards' steep driveway—I'm not sure how the driver had managed it—forcing me to park along the private road. I had located the professor's dead body only the day before. How had his wife managed to hire movers to begin emptying her house the very next morning?

As I stepped into the mud, I noticed a flag of yellow police tape flapping in a tree and a latex glove wrapper dropped by some careless deputy.

The movers were all dressed in coveralls. There seemed to be enough men working around the house to field a baseball team. I watched several of them carry some blanket-wrapped pieces of furniture down the walkway and up the ramp of the van before one of them made eye contact.

"Is Mrs. Westergaard here?" I asked.

The accent was straight out of South Boston. "Yeah, she's here somewheres inside."

By the light of day, the building seemed like an unfamiliar place—neither the shadowy horror show that Charley and I first witnessed nor the ghostly lit structure I'd toured via video at the sheriff's office. It was just a mansion with tall windows and high ceilings, a place you wondered how any maid could ever clean. A draft blew through the open doors, causing the small hairs to lift along the back of my neck.

I found Jill Westergaard in the living room, overseeing the removal of the couch with a steaming cup of tea in her hand. She wore the same trench coat I'd last seen her in, but the rest of her outfit was new: brown turtleneck, blue jeans, and some sort of moccasin-type shoes that probably retailed for more than my week's salary.

"Please be careful with that," she was telling two men who were attempting to wrap a blanket around the sofa. "That davenport belonged to my mother."

I coughed to make my presence known. "Mrs. Westergaard?"

When she turned to me, I noticed that her face was done up with eyeliner and lipstick. The makeup was very subtle; it had been carefully applied. Her bleached-blond hair appeared freshly washed. The whites of her eyes were clear. Not for an instant would I have guessed that this was a woman in mourning.

"Thank you for coming," she said without smiling.

"It was no trouble."

"I doubt that's true. What did you do to your hand?"

"I broke it chasing some vandals in the woods."

My answer didn't seem to interest her. She shook her golden head in the direction of the back porch. "Do you mind talking outside, to get out of the way of the movers?"

"Not at all."

I followed her through the living room. The shattered lamp had been removed and the glass vacuumed up. A towel, I noticed, had been placed carefully over the bloodstain on the carpet.

She stood against the porch rail, with her back to the ocean. A brisk sea breeze was blowing off the water, but the view was spectacular. I spotted a raft of eiders bobbing along in the current. In the distance, a tanker was crawling up Penobscot Bay, making for the oil piping station at Searsport.

"I owe you an apology," she said. "You were right about Hans."

"That's not necessary, Mrs. Westergaard. In fact, I wanted to apologize to you for dismissing your concerns."

"No, you tried to warn me. I can't believe I was such a fool."

"Don't be too hard on yourself."

She found her sunglasses inside her coat pocket and put them on. I saw myself reflected in the lenses. "That's easy for you to say. You didn't hear me insisting to the detectives that Hans couldn't possibly have been fucking Ashley Kim."

"You were in denial."

She took a sip of tea to recover her composure. "I remember telling you how well I understood Hans, how there was no way he would have chosen a twerp like Ashley over me. I still have no idea what he saw in that kid. But you never really know someone until your relationship with them is over."

"What do you mean?"

"At the end is when all the secrets come out. I never would have imagined Hans could have committed suicide, let alone murdered someone. He had too much self-regard to take his own life."

The last time we'd spoken, she'd been certain that her husband was also a victim. "You don't believe he killed himself?"

"I never would have believed it was possible. But I never believed he was having an affair with Ashley, either."

I chose my next words with care. "You might not know this, but I was the one who found his body yesterday."

"Of course I know it," she said brusquely. "That's why I asked you to come here."

"What did the investigators tell you?"

"They told me that his throat was slashed. Then they asked me if Hans had any enemies."

So Menario was continuing to look at alternate suspects. I was relieved to hear he hadn't believed

Danica Marshall's assertion that this case was a murder-suicide.

"*Did* your husband have any enemies?"

"No one except the rest of the Harvard Business School faculty, the executives he excoriated in his book, and many of his former students. Hans was an arrogant man who never minded being disliked. But I doubt he ever did anything in his life to make someone decide to murder his girlfriend before slashing his throat. Then again, what do I know? I thought he was a faithful husband."

The sea breeze was beginning to flay my exposed skin. There were so many questions I wanted to ask. "What about Ashley? Did she have enemies?"

"I have no idea. We weren't girlfriends, for Christ's sake. Hans and I had her up here last summer, visited some lighthouses, bought lobsters off the dock in Seal Cove, had a few too many drinks." The bottom half of her face, beneath the sunglasses, was contorted, but her forehead remained smooth. "These are the same questions Detective Menario asked."

"Did he mention the name Erland Jefferts?"

"You mean the man in prison everyone says is innocent?"

I was somewhat surprised that she recognized Erland's name, until I realized how much publicity Ozzie Bell had stirred up for him in the Maine media.

My hand was burning like a three-alarm fire. "It might sound ridiculous, but I wondered if there was some sort of connection between your husband and Jefferts."

"What sort of connection?"

"Had he been following the controversy over Jefferts's conviction in the papers?"

"I'm not sure what you're suggesting," she said warily.

"I'm just trying to make a connection."

She put two and two together very fast. "You don't think Hans's death was a suicide. You think whoever killed the Donnatellis' daughter also murdered him?"

It irked me that she gave no consideration to Ashley Kim. And I was about to protest that I actually *believed* Erland Jefferts had killed Nikki Donnatelli, when the weight of what she'd said smacked me in the temple. "You know the Donnatelli family?"

"Of course I know them. I remember Nikki from when she was a toddler."

Now I was completely confused. It was my understanding that the Donnatelli family hadn't owned property in Maine for seven years. "Didn't you just move here, Mrs. Westergaard?"

"My family has had a summer cottage on Parker Point for three generations. I learned to swim off the dock in town. I practically grew up in Seal Cove."

It took me a while to absorb the importance of what she was telling me. "I thought this was a new home."

"It *is* a new home," she said, "built to replace the falling-down cottage my family has always owned here. This was supposed to be my dream house. I spent years designing it and supervising the construction. And now I can't even stand being inside it for more than five minutes without wanting to vomit."

That explained the movers. She must have known days ago that even if her husband was found alive, she could never live in this house again.

"It must be difficult."

"Let me tell you what's difficult." Her voice climbed in pitch. "My family's been coming here for a hundred years, and still I've got illiterate clammers calling me a 'summer person' or, worse, a 'Masshole.' As far as I'm concerned, I have a far deeper connection to this place than people like you. And through no fault of my own, I am losing that connection forever. Being forced out of your favorite place in the world is a tragedy I hope you never have to experience, Warden Bowditch."

Her predicament brought to mind the situation Charley and Ora were going through in Flagstaff. I didn't much care for Jill Westergaard, but her speech did engage my sympathies.

"Stanley Snow told me you were selling the house."

"*Stanley* did?"

"We ran into each other last night at the Harpoon Bar."

"The Harpoon?" She brought her hand to her mouth reflexively. When she took it away, I saw that she had smeared her lipstick at the corner of her mouth. "That wasn't very discreet of him. What else did my caretaker tell you?"

"Only that you were upset."

"You're damn right I'm upset!" She flung her hands wide and accidentally knocked the mug from the railing onto the rocks below. "Who wouldn't be upset?"

It had been a mistake to come here, I realized. I was only making her more emotional. "Maybe it would be better if I left."

She grabbed my good arm with sudden fierceness. "Who are you? What's your involvement?"

"Excuse me?"

"First you break into my house and find Ashley, and then a week later you discover Hans's dead body in the forest. That's not a coincidence. You're involved in this somehow."

I wasn't certain if I'd just been labeled a murder suspect. "I've just been doing my job," I explained.

"As a game warden?"

"Yes."

358

"That's a lie," she said hoarsely. "Stanley told me about you. He says you're a guilt-driven man obsessed with what happened to Ashley Kim. I want to know why."

Was this the real reason she'd summoned me to her house? I'd assumed that her apology, however unwarranted, was genuine—that she'd only wanted to confess how deluded she'd been before. Now I began to wonder whether this calculating woman had played me for a sucker.

I didn't know how to defuse the situation except with candor. "I found Ashley's car on the night she disappeared, and I suspected something had happened to her."

She laughed at me. "So is this some kind of *mission* for you? Are you trying to atone for your incompetence?"

"I need to go now. You have my sympathies, Mrs. Westergaard."

"I don't care if you have a guilty conscience," she said. "You'd better stop sticking your nose into my life!"

Her threatening words chased me out of the house and up the streaming driveway to the top of the hill. It was obvious that Jill Westergaard knew how to push my buttons. The question was why she kept doing it.

Back at my Jeep, I did my best to scrape the mud off my boots with a fallen spruce branch. I replayed the conversation in my head but recalled nothing that helped explain this enigmatic woman. Ora Stevens had told me that people grieved in different ways. Maybe Jill Westergaard needed a scapegoat.

I did a U-turn and headed back to civilization. When I got home, I would abide by Sarah's wishes and make my promised call to Kathy Frost. As I pulled onto the Parker Point Road, I passed a white pickup going the other way. Glancing in my rearview mirror, I saw its brake lights flash, as if the driver had recognized my vehicle, too. Then Stanley Snow's truck shot forward again at a high rate of speed.

34

The fire on the Drisko property was first reported by an exhausted lineman from Central Maine Power. The electrical worker was suspended thirty feet up in the air in his bucket, repairing a balky pole-mounted transformer—a casualty of the previous week's ice storm—when he spotted a wisp of smoke rising from a distant wooded ridge. At first, the lineman wondered if it was just someone burning brush in his yard, but as the cloud began to boil up in an oily mass, he quickly got on the radio to his dispatcher, who called in the fire to the Knox County Regional Communications Center, which, in turn, sent word out across the airwaves to the state police, the Seal Cove Volunteer Fire Department, and every other available first responder. That was how I learned about the inferno.

"Attention all units, Seal Cove," came the call on my scanner. "Structure fire, Five Town Farm Road, time out, nine thirty-five."

From Parker Point, I didn't have far to drive.

I was one of the first men on the scene.

Two pickup trucks with spinning red balls clapped to their dashboards had pulled up outside the Driskos' fence. Flames were shooting through the roof of the trailer and dense smoke poured from the vents and front door.

One of the volunteers was already fully outfitted in all his gear but was struggling to pull a scuba-type tank over his shoulders. The other man, who still had his fire pants around his ankles, kept looking down the drive, waiting for real help. I knew that most local firemen gathered at the station and rode with the town trucks, but all of the volunteers I knew kept their personal turnout gear—boots, pants, coats, gloves, and helmets—bagged in their vehicles.

The first fireman had pulled on his helmet and was plodding heavily toward the building as I leaped from my truck.

"Wait!" I shouted after him. "They have a pit bull!"

The fireman didn't hear me. He just forged

through the gap in the barbed fence. No dog rushed out to attack the intruder. Vicky wasn't tied to her usual post. Maybe she was out back. I listened for barking, but the only sound was the crackling of the fire.

I stumbled forward to get a better view. Heat radiated down the slope, making my eyes water and smart. Peering through the smoke, I discerned the flatbed pickup, the beat-up Monte Carlo, the two ATVs.

Christ, I thought, both of the Driskos are inside there.

"Aren't you going in?" I shouted at the other volunteer, who was still struggling awkwardly into his coat.

"I'm not certified," he said over his shoulder.

I was startled to realize the man I was addressing was Hank Varnum. Then I remembered he lived around the corner. That's why he originally thought the Driskos were the ones harassing him.

"You can't let him go in there alone, Hank."

The lanky grocer then did something nonsensical. He tugged on his Lincolnesque whiskers. "I can't go in," he said. "I have a beard."

"What are you talking about?"

"The mask won't fit on my face because of the beard. You can't get a tight seal."

"Who's the guy who just went in there?"

Varnum held up a dog tag. The standard practice among volunteer firefighters is to leave a name tag, usually kept attached to the helmet, with someone outside the structure before going in. That way, the incident commander will know who's inside the burning building.

"It's Guffey," he said.

"Dane Guffey?"

"We always go inside in teams of two," said Varnum. "But Dane wouldn't wait. He was here when I showed up."

"I think both of the Driskos might be in there," I said.

"Oh, damn." He grabbed the radio from his truck and shouted into it: "Dispatch, this is Unit Fifty-one. I am ten twenty-three at Five Town Farm Road at nine forty-nine." He coughed into his fist. "We have possible multiple ten forty-eights."

I glared at the burning mobile home. Should I try following Guffey inside? I wondered. I figured if I crawled on my hands and knees, maybe I could help him. But the heat, even from fifty feet away, was too intense. And without a breathing apparatus, the carbon monoxide would knock me out in seconds.

Varnum looked at me helplessly. "I'm afraid one of those propane tanks is going to blow. That damned Guffey! He knows we're not allowed to go into the building until the chief arrives." He glanced down the rutted driveway, but no more help seemed forthcoming.

In Seal Cove and other rural communities, the members of the volunteer fire department half-jokingly refer to themselves as the "Cellar Savers." Because it takes so long for the team to respond, very often the only thing left of a burning building is its foundation. Every small-town fire department in Maine has its own rules—some departments are exceedingly well run—but I seemed to remember that the Seal Cove volunteers had a reputation for ineffectuality.

With their home ablaze, the words spray-painted on the Driskos' makeshift fence seemed to take on a new and absurd meaning: KEEP THE FUCK OUT! WARNING, DANGEROUS DOG! TRESPASSERS WILL BE SHOT. I didn't think Dave and Donnie had ever imagined a day when they would be desperate for visitors to disregard those signs.

"You've got to move your vehicle," Varnum told me.

"What?"

"We need to be able to get the pumper in close to the trailer."

By the time I'd pulled my Jeep out of the way, more vehicles had arrived: random volunteers, some already in their coats and helmets. Men were shouting at one another. "Did we call for mutual aid?"

"What are you, stupid? It's a frigging trailer."

"Hank says there might be bodies."

"Guffey's inside, alone."

"Those propane tanks are going to blow."

A stocky old man I didn't recognize was pulling on his own air tank. He handed Varnum his dog tag. "Tell Milton I couldn't wait."

A downwind pushed the smoke at us suddenly and we staggered away from the fence, our arms raised to protect our eyes, squinting into the billowing fumes. The smell was an acrid mix of burned metal and melting plastic, which made me choke violently and turn away.

"Where's the dog?" I asked the men around me. "The Driskos have a pit bull."

The volunteers looked at me like I'd just escaped from a mental ward. But the absence of the Driskos' ferocious watchdog seemed important: a key to what we were watching unfold.

Ignoring me, the firefighters continued their frantic conversation.

"We've got to turn off the electricity before the pumper shows. Did anybody throw the breaker?"

"Where are we going to get water? Did you see a stream on the way up?"

"There's a pond down the hill, I think."

After what seemed like an eternity, two fire-fighters came backing out of the door of the trailer, dragging a crispy black-and-brown thing that might once have been a human being. Men rushed forward to help them. I took a step forward myself—a reflex action.

Just then, one of the propane tanks at the back of the building exploded, and we were all thrown off our feet. I landed facedown in the mud. When I looked up again, men were scurrying back from the building, terrified that the gas tanks of the Driskos' vehicles, or some hidden cache of explosives, might detonate next. Guffey and the other man who'd gone inside had dropped the incinerated body, but they bravely returned to haul it outside the perimeter of the fence.

At that moment, the pumper truck came screaming up the road. If anything, the scene became even more chaotic as men gawked at the charred remains of either Dave or Donnie Drisko. The eye sockets were gooey and the gums were burned back from the teeth. Other men scrambled around to unroll hoses. The chief arrived, a tubby little character who ran an auto-repair shop in town that specialized in bilking out-of-staters. He began barking orders.

The firemen pulled this immense canvas object out of the pumper truck and then unfolded it next to the vehicle. It looked like a kid's swimming pool, only on a giant scale. The tanker truck arrived and began dumping water into the pool. The engine inside the pumper truck functioned basically like an enormous squirt gun, sucking water from the canvas pool through one set of hoses and then blasting it out again at high pressure through others. The firemen used this second set of hoses to fight the fire.

Whenever the tanker truck became empty, the driver would rush away down the road to the nearest stream or pond to replenish the water supply and then would come racing back to refill the canvas pool. In a land without fire hydrants, this is how you fight a fire, and if you are skilled or lucky, it's how you keep buildings from burning down.

The Cellar Savers were neither skilled nor lucky.

The Driskos' trailer was made of aluminum, so it didn't collapse. But the fire gutted the structure completely. And it took the state fire investigator a long time to collect the remains of the other Drisko.

Was it Donnie or Dave? Even at the end, no one could tell them apart.

35

I spent the afternoon at the scene of the fire, waiting and hoping that the cause of the blaze would be quickly ascertained. An investigator from the state fire marshal's office had been summoned from Augusta, but determining the origin and cause of the fire would likely be laborious. Figuring out whether it was an accident or arson might take days. But I was hopeful for a quick answer.

Passing out drunk with a lighted cigarette seemed like something one of the Driskos might do. Father and son had both seemed destined for fiery ends. So I decided to stick around the smoldering trailer because I was curious. And I wanted to meet the mysterious Dane Guffey, who had materialized out of the past to haunt my recent conversations. I needed to ask him why he had resigned from the sheriff's department. What had he been doing in the seven years since he'd arrested Erland Jefferts?

To keep myself occupied, I made a wide circle around the Driskos' wooded property, looking for their pit bull. I figured Vicky must have broken free of her rope. Maybe the fire and smoke had given her that extra energy to escape. Having a vicious dog running loose through these woods would be dangerous to the local wildlife, not to mention the local children. For all their small-man bravado, I think the Driskos had been secretly scared of her, too.

The forest floor was sopped. I found no dog prints anywhere. At the very least, I could conclude that Dave and Donnie hadn't been in the habit of letting their watchdog free to chase deer. The hollows between the oaks held pools of water that would soon fill with mating wood frogs and spotted salamanders. So far, the amphibians had failed to emerge from their hibernating places. To me, spring never truly arrived until I heard my first frog.

Eventually, I returned to the commotion. I leaned against the side of my Jeep, watching the volunteers scurry about in coats and boots that seemed too big for them, like boys playing firemen. Dirty smoke drifted through the tree-tops. The air carried the sour odor of wet ashes. I reflected on my last visit to this trailer and my subsequent confrontation with Dave and Donnie at the Harpoon Bar. I'd been struck by how glee-ful they'd seemed on both occasions. How had Dave responded when I told him he seemed exceptionally happy? "You have no idea."

What had he meant by that? The Driskos must have understood they were still murder suspects. There was evidence, in the form of deer hair and blood, tying them directly to Ashley's last known whereabouts. So why had they been strutting around the Harpoon like little red roosters?

Was it possible they'd known the identity of Ashley Kim's abductor? If they'd been on the scene that night, grabbing that deer, had they witnessed something they only later understood as significant? Rather than going to the police—since no reward had yet been offered—I could imagine them trying to extort money from the murderer. Had the Driskos made a fatal error in threatening the wrong man with exposure?

They'd been drinking with someone that night at the bar, a bald man who'd kept his back to the darkened room. Stanley Snow was bald, and I'd run into him in the rest room. I'd also just passed his speeding truck hours earlier on my way home from Parker Point.

Snow had keys to the Westergaard house. But what motive would he have had to kill his employer and rape and murder an innocent young woman? As a local boy, he would have known the particulars of Nikki Donnatelli's death well enough to copy it. In all the reading I'd done about Erland Jefferts, I realized, the caretaker's name had never come up. He was just about the only guy in Seal Cove whom the J-Team hadn't added to its list of potential predators. That seemed odd in and of itself.

God, I was driving myself crazy with questions, especially when the likelihood was that Dave or Donnie had just passed out with a smoldering cigarette.

My friend Deputy Skip Morrison had shown up in his Dodge Charger to direct traffic away from the fire. But there was no traffic to direct on the dead-end road, so instead he had wandered up the hill to watch the firemen hose down the burned-out shell of the trailer.

"What are you doing here?" he asked.

"I heard the call on the radio."

"I thought you were on leave."

"I am."

He shook his head at me and chuckled. "So much for the Driskos."

"Did you hear if anyone found any trace of their dog? They owned a pretty vicious pit bull."

"Guffey said he saw a crispy critter inside."

"That's weird. Dave told me she never went indoors."

"Maybe he made an exception occasionally."

"I think they were afraid of her. *I* was afraid of her."

"Well, it sounds like she perished in the fire. Wherever Dave and Donnie are at the moment, I'm guessing it's just as hot as where they left."

I spotted Hank Varnum standing in a circle of volunteer firemen, some of whom I recognized and some of whom I didn't. They were rolling up their heavy hoses, but they didn't seem in any rush. "Excuse me for a second, Skip," I said. "Hey, Hank!"

The tall grocer had ashes in his whiskers. He stuck a long finger out in the direction of my splint. "I heard you crashed your ATV chasing Barter. How's your hand doing?"

"It's all right."

"If that kid dies, that son of a bitch should be tried for manslaughter."

"He's already facing a slew of charges, including child endangerment and felony OUI."

"What about the damage he did to my trees? How is he going to make restitution for cutting down those oaks?"

"Calvin Barter is going to jail, Hank," I said, beginning to feel exasperated with his abiding anger. "And his son suffered a potentially fatal head injury."

"I was sorry to hear about the boy," he said, not sounding particularly sorry to my ears. "Is that what you wanted to tell me?"

"I wondered if you could point out Dane Guffey to me."

"Over there." He indicated a man sitting on a stump, apart from the others. Guffey had removed his helmet but was having trouble tugging off one of his boots. Even from a distance, I knew I'd never seen the man before. He was a chunky guy with a weak chin and a forehead that extended beyond the peak of his skull. He was the spitting image of his old man.

I left Hank and walked through the black streams flowing from the charred mobile home down the hill. "Guffey?"

His cheeks were sooty and a strong smell of smoke came floating off his body. He was panting as if he'd just run a marathon. "Yeah?"

"I'm Mike Bowditch."

He narrowed his eyes and spat on the ground. The spittle was black. "You're the warden who came to my house last night. My dad gave me your card. He said you wanted to talk with me. What for?"

I chose not to answer his question. "I admire what you did back there. Going inside that burning building alone like that."

"Tell the chief," he said in a smoke-parched voice. "Milton says the internal attack team can't go into the structure until he's on the scene. So now I'm in the doghouse."

"Why did you do it?"

He finally got his boot loose. He tossed it on the wet ground and pulled a rubber gardening shoe onto his stockinged foot. "I knew Dave and Donnie were inside. Their vehicles were out front. And those guys never walked anywhere they could ride."

I tried to make my next question sound natural. "How did you know so much about them?"

"As you know, I live just down the hill. Are you ever going to tell me why you came to my house last night?"

"I met Erland Jefferts yesterday," I said point-blank.

He didn't roll his eyes, but his expression revealed the depths of his annoyance. "That's one subject I'm done talking about."

"I just have a few questions."

"Well, I'm not going to answer them."

"It has to do with that so-called murder-suicide on Parker Point. You must have heard about it."

"I heard about it," he said. "What does it have to do with me?"

"There were similarities to the Donnatelli killing."

"So?"

His indifference to the death of two people shocked me. "You used to be a deputy, Guffey. The state police are trying to catch a murderer."

"Yeah, I used to be a deputy. For about eight months." He stood up from the stump he'd been sitting on, and I realized that I'd underestimated his size. He was much taller and a hell of a lot heavier than I was.

"It doesn't bother you to think a man might get away with murder?" I said.

"It wouldn't be the first time."

"What does that mean?"

"Ask your friends on the J-Team. While you're at it, tell them to stop slandering me in the newspapers."

"They're not my friends. And maybe if you stopped lying about Jefferts, they'd get off your back."

My jujitsu must have worked, because he poked me hard in the ribs. "Everything I put in my report was the truth. I can't be held responsible for what Winchenback said."

"What did he say?"

He ran his tongue across his teeth and spit again, but nothing much came out.

I repeated the question. "What did Winchenback say?"

Guffey began gathering his turnout gear and stuffed it into its oversize bag. Over his shoulder he muttered, "I told you I'm done talking about it."

"Where can I find Detective Winchenback, then? I'll ask him myself."

He gave a snorty laugh. It reminded me of the sound a neighing mule makes. "Sennebec Cemetery. Six feet under. Cancer of the tongue, ironically."

"So Winchenback lied in his testimony," I said.

"I never said that."

"But it's why you quit the sheriff's department." It was a wild guess, but I knew instantly from the way his back muscles tensed that I was correct.

Guffey threw his turnout bag on top of a pile of planks in the bed of his pickup. "I quit for a bunch of reasons, and they're none of your fucking business. What do you care about my life anyway?"

"I care because I was the one who found that dead girl, and I want to nail the bastard who raped and smothered her."

"Good luck with that."

"I don't think you're as cynical as you pretend to be." Hadn't Sheriff Baker said almost those exact words to me a few days ago?

"I'm going home now." Evidently, Guffey was as jaundiced as he seemed. He reached for the truck door handle.

I felt my opportunity to learn something from him slipping away. Anger and desperation caused me to grab the top of the door as he slid behind the wheel. "I don't know what happened to make you curl up inside a shell. But if this psychopath kills another person, you'll have blood on your hands."

He yanked the door closed so hard, I had to snatch my hand away to avoid having my fingers amputated. "Go fuck yourself," he said through the window.

I had to shout to be heard above his revving engine. "You think Winchenback and Marshall railroaded Erland Jefferts, don't you? You think someone else might have killed Nikki Donnatelli and planted evidence to incriminate Jefferts."

He glanced in the rearview mirror to see if the coast was clear to back up. "Read my report."

"If Jefferts didn't do it, who did?"

"I'm sure your buddy Hutchins has some ideas."

"Curt Hutchins? The state police trooper?"

To my surprise, he rammed the gearshift into park. The truck sat where it was, idling. Whatever dark secret Guffey was keeping wanted to come out. "Ask him why the J-Team hasn't dragged his name through the mud like they did mine."

I thought I understood what the ex-deputy was getting at, but I wasn't certain. "Do you mean Curt Hutchins was living around here seven years ago?"

"Living around here?" Guffey snorted again. "He and his buddies were drinking at the Harpoon the night Nikki vanished."

36

I'm not sure I staggered, but I definitely felt the mud slide beneath my feet. "Did the police ever look at Hutchins as a suspect?"

"Why should they?" said Guffey. "Winchenback had a 'confession' from Jefferts."

I was stunned. "Well, what do you think?"

"It doesn't *matter* what I think." The ex-deputy threw the truck into reverse again. "That's a lesson I learned seven years ago."

I watched the former deputy swing his pickup around and then rumble down the wet hill and out of view.

Now what? I wondered. Should I call Menario and tell him what Guffey told me? But why would the detective listen to me about Hutchins or anything else? Sheriff Baker might believe me. I reached inside my jacket for my phone and instead encountered the grip of my pistol. I kept forgetting that I'd lost my cell.

I saw Morrison ambling down the hill toward his police cruiser. "Skip!"

He turned to wait for me. "Can I borrow your phone?"

Grinning, he offered me his cell. "You're not going to call one of those phone-sex numbers, are you?"

It occurred to me that if I called the sheriff and mentioned Hutchins's name as a suspect, I'd be incriminating him without any evidence—exactly what Ozzie Bell and the J-Team did to half the men in Seal Cove. For whatever reason, the trooper had allowed me to drive home the previous night. It seemed pretty low to repay his leniency by making him the subject of a homicide investigation based on nothing but Guffey's hearsay.

"Maybe you can tell me," I said to Skip. "Is Hutchins on duty today?"

"I heard they put him on paid leave while Internal Affairs finishes its proctological exam."

"Ouch."

"You got that right, brother."

The only fair thing to do was talk with Hutchins man-to-man. I owed him that courtesy at least. I said good-bye to Morrison and started my Jeep.

But as I drove north along the crooked peninsula, I began to wonder about the wisdom of confronting the man in his own home when I was suffering from a broken hand and acute

Vicodin withdrawal. If Hutchins really had murdered two young women, what did I imagine would happen—that he would just admit his guilt and accompany me to the Knox County Jail for booking?

As had been the case the previous week, I saw a state police cruiser parked in the drive. The Dodge Durango wasn't there, but a set of wet tire tracks led across the asphalt to a closed garage door. The lawn was the same muddy mess, although a few green shoots were pushing up in random places and the red buds of the sapling maples had started to swell.

I climbed out of the Jeep and took a deep breath. Behind Hutchins's house, mauve-colored hills rose in the distance. A kettle of turkey vultures—I counted twenty-one birds soaring in tight spirals—wheeled overhead.

When I looked down again, Hutchins was standing on his front step with the door swung open behind him. He wore jeans and a white T-shirt with stained underarms. He was barefoot and unshaven. He didn't look well. There was an unhealthy pallor to his skin.

"You didn't have to drive all the way over here." It sounded like he'd been expecting me.

"I thought I should."

He shrugged his massive shoulders. "Let me go get it."

Then he disappeared inside the house.

Get what? I felt as if I'd wandered into the middle of a Shakespeare play.

There seemed to be something different about the place. Then I realized that all the shades were drawn. It made me think of the Driskos' trailer. Lonely men liked to live in caves.

But Hutchins was married. I tried to remember the name of his wife. Katie, was it? I remembered her skittishness at meeting me, the sunglasses, the way she kept her face turned away when we spoke. Had she been hiding an injury?

I marched up the flagstone walkway to the front stoop and ran smack into Hutchins. I kept forgetting how big a bruiser he was until I found myself looking up at the cleft in his chin. Standing so close, I could tell he hadn't applied any deodorant that morning.

"Here." In his enormous hand was my cell phone.

"Where did you find it?"

He frowned, as if this question was one he'd already answered. "On the roadside after you drove off."

"If you had the phone with you last night, why didn't you just drop it off at my house? I know you followed me there."

"I got a call from my troop commander, telling me I was suspended. I just called your house to tell you I'd found it. If you didn't get the message, what are you doing here?"

"I just spoke with Dane Guffey."

His smile was wide, and I detected the smell of beer on his breath. " 'Dane the Stain!' That's what we called him in high school. Where did you run into Dane? The guy's a fucking hermit."

"This morning, at the Drisko fire. It turns out Guffey's a volunteer firefighter."

"What Drisko fire?"

I realized that Hutchins hadn't heard the news. From his disheveled appearance, he looked like a troglodyte who'd just emerged from a cavern. "The Driskos are dead. They burned to death in their trailer this morning."

The look he gave me was pure, unadulterated surprise. "No shit?" He rubbed his stubbled skull. His crew cut was so short, he might have appeared bald from a distance. "Hey, do you want a beer?"

Before I could answer, he turned and disappeared back into the darkened hall. Did he expect me to follow him? My good hand drifted into the pocket of my coat and felt the reassuring heaviness of the Walther. After a long hesitation, I stepped inside the shrouded house.

Something about the place was different all right. And it wasn't just the drawn shades.

The last time I'd visited, the rooms had felt empty, but now they literally were. Most of the furniture was missing. Nothing was hanging on the walls, and the floors were bare. I'd thought

Hutchins and his wife were moving in. Now I realized that they were moving out. It was the second time that day I'd walked through a building in the process of being vacated in a hurry.

I found the trooper in his den, seated on a sofa in front of a huge flat-screen television. The sofa and the TV were the only furnishings in the room. The screen showed college basketball players racing up and down a parquet court. It was the NCAA tournament again. The sound was muted.

"Want one?" He held up a six-pack of dangling cans held together with plastic.

The room flickered with the bright red-and-blue light coming from the television. He unsnapped a beer from the plastic ring and held it out to me. I took the can and opened it, but I didn't drink.

Hutchins cracked one for himself and continued staring at the screen. "On top of everything else, I'm losing a bunch of money on this game."

"It looks like you're moving out," I said. "Where are you going?"

"Nowhere."

That's when the realization belatedly arrived. "Where's Katie?"

"Who knows and who cares."

I studied the scene in front of me carefully. Hutchins had his long legs stretched out in front of him on the bare floor. I noticed that the arm of the couch had been gnawed down to the wood. "She left you?"

"I kicked her out." He swiveled his head around on his thick neck, giving me a heavily lidded look. "She was cheating on me. Can you believe that?"

"How did you know?"

"She kept denying it, but I knew she was lying," he said. "Sometimes you just know things. You see it in their eyes. Like when you pull someone over and ask them if they've been drinking, and they say, 'Yeah. I had two beers.' Why is it that every drunk always claims to have had two beers? You ever wonder that?"

I remained motionless.

"I always knew Katie was going to be my downfall," he said. "We should never have gotten married. I don't think I ever loved her. But somehow we ended up getting married. I can't even remember why."

"What do you mean, she was your downfall?"

"You know what I mean."

"No, I don't."

He gave me a look, like I was an imbecile. "I *followed* her. That's what I was doing that night. She told me she was going to the movies."

On the night Ashley Kim was abducted, Hutchins claimed he'd had car trouble—that was why I'd been rerouted to the crash scene—when in reality he'd been stalking his own wife. "I drove to the theater in Thomaston, but Katie's SUV wasn't in the lot. When I got home that night, she was asleep. I woke her up, and she gave me a bullshit story about the movies. That's how I knew she was cheating."

That explained the bruise on her face the next morning. I felt a sudden urge to pistol-whip the wife beater.

But Hutchins gave me an imploring look. "What would you have done, Bowditch?" He honestly seemed to want my opinion.

"I would have trusted her."

His lip curled. "That's a load of crap. Wait until your woman starts fucking another man, and then come here and tell me how noble you acted when you found out."

The thought that Hutchins believed we were blood brothers turned my stomach.

"Why didn't you arrest me last night?" I asked.

"I felt sorry for you."

"You felt *sorry* for me?"

"Look at you, man—you're a fucking mess. We're both fucking messes."

My first impulse was to tell him he was wrong. But then I heard Sarah's voice in my head, pleading with me to get help, and I remembered the contempt in Jill Westergaard's voice as she accused me of being on a mission to atone for my guilty conscience; I thought of the Vicodin and the whiskey and all my troubled dreams, and the words choked in my throat. Hutchins was right: We were both fucking messes. It took staring into this ugly mirror to see how far I'd fallen.

He gulped down his beer like a man dying of thirst. "So what did Dane the Stain say about me?"

I wondered if he'd forgotten that earlier part of our dialogue. "He said you were at the Harpoon seven years ago, the night Nikki Donnatelli disappeared."

"So what?"

"He suggested you might have had something to do with her death."

"Dane thinks I killed that stuck-up waitress? That's pretty hilarious."

"I disagree. What do you mean, she was stuck-up."

"She thought she was better than us natives. Jefferts said he got in her pants, but that was just another of Erland's lies."

"Tell me about Jefferts."

"Oh, Jesus Christ!" he exclaimed and threw his empty can against the wall. I dropped my own beer on the floor and went reaching for my handgun. But then I saw that he was screaming at the basketball game on television. "These assholes can't play defense."

I looked down at the can on the ground, the puddled beer around my boots. Hutchins hadn't seemed to notice the spillage.

"I guess it won't be long before the newspapers start saying I murdered both those girls," he muttered. "That'll be interesting."

I kept my hand on the butt of my pistol. "You might want to tell Menario yourself first."

He swung his head around to look at me again. "Tell him what?"

"Tell Menario the truth about where you were the night of the accident."

"Thanks for the advice."

"What if he interviews your wife about what happened?"

"You leave Katie out of it."

Hutchins was a paranoid, self-pitying bully, but looking at him now, slumped in his stinking undershirt on his stinking sofa, I didn't believe he had murdered anyone. "If you don't tell Menario the truth about that night, I will."

"Is that a threat?"

"More like a promise."

He waved his hand like a tyrant king dismissing one of his vassals. "Get the hell out of here, Bowditch. Go home to your girlfriend. I'm sure she's as pure as the driven snow."

For the past few minutes, a revelation had been trying to bust through into my conscious thoughts. My gaze went to the chewed-up arm of the sofa again. "What happened to your dog?"

"The bitch took him," said Hutchins. "Can you believe that? She took my damn dog."

37

The day was dissolving into darkness by the time I escaped from Hutchins's cave.

I had no doubt that, under the wrong circumstances, he could be a very dangerous man. The idea that this thug identified with me, that he thought we were kindred spirits, bound together by mutual bad luck, a hatred of women, and who knew what else, sickened me more than anything he'd actually said.

I pulled the Jeep over onto the shoulder of the Catawunkeg Road to think through Hutchins's story. He had been at the bar when Nikki disappeared. He had been at the crash scene when Ashley disappeared. He was a police officer. Women would trust him.

He could have easily shown up at the crash scene while Ashley Kim was still there and offered her a ride to Westergaard's house. The next day, he could have sneaked back to Parker Point to rape her and abduct the professor. I remembered how Hutchins had gone alone into the house after Charley and I had broken in and the countless minutes he'd spent inside. Had he been searching for incriminating evidence he might have left behind?

I'd begun to wonder if I'd just escaped a close encounter with the Grim Reaper.

But if Hutchins was a cold, calculating killer, how could I explain the drunken mess of a man I'd just found at his house? He'd permitted me to walk into his den, accuse him of murder, and then waltz out again, unharmed, when he could have shot me and dumped my body at the bottom of a flooded quarry.

Something didn't add up. It was as if I were standing too close to a painting in a museum and could only see splashes of color, when what I really needed to do was take a step back. Only then would I see the larger design.

I needed to return to the intersection where my involvement in this all began, back to the accident scene on Parker Point.

As the temperature had warmed through the course of the afternoon, a fog had crawled up from the sea. Chilled by arctic currents washing down from Labrador, the Gulf of Maine remained unbearably cold all year long. When the sun heated the land, a mist would creep in from the coves and harbors.

I drove directly to the site of the accident. The rain had fallen and the snowplows had come along and scraped the deer blood from the road. I pulled my Jeep over to the approximate place I'd first parked and tried to re-create the scene in my head, but my memories already seemed to be dissolving. The angle of the wrecked car along the road, the location of the blood pool, the places where I'd set up my hazard markers—all the details were melting away into a gray haze.

What if Ashley Kim's homicide was never solved? Sarah had reminded me of the sad litany of unsolved murders in Maine. Every day that went on without a break in the investigation suggested that Ashley Kim was herself dissolving into some sort of fog. Without the closure of an arrest and conviction, the woman would become a kind of ghost. In time, her name would cease to refer to a specific person—an intelligent young woman from Massachusetts who had found herself in the wrong place at the wrong time—and become a local watchword for fear. People in Seal Cove would tell their daughters about her in whispers.

How did that old legend of the vanishing hitchhiker go? A traveling salesman sees a young woman standing along a roadside at night. He stops to give her a ride. She provides him with a street address, then sits mutely while he drives her home. When the salesman arrives at the house, he goes around to the passenger door to let the pale girl out, only to discover she's disappeared. He knocks on the door, and the man who answers tells him that his daughter died in a car accident one year earlier, at the very spot the salesman saw the apparition.

A car came rushing past me out of the fog. It

didn't have its headlights on, so it seemed to materialize out of nowhere and then disappeared just as fast. My heart clenched up before it began forcing blood back through my circulatory system.

Think, I told myself. Try to remember.

I felt a sudden need to hash over these mysteries with Charley. On my own, I seemed to be getting nowhere. At the very least, I needed to stop telling myself ghost stories.

Bracing the steering wheel, I reached into my pocket for the mobile phone. I tapped in the old pilot's number. It took me half a minute of utter silence to realize the cell was dead. Maybe the battery had gotten soaked while lying in the mud. For some reason, it reminded me of my visit with Erland Jefferts. Had he mentioned something significant about a mobile phone?

Or maybe I was misinterpreting the message that was trying to push its way through from my subconscious. Someone had used a nearby pay phone to report the deer/car collision. The identity of the unknown caller seemed to be the key to all this.

The man who had reported the crash had called from outside Smitty's Garage, two miles down the road. I restarted my engine and pulled carefully back onto the pavement, headed south.

The garage was a drab little building assembled out of cinder blocks, asphalt shingles, and broken windows. Across the road, a lane led down to the fishermen's wharf. Two antique gasoline pumps stood ready out front, but their tanks had run dry ages ago, back when gas sold for less than a dollar a gallon. The garage had been out of business for years, and the fading sign above the bays was the last remaining legacy of the late Mr. Smith.

For some reason, the local phone company kept a pay phone in operation here. It was just a hooded metal box bolted to the cinder blocks. Vandals had stolen the phone book—its snapped chain dangled to earth—but the phone itself was functional. I lifted the receiver to my ear and heard that distinctive hum a disconnected line makes. Seven nights ago, a man had used this phone to call the Knox County Dispatch to report a deer/car collision.

What had he been doing here? Smitty's was pretty close to the end of the road, which suggested that the caller might live somewhere between the garage and the tip of the peninsula. At the very least, he must have known of the phone's existence; this dark crossroads wasn't a place you happened by.

Because of the mist, I could only see a short distance, but the briny smell of the sea was pungent here. The turnoff to the commercial fishing wharf beckoned from across the road. I decided to take a drive down to the water.

• • •

It was March, and with the exception of two fishing boats floating in the harbor, the local fleet was still in dry dock. At the edge of the parking lot, I passed the hulking shapes of lobsterboats balanced on cradles. Most were still cloaked against the elements in tight casings of white shrink-wrap. The sight of these ghost boats recalled the pale sheets the movers had thrown over the furniture in the Westergaard house.

The fishing wharf consisted of a steep boat launch beside a dock that teetered on piers above frigid gray waters. A shingled warehouse sat atop the pilings, which were slathered with black tar to keep marine worms from chewing through the wood. Towers of yellow-and-green lobster traps were arranged along the wharf, waiting to be returned to the bottom of the Mussel Shoals channel. On the far side of the dock was the lobster pound: a fenced-in rectangle of the cove where the fishermen dumped their daily catch. Lobsters could be kept alive in that salt-water corral for weeks before being hauled up for shipment.

The parking lot was empty of vehicles, but there was a glow in the upstairs window of the fisherman's co-op. I pulled up to the garage door and got out. The smell hit me at once. Even after the long winter, the lobster traps stank of rotten bait.

I peered around me into the mist. The air was damp and very still. I could hear the waves slapping against the pilings and, in the distance, the repeated moans of a foghorn out in the channel.

I wandered over to the lobster pound's gate. The enclosed area was about an acre in size and fenced against predators. At night, lobsters will creep into the shallows, where scavengers can pick them off one by one. Raccoons will crack open their shells to get at the green tomalley, leaving all that precious meat to waste. Many lobstermen topped their fences with razor wire and used dogs to scare away the little bandits.

But of course the wiliest predator is man. I knew of thefts along the Down East coast where robbers arrived in the night to steal thousands of dollars' worth of lobsters from these pounds. In almost every case, the heist was an inside job.

I slid my left hand into my pocket to feel the reassurance of my pistol and glanced over my shoulder at the warehouse. The entire wharf seemed abandoned, but a sallow light burned in one window. I crossed to the building and tried the door. It was locked. I pounded on the wood with my fist, but there was no answer.

Smell is the sense closest to memory. The stench of decomposing herring sent me time traveling; I remembered my days as a lobster-boat sternman, stuffing mesh bags with alewives, trying not to vomit. That was the summer Erland

Jefferts had abducted and tortured Nikki Donnatelli. Jefferts had been a sternman, too.

There were two lobsterboats riding at anchor in the harbor. My eyes had flitted over the blurry names painted on the transoms when I'd arrived. Now I squinted to read them. The first boat was the *Hester*. The second, farther out, was the *Glory B*—the very same boat Erland Jefferts had been been working on the summer Nikki Donnatelli was murdered.

38

Back at the pay phone outside Smitty's Garage, I dialed information and asked for the number of Arthur Banks in Seal Cove. It was common knowledge around town that he was the owner of the *Glory B*. A computerized voice asked if I wanted to be connected directly with the Banks residence. Needless to say, I did.

A woman answered. The warble in her voice told me she was elderly. "Hello?"

"Is this Mrs. Banks?"

"Ye-es?"

"This is Mike Bowditch with the Maine Warden Service. May I speak with your husband, please?"

She paused, as if waiting for me to continue. "Arthur passed away last fall."

"Oh, I'm sorry." I usually read the obituaries in the local paper, but I had been so preoccupied by my father's misdeeds over the autumn that I had missed a great many things during those months. "Maybe you can help me. Do you know who owns your husband's old lobsterboat?"

"The *Glory B*? Why, Arthur left it to my nephew, Stanley."

"Stanley Snow?"

"Ye-es."

What were the odds the Westergaard's caretaker would now own Jefferts's old boat? Here was the connection I'd been searching for; I just needed to understand what it meant. "Mrs. Banks, what can you tell me about Erland Jefferts?"

When she spoke again, it was with audible caution. Jefferts's name had that effect on a lot of the local people. "He just worked on Arthur's boat that one year."

"At the same time as your nephew?"

"The two boys were friends when they were little. Stanley's mother is a Bates. He and Erland are second cousins."

"They were friends," I repeated quickly.

She must have sensed that my interest had unhappy implications for her nephew. "That was a long time ago! Stanley was just a boy." The receiver seemed to be shaking now in her grip. "Excuse me. I have tea boiling."

Before I could wish her good night, the phone clicked and went dead.

I pumped my last quarters into the slot. I keyed in Detective Menario's cell-phone number and waited. My call went straight to voice mail.

"This is Bowditch," I said. "I'm calling from that pay phone on Parker Point. I think Stanley Snow was the anonymous caller who reported Ashley Kim's accident. He owns a lobsterboat at the fisherman's co-op here. And he met with the Driskos at the Harpoon Bar before they died in that fire. Erland Jefferts is his cousin. They both worked on the same lobsterboat. There are way too many connections here for this to be a coincidence. You need to find Stanley Snow."

I kept rambling until the last of my change ran out.

I didn't trust Menario. It was easy to imagine him receiving my message and hanging up without even listening to it. In his mind, I was the man who cried wolf.

The tide was dropping in the harbor. I could smell seaweed through the gathering mist as the receding ocean exposed slimy beds of dulce and kelp. On nights like this, the Vikings had believed that trolls crawled out of the sea to steal babies from cradles.

The fact that Jefferts and Snow were distantly

related was no great shock; Erland had cousins all over Seal Cove. Most of them, however, had come to his defense before and after the trial. When looking through Ozzie Bell's box of files, I'd read letters and petitions signed by dozens of family members. But not once had I encountered the name Stanley Snow in those documents.

Why?

I needed to call Charley. He was the only person I trusted to act upon the evidence I'd unearthed. With luck, he could persuade some of the higher-ups in the state police to put out an all-points bulletin for Stanley Snow. I tried my cell phone again, but it was still short-circuited.

I began pawing around inside my Jeep, looking for coins. I found a handful of useless pennies in the cup holder—not enough change to make another call.

Erland Jefferts came wandering into my head, unbidden. I remembered that Arthur Banks had signed the J-Team's letter to the attorney general asking for a new trial. Half the town had. So why hadn't Erland's cousin and boyhood friend, Stanley Snow?

In the back of the Jeep, I found Ozzie's forgotten files. I switched on the rear cargo light and began paging through the overstuffed folders. My fingers stopped on a document I'd only skimmed the previous week.

It was an inventory of items the state police

had removed from Jefferts's person and his truck on the morning he was arrested. The list went on for pages: a Swiss army knife with a broken saw blade; a green plastic trash bag; an unopened pack of Camel cigarettes, slightly crushed; a single twenty-dollar bill; four quarters, two dimes, and fifty-seven pennies; a pair of sunglasses tucked above the visor; a permanent black marker; a tangle of polypropylene rope; an empty pint of Allen's Coffee Brandy; a sawed-off baseball bat; a single Magnum condom in its wrapper; needle-nose pliers; a crushed ATM receipt showing a balance of $168 in his checking account; six Bud Light bottle caps and an empty bottle; and, of course, one roll of rigging tape.

Something was missing.

I needed to speak with Charley. He had the clout to mobilize a search for Stanley Snow. The word of a legendary game warden still carried some weight in Maine. And maybe my friend could help me understand what it was in this box that I was failing to see.

I closed the cargo hatch, slid behind the wheel of the Jeep, and sped off for home.

When I pulled up to my front door, I noticed that my patrol truck was the only vehicle in the yard. At first, it puzzled me that Sarah wasn't home; then I remembered her mentioning something about parent-teacher conferences. I glanced at my dashboard clock and saw that it was just past five. She would go ballistic when she learned about my day. I still needed to set up an appointment with the Warden Service's psychologist, I realized. It was the least I could do.

I had some trouble with my keys at the door: I dropped them once, trying to get the right one into the lock, then dropped them again. Inside, the house was cold and dim. The birch logs in the woodstove had burned away to ashes, and a draft had discovered some previously unidentified crack in the cedar shingles. The faint odor of bad fish told me that the trash can in the kitchen needed to be emptied. The sensation of returning to an empty house made me think of the weeks after Sarah had moved out. These days, I often ended my patrols with a feeling of déjà vu.

Awkwardly, I slid my coat off and hung it on a hook by the door.

I heard the floorboards creak and was just turning my head when a sharp pain exploded along my right biceps. I fell back against the wall, aware that I was being assaulted but unable to do more than raise my splinted hand against my attacker. The metal crowbar came down hard on my forearm. I howled in agony and kicked out with my legs, but the intruder leaped back.

I was left to squirm there for a moment, blinded by tears, before my assailant tapped me, almost delicately, on the forehead with a steel club. There was an instant of achingly hot light—like a flashbulb going off at point-blank range—and then I ceased to see.

I came to as my attacker was slinging my limp body onto the sofa. Whoever it was must have torn the splint off my wrist, because my first sight was of my own corpse-colored hand. My eyes were watery and had trouble focusing.

For a moment, I didn't know where I was or what had happened. I was as disoriented as a surgery patient emerging from anesthetic. If a voice had whispered that I'd been in a car crash, I would have believed it.

I felt a boot kicking my shins and then heard a high-pitched voice say, "Sit up."

As I did, a weight shifted inside my head like a bocce ball rolling around inside my cranium. Something was standing over me. At first, it was just a shadow. Then, as my pupils began to function once more, the shadow became a man.

He was a tall, balding man with darting eyes. He had bulbous cheekbones and a jutting jaw. He was wearing a dark peacoat, oil-stained work pants, and heavy rubber boots. In one gloved hand, he held a crowbar. In the other, he clutched a rectangular bottle of amber liquid, which he thrust into my face.

"Drink this," said Stanley Snow.

I blinked and tried to speak, but my tongue wouldn't obey. I cradled my useless right arm against my chest.

"Drink it!"

It was my own half-empty fifth of Jack Daniel's. He must have found the whiskey in the cupboard. A fishy scent came wafting off his clothes, the stench of rotten bait.

I pulled the words up out of my larynx. "The cops know it's you, Snow."

The sound of his own name being uttered caused the Westergaards' caretaker to catch his breath. Slowly, he took a seat in the chair across from me, but his posture remained as tight as a coiled spring. He set the whiskey bottle on the table between us. "Bullshit."

"I called Menario." My voice sounded as if I had gargled with drain opener.

"No, you didn't."

"I called him on the pay phone at Smitty's. I told him you owned the *Glory B.*"

Every muscle in his body became utterly still. "What else did you tell him?"

I understood that Stanley Snow was going to kill me, but I was too weak and in too much pain to defend myself. All I could do was try to gather my strength and wits.

"She knew you," I croaked. "Ashley Kim."

He leered at me with a gargoyle's smile. "She thought she did."

"She met you with the Westergaards last summer."

"That slant-eyed slut." He leaned forward and waved the crowbar in my face. I followed the motion warily, as if it were a swaying cobra that might suddenly strike. "She came up here to get fucked. She got fucked all right."

My head and hand were beating to different drummers, but my thoughts were beginning to flow freely again. Hans Westergaard had told his caretaker to get the house ready. Had he mentioned—master to servant—that he was bringing his mistress? Snow had been lying in wait for Ashley to arrive.

"But why Westergaard?" I asked.

"He shouldn't have cheated on Jill. He had no right to do that."

"You killed Ashley for her?"

He snickered but didn't answer my question. He just scratched his nose absently.

I needed to keep talking, keep stalling. "The police know it's you, Snow."

The crowbar stopped waving. "There's nothing they can pin on me. It's pretty easy to set up alibis. Just drop in on some diners and gas stations. Make sure people see you. Collect receipts. If you turn on the TV loud in your apartment, people will swear you were there all day."

In my mind I saw his white pickup truck with the snowplow parked outside the Square Deal

Diner. I saw his face sneering at me from the other end of the counter the morning after Ashley Kim disappeared. Even then, he'd already been readying his alibis.

"They'll connect the dots."

"Cops are dumb," he said. "Including you." He was trying to project self-assuredness, but I detected a hint of desperation behind the bluff.

"I know you killed the Driskos. They saw you at the crash scene with Ashley. They demanded money to keep quiet."

Some of the confidence drained out of those quick-moving eyes. "What else?"

"You murdered Nikki Donnatelli."

"Strike one," he said with a one-sided grin. "Jefferts killed that girl. A jury said so."

"You used to be friends."

"That's what Erland thought."

So why hadn't Jefferts named Snow as an alternate suspect? He'd named every other degenerate in Seal Cove. "You pinned the murder on him."

His eyes became merry. "There's proof I didn't."

"What kind of proof?"

He reached inside his peacoat and removed something from his inner pocket. It was a cell phone. "I've got a 'Get Out of Jail Free' card."

I was baffled. How would a cell phone enable him to avoid prison? "Is that Jefferts's?"

"No, this one is mine, but you're getting

warmer. That's strike two, by the way." He dropped the phone and raised the crowbar, clutching it with both hands, imitating a batting stance. "You know what happens with strike three, right?" He swung the club. It whistled through the air above my head.

"You're going to beat me to death?"

"I'm considering my options."

"You're out of options, Snow."

"That's what you think." He said this with such calmness that I was completely unprepared when he came vaulting across the table at me.

Snow was quick and agile for such a gangly man. He tossed aside the crowbar and grabbed the whiskey bottle and knelt hard against my chest, pinning me to the sofa. With his free hand, he pinched my nose and began pouring scalding whiskey down my throat. I clamped my teeth shut, so the liquor spilled down my shirt, but he held my nostrils firmly, waiting for me to gasp for breath. When I did, he emptied the bottle down my gullet.

After he'd finished, he backed off, leaving me hacking. My insides burned like I'd swallowed acid. I could feel the whiskey trying to come back up.

"This is a pretty shitty little house," he said, shaking his head sadly. "I guess they don't pay game wardens crap. No wonder you're so depressed."

I coughed and spit, trying to vomit up the alcohol. My eyes had become gushers again, so he appeared blurred to me once more. I became aware of Snow stooping to retrieve his crowbar from the floor.

"Do you know how long I've been waiting for that pretty girl of yours to come home?' he asked.

I tried to sputter out something but couldn't.

"I've been having trouble getting your gun safe open." He gestured with his crowbar to the bedroom. "You mind telling me the combination?"

"Fuck you."

"Figured you'd say that."

He smacked my right arm again with the steel bar. I managed to move the wrist at the last second so that the blow caught me on the muscle of my forearm. Pain traveled up the median nerve and into my spinal column.

Snow peered at me from beneath his Frankenstein brow. "Yeah, I know all about you. Your old man shot himself, right? And Ruth Libby said you blew the head off some Indian. And now Calvin Barter's boy is gonna be a vegetable because of you." He began rocking back and forth on his boot heels. "No wonder you're such a basket case, Bowditch. When I saw you at the Harpoon, I said, 'That guy's gonna blow his brains out some night.' " He let out a fake yawn. "What's the combination to the safe?"

His plan was to make my death look like suicide. It would seem that I'd swallowed my gun out of guilt for Ashley Kim, Hans Westergaard, Travis Barter, and every other reason I had to feel depressed. And the state police might even believe it, too. Would Charley and Kathy, though? What about Sarah? In my heart of hearts I feared that everyone I knew would accept the evidence that I had committed suicide, just like my cowardly father had.

"Two suicides in two days, Westergaard and me," I said. "No one will believe it."

"Maybe, maybe not."

The whiskey came surging into my blood-stream. "I'm not going to tell you the combination."

He plopped down suddenly in the chair. The legs squeaked across the floor. "Maybe you're right. Maybe we should wait for Sarah to come home."

He reached into his coat sleeve and, like a vaudeville magician performing a trick, drew out a wad of cloth. It was a pair of Sarah's underpants. He dangled it between us and then pressed the cotton against his nose and inhaled loudly.

I snarled at him and tried to rise, but he pushed me back with the curved end of the crowbar.

The alcohol was beginning to zap the nerve connections in my brain. Sarah was due home any minute. The thought of this monster raping the woman I loved in front of my eyes was the most horrific thing I could imagine.

Dear God, I prayed. *Please don't let him hurt her. He can kill me and it will be all right, but please don't let him hurt Sarah. I won't fight him if you just make him go away afterward. I'll trade my life for hers, God. I'll do whatever you want me to do, but please, God, don't let him hurt her.*

"So what's it going to be?" Snow asked.

My eyelids were getting heavy. There was no escape. All I could do was save Sarah. Let him shoot me with my Walther and maybe he'd go away before she came home.

Except the Walther wasn't in the safe. My off-duty weapon was still in my coat pocket.

"The combination is forty-three fifty-five," I mumbled.

"You'd better not be fucking with me."

I closed my eyes and shook my drowsy head to indicate that I was being truthful.

Snow flicked my nose with his finger. "Don't pass out on me yet."

I squeezed my eyes shut, as if I were slipping into unconsciousness. I heard him give a hyena laugh and then I heard the stomping of his boots as he left the room. It wouldn't take long for him to realize the combination was bogus.

The whiskey had numbed much of the pain in my body, but the booze had left me uncoordinated. It took all my strength to sit up on the couch. I leaned my weight on my good arm and tried to get my feet under me, but it was as if my legs had turned to spaghetti. I crashed forward onto the pine floorboards. I tried to crawl toward my coat, which was hanging beside the door.

Snow sprang from the bedroom and stepped hard on my spine. "Where do you think you're going?"

I could barely breathe with his weight crushing me. "It's twenty-one fifty-four," I gasped.

"What?" He removed his boot but held it ready to crack my spine.

I flopped onto my back. "The combination is my call number." This was the truth; I didn't figure I could lie to him twice.

Snow cocked his head suddenly and a smile oozed across his lips.

I didn't understand why he was smiling.

Then I heard the puttering of a car engine. Blue-white headlights pierced the front windows as Sarah's Subaru turned into the dooryard. I could feel my swollen heart pumping hard against my sternum.

Snow stepped out of the light. I rolled my head toward him and saw his sick, goblin leer.

"Just like Ashley and the professor," he said.

The car door slammed as Sarah got out.

It took everything in me to shout her name.

Snow kicked me hard in the head. "That was stupid."

He yanked open the door and went leaping down the front steps like some long-legged hunting dog. I felt myself on the verge of blacking out again, but fear kept me awake. I got up on one knee and then collapsed forward against the hanging coats, bringing down a pile of wool and Gore-Tex on top of me.

I heard Sarah shriek out in the yard. But I didn't allow myself to be distracted.

Focus, focus, focus.

I found the pistol in the pocket of my jacket with my left hand and pulled back the hammer with my thumb.

Snow had left the door hanging ajar. Mist drifted into the house on the breeze. When I crawled onto the front stoop, I saw him stretched on top of Sarah in the mud, pummeling her. She kept screaming my name over and over.

Carefully, I raised my left arm. I watched the barrel of the pistol weave back and forth. I steadied it with my shattered hand.

"Snow," I mumbled.

He didn't hear me above Sarah's screams.

"Snow!"

As he twisted his body and rose up on his knees to face me, I shot him through the chest.

39

The next thing I knew, I was waking up in the hospital. My throat was scraped raw from the tube the doctors had used to pump my stomach, and there was a ringing in my ears, like a phone from a distant room, that just wouldn't stop. I tried to rise on the pillow but felt instantly dizzy, as if I'd been spun around in a circle half a dozen times. I bent my elbow slightly and discovered a fat IV needle taped to the big vein that ran along my left forearm.

Most people who suffer from a concussion experience amnesia—they can't remember the incident that caused the head trauma.

I remembered everything.

With my blurred vision and the splint on my hand, it took me a few moments to push the call button. The woman who answered wore blue-green scrubs; she had wiry black hair and dark, tired-looking eyes. It took me a while to recognize her as the ER nurse I'd met the night of the ice storm.

"Where's Sarah?" I rasped.

The woman touched my hand and nodded. "She's resting comfortably."

The little blond doctor appeared around the edge of the ICU curtain. Dr. Tennis Shoes wasn't smiling this time. He leaned close to the nurse.

"How's he doing?" he asked, as if I weren't awake and looking right at him.

"He just asked about his girlfriend."

His whisper was loud enough for me to hear. "Did you tell him she lost the baby?"

The nurse grabbed him forcibly by the biceps and shoved him away from my bed. "Doctor," she said sharply, "I need a word with you, *please.*"

Later, before the drugs shoved me back into unconsciousness, I found myself remembering the night my mother announced she was divorcing my father.

During their nine-year marriage, my mom miscarried twice.

I learned about the first time long after the fact. It was just one of those things when the uterus rejects the fetus.

The second miscarriage was different. I was nine years old, and one warm spring evening, my dad told me I was going to have a little brother or sister. He announced the news at the dinner table while pounding down the last can of a six-pack. My mom was washing dishes at the sink, and I remember her turning around with a look of utter horror, which confused and frightened me. They must have had some tacit agreement not to tell me about the pregnancy.

My mother hurled the bowl in her hands at my father's head, but he ducked, and it shattered against the fake-wood wall of the trailer. Usually, when my mom did something like that, she would scream and rage at him, sometimes even claw his face. This time, she just walked out of the kitchen while my father laughed softly to himself. He seemed to be enjoying a cruel joke.

A few days later, my mom took me to stay with the Coles, who lived down the road. They were a nice retired couple who sometimes baby-sat me when my mom attended one of her Dale Carnegie courses in Farmington or visited my aunt in Portland. She didn't trust my dad to watch me for any length of time, because sometimes he would just stay out all night, drinking at his favorite roadhouse, the one where the waitresses became strippers after dark.

On this occasion, she was gone for three days. While she was away, I began thinking what it would be like to have a little brother or sister. I decided it wasn't a prospect I welcomed. The whole pregnancy thing baffled me. I knew where babies came from—my father had shared the facts of life with me, using *Playboy* magazine as an instructional guide. It was more that I'd been oblivious to my mother's condition. I'd noticed she had been gaining weight, because she never gained weight; to this day, she could still wear clothes she had worn in high school.

But I was just a kid, so what the hell did I know?

When my mom came home from wherever she'd gone, she looked ashen and thinner, and she hugged me so hard, I could barely breathe. In the car, riding back to our mobile home from the Coles', she told me that she'd had an accident and was no longer pregnant.

"What happened?" I asked as the wind rushed in around my ears.

"I fell," she said.

"What happened to the baby?"

"He's in heaven."

She must have stopped at the house to break the news to my father before she came to fetch me, because when we got there, the door was ajar and his truck was gone. He didn't return for three weeks, and when he finally did, my mom announced they were getting a divorce and that the two of us were moving to the big city, which was how she always referred to Portland.

My mother was a strict Roman Catholic. She attended Mass every Sunday and still said the Rosary. It didn't occur to me until much, much later what she'd done.

When I woke again in the hospital, Sarah was sitting in a chair at the foot of my bed. She was wearing Levi's and a black turtleneck. Her lower lip was swollen, and I late discovered that she had purple-and-black bruises across her abdomen.

Her hair appeared greasy for the first time I could recall, and the shadow behind her eyes was visible for any fool to see. She leaned forward and called my name, summoning me from sleep.

"Stanley Snow is dead," she said.

My voice was still barely a croak. "Good."

"I thought he was going to kill you. I thought he was going to kill us both."

"Me, too."

She came around to the side of the bed and touched my hand. "The doctor said you have a concussion but that you're going to be OK."

"What about you?"

"Just some cuts and bruises." She said this while looking at my IV bottle.

I had a hard time getting the next words out. "Why didn't you tell me about the baby?"

My question startled her. Her eyes widened and she leaned back slightly, and I could see her trying to decipher how I could have discovered her secret. After a moment, she breathed out again. Ultimately, it didn't matter how I knew.

"I was going to tell you, but you weren't ready and—I think it was because I was afraid."

She waited for me to answer, not knowing if I would respond with anger or with tears.

"You didn't need to be afraid," I said.

She didn't speak, just squeezed my hand harder.

40

Two days later, the gentle yet hulking prison guard named Thomas escorted me into the Maine State Prison's visiting area. I had received special permission to see a prisoner on such short notice. Once again, I had an appointment with Erland Jefferts.

When I'd called Ozzie Bell to arrange the visit, he'd been ecstatic. He'd heard the news about my fight with Stanley Snow, and although he voiced concern for my girlfriend and myself, he couldn't suppress his giddiness. He was so upbeat, he didn't bother asking me why I wanted to talk with Jefferts alone.

I didn't have long to wait. The model prisoner came through the door with the biggest shit-eating grin I'd ever seen.

"My man Bowditch!" He looked neat and clean in his blue denim outfit. His wavy blond hair was wet and combed carefully back behind his ears. He surveyed my bandaged head and new sling and shook his head with amusement. "You look like half a mummy, dude."

"Have a seat, Jefferts."

The inmate and I faced each other across the table. He waited for me to start the conversation, but I was in no particular hurry.

"I guess I should start by thanking you," he said. "I can't believe it was Stanley. He was, like, the last person I ever suspected."

I tried to remain still as I spoke. "Why was that?"

He gave me one of his patented movie star smiles. "He just seemed like this honest, hard-working type of guy. He never got too high or too low. 'Steady Stanley,' I used to call him. I don't think I ever saw him drink a beer. But I guess that's how psychopaths are—cold and calculating."

"Some are," I said. "But then you have killers like Jeffrey Dahmer, people who are complete alcoholics. My father was a drunk."

He leaned back in his chair. I was certain he didn't know what to make of my subdued manner. Maybe he figured I was sedated.

"Well, in any case," he said, "Stanley wasn't a drinker."

"Do you remember the last time you saw him?"

"The dude never visited me. Not once in seven years. And he was my own cousin. But it makes sense now, in retrospect."

I shook my head. The motion was like a flare going off inside my brainpan. "I meant the night Nikki disappeared."

"He came out into the parking lot after Folsom tossed me out of the bar. He said I was too drunk to drive, but I told him to get lost. I guess he must have seen how wasted I was, and that was when he got the idea to pin the murder on me. It was probably when he stole the tape out of my truck, too."

"You never mentioned in your court testimony that he was at the Harpoon."

He brought his hands together, laying one over the other. "I was pretty wasted."

"How do you think he found you passed out in the woods?"

"He must have followed me around that night."

"When do you think he abducted Nikki?"

He gave a halfhearted shrug. "Good question."

"It looks like you'll be getting a new trial," I said placidly.

He flashed that brilliant smile. "That's what Ozzie says. There's just no way they can railroad me again after what Stan did. It's open-and-shut, man. Open-and-shut."

"How so?"

He seemed bemused by my question. "It all makes sense now, right? At the trial, my lawyer argued that I couldn't have killed Nikki, because she died while I was in police custody—on account of the rigor mortis evidence. Snow killed her after they arrested me, just like we always said happened. But that bitch Marshall was so hot to nail me, she denied the state's own science.

The newspapers are going to crucify her now."

I sat there quietly.

Jefferts seemed to sense something was amiss. "Are you OK, man? You don't look so hot."

"No, I'm not OK," I said. "Your accomplice just tried to kill me and my girlfriend."

"My accomplice?" Jefferts tried to shake the accusation off by pretending he hadn't heard me correctly. But he'd heard me all right.

"You remember the last time I was here?" I said. "I asked you what you did after you left the Harpoon that night, and you said something that struck me, but it took me a while to figure out what it was. You said you drove around and called some of your friends on your 'CrackBerry' to find out if there were any parties going on."

He smiled again, but this time without showing his teeth. "I'm not following you."

"Well, I remembered the inventory of items the police recovered from your truck. There was a lot of crap there, but no BlackBerry."

Jefferts stared at me silently for a few moments, without expression. "I must have lost it."

"Either that or someone stole it."

"That's a possibility."

"There was another thing that had me puzzled. I read Ozzie Bell's files, and Stanley Snow was never mentioned. All of your other cousins attended your trial or signed letters demanding that you be pardoned. Snow never did either of those things, and I wondered why."

He adjusted his shirt collar but didn't respond.

"The J-Team has been pretty aggressive in naming other people as potential suspects in Nikki's murder," I continued. "Calvin Barter, Mark Folsom, the Driskos, and half a dozen others. Why not Stanley Snow? The rigging tape used to suffocate Nikki had been exposed to salt water, so it might have come off his uncle's lobsterboat, the *Glory B*. If your defense team was throwing darts against the wall, how come one didn't hit your buddy Stan?"

His eyes were hooded now. "You should ask Ozzie that."

"I asked Sheriff Baker. He said you told the J-Team to leave Stanley out of their witch-hunt."

"Because I didn't think he did it. He was my friend and I didn't think he did it." He crossed his arms over his chest and leaned back in his chair. "Simple as that."

"All along, you've been presenting everyone with only two choices. Either you're totally guilty or you're totally innocent. Nobody ever considered the possibility that you might first have been complicit in Nikki's abduction—and then later been played for a patsy by your cousin."

Two bursts of color appeared on Jefferts's cheeks. "Go to hell."

I decided not to respond to the personal attack.

"You did say one thing that I believed. I think you and Nikki did fool around a little. Mark Folsom said he threw you out of the bar that night because you grabbed Nikki, but I bet there was some history there. My theory is that you waited for closing time to apologize. I think that somehow you sweet-talked her into going for a ride with you."

"That's bullshit."

"There's no way Nikki would have gone anywhere with a troll like Stanley Snow."

Beads of sweat had appeared along his forehead. "You're just making this shit up."

I continued my story. "You drove Nikki to your secret spot down lover's lane, and then something happened. Maybe you tried to force yourself on her and she said no. Whatever happened, you knocked her senseless, because the coroner's report said she had a wound on her forehead that no one could explain. She was hurt, and you panicked. That's when you called 'Steady Stanley' for help."

Jefferts restrained himself from flying across the table. "Fuck you."

"When Snow showed up, he found you passed out from drinking a gallon of booze. Even better, Nikki was out cold, too. Here was this hot little waitress lying helpless in front of him, this stuck-up rich girl. I'm guessing it was then he realized he could rape her and pin it on you.

So your good friend—the man you called for help—snatched her away and left you lying in your own puke."

On the tabletop, his hands were balled into bony fists. "You can't prove any of that."

"The only evidence linking Snow to Nikki's disappearance was the call you made to him from your phone, asking him to come help you deal with her. He needed to get rid of it. That's why the police never found a BlackBerry in your truck."

He settled back in his chair, composing himself. "That's a nice story," he said with a twitchy grin. "But I'm getting a new trial, Bowditch, and it's all thanks to you. After Stanley killed those people, there's no way they'll be able to prove guilt beyond a reasonable doubt. Within six months, I'm going to be out of this shithole."

I rested my good elbow on the table and dropped my voice to a whisper. "Do you want to hear a secret? When Snow was beating the crap out of me, he did something strange. I was too fucked-up to understand what he meant at the time, but he held up his cell phone and told me it was his 'Get Out of Jail Free card.' What do you think he meant by that?"

"Who the fuck knows?" he asked, but I could tell he did know.

"He kept your message, Erland, from the night you called him. It's what he's had hanging over

421

you all these years, the reason you never gave him up to the cops. He told you that if you ever mentioned his name to anyone, he'd just play the message, and any hope you had of ever getting out of here would go up in smoke."

Jefferts's mouth went slack with disbelief. "I have no clue what you're talking about."

"Stanley Snow dropped his BlackBerry inside my house, Erland. Whose message do you think was on it?"

Kathy Frost was waiting for me outside the prison. It was another dreary, misty day. A light rain had fallen near dawn, stopped for a while, and then started drizzling again. The extended forecast called for more of the same. It was mud season, after all.

My sergeant opened the door of her patrol truck for me and helped guide me inside. Then she went around to the driver's side and climbed behind the wheel.

"How did it go?" she asked.

"I think I scared him."

She started the engine. "So you told him about Snow's cell phone?"

"Yep."

She pressed on the gas and turned the truck in the direction of the prison gate. "I don't suppose you mentioned that there was no message on it from Erland Jefferts."

"I didn't say there was—not in so many words."

"His defense will subpoena it. They're going to find out you were lying to Jefferts."

"By the time they do, Menario's going to have found the actual phone with that message. Snow must have kept it somewhere safe. It was his ace in the hole in case Erland ever tried to strike a plea bargain."

I could feel her looking at me out of her peripheral vision. "That's high-stakes poker, Grasshopper."

The windshield was fogging up. I reached down and hit the defroster. "It's my ass on the line, not yours."

She scratched her nose absently. "My question is why Snow stopped killing for seven years and then started again. He must have had other opportunities. I guess we'll never know what really happened."

I'd thought a lot about this question over the past forty-eight hours, trying to piece together the sequence of events that occurred the night Ashley Kim vanished. Snow had known that Hans Westergaard was secretly driving over from Bretton Woods to meet his mistress, and he must have plotted an ambush. My guess was that he'd already attacked and tied up the professor before Ashley hit her deer. Snow had probably answered the phone when she called Westergaard asking for a ride. She knew him from her visit to Maine the previous summer, knew he was her lover's caretaker, and thought nothing of blithely getting in his pickup.

What Snow hadn't counted on was that the Driskos would arrive at the crash scene while he was there. Dave and Donnie weren't the sharpest tacks in the box, but even those morons could put two and two together. And so father and son embarked upon their ill-fated scheme to blackmail him.

The medical examiner had determined that Ashley Kim and Hans Westergaard died within hours of each other. Snow had evidently kept them imprisoned in the house overnight while he repeatedly violated the young woman. Had he made Westergaard watch? My gut told me he had.

The next day, Snow had left the unfortunate couple alive in the house so he could set about creating alibis for himself. I had seen him at the Square Deal Diner that morning. Sometime later in the afternoon, he had returned to the cottage to rape Ashley Kim one last time before he smothered her to death. He'd then driven Westergaard's Range Rover to that isolated road in the woods, where he'd cut the man's throat with a kitchen knife. He removed whatever bonds he'd used to immobilize his captive and then hiked out of the forest. By the time I found the Rover, the ice storm had erased whatever footprints he might have left. Snow figured that if fiber evidence placed him inside the vehicle, he could always claim that the professor let him use the SUV from time to time.

The unanswerable question was what had incited this killing spree. Snow had already gotten away with murder seven years earlier. There seemed to be something about sexually active young women—Nikki Donnatelli, Ashley Kim—that brought out the demon inside his shriveled little heart. Kathy was assuming that the only murders Snow had committed were the ones in Seal Cove, but who was to say that investigators wouldn't link him to the slayings of luckless women elsewhere?

"Maybe Snow secretly wanted to be caught," I said. I'd read that some serial killers crave the celebrity that comes from being caught; they secretly want to be as famous as John Wayne Gacy or Ted Bundy, and so they begin to sabotage themselves.

"Do you believe that?" Kathy asked.

"He was a lot more careless this time around." I ran my fingers lightly across my bandaged skull and felt the bump on my head. "He knew he'd fucked up Westergaard's fake suicide. He was boasting to me about his phony alibis and how dumb cops are. But he knew it was only a matter of time until Menario caught up with him. He was desperate, or he wouldn't have come after Sarah and me."

"What do you guess Westergaard's wife's role was in this?"

"Snow seems to have had a crush on her, but I don't think she put him up to it, if that's what you're asking."

We drove along without speaking, listening to the rhythmic back-and-forth swish of the windshield wipers. "How's Sarah doing?" she asked.

"How do you think she's doing? A madman broke into our house and tried to kill her."

I didn't mention the baby. Sarah had been sobbing uncontrollably for two days, and I couldn't make her stop. Neither of us could bear to return to our house. Instead, Kathy and Sarah's sister Amy had packed a week's worth of clothes for us, and we'd moved into the motel behind the Square Deal. Eventually, Sarah and I would need to talk about our trauma, but neither of us had the heart to yet. I'd begun to wonder if we ever would. Maybe the Reverend Davies could help us. I had a counseling appointment with her to discuss the shooting.

"I heard the Barter boy came out of his coma," Kathy said.

This was news to me. "What's the prognosis?"

"He spoke to his mother."

The St. George River came into view through the fog, a rushing wide brown expanse carrying tons of mud out to sea. I turned my head to face the window.

"Tomorrow's the first day of open-water fishing season," she said. "You're welcome to ride along with me if you want."

I felt a jolt of pain travel from my shoulder down to my fingers when I changed position. "Do you know what else tomorrow is?"

Kathy looked at me with her peripheral vision. "April Fool's Day."

"Tell me about it," I said.

EPILOGUE

The blackbirds were singing and the spring peepers were calling in the cattail marsh behind the Square Deal as I stepped out of my Jeep. I still hadn't returned to active duty—the hard plaster cast on my right wrist had delayed that prospect indefinitely—but my bruises had begun to heal, and I could stand up in the morning without a lead weight pressing against the backs of my eyes. It seemed like a long time since Sarah and I had moved home from the motel, but I was surprised to realize it had been only two weeks. If nothing else, the leaves bursting from the trees and the bright violets sprouting underfoot suggested that we had finally turned the page on mud season, even if it was only a lie we told ourselves to reawaken our dormant hopes.

"Hey, Mike," Dot Libby said as I came through the door.

She wore a bright orange wig to cover what the chemotherapy had done to her head, but there was a hint of color in her cheeks that hadn't been there the last time I'd come in. From her energy level, you'd never have known she was battling breast cancer.

"How are you, Dot?" I asked.

429

"Right as rain." The tangerine color of her wig made me think of the Barters, but Calvin was still in jail, his son was on the mend, and for the moment I could relax about those worries. "Your handsome gentleman friend is waiting for you."

I was always surprised to hear a woman call Charley Stevens attractive, but maybe they saw his inner glow—like the candle inside a jack-o'-lantern.

Charley rose to his feet as I approached our regular booth. "Don't you look an awful mess," he said by way of a greeting.

"Thanks for coming down, Charley." There was already a cup of coffee waiting for me. My body still ached every time I had to bend down to a sitting posture.

He sipped from the steaming mug. "I reckoned I'd visit the transportation museum while I'm here and take a look at those old biplanes. Maybe I can bamboozle them into letting me take one for a spin."

"How's Ora doing?"

"We've got Stacey living with us again. She's helping us clean out the Flagstaff place, but she and the Boss don't see eye-to-eye on most things, so it makes for some awkwardness. Stacey's not quite domesticated in some respects. She's hoping I can finagle a job for her as an assistant wildlife biologist, but that's a tall order. At least that Colorado district attorney declined to press charges."

"I'd like to meet Stacey one of these days."

"I'm not sure that would be wise," he said cryptically. "How are things back on the home front?"

"Better," I said. "At first, Sarah was crying all the time. She didn't want to move back into the house after everything that happened." I took a sip of coffee to loosen my stubborn tongue. "But she's been doing better this past week."

"I'm glad to hear it," Charley said, but his expression remained concerned. "Do you know if it was a boy or a girl?"

He was the one person I'd told about the miscarriage. "It wasn't anything yet."

He stroked his large chin, waiting for me to say more, but I was done with that topic.

I found myself staring at the place mat. "I've been thinking about something Jill Westergaard told me. She said, 'You never really know someone until your relationship with them is over.' Do you believe that?"

He considered the question a while. "Ora and I are still together, and I think I know her fairly well," he said. "She certainly knows all my sorrowful imperfections."

"I never really knew my father," I said.

He warmed his hands on the coffee cup. "Your old man was more of an enigma than most, but he wasn't quite as mysterious as you make him

431

out to be. If you search your memories, I bet you'll find a trail of bread crumbs."

A revelation landed hard on my head. "You knew he killed Brodeur and Shipman—you knew it the whole time we were searching for him. So why didn't you just come out and tell me?"

His entire face wrinkled when he smiled. "An old philosopher once remarked, 'You can't teach a man anything. You can only help him find it within himself.' Or something like that."

"When did you ever read philosophy, Charley?"

"Oh, I never did, but Ora likes to quote that line to me when I'm lurching from one mishap to the next." He raised his long index finger to catch Dot's attention. "What's this I hear about the J-Team suddenly getting cold feet?"

In the days following the shooting, Ozzie Bell and his cohorts had come out with full-throated calls that Jefferts be pardoned. The big newspapers issued editorials arguing that Maine's most famous inmate should receive a new trial. It all seemed to be building to a scandal that would shake the foundations of power and bring the attorney general's office crashing down. And then, like a balloon with a slow leak, the air seemed to go out of the story. I'd just heard on the radio that the J-Team had dropped its motion for a new trial. In fact, the group—with the notable exception of Lou Bates—was giving up the ghost.

"It sounds like Menario finally found a certain cell phone among Snow's possessions," Charley said.

"Sheriff Baker told me there's going to be a news conference later today."

"That was thoughtful of the sheriff to give you the heads-up."

"Dudley's a good man," I said.

After we'd finished lunch, Charley shook my hand so hard, I thought my arm would pop out of its socket. I'd be back on patrol in no time, he said, and summer in the Maine woods was a balm to soothe even the most troubled of spirits. I accepted his well wishes and followed him out to his vehicle.

"One last thing," he called to me through the window. "The Boss gave me a message for you. She said, 'Tell him he should call his mother.'"

I promised I would.

In fact, I had already telephoned my mother at her winter home in Naples. My photograph had been all over the news again, and the media inevitably dredged up the bloody events at Rum Pond. If ever there was a chance to talk with my mom about my dad, this seemed to be it. I was hoping that she might share some insight into his misbegotten rage and loneliness. What caused her to forgive his cruelty and self-centeredness? I wondered. Was it her own guilt over their lost child?

But when I tried to broach these questions, she cut me off quickly. "We'll be back in Scarborough at the end of the month," she said. "Why don't you and Sarah come down, and we'll all have dinner? I'm going to play tennis with Jane Rittmeyer. I can't wait to see you, Michael."

Denial has deep talons, I thought.

The front door was ajar when I arrived home. I found Sarah at the kitchen counter, with a pen in hand. She was dressed to go out; she wore boots over leggings, a cashmere top, and the expensive new leather jacket her parents had given her for her birthday. Her complexion was radiant, her hair perfect. I couldn't remember her looking more beautiful, although I knew her stomach was still bruised.

"I was just leaving you a note," she said. "Melissa and Nicole invited me out for sushi in Rockland. They thought I needed a girl's night out."

"That's all right," I said. "I'll make a sandwich."

"I won't be late." She kissed me on the cheek.

"Sarah, I need to talk with you about something."

"Mike, I have to go."

"I know you do."

She paused in the doorway with the keys in her hand, and then she came back and sat down

434

on the sofa. She patted the cushion, indicating I should join her. I couldn't look at that couch with-out thinking of Stanley Snow attacking me there, but I took a seat. She put a hand on my knee.

"What would have happened if we hadn't lost the baby?" I asked her.

"Probably the same thing," she said. "It would have just taken us longer to get to this place, and it would have been a whole lot more painful for all of us."

"I know I should have listened to you," I said. "You kept trying to talk to me, and I was never there."

"You were trying to solve a crime. You *did* solve a crime."

"I keep thinking I could have done something differently."

She shook her head and met my eyes, and I realized she would probably never look at me this intimately again. "We're just not meant for this. I don't want to be a nagging, resentful person; that's not who I am. At least I hope I'm not."

I gave her a playful nudge. "I didn't make it easy for you, did I?"

"You saved my life."

"That's a nice way of saying I nearly got you killed."

"No, it means you're a hero. You just don't believe it, for some reason. I hope someday you will."

She stood up and began removing her jacket.

"What are you doing that for?" I asked.

"I feel like I should pack."

"It can wait," I said. "Go have dinner with Melissa and Nicole."

"It doesn't feel right to just leave you here alone."

"You don't need to worry about me."

Sarah protested awhile longer, but eventually I persuaded her that she needed the company of her friends. There was no rush now that we both understood what needed to happen. Before she left, she kissed me on the lips. I stood in the open door until her little white Subaru disappeared through the trees.

It was a glorious afternoon. The river was high in the tidal marsh, and I could hear the sound of rushing water through the budding alders and the leafing poplars. The beautiful liquid song of a brown creeper carried down to me from one of the pines.

I closed the door, went into the kitchen, and took a jelly glass from the cupboard. I filled it halfway full of whiskey, then added a splash more. Outside, the tide was rising, and a sea breeze drifted in through the open window. The late-afternoon sun caught the amber light of the whiskey as I raised the glass. I saw my beautiful marsh refracted through the tawny color of the alcohol before I dumped it down the drain.

AUTHOR'S NOTE

It would have been very difficult to live in Maine for the past two decades and not have heard of the Dennis Dechaine case. In 1989, the Bowdoinham farmer was convicted of the rape and murder of twelve-year-old babysitter Sarah Cherry. Since that time, Dechaine's supporters have fought to free him from prison, contending that scientific evidence proves he could not possibly have committed the homicide. While I drew inspiration from the Dechaine case—and learned much about the state's legal and correctional systems from James P. Moore's book about it, *Human Sacrifice: On the Altar of Injustice*— this novel is not meant as my commentary upon the investigation or trial. *Trespasser* is entirely a work of fiction, and none of the characters, organizations, or events depicted have real-life counterparts.

I am grateful to Maine Warden Service Corporal John MacDonald, Warden Joe Lefebvre, and Warden Service Pilot Dan Default for answering my many nitpicking questions about their difficult work, and to Knox County Sheriff Donna Dennison for sharing her time and expertise. I also appreciate the help of Baxter State Park Ranger and fireman Andrew Vietze for his information on the difficulty of fighting rural house fires. As is always the case, mistakes of fact in this novel are my responsibility alone, although I will admit to taking dramatic liberties when they served the story.

Thanks to the early readers of the manuscript—Monica Wood, Cynthia Anderson, and especially my wife, Kristen Lindquist—for their wise suggestions on how to improve the book. I owe a debt, too, to my colleagues at *Down East* for supporting my sideline writing novels, and to my family for their unflagging encouragement.

Finally, I would like to thank my editor, Charlie Spicer, who thoughtfully guided me through several revisions, and to the team at Minotaur Books, including Andrew Martin, Matthew Shear, Matthew Baldacci, Hector DeJean, and Allison Strobel, who have demonstrated such faith in me and my work. Last, I extend my gratitude to Ann Rittenberg, the best agent a novelist could hope for.

Center Point Publishing

600 Brooks Road • PO Box 1
Thorndike ME 04986-0001 USA

(207) 568-3717

US & Canada:
1 800 929-9108
www.centerpointlargeprint.com